The BODY THE DIAMOND and the CHILD

The BODY THE DIAMOND and the CHILD

R S LEONARD

rsleonardbooks.com
Copyright © 2022 R S Leonard
All rights reserved.
Ebook: ISBN 978-1-7395889-0-8
Paperback: ISBN 978-1-7395889-1-5

Edited by Laura Gerrard
Cover art by Damonza
Layout by Damonza

For mum
Though her mind be now muddled
her heart stays true

The Times

LONDON, TUESDAY, MAY 29TH, 1804

FAMOUS DIAMOND STOLEN - *A most shocking story has come to our attention concerning a famous jewel, known as the Celestial Light, which has been in the possession of the Countess Annabel Darby, bequeathed to her by a fond former father-in-law, The Lord William de Lacey.*

The disappearance of the diamond was discovered on Sunday morning last following one of the Countess's select evening parties, the details of which our readers will have found reported in these pages. The Darby townhouse has been thoroughly searched by officers of the law, but to no avail. However, it is known that one of the Countess's manservants fled from the house just yesterday, a man who has not been unfamiliar with the wrong side of the law. The Lady, who is engaged to the third Baron de Vere, is said to be in great shock and has been taken ill. We understand that she will be retreating to her Hampshire estate to recover.

Our readers may be interested to hear some of the stories that surround this notorious stone, the veracity of which they may well be able to judge for themselves. The Celestial Light, a flawless diamond, is thought to be one of the largest in the world, being the size of a small hen's egg. Passed down from Mughal emperor to Mughal emperor, it was once set in a great throne – known as the King Cobra - made in the design of a snake, which was encrusted with many other brilliant jewels. As the empire's power dwindled and wars raged, the throne was broken up and the jewels scattered in several directions. It is not fully known how the Celestial Light came into the hands of the Lord de Lacey, but it is thought that one of the last in line of the Mughal emperors gifted it to the gentleman, who was renowned for his valour, in gratitude for some great military and personal service, rather than let it get into the hands of a bloodthirsty Persian conqueror.

The diamond is thought to absolve its possessors of their sins, and this has the happy side-effect of making them look younger. However, those with particularly vicious souls should beware, for the diamond will pass its divine judgement on these possessors and turn their inward corruption outward, so that their bodies will decay. But those luckier souls who are blessed with a new purity may have also to contend with a state of possessive mania, since the diamond will be so coveted by others that the least grasping soul alive is transfixed at the sight of the jewel, and longs to make it their own.

Fantastic fables aside, we wish the upholders of the law a speedy recovery of the jewel, a just punishment for the criminal, and a swift return to health for the good Countess.

Chapter 1

The strange events that occurred in the county of Hampshire, England, in the year 1804, began with the discovery of the dead body of a woman, heavy with child.

One morning at the end of May, the Reverend Jonathan Millbrook and his good lady wife, Anne, were walking the few steps from church to the rectory after clerical duties were done. Anne, who was frail, and really not cut out for the role to which providence had been pleased to call her, was leaning heavily on her husband's arm and turning her face inwards against the brightness of the day, which seemed to be chastising her for her melancholy.

Not far from the iron gate, Anne was puzzled by the sight of something lying on the path about midway between the gate and the house. As they got closer, she realised that it was a person, a woman. Someone must have been taken ill.

'John, John, look.'

The reverend, smiling and humming his favourite hymn, *Love Divine, All Loves Excelling* – which he had sang particularly well that morning, he thought – awoke from his reverie and looked in the direction to which his wife was pointing. He stared, then let go of Anne and rushed through the gate and up to where the body lay. It was, indeed, a woman, dressed in pale grey, lying face down, a rather smart black bonnet to the right of her head. Her arms were spread out at ninety-degree angles, so that she looked like she was being crucified on the cross. John knelt down and carefully turned over the woman's body, wincing when he saw her face: her skin was dark, but her pallor grey to match her dress. He quickly felt for the pulse on both her wrists. Yes, she was dead.

Anne, who had followed her husband through the gate stood watching the scene, feeling strangely removed. There was her handsome husband, with his brown eyes and curling brown hair and whiskers, crouching down and looking solemnly at this woman – dead, she was sure – lying in the shape of a cross. Anne was driven by a sudden impulse to sit next to the woman and touch her face. She went near to the body and knelt down.

'No, Anne. Go inside, dear,' said Jonathan. 'This is not a sight for you. Please. Get some help. Where is everyone today?' He looked towards the house, frowning.

'I will,' said Anne, but she did not get up. Instead, she followed her impulse and reached out a hand to touch the woman's face. It was cold, stiff. 'Is she a negro, John?'

John almost smiled. 'Yes, dear. They really do exist, you know; not just in our emancipation pamphlets and tracts.'

'I think she is – was – with child. Look at her belly. Oh, poor thing.' Anne started to cry.

'Go inside, now. I insist.' John helped his wife to get up and shouted for assistance. 'Samuel? Mary? Where are you?'

Mary, the cook and housekeeper, a very handsome woman of about thirty years of age, appeared a minute or so later from the west side of the house, looking flustered and brushing flour from her long, chequered apron.

'What's this, sir?' she asked, approaching the scene, then stopping suddenly to take it in.

'I cannot tell you, Mary, apart from what you see with your own eyes. Please get Anne inside and put her to bed. And get Samuel here, now.'

'Yes, sir.'

Mary took Anne's arm somewhat brusquely and pulled her towards the house.

'There, there, mistress, there, there.'

Anne allowed herself to be guided but could not help turning round for a last look at the strange scene, the woman's grey outline and her husband's dark clerical costume like smoky smudges against the sun and small white clouds in the sky.

Mary took Anne up to the main door of the house,

and banged loudly – that would rouse everyone. Joseph Carter, a village labourer's boy who ran errands for the Millbrook family, finally opened the door, peeping his head around the edge nervously, astounded by his own boldness.

'About time! Joe, quickly, the master needs you – over there. And where's Samuel?'

'He's in the grounds somewhere.'

Mary sighed. 'Well, you get to the master, and I'll find Samuel directly.'

Joe, a short, thin boy of about eight years old, nodded, wide-eyed, and hurried over to the reverend while Mary pulled Anne inside and up the main staircase, through her pretty green dressing room and into the bedchamber.

'Get out of your outer things, now, and then you can rest,' said Mary, helping Anne off with her shawl and bonnet, and sighing as she spotted dirt marks on Anne's pink gown, from the kneeling down, which she would have to clean. Then she pressed her mistress downwards to sit on the bedside chair while she deftly unlaced her neat brown boots, noting, as she often did, the tiny feet and slender ankles. 'Now get upon the bed and lie down, mistress. I'll go and fetch something to soothe you.'

Anne did as bid, watching the housekeeper's buxom form disappear, in awe, as she often was, by her beauty, which was of quite an exceptional kind. Mary's strong, perfectly sculptured features, smooth olive skin, large brown eyes and glossy chestnut hair would have made her a model for a Leonardo. Her upright bearing and fine curves gave her the air of a ship's masthead, and her plain, housekeeper's dress only served to enhance, rather than diminish, her beauty. Anne was a bit afraid of her, as she was of many strong-willed people, and was also slightly intimidated by Mary's general capability and nimble hands, and felt her own feebleness and inadequacy as mistress of a house.

She continued to cry a little as she thought of that poor woman and her unborn child. Who was she? Where did she come from? She remembered now the plain metal band on the second finger of her left hand, so perhaps, at least, she was not a fallen woman. Was there a husband somewhere, searching anxiously? She had never seen a negro before. Only an image on a coin of a supplicating man in chains – 'am I not a man and a brother?' Then there was this woman, dressed just like she, Anne, would. She wished she could shake the woman and wake her up, talk to her, keep the child alive. How glad that would make her.

Mary reappeared in her heavy, bustling way, offending Anne's ears. Anne was sensitive to noise, especially when she was feeling low and exhausted, which seemed to be most of the time of late.

'Here we are, mistress. A good cup of chocolate for you, with a little tonic to help you rest.'

'Thank you, Mary.' Anne took the dainty china cup and sipped the chocolate carefully. The brandy that was in it begin to warm her a little.

'Is there no sugar?' Anne ventured.

'Yes, ma'am, and your usual amount is in the drink along with your usual tonic. Your sweet tooth must be getting worse.' Mary checked herself. 'Drink up, mistress; it really will do you good.'

Anne lowered her large grey eyes and did as told, if only to get rid of Mary, then put the empty cup down on the bedside table and closed her eyes.

Mary took the cup and stood watching her mistress for a few moments. She stared at Anne's fair, slender form, half envious, half contemptuous, comparing it with her own, more vibrant looks. She left the room, frowning as she went, and clomped down the staircase to find at the bottom Samuel Cole, butler, groundsman, and many more things besides, who had just discovered the scene outside.

'Well, Mary, this is a bad business,' he said, nodding towards the front door. 'But I shan't stop now; there's much to do.'

'Aye, and there's Madam dreaming away upstairs, after her usual attack of the nerves, and the rest of us left to manage.'

'Mind your tongue, Mary, and show some respect. She's a poor, weakened creature, what with all her sorrows and still no children to love. And there you are with your two fine boys.'

'We all have our crosses to bear.'

'Very true, Mary, and so where is your womanly compassion?'

'Long dried up, Samuel, like the rest of my life.'

Samuel gave Mary a stern look with his pale blue eyes. 'Well, we've not time for this now.' He turned away from her, and Mary watched him go. Sam was a widower, a well-looking, slightly weather-beaten, man, of eight and thirty, with sandy hair and a broad chest. She walked to the kitchen, her face grim, her right hand tightly gripping the cup as if it was full to the brim of her own bitterness.

Sam joined the reverend and Joe and the three of them lifted the woman's body and carried it somewhat clumsily to the back of the house, and then into an old and very cold parlour, now used mainly for storing ale, cheese and fishing tackle. They lay the woman on a low bench, and Joe, feeling his throat constricting with the effort not to cry, tucked in the woman's arms and legs to create what he hoped was a dignified neatness.

'We left her hat,' he said.

'Never mind, Joe. Sadly, she'll not be needing it now,' said Samuel, patting Joe's shoulder.

'I must get it for her.'

Joe had a strong feeling, perhaps stemming from his mother's constant anxiety about forgetting to cover her head before leaving the house, and the shocking reputation she would thus acquire, that the dead woman must be reunited with her bonnet. He ran back out to the front grounds, picked up the black, silk bonnet and carried it with both hands, arms outstretched as if it were a fine meal on a silver platter, back to the room where the body lay. He tried to place the bonnet on the woman's head. This exercise was not a success, him not having the smallest notion how to put on a woman's hat, not least onto a head not upright. He settled at laying the bonnet close by the right side of the woman's head, the black ribbons falling over her shoulder. He patted the ribbons. There, that was better.

The reverend smiled at him. 'Thank you, Joe. Now come with me to my study while I write a short note for the Coroner. I will give you the direction. He is just off the High Street, you know, and you can run thither in no time. If he is at home, wait for his response. If not, leave the letter at the house.' He turned to Samuel. 'We will need to have an inquest, and soon, and get the poor woman buried.' He turned back to Joe. 'Follow me, Joe. When you have done your duty, you can have a good meal in the kitchen, here, and then return to your mother.'

Joe smiled at the thought of the good feed ahead, then frowned at himself for committing such an unseemly act in the presence of death. He followed the reverend out of the room, turning once, as Anne had done, to take a final look at the woman. Samuel stood for a few moments staring at the body, then picked up a rough blanket from a nearby shelf and placed it carefully over her, bonnet and all.

As the reverend, Joseph and Samuel were lifting the woman's body, a slightly battered, chocolate-coloured gig drawn by shabby, old bay horse was moving quickly and shakily down the lane at the front of the church. The driver, a tall, older man, and his passenger, a small, neat woman in a cornflower blue bonnet, were laughing. As the cart and horse passed the rectory, the woman noticed the unusual scene and her small, round spectacles slid towards the end of her nose as she stared. A jolt of the gig brought her eyes back to the road ahead, and she settled back to bear the rest of the journey home, her face now sombre and thoughtful.

Chapter 2

A GIG PULLED up into the courtyard of a fine old manor house, and the driver, more nimble than he looked, jumped out first and then walked round to the other side of the cart to help his passenger. The woman pushed back her spectacles, took the man's hand and stepped down lightly, placing a silver, amber-topped cane on the ground before her, which she used to support a slight limp in her right leg.

'Welcome home, ma'am,' said the man in his soft Highlands brogue. He smiled and gestured towards the house and grounds. 'I cannot tell you what a pleasure it is to have you here again. Mrs Campbell has been all aflutter with excitement and has been cleaning and baking as if the Good Lord himself was about to pay us a visit.'

'Thank you, Gabriel. You and Mrs Campbell were always so kind. But I am afraid it is only poor old sinner me, Miss Swinglehurst, come home, so I hope I am worthy of your attentions.' She paused, looked up at his long, angular face and grinned. 'Are there queen cakes?'

'Oh, enough to feed all of Hampshire, and most of London, too, I shouldn't wonder.'

Miss Swinglehurst laughed her slightly throaty laugh and kissed Gabriel on the cheek. Mr Campbell, a long-limbed man of two and sixty years of age, smiled from one large ear to the other, which exposed his long teeth, as well as the prominent absence of two of his bottom ones.

'The sound of that laugh takes me back, Miss, and does my heart good to hear, though I wish your good father and mother were still with us to hear it.'

'So do I, Gabriel, so do I. I must confess that I am feeling a little tearful already.'

'Well, miss, it's only natural. Mrs Campbell is fond of a good weep, even when she's only burnt a pudding, or sometimes when she hasn't, if it comes to that.'

Miss Swinglehurst laughed again. 'Oh, Gabriel, will not you call such an old friend as me Freddy? Or perhaps Fredericka, if you like something more formal, being so upright as you are? I know it is not considered dignified for a lady to own her age, but I am two and thirty years of age, now, you know.'

'No, Miss, I couldn't think of it. I hate to disoblige you, but think of your father, and I once his servant.'

Freddy sighed and smiled. 'As you wish, Mr Gabriel Campbell, as you wish.'

The pair walked slowly towards the house, the small, compact Freddy leaning on the tall, slightly stooped Gabriel, and pressing on her cane with her right arm. Just as they were approaching the door to the kitchen on the east side of the house, an old, brown Newfoundland dog came walking, a little heavily, towards them from the back of the house.

'Why, it is Flip,' said Freddy, as the dog attempted to jump up to her with his aging legs and to lick her face. 'Do you think he remembers me?'

'I should say so, miss, by the welcome he's given you and that smile on his face.'

Freddy unlinked her arm from Gabriel's, laid her stick aside, and knelt down to snuggle the dog, who was panting and wagging his tail with excitement. 'He must be eleven years old, now, and what a bear he is. I remember him as just a bundle of fur with those sad, drooping eyes in the middle.'

'Yes, he'll soon be as long in the tooth as I am. He's reached a good age, but I hope he's got one or two more years in him yet.'

Flip had been a present to Freddy from her former fiancé, Charles Ingleby, a naval officer. The dog was to keep Freddy company, Charles had said, before he went off to the war in early 1793. The puppy had not been in the house above five minutes when it drank up a tankard of flip, Gabriel's favourite tipple, and then quickly brought the hot mixture of rum, ale, sugar, eggs and nutmeg back up onto Mrs Campbell's newly polished kitchen floor And so he was christened. The sight and touch of the dog now brought back to Freddy Charles's green eyes and flushed face as he gave her the present. It moved her, but did not pain her, to think of Charles now; it felt more like a nostalgia for childish things that had long been put away. Realising this eased her heart a little, and she compared it to the unbearable grief she had undergone, when he had died from sickness at sea not long after the war had begun, and this less than six months after the death of her beloved father. She had fled to London in consequence.

Freddy now got up as the heavy oak door to the kitchen opened inwards to reveal Mrs Margaret Campbell, who was as short and round as her husband was tall and bony. She was wearing a mauve-coloured, striped gown of the fashion of twenty years before, and a crisp, white kerchief and linen cap, which set off her mildly freckled, beaming face.

'Freddy Swinglehurst, it's you at long, long last!'

'Yes, it would be appear to be,' said Freddy, laughing, and kissing Margaret, who took Freddy's small oval face in her hands and then kissed her repeatedly on the forehead and cheeks.

'Eleven long years, Fredericka. And you, like a female vagabond, galivanting off here, there and everywhere – well, to that smoky, nasty London, at least. And I can still remember the day you left, and broke our hearts, and your own as well, I know it. But now you've seen sense – better late than never, I suppose - and are home for good, where you belong, and we can't believe our happiness. But come in, come in. My best queen cakes won't eat themselves, and I don't need any more padding, to be sure.'

Freddy stepped inside the hot kitchen and smiled as her eyes wandered over the old place with its clean, limewashed walls. There was the jumble of copper pots and pans hanging over the hearth, oven and fireplace. Best of all, there was the battered oak table on which lay the old pewter tea pot next to a large plate of cakes.

'Sit down and eat and drink, then,' said Margaret. 'And Mr C, are you going to take our treasure's bonnet or stand there all day gaping?'

Gabriel smiled and did as bid. Freddy sat down and Flip settled himself against her feet under the table. Margaret could not resist taking Freddy's face in her hands and staring happily a her delicate, perfectly balanced features, excepting one brown eye and its brow slanting at a slightly lower angle than the other, which gave her a quizzical, mischievous look, even with her spectacles on. Margaret kissed her thrice more before setting a teacup in front of her and then picking up the sugar tongs.

'Oh, Mrs C, I am not sure I should. I am trying to eat less Caribbean sugar.'

Margaret's round face looked aghast. 'Whatever for, my love? Why, I never knew a child – and then a young woman, for that matter – who loved sugar as much as you did. I used to catch you with your fingers in the jar, just before your bedtime. Do you remember?'

'I do. I can still taste those crystals scratching my tongue, then melting in my throat.' Freddy grinned and sighed. 'But tis this slavery business, you know. I am trying not to eat West Indian sugar. But we can get sugar from elsewhere. Aphrodite, when she visits next week, is going to bring some that has come all the way from the East Indies.'

Margaret looked a little saddened and glanced at her husband. They both sat down.

'Well, my dear, we can only applaud you for your sentiment,' said Margaret, 'but it feels very unfair that you have to deprive yourself of so small and yet so great a pleasure when you've never done anything wrong in your whole life. Tis true, I don't know a great deal about these things, excepting what Mr C here tells me.'

'It's a very large matter, with many complex aspects to it, and we must keep fighting for what is right,' said Gabriel, looking thoughtful. 'Perhaps we should be boycotting the sugar; aye, perhaps we should. However, let's use this new sugar of yours when it comes, and in the meantime, try not to make yourself uneasy. Our current batch of sugar is already here and in use, so you refusing it won't really help anyone.'

Freddy smiled and brightened. 'That is true enough, and by the time it runs out, we will have Affy's. How clever you are, Mr C! Well, I will have two lumps in my tea, if you would be so good, Margaret, and a few of those cakes.'

Margaret beamed, relieved. There was a good deal

of sugar in her cakes and she had been looking forward for so long to seeing Freddy eat some of them. Feeling slightly sheepish, she dropped two lumps into Freddy's cup, who smiled at her reassuringly, and poured the tea in what she hoped was an elegant fashion, then put three of the queen cakes onto a plate and pushed it proudly towards her treasure.

Freddy took several sips of the tea, then picked up one of the cakes and bit into it. She closed her eyes as she tasted the delicious combination of currants, sugar and rose water, made some slightly undignified sighing noises, opened her eyes, and grinned at Margaret and Gabriel. Ladies were not meant to be gluttonous, and to show too keen a pleasure in the business of eating, but Freddy no longer cared for such ideals, and felt a child again in her old kitchen. 'Nobody's queen cakes are as good as yours, Mrs C,' she said.

'Of course they're not,' said Margaret, delighted. 'There, that's better, isn't it?'

Freddy took another cup of tea, ate the other two cakes, and sat happily at the table for about an hour, picking up the gossip from Margaret, who had an ear to the ground not only in the surrounding villages but in most of Winchester, Southampton and Portsmouth too.

'Do you see much of Jonathan Millbrook and his family?' asked Freddy.

'Oh, yes, dear. He is a fine man, as he was a fine boy, as you know. His wife, Anne, is a very good, genteel sort of creature, though she has not borne any children, which makes her a little melancholy, I believe. She has a cousin, a Captain Henry Lefroy, who visits when he's on dry land, and what a charming man.' Margaret smiled a little girlishly. 'He's currently renting a fine house on College Street in Winchester. And, only think, he knew something of your father. You will meet him soon, I am sure.'

Freddy smiled. 'I shall look forward to it. But has anything strange happened at the rectory? When Gabriel and I drove past earlier, the reverend, another man, and a boy were picking up a woman from the ground, who may have been sick, or even deceased. I cannot be sure, but I think her skin colour was like mine, and she was with child.'

'Good gracious,' said Margaret, 'who could she be? There's been nobody of that description in the village, or even in Winchester, as far as I know. She must be a visiting friend of theirs. Dear, oh dear; I hope she's recovered. I imagine the other man you saw will be Samuel Cole, the butler and groundsman and everything besides, and the boy Joe Carter, from the village.'

'I may call at the rectory tomorrow,' said Freddy. 'It will be pleasant to see the reverend after all these years and we may be able to offer some assistance.'

'Yes, that's a very good thought,' said Margaret. 'Well, my love, you may have come home to a local mystery. And not only that. Have you heard the news of Lady Darby's diamond? I got it only this morning from the butcher in Winchester, which he got from someone who'd just been in London. It will surely be in the *Chronicle* soon enough. They say that she will come home to her Hampshire estate because she is so cut-up.'

'What news about the diamond?' asked Freddy. 'I have not heard this, though I have not been reading my newspaper recently. What has happened?'

'Why, it has been stolen, my dear.'

'Stolen? Well, I never. But, stay, the story may be in *The Times*. I have a copy of yesterday's paper in my luggage.'

Freddy got up, opened her leather travelling bag, pulled out the newspaper and placed it on the table.

'There it is on the front page,' she said, pointing at the article, and even Gabriel got up to take a look, though he could not see much without a magnifier.

'I was at that evening party,' Freddy continued, in astonishment, 'but I left early. I remember thinking how well and how young the countess looked; her countenance, and whole being, thinking about it, seemed sort of glowing. Though, indeed, it was difficult to take one's eyes off the diamond, which was hanging round her neck. As they say, it is very seductive, and seems to draw one in.'

'So you didn't see anything?' asked Margaret eagerly.

'No, I am afraid not. How frustrating. I shall give it some thought, though.'

Freddy yawned. She was growing sleepy to the sound of the ticking kitchen clock.

Margaret noticed Freddy's slouching body and fluttering eyelids.

'Well, dearest, I've managed to exhaust you already, and you back home not yet an hour.'

Freddy opened her eyes and straightened herself up. 'Not at all, Mrs Gabriel. All this excitement makes me want to stay wide awake, and yet I am very tired, and it is so snug and safe in here, with all the familiar sounds and smells, and Flip keeping my feet warm, that I feel just like a child again ready to curl up and dream sweet dreams.'

'May you always have sweet dreams in this house. And you'll always be snug and safe with us. Won't she, Gabriel?'

'That she will, Mrs Gabriel, that she will.'

Freddy looked at them both, beginning again to feel a little tearful. She took Margaret's hand and kissed it, then got up and kissed Gabriel on the cheek.

'You get off up the stairs, now, dear,' said Margaret, 'and we can send your dinner up when the time comes, if you like, and you can have a bit of peace for today. I remember that look from old and it means that little Freddy needs a good rest and some time on her own for reading all those novels that are far too grown up for her. Though, I grant you, you're old enough now to be reading *Tom Jones*, even if it is a little too spicy for my liking.'

Freddy laughed and looked at her old friends gratefully. 'Oh, I've read plenty spicier books since then, Mrs C.'

'I do not wish to hear it, my dear. You'll always be a girl to me, and I'd be quite happy if you stuck to the Bible.'

Gabriel grinned at Freddy and handed her a wax candle in a fine silver holder.

'Up you go, Miss. Some of the places are a little dark, despite the sunlight, so take this, just in case. One thing you'll find you won't be short of at home is light. Mrs Gabriel has quite shocked the village with her recent rejection of tallow, and her profligate purchase of wax.'

Gabriel escorted Freddy out of the kitchen and through the ground floor to the base of the main staircase, then stopped, nodding at her encouragingly. He knew that she would want to do the rest alone. Freddy smiled at him, pressed his hand, then turned to face the stairs.

Gabriel returned to the kitchen and sat back down on the chair opposite his wife. They smiled at each other, and a few tears slid down Margaret's rosy cheeks.

'Are you well, my dear?' asked Gabriel, laughing a little and taking his wife's hand.

'I couldn't be happier. It's like our own dear daughter has come home and my heart's so full just now it might well burst.'

'I confess that I'm a little shaken up myself.'

'I can tell you are, you old goose.' Margaret pinched her husband's cheek and beamed at him through her tears. 'Now what about this poor woman in the grounds of the rectory? What did you see?'

'Very little; I only glanced as we drove past the scene. I was keeping my eye on the road, my dear, as you often remind me I should.'

'Glad I am to hear it. Though tis a little vexing that you should pay heed, at last, when a little more attention the other way might have proved useful. Well, we will learn more tomorrow, I am sure, and no doubt more in time about that diamond.'

'With you and our intrepid Freddy looking into matters, Mrs C, I do not doubt it.'

Chapter 3

When Gabriel left her, Freddy slowly ascended the stairs, the tapping of her stick responding to the ticking of various clocks. She could remember every nook and cranny of the old manor house, which had been built after the Restoration and then improved and extended over the years so that it was now of no particular style. As a child and young woman with a vivid fancy, she would imagine bloody daggers, ghosts and secret chambers, and her heart would thrill with terror and delight. Her father, an antiquarian with a romantic soul, had fallen in love with the place on his return to his native Hampshire late in the year 1763 after the wars. He rented it from the old squire, who had built himself a shiny new manor house in the Palladian style, and then had managed to purchase it from him, so leaving something solid for his daughter and shelter and security for the good Campbells while they lived.

Many of the rooms' interiors on the first floor were draped in dust sheets, but Freddy could still see her father in each, smiling up at her or frowning over the accounts, his bright yellow hair shining in the sunlight; then, years later, his white head bent as he dozed. She stopped at the door to his study, reached out to touch it and push, but her heart failed her. It had been Admiral Swinglehurst's favourite place, crammed with naval paraphernalia and clocks. The admiral had a passion for predicting the weather with his collection of barometers and notebooks. Freddy would ask him, 'can you tell me what weather we will have today, sir?' and the admiral would stroke his chin and set to examining his scribblings, and Freddy would laugh and say, 'Perhaps I will just step outside and see for myself.' She turned away. Tomorrow would do well enough, when she was feeling stronger.

She made her way to her dressing room, which was newly decorated in yellow trellis wallpaper with a green foliage border, and smiled. Margaret had managed the business for her with Joseph Trollope & Sons in London. She had instructed Margaret by letter, saying simply that she wanted it to be pretty and full of sunshine, in honour of her mother, who had come from Barbados. Freddy walked slowly round the room, running her fingers over the new fabrics and upholstery, and the curves of the dressing table. She moved over to one of her father's old desks, which had been placed next to the window looking out onto the front grounds of the house. It was a standing desk, and she remembered as a small child being lifted up by her father, who would guide her use of ink and paper until she had written her name in large, looping letters.

How pleasant it all was. She gave a deep sigh, took off her spectacles, dropped into the newly upholstered easy chair and closed her eyes for a few moments. Then she unlaced and pulled off her boots and threw them to one side, picked the pins out of her dark, curly hair and shook her head to let it loose. She spotted her luggage, which Gabriel had brought up for her, opened the largest trunk, and rooted inside, finally pulling out a man's white linen shift and some buff-coloured pantaloons. She struggled and wriggled her way out of her gown, petticoats, stockings, shift and stays, breathing a sigh of relief as she did so, and put on the shirt and trousers. Then she went over to the desk, on top of which sat a bottle of claret and two glasses. She poured herself a large glass of wine, then opened one of the desk's small drawers and took out her father's old pipe. With swift expertise she tapped some tobacco, which she kept in a leather pouch inside her sewing box, into the pipe and lit it with a wax taper. She smiled as the pipe's aroma – her father's aroma – filled her nostrils, and carried it, with the claret, back to her comfortable chair.

As she puffed at the pipe and sipped her claret, she thought about Annabel Darby and her diamond. How vexing that Freddy should have been present on the very evening it was stolen and yet not noticed anything suspicious. She remembered the Countess's exceeding happiness, yet strange nervousness, the way she fluttered from guest to guest, her eyes darting, her head jerking. Despite the stories about its magical qualities, could one really be happy possessing such a thing? Freddy now remembered some rumours she had heard about its provenance. One suggested that the Lord William de Lacey had in fact stolen the diamond in India in cahoots with a dishonest British East India Company officer and a disgruntled Court eunuch. Another said that he had simply purchased it on the Amsterdam market, with the help of a little skulduggery. Whatever the truth, de Lacey had gained sole possession of the stone, and gifted it to Lady Darby, to whom he had taken a shine, in his will, much to the rage of his family. Freddy smiled at the newspaper's description of a valorous de Lacey. In real life, he was known as 'mad Bill' due to his more than friendly inclination towards the dogs and horses on his Northamptonshire estate, and his propensity for shooting a little more than the local wildlife.

Freddy felt a little sorry for the Countess, whom she liked very much; they had been friendly acquaintances, if not friends, for years, the Countess having known her father. She hoped that the lady's change in circumstances would not affect her forthcoming marriage to the Baron de Vere. At the party, there had been speculation – and much ribaldry – that it was not the diamond but the prospect of her approaching union with husband number six that had caused Lady Darby's latest rejuvenation. The Baron de Vere was fifteen years her junior (the Countess being five and sixty), had the gout in just the one foot, and was even thought to own several teeth that had not been procured by the hands of a resurrectionist.

Imagine having had six husbands, Freddy thought. She felt quite fatigued at the thought of having one. Of course, there had been Charles all those years before, and they would have been happy, she was sure. They might have lived here with her father, and the Campbells, and there may have been children running round the garden with Flip. But she was such a different being now, so altered by her life experience, so grown into her peculiar independence – as the world saw it. She was content to remain single, and though she joked about becoming the village spinster, her intent was serious. Nor did she mourn for the children that she might have had, or would not have; she had never had that yearning.

In fact, she had once taken some help to get rid of the beginnings of a child inside her, the result of a sordid encounter with a man she had barely liked. She tried a few of the usual methods on her own - gin, scalding hot baths, purgatives and pills 'to remove obstructions', throwing herself down the stairs. Thankfully, her attempt at the latter was a little half-hearted, and she only damaged her right leg, though the baby remained. Finally, she confided in her dear friend, Lady Lavinia Ingram, who had taken her to a very discreet and expensive doctor. Freddy still squirmed at the remembrance of that pointed implement – whatever it was – that had been pushed inside her. The pain had been dreadful, even though she had prepared herself by taking a large dose of laudanum. She had been fortunate, she knew, not to sicken afterwards, and had recovered well.

Whilst the social disgrace of having the child would have been terrible and great, she knew that some of her motivation for her action was a terror of giving birth – had not her poor mother died from that act that was supposedly so natural and everyday? – and the rest of her motivation a desire simply not to have a baby. Was she wicked? Many would have said so, but thankfully she could not feel so in her own heart. She had never regretted her action, only felt a pang of guilt sometimes when she encountered those truly suffering for the want of children. Her dear Campbells were of these number. She had never known them to be self-pitying or bitter about it, though they must have suffered terribly, perhaps Gabriel even more than Margaret. She remembered Margaret telling her about a still birth, a girl, which had followed several miscarriages, and that Gabriel could simply not comprehend why an infant would take the trouble to come into the world fully formed but not to stay in it.

Freddy gradually dozed off as her mind wandered over old times, and she woke some hours later feeling brighter, and ready to go downstairs and be back in the company of the Campbells.

She made her way down to the kitchen, yawning and stretching as she went, and appeared at the open door, smiling as the smell of roasting meat filled her nostrils. Flip got up from under the table, wagging his tail, and padded over to her. Margaret was busy at the stove, Gabriel was sat at the table, facing her, and there was another man in the room, sat with his back to her.

'Miss Swinglehurst,' said Gabriel, giving her a peculiar look, then smiling. 'Are you well rested?'

'Yes, thank you, Gabriel, and now I have followed my stomach down to Mrs C's good kitchen.'

Margaret turned round, her faced flushed. 'Freddy, dearest.' Then she stared. 'Good gracious, my love, are you quite well?'

'Perfectly so, Mrs C. Why should I not be?'

'But what are you wearing?'

Freddy looked down at herself, and realised that she was still wearing the pantaloons and shift, and her bountiful hair was doing quite its own thing by sticking out in every which direction as well as down her back. At that moment, the strange gentleman turned round and got up. He was tall and very slim - though his off-duty blue naval uniform became his figure very well – and he had light brown hair, bright blue eyes, a slightly long nose and a very glowing complexion. Certainly not unhandsome, was Freddy's first thought.

'We have just been talking of you, dear,' said Margaret, 'though perhaps I did not stress quite enough to the captain what wild ways you will have picked up in London.'

Freddy stayed rooted to the spot, and giggled in that

slightly silly way she found so irksome in other women finding themselves in the presence of handsome sailors.

The captain smiled at her, and reached out his hand to shake hers.

'Captain Henry Lefroy, at your service, Miss Swinglehurst,' he said, in a rich, deep voice with an Irish accent. 'It is an honour to meet you; I have heard so much about you. I see you are quite ahead of me in the mode with those trousers; I am afraid I am still attached to my breeches.'

Freddy giggled again and found herself staring at the captain's breeches. She forced herself to look up at his face.

'Well, I must make my departure,' said the captain, 'but I hope we can become better acquainted soon, Miss Swinglehurst. Thank you for your hospitality, Mrs Campbell, Mr Campbell. I will be in touch about that horse.' He shook Gabriel's hand, smiled at Margaret and quit the kitchen by the door that led outside.

'Upon my soul,' said Margaret, sitting down. 'I've never been so embarrassed in my entire life. What will he think of us? We drove him away – he couldn't leave fast enough. Did you see the expression on his face? And that talk of pantaloons, and breeches! We'll be the scandal of the neighbourhood.'

Margaret, though truly a little shocked at Freddy's appearance, had a healthy sense of humour, and started laughing. Freddy, laughing too, stood behind her and put her arms around her neck.

'I am very sorry, Mrs C. This is just a little costume I wear for my leisure when at home, and I quite forgot that I no longer live alone.'

Margaret kissed Freddy's right hand and turned to face her. 'No, my dear, you no longer live alone, and don't you forget it; you're back with your family now. And I'm sure you can wear whatever you want, though if we don't want to terrify the neighbours it might be advisable during daylight hours at the least to wear something a little more formal – and designed for the female of the sex – and tidy up that beautiful hair of yours. But if you're wanting to keep the crows from attacking farmer Denton's corn then you'll be doing a fine job.'

Freddy laughed, kissed Margaret on the top of the head, then sat down next to her. Gabriel, laughing too in his slow, measured way, had also sat down, opposite his wife.

'He is a very handsome man, is he not?' said Margaret, looking slyly at Freddy.

'Mr Campbell?' said Freddy. 'Aye, he is indeed, or you would not have married him, I am sure.'

'You know very well that I mean the captain, Henry Lefroy.'

'Agh, well, you should have been more specific. He is not ill-looking, I suppose.'

'Not ill-looking, child? He is the very picture of handsomeness.'

'He is a little shiny.'

'Shiny? He is not a boot, Fredericka.'

Freddy giggled 'I just meant that he was sort of glowing. Oh!' She put her hand to her mouth and gasped with mock horror. 'What if it was he who stole the famous diamond? Perhaps it was in the pocket of his waistcoat at the very moment he was speaking to us.'

'Fie, what nonsense you are full of today, my love, but I confess it does my heart good to hear it, and to have you here again at our table, with or without pantaloons.' Margaret reached for Freddy's hand and kissed it twice. 'Well, I doubt we shall see the poor man again. I am still blushing at the thought of that breeches talk.'

Freddy laughed. 'The captain began the subject, I believe; it was all his doing.'

'She is right, Mrs C,' said Gabriel, grinning at his wife.

'I believe she is,' said Margaret. 'Well, never mind that now. He brought us news from the rectory.'

'Indeed,' said Freddy, looking more serious, 'and what is the situation there? Who was the poor woman?'

'They do not know,' said Margaret. ''Tis a great mystery, apart from the fact that the poor creature is dead, as you thought, and was quite full with child – God rest both their souls. The reverend and his wife found her in their grounds on returning from church this morning, and she is a complete stranger to them, and to Mary, their housekeeper, and Sam and Joe, whom I mentioned before.'

'That is most peculiar,' said Freddy. 'How did she end up there if she was not known to anyone?'

'I cannot tell you. The reverend and Anne can only think that she wandered there, perhaps in distress and seeking spiritual comfort, and had asked someone the way to the nearest church or church man.'

'It is possible, I suppose,' said Freddy, 'in which case she must have spoken to somebody, or at least have been seen. We must find out who she is. There may be people missing her – friends, and a husband, perhaps?'

'Yes,' said Margaret, 'I forgot to mention that she wore a wedding ring.'

'Oh, dear. It is all very sad.'

Margaret turned to look at her husband, who was looking very melancholy. 'There, my love,' she said to him, 'try not to take it to heart so. Tis most tragic but we will do what we can to help.'

'I know, wife,' said Gabriel quietly.

Freddy got up and put her arms around his neck, as she had done with Margaret, breathing in his Gabriel scent, a comforting mix of oak, soil, horses and tobacco. 'Dear Gabriel, I forgot how good you are, and that you are not quite fit for this world that can be so cruel. Papa always said so, did not he, Margaret?'

'Aye, he did, and poor Mr C has only grown more tender with the years. Come now, husband, and get yourself cleaned up before dinner. Just because we have a wild woman in the house does not mean that the rest of us can abandon all priority. I suppose next you'll be wanting to come down to breakfast in a lady's gown, sir?'

Gabriel laughed, as his wife had intended, and

endeavoured to brighten up, but he could not help but feel that this business of the dead woman was a very bad one indeed, and that there was more evil to come.

Chapter 4

Freddy woke up the next day manifesting signs of a heavy cold, and Margaret, terrified that her newly-returned treasure might take an infection, insisted she stay at home, and be nursed. Freddy, though anxious to discover more about the local mystery, found herself relieved to spend most of the day in bed, and be fussed over and fed ginger tea and negus by Mrs Campbell. The following day, however, she was feeling a little better, and the day was so bright and mild that Margaret allowed her to go out for a walk in the mid-afternoon, and thus attempt to satisfy her curiosity.

She set off happily, leaning slightly on her silver cane and smiling a little as she walked up the blooming lane in the direction of the rectory, which was but a fifteen-minute journey by foot. She wondered if it was perhaps a little forward to turn up unannounced after so many years, but then the Campbells were still friendly with the Millbrooks, and there seemed to be little formality in their interactions. Besides, after appearing to Mrs Millbrook's cousin in the guise of part gentleman, part scarecrow, social scruples now seemed a little redundant.

Not far from the rectory, she spotted the reverend himself, coming upon her from a side path. He stopped and stared. She drew closer and smiled.

'Reverend Millbrook,' she said, looking up at him from behind her spectacles, her head cocked slightly to its left side. 'Do you not know me?'

The reverend laughed. 'Miss Fredericka Swinglehurst, as I live and breathe. I knew that you were coming back to Hampshire, but I was not sure exactly when. And here you are.'

'Here I am.'

'It has been so long. Are you well? And what have you been doing with yourself all these years?'

'That is a lot of information to impart at once, sir, and I hope we can talk at length in due course. But rest assured, I am well.'

'Are you heading in any particular direction? If you do not have any pressing business, why not come back to the rectory with me and take tea? My wife, Anne, gets lonely, I am sure, and would be delighted to make your acquaintance.'

'Thank you, Reverend.'

'Oh, none of that Reverend stuff. Call me Jonathan. Or John, if you like, as you used to of old.'

Freddy smiled. 'Well, maybe Jonathan. I was just

taking the air, and have no particular business. In fact, I was wondering if I should call, and now you have solved my dilemma.'

'Capital. But, come, take my arm. You do not look as strong as you used to do, though I know – if you will forgive my impertinence – that you once had sorrows enough to weigh down any poor soul.'

Freddy was moved by the reverend's easy compassion, and took his arm, and they walked companionably together to the rectory. The shape of Jonathan next to her and the sound of his voice brought back some of Freddy's childhood and youth. They had been great friends, and used to run half wild in the village, play cricket in the grounds of the Swinglehurst residence and pretend to be sailors on the high seas of the garden pond. Jonathan had been a handsome boy, broad and tall with fine brown eyes, and the promise in the boy had been fulfilled in the man of five and thirty; the few grey hairs he now bore only added the requisite gravitas. They had kissed once, Freddy remembered, suddenly, when one summer's evening they had been sat under the great beech tree at the back of the old manor house, making paper ships and eating apples. It had been strange, and felt silly, and they had both laughed and gone back to being brother and sister, for she had always wanted a brother, and that was how she liked him best.

They arrived at the rectory, which Freddy remembered as being an unusually grand affair, with three large meadows, ample stabling and two workers' cottages.

Now it seemed to look even smarter, with fresh paint and new windows; and some kind of refurbishment and extension was also taking place. Freddy was shown into the front parlour, where they found Anne Millbrook sat peacefully, sewing. She started up at the sight of them.

'Do not take affright, Anne,' said Jonathan. 'Look who I have carried home to meet you. You know that I have spoken to you about Miss Swinglehurst and her good father, the admiral? Miss Swinglehurst has come home to the Campbells after many years away.'

'It is a pleasure to meet you, Miss Swinglehurst,' said Anne, moving over to Freddy, taking her hand, and trying not to stare too much at her face. Another negro, she thought. How strange that she should see two such people in the space of a week after never having met one in the whole of her life.

'Pray, sit down, sit down, Miss Swinglehurst,' said Jonathan. 'I will get Polly to bring an extra cup with the tea.' He disappeared.

'What a neat, pretty parlour, you have,' said Freddy, taking a seat and smiling at Anne. 'That yellow dotted paper is just perfect. And how it becomes your style of beauty.'

Anne smiled at Freddy. How peculiar she looked, Anne thought, with those ugly spectacles and that cane. She must be a spinster. Then again, her green and white muslin gown was rather pretty; and how softly she spoke. It was very soothing. Anne had not long been suffering Mary's grating tones.

'Thank you, Miss Swinglehurst,' she said. 'How kind of you. It is newly done. Mr Millbrook – Jonathan – insists on satisfying my every whim, whether I wish him to or no.' Anne smiled and gestured to the pile of furniture and decorating catalogues that lay on the delicate rosewood sideboard, then began to twist the large diamond ring on her right index finger, one of the many jewels that she wore.

'That is, indeed, the best kind of husband,' said Freddy, laughing a little.

'I dare say it is,' and Anne, also laughing. She looked around again. 'I confess that this is my favourite room in the house. I find my peace here.' Anne was surprised at her own frankness.

'We all need somewhere to find our peace,' said Freddy.

Anne felt herself close to tears. 'Yes.'

The young maid, Polly, who was already on her way to the parlour with refreshments for her mistress, now appeared. She was just putting a tray down on the tea table when she caught sight of Freddy, jumped slightly and dropped everything on the floor, the hot water from the urn spilling on the rug.

'Sorry, miss; I beg your pardon, ma'am,' spluttered Polly, starting to cry. Polly, not yet fifteen, was a pretty girl with a slightly pointed chin, flared nostrils and wide green eyes. She was also a gangly, awkward thing, whose long, bony arms seemed to hinder rather than to help any task she attempted.

'Never mind, Polly,' said Anne, calmly. 'Clear it up, there's a good girl, and you can bring some more. We need to get those slender arms of yours strengthened.' Although Polly would have been dismissed ten times over from other houses, Anne found that she was not angry when Polly broke things, even when it was the best china (though she did hide that fact from her husband). Sometimes she felt a small thrill of excitement seeing things break, and for a brief moment imagined rampaging through the house, smashing things up.

'Please, let me help you,' said Freddy, reaching down to pick up two Worcester china teacups, still intact. Polly turned to look at her, a strand of thin hair falling from underneath her cap to cover one green eye; she could not help but stare a little. Freddy smiled at her and Polly smiled back, a solitary tear dropping onto the blue and white china teapot she was holding.

'My mother used to drop things all the time,' said Freddy. 'Or so my father told me, for, alas, I did not get the opportunity to meet her. He used to trail after her with his hands extended, waiting for something to fall.'

Polly's smile grew broader.

'He brought her home to Hampshire from across the oceans, from a beautiful, sun drenched place called Barbados, where the air is as thick as treacle and they have the tastiest fruit in the world, a large, yellow thing called a pineapple.'

'And have you been to this place, Bar-bad-os?' asked Polly, pronouncing the word slowly and carefully. Then she glanced sheepishly at her mistress, aware that she should not be getting above her station by asking bold questions of visitors. Anne smiled at her, reassuring her that she had not done wrong.

'No, I have not,' said Freddy. 'Perhaps I may, one day; though some very sad things happen there, so I am not so sure. However, I have eaten several pineapples.' She grinned.

The reverend appeared, took in the scene, and sighed. 'There you are, Polly. Not again? Well, never mind, finish clearing up, now, and get along with you.'

Polly did as she was told, then attempted a curtsey whilst holding the full tray, and nearly dropped it again, before shuffling out of the room.

'Depend upon it, Miss Swinglehurst,' said the reverend, 'if there is something in a house worth breaking, that girl will do the job.'

'She will acquire a little more grace in time, I am sure, and grow into a swan,' said Freddy, smiling.

'What news of the inquest?' Anne addressed her husband, her peace now replaced by anxiety.

'Do not upset yourself, my love,' said Jonathan, sitting down. 'They found it was her heart, poor woman, and so she died a very natural if very unfortunate death. Mr Winkworth is burying her today, and will do it very decently.' He looked at Freddy. 'Forgive me, Miss Swinglehurst, you may not be aware of the terrible business occurring here just in the past few days. We found the dead body of a woman – a woman with child – in the front grounds here at the rectory, of all places, and it is all a terrible mystery. An inquest was held this morning at the Hog and Gibbett Inn. The surgeon found weakness in the woman's heart, and suspected that she had borne some great sorrow – wandering here as a stranger as she did - so that the combination of these two things had caused the heart to fail, and so the death.'

'Poor creature,' said Freddy. 'Yes, I had heard something of it. But what if her friends are looking for her? You mention that she is being buried today. How will they know? How will they find her?

'I am not sure,' said Jonathan, 'it is very difficult. We wanted to treat her with dignity, and you know she has no burial rights here as a non-resident of the parish, and then if there was suspicion about a possible suicide, a Christian burial would be entirely ruled out. We thought it best to bury her quickly and let her rest in peace. The alternatives could have been far worse.'

'I see, yes, and I am very glad to hear about the compassion of the parish in this instance. Nevertheless, it would be helpful to try to discover more about her, for her friends' sake.'

'Oh, yes,' said Jonathan. 'Winkworth – my curate – and I will be sure to continue to make enquiries.'

The door was pushed open and Mary appeared with a tray.

'Begging your pardon, sir,' said Mary, 'I thought it best to do the job myself, what with Polly the way she is.' Mary rolled her beautiful eyes and gave her mistress a quick, hard look as she put the tray down on the table.

Freddy noticed, and wondered why Anne put up with such impertinence. But what a remarkably handsome woman Mary was; it was a pleasure to look at her. Mary turned to Freddy, smiled tightly, curtseyed and left the room.

Anne began to look upset, then got up abruptly. 'Please forgive me, Miss Swinglehurst; I feel a little unwell.' She smiled weakly at Freddy and hurried from the room.

'Oh dear,' said Freddy. 'Poor thing. Shall I go after her?'

'No, thank you, Fredericka. I find she is best left alone for a short while when she has these little turns.'

'If you do not mind me saying, Mary's manner, for a servant, seems a little haughty.'

'Not at all,' said Jonathan. 'Her manner does leave much to be desired; I will have to check her about it, and not for the first time. She is such a good housekeeper, however, that we are loath to lose her. But it was not Mary that upset my wife. It is the dead woman. Anne was the first to notice the body. She is very delicate at the best of times and gets upset so easily. I think the worst thing for her to bear is that the woman was with child. We have not been blessed with children, you see, and it is a very painful matter for her.'

'Oh, Jonathan, I am sorry. Poor Anne. And you? How do you bear it?'

The reverend gave a short laugh. 'I have never been asked that question. I suppose I bear it as well as I can, as well as any man can. The most difficult thing is my position here. I give my sermon in church, sometimes, and I can see the looks of contempt - or perhaps of pity - on the faces of some of the congregants. How can he preach the word of the Lord, they are thinking, the message to go forth and multiply, when the Lord has seen fit to make them barren?'

'No, Reverend. People are kinder than you think. Your sorrow is your burden, and you bear it, as they have to bear theirs. Surely that makes you a better priest?'

Jonathan looked at Freddy, and smiled. 'Dear Freddy, you always did have that way of making one feel special, and of smoothing over one's flaws and defects until one thinks oneself quite a king. I am not a particularly amiable fellow, am I, thinking about my own vanity rather than Anne's womanly grief? I confess that I sometimes resent being in this parish. I saw myself once as Bishop of Winchester, or even of Westminster. What a pompous fool I am!'

'No. You were always ambitious, and surely that is something to be applauded. You are still young. There is time.'

Jonathan laughed. 'I do not feel young; and I am five and thirty. I grant you, there is still time to rise. But I do find myself feeling at times as if my best life has passed.'

'Nonsense.' Freddy laughed. 'Oh dear, I sound just like my father used to! But you do have your whole career ahead of you; you must not give up. In the meantime, I am sure you do much good here.'

'I rather doubt that. And if I were less selfish, and wanted truly to do good, I would take myself off to an impoverished parish, confine myself to a scanty pittance, and do something for the sick and needy. Us Winchester clerics live so well, and grow so fat and gouty, it is quite shameful.'

'No, sir, I do not believe this picture you are painting. Mr Campbell tells me that you are quite the philanthropist, and commit a great deal of your time to fighting against the slave trade.'

'I give lectures and try to raise funds, it is true, and I travel a great deal to do so. But then I neglect my poor wife; I feel I enjoy my cause too much.' Jonathan smiled at himself. 'Well, well, listen to me discoursing on and on about my wrongs and sorrows, as if you were my great confessor. Poor Fredericka, you must be regretting accepting that invitation.'

'Not at all, Reverend. It is a pleasure to be here.'

'But, pray, tell me how you do. You look a little frailer than you used to do, if you will beg my pardon for saying so. Though I can still see the quaint little face of the old Freddy smiling at me from behind those spectacles. I remember you were thought to be quite the beauty once. I never noticed it, but apparently you were.'

Freddy laughed. 'Why, thank you for the fulsome compliment, sir. No, I am quite sure that I was never considered a beauty. I was too small and odd-looking, like a boy. Even in my finery. Do you remember that summer ball at the great house? It was in the year 1792. Well, I was dancing very happily with Charles, and I overheard the Lord de Vere describe me as "not bouncing and buxom enough" for his tastes.'

'The Countess Darby whom he is about to marry is certainly bouncing and buxom. You could port a ship in that bosom of hers. I once saw her struggling for not less than fifteen minutes to get out of his carriage.'

'Reverend, do not be wicked.'

The reverend puffed out his cheeks and stomach, and mimed a struggle to get out of his chair.

'Stop! Poor old Annabel Darby. I do like her so. She is so enthusiastic, for an aristocrat. I find it infectious. And she has always been so very kind to me. Have you heard about the diamond?'

'Indeed, yes. She must be terribly shocked, and I hope de Vere is not having second thoughts. I fear that the stone was a crucial part of the bargain from the gentleman's side. I cannot help but wonder about that diamond. Nobody knows how the de Lacey family really came by it. It appears to be more celestial blight than celestial light.'

'I quite agree with you. But, stay, I forgot to mention that I met Anne's cousin, the captain, the other day, but only for a few minutes. He called at the old manor house. The Campbells speak very highly of him. It must be pleasant for your wife to have a family member close by.'

'Yes, they are great friends, and he does her a deal

of good. I am afraid that he is not so fond of me, however. We cannot seem to find each other's good points. I find him a little too serious, and by trying to poke some humour out of him I turn myself into a buffoon.'

'Oh dear; family connections can be rather trying, I know, though I have been exceeding fortunate in my own.'

'That you have. How are the Campbells? I have not called for a while. You must have missed them.'

'They are well, thank you, and, yes, I have missed them a very great deal.' Freddy hesitated. 'I should have come to them sooner. For a time, in London, I became a person that I did not like. The Campbells are so good, so pure, that I felt they would see my taint, or that I would taint them in some way.'

Jonathan looked concerned. 'Freddy, I am sure that could never be the case.'

'Thank you, but I assure you it was. But I am home now, and Gabriel and Margaret are like second father and mother to me.'

'What has brought you back after all this time?'

'I have come to stay, and to settle. I found that I grew tired of the noise and throng of London, and was craving fresh air, green fields and broad skies. Come the summer, I shall take my father's old bath chair to a sunny corner of the garden, and spend all my time reading scandalous novels, gossiping with Mrs C and eating her queen cakes. I will grow as fat as my hair grows white, and fade contentedly into the grave to the sound of the larks singing and the fragrance of Hampshire lavender.'

The reverend laughed loudly, which, Freddy remembered, was like the pleasant barking of a dog. 'I see that you have not lost your poetic sensibility,' he said. 'But I do hope you are not quite ready to shuffle off this mortal coil, not when we just have you back amongst us.'

'Fear not, I shall stay a while yet. Mrs C is making a new batch of queen cakes.'

'Agh yes, the famous cakes. But did you never want to marry? Forgive an old friend yet another impertinent question. I quite shock myself, today, with my bold inquisitiveness.'

'I do not mind.' Freddy found herself blushing a little. 'No, I did not want to marry. There was nobody who seemed to compare to Charles, or perhaps I could not see them clearly. I liked one or two gentlemen – if that does not sound too profligate – but it never quite felt real. I suppose that I was not really myself at that time, and the gentlemen who sought me were seeking that strange self, and so not really me.' Freddy smiled. 'You see that I still talk in riddles.'

'Aye, poetic riddles.' But I am truly sorry about what happened to Charles, and for your other sorrows.'

'Thank you, Jonathan. I am very glad to see that you are so happily matched. Anne is so gentle, and what a delicate beauty she is with those large grey eyes and perfectly drawn brows, like the finest porcelain vase.'

'Yes, she is both of those things, and more; she is my dearest life.' Jonathan smiled. 'In fact, if you do not mind, I will go to her now that she has had her little time alone. I cannot be easy myself when she is suffering. We have not even drunk our tea.'

'You must go,' said Freddy, 'and what a thoughtful and attentive husband my old friend has turned out to be.'

'I flatter myself I have.'

'It does my heart good to hear you. In fact, I should also be getting home. Margaret will be feeling anxious, and suspecting I have been kidnapped by highwaymen. She will send out poor Mr C to find me, and he will drive even more alike to a madman than usual and chaos will descend across Hampshire.'

Jonathan laughed. 'Samuel can take you in the curricle. Will you not struggle with that bad leg?'

'Thank you, but there is really no need. I would prefer to walk, and tis such a short journey. I believe that I am already quite the celebrity in the village and no harm can come to me strolling alone. As to my leg, it is really not that bad. I had a small accident a few years since and use the stick more from habit than necessity. I rather like it. It gives me an air of romance, like a tragic heroine in a novel.'

The reverend laughed again and shook his head. 'A poet, an original, a mystery. Still the same old Freddy, after all.'

As Freddy walked back through the front grounds of the rectory, she noticed Mary stood near the side of the house very close to a tall man, with whom she was in animated conversation. The man looked familiar, though he had his back to Freddy's view. It looked like Captain Lefroy – and she felt a slight nervousness at the thought - though she could not be sure. She supposed he must be quite familiar with all of the household, being Anne's cousin and a frequent visitor. Still, it looked a little odd. Then again, bearing in mind the combination of what sailors were – naturally excepting her good father and her former fiancé – and Mary's great beauty, she would not be surprised if there was some kind of intimacy between them. Perhaps this explained Mary's bold manner? Did Jonathan know about it? Did Mrs Millbrook?

Chapter 5

A couple of days after Freddy's call at the rectory, not that far away in the neighbouring city of Southampton, a man was walking leisurely along a ramshackle street in a very poor neighbourhood close by King Street. Onlookers would have noticed a short, stocky figure in dark clothes, his head covered by a black hood. He stopped twice to cough, loudly and hoarsely, and then to breathe out, rasping, and take a few minutes to let his lungs clear, and his breathing steady. It was early evening, but still light; he felt most comfortable in the dark these days but the season was against him. If anyone caught a glimpse of the man's face, they looked away quickly; with its even features and slightly heavy brow, it would have been unremarkable except for its skin - yellow, scarred and dotted with sores. A child later told its mother that he had seen the grim reaper himself walking down the street, and his mother simply nodded and said that yes, death was indeed a frequent visitor there.

The man knocked at the door of a rough lodging-house, which was answered by a greasy, slovenly woman of about thirty years of age. She was holding a baby that was smeared with dirt, while another, equally filthy, child of about two years of age clung to her legs. The woman, Mrs Sally Smith, was the elder sister of a David Barber, former under-butler at the Darby townhouse in London. Mrs Smith stared at the visitor's face, her small blue eyes full of their usual despair.

'Good evening, ma'am,' he said. 'Do not vex yourself; I'm not contagious.'

Mrs Smith shrugged; she had long given up trying to stave off disease; God gave and he took away, and that was that.

'I'm here to see your brother; he might be expecting me.'

'Yes. Come in. Davey's in the cellar.'

'You don't want to ask my name, madam?'

Mrs Smith shrugged again. It was perfectly obvious to her who he was. The man stepped into the house, where another scrawny child, a girl of about five years old, was stood, wiping some grubby tears from her cheeks. Mrs Smith pointed to a broken, half-open door on the right of the hall place, which led downstairs, then turned to go back upstairs, saying as she went:

'I don't want anything to do with what he's done or might do. I try my best to be respectable, which isn't easy here, but just keep me out of it.' The girl picked up the toddler with both her thin arms, and carried him up the stairs, following her mother, once turning round awkwardly, to get a final look at the strange man's face.

The man made his way down the broken stairs to the dank, foetid cellar room, shivering slightly, despite the warmth of the day.

'Mr Barber,' he said, looking at the man squatting on some broken bricks, which served as a chair. Barber was a few years younger than his sister, had a florid complexion, fair hair and a squashed nose, and his face was marked by several bruises and cuts.

'Mr Short, sir.' David jumped up and went to shake Mr Short's hand. He was reluctant to do so – was his disease catching? – but felt the need to be conciliatory given the mess he had made of the theft, and not least the fact that he was terrified of the man. 'Sit down, sir, sit down.' Barber smirked and simpered as if he was still performing his butler duties for the Countess. 'I'm sorry for the nature of our meeting place, but I must lie low a while until I can get away.'

'I hope you're not planning to run away with a certain jewel, Mr Barber?' said Mr Short, sitting down on a deal chair, which David had kept free for him. Short's tone was civil – too civil – slightly sneering, and with a hint of menace in it.

'Oh no, sir, of course not, sir.' Barber sat back down. 'If only I had it. We'd all be counting our guineas now instead of where we are.' He quickly glanced round the room in a fidgety manner, which was bare apart from the bricks and the chair, some straw covered by a rough blanket, which served as the bed, and a large, cracked pewter vessel, which was used as the piss pot and repository for all other filth.

'Why didn't you make contact with me sooner?' asked Short.

'I couldn't, sir. I wasn't able to get away on the Sunday, as the household was in uproar and the constable was questioning us all and searching for the jewel. Suspicion was beginning to fall on me. They didn't know anything; it was only due to the spite of the other servants, I'm sure – hang them all! Anyway, I had to make the decision to flee from the house in the early hours of Monday morning; as you see from my face, I had a little trouble with the law. I managed to get to Sarah, and tell her what happened, and told her to pass that onto you. Then I had to run, and made my way hither, as I told you I would if things got too hot; I didn't want to end up facing the noose without having had any previous joy for it.'

'You say that the jewel disappeared, so you're telling me that you didn't take it? Didn't you even try?'

Mr Barber looked sheepish. 'I did take it, sir, and all as instructed, but left it alone for a brief moment, only the very briefest moment, I swear to it, and then it was gone.'

'Are you lying to me?'

'No, sir, I promise you.'

'You're a greater simpleton than I thought, then. Why did I trust you with this?'

'It was just one moment's inattention. I can't quite believe it myself. I've done other jobs, as you know, sir, and not the smallest thing went wrong. I pride myself in my work. I'm quite renowned for my proficiency, and…'

'Oh, stop your mouth, Barber. What do you think happened to the diamond? Tell me how it disappeared. Give me the full story, and nothing but the truth, mind.'

'Yes, sir. It was quite late in the evening. As planned, I got the drug into the Countess's drink, and also in one for her lady's maid. It didn't take long to encourage Miss Baines to take a little nightcap; she rather likes me, I think. It was all very smooth. The guests were leaving and the Countess grew so heavy that she had to retire before they'd all quite gone. Miss Baines went after her, as usual, to help her mistress undress, and I followed them upstairs, at a quiet distance, and got near to the dressing room. I could see that the maid took off the necklace from around her lady's neck and placed it on the dressing table next to the locking box. Then she helped her off with all the layers and nonsense that these women wear, which seemed to take an age. They were both so drowsy by this point that the Countess dismissed Miss Baines, who dragged herself to her chamber a few doors down – she didn't seem to notice me - and the Countess staggered through to her bedchamber and must have crawled into her bed.

'I waited a few moments, looked about me, then

went into the Countess's dressing room where the necklace was waiting snugly on the table, as if waiting for me. I picked it up, easy as you like, and held the stone in its setting.'

David paused, assumed a slightly dreamy expression, and stroked his left palm with his right hand, as if he was still touching the jewel.

He continued. 'I felt a sort of glow of power – it must be true what they say about the diamond; anyone could be king of the world with that in their hands. Oh, what I would do.'

Barber stopped again, closed his eyes, smiled, and held out both his arms, palms upwards, like an eastern god basking in the sun. The rough skin of his face gleamed for a second or two, and then for the shortest, barely perceptible moment, his skin became a red-raw, open wound of sores, pus ran down his cheeks and chin, and his eyes glowed a sickly yellow.

Mr Short blinked, wiped the sweat from his brow, and looked at David with contempt. 'You would be a worse fool than you are now,' said he. 'Drop that ridiculous pose and get on with the tale, Barber.'

David opened his eyes and wiped the smile from his face. 'Yes, Mr Short. I got near to the door, but then heard the sound of someone coming. It wouldn't have done either of us much good, sir, for me to be seen with the gem hot in my hands, so I placed it inside the Countess's sewing box, chain and all, which was on a shelf near the door – rather a clever place to put the jewel,

I thought, nice and innocent looking. Then I quit the room and walked up the next pair of stairs for a few moments until the noise had gone.'

In fact, David, on hearing the noise, had been in a state of great panic, and had put the necklace in the fine, lacquered workbox only because it was in his eyeline – he would have dropped it on the floor, otherwise – and hurried out of the room and up the stairs with great clatter and bluster. He was an ignorant, sly fellow, with a great deal of self-consequence, prone to fits of violence, who had got lucky in the past with some petty criminal activities that went undetected but was hardly up to anything that required a cooler brain and a courageous heart.

'Then you went back?'

'Yes, sir; the noise stopped and I'd been gone barely a few moments.' It was actually fifteen minutes, when he had stood on the second-floor landing place with his heart beating wildly and his body sweating. He had almost given up on the whole venture, but on finding all quiet when he walked back down the stairs and past the Countess's room, he went back in on impulse and opened the workbox. 'The box was empty.'

'You didn't see anyone at all? Surely there must have been someone around.'

'No, I swear it, sir. But, yes, somebody must have been there and taken the stone – that was the noise I heard. I went back down to the ground floor to help with the clearing up; I knew I'd be missed and that the other servants would be grumbling about me. I was on the lookout for the diamond all the time, and even got up in the night to search where I could.' Mr Barber had not left his bed. He had spent a sleepless night listening to the loud snoring of the groomsman, with whom he shared the room, terrified that at any moment the authorities would bang on the door and cart him off to gaol.

'And you said you made contact with Sarah?'

'Oh yes, sir; we were to meet on Monday last at midday, as you know, but I managed to get her up early that morning with the help of the housemaid at her lodgings. I told her what had happened and asked her to tell you, and I said she should wait for the gentleman to come, as planned, in the next few days. She was very upset that I didn't have the diamond to pass on to her, and said the gentleman might be angry, and she went away in a state of confusion. I don't think she can grasp even the commonest idea, like most of these stupid moors that we see everywhere now. I don't know why the gentleman was wasting his time with that animal whore – some men have the most peculiar taste. They mate with apes, you know. I heard that somewhere. I'm sure you've seen it with your own eyes. You know what to do with the likes of them, sir – you understand me.'

'Shut up your filthy mouth, you devil.'

'What? What have I said?'

'Just keep your dirty opinions to yourself, and know your place, before I smash that useless head of yours against that wall.'

'All right, sir, yes sir, as you wish. I was only saying.'

'Well, don't; I'm already as tired as a man could be with your whining tones. Sarah has disappeared, it seems. I called at her lodgings that Tuesday, and a few times since, and her landlady hasn't seen her since that day. I did not speak to the housemaid, however; what does she know of the business?'

'Oh, nothing at all. I befriended her in case I needed to get to Sarah quickly. A little charm goes a long way, I find.'

'You are quite the lady's man, Mr Barber.'

David was about to smile conspiratorially, when he registered the sneer on Short's cracked and scabbed lips.

'I need to find Sarah,' said Short. 'I hope, for your sake, that you've not made a plan together to make away with the stone, for you wouldn't live long to enjoy it, my boy.'

'Of course not, Mr Short. I wouldn't be here now, would I, if I'd dared to do such a thing? And I wouldn't have given you my sister's address, open and honest, so that you could find me.'

David had not wanted to give the address to Short, but was not given much choice when he had agreed to be involved in the scheme. Besides, he had not doubted of its efficacy, and thought that he would by now be rioting in lust and luxury. When the theft failed, he had contemplated fleeing as far away as possible, but he had nothing to run with, and had decided that he should take his chance with Short, and a play of humble honesty, with the hope of still getting something from the plan, or at least of getting away a little better prepared.

'Now,' said Short, 'assuming I believe what you've told me so far, do you have any suspicion as to who could have taken the diamond? Another servant or even a visitor to the house that evening? If we can find it again, there might still be a little something in the business for you, but if we don't, it looks like you'll be stuck in this hole for the rest of your life.'

'Well, I'm not quite sure, sir, but there could be someone.' David looked at his companion slyly. 'I'm a bit hesitant to suggest it now that you seem so sensitive about our blackamoor men and brothers. But it's the head-butler, another coal-faced fellow in our midst. He's quite a favourite with the Countess. The women do love them, don't they? She's a lusty jade, that Countess; always fucking someone like a bitch on heat.'

Mr Short got up, raised his left fist, and punched Mr Barber hard to the left side of his head. David's body jerked sideways and he fell from the bricks.

'What did I tell you about keeping that vile mouth of yours shut?' said Short. 'You're a disgrace to the human race. Do you know what I used to do to those who disobeyed me on my plantation? I got someone to shit in their mouth, then tape it up for hours on end until they were gagging and bawling like a baby. And that was just me warming up. What I'm thinking now is that those who talk as much shit as you do deserve a bit of shit in their mouths, so if you don't pay heed and stop spewing your filth at me, I might have to give you a little present.'

David was whimpering on the floor, his body curled

up, his head bleeding. 'I didn't mean it, sir; I didn't mean anything by it. I couldn't be more sorry, sir, if I've caused offence. It's just my way of talking, just a little fun, if you like. My mouth does run away with me, sometimes; I'm a foolish fellow, but I don't mean anything by it, really; it's just a bit of nonsense.'

'Just get up off the floor and tell me the name of this butler.'

David got up slowly, cowering and still crying a little as he sat back down on the bricks. 'Matthew Lane, sir. It's just an idea, though, just a thought. I don't know anything for certain.'

'Well, I'll find out, Mr Barber. Now I shall leave you in peace. And just a reminder, my man; don't even think about trying to cross me in any way, or your next gift after the shit will be me stringing you up by the balls and setting some rabid dogs on you. They'll make quick work of your tiny prick, I can assure you.'

David swallowed. 'Yes, sir. No, sir. I won't say a word, ever, to anyone; on my life, Mr Short.'

'I wish you good day, Mr Barber.' Mr Short smiled.

Adam Short made his way up the stairs and through the vestibule, quitted the house and set off in the direction of his lodging house. He walked slowly, whistling a tune as he went. He was feeling quite exhilarated. How the old adrenaline had rushed back when the violence stirred within him. He did not have long to live, he knew. All he wanted now was to get a bit of money for his love and their children, then – if he lasted that long –

to get back to Antigua to die. He had expected no more pleasures – great or small – from the time he had left, but it seemed he was wrong, and there were still some tiny kicks of joy to be had after all.

David Barber finished his crying, then went crawling up stairs to his sister, who patched him up a little and gave him a couple of coins. He must get far, far away, he thought. He had once contemplated going out to the West Indies himself, thinking that the slavery business would suit a fine fellow like him. But now the idea appalled and terrified him. He could imagine being pursued across the Caribbean by that mad bastard, Short, and tortured to death. No, Australia might be the best place. He had heard that it was very far away and surely nowhere near the Indies? Perhaps he could get himself transported.

'Don't come back this time, Davey,' his sister said, as she closed the front door on him.

Chapter 6

Freddy, still feeling unwell after her call at the rectory, spent the next five days settling into her old home. The weather had also taken a cooler turn, and so she was content to wander through the house and grounds making plans with the Campbells; Flip, if he had the energy, would plod slowly after them. The dead woman was on Freddy's mind, and she was determined to find out more if she could – it saddened her to think of this woman and her unborn child lying alone in strange ground, with nobody to visit them. At night, or in dozing, fevered daylight moments, the story of this woman and that of the Celestial Light would combine together to produce strange dreams. In one, the woman knocked at their kitchen door, which Freddy, dressed in her gentleman's garb and a sailor's tricorn hat, would answer, to find her standing there smiling, the diamond in one hand and her tiny, wrinkled baby in the other, as if both were of equal weight, like two plums she was about to juggle. Freddy was pleased that her good friend, Aphrodite Sweet, was arriving from London that Thursday for a few days' visit. It would be a relief to talk to her, and she also planned for them to go into Winchester together and make some enquiries.

Margaret had been upon the gad around the village, which was all abuzz with the news, and was giving Freddy intricate and colourful, if not especially informative, daily updates. Reports ranged from various sightings of the woman – apparently in different places at the same time, or even when she was already dead – to suggestions that there must be a murderer on the loose. Even Margaret, however, drew the line at one notion that the Reverend Millbrook worshipped the devil, and required the sacrifice of half-formed children. Freddy missed a call by Captain Lefroy, being asleep in her chamber. She was half disappointed, being quite intrigued by the man, half relieved; if he was the man she had seen in that furtive manner with Mary, she felt that she could not quite trust him.

Another strange, but rather wonderful, thing, happened at this time. One afternoon, Freddy was sat in her comfortable chair in her dressing room, half dozing, half reading the *Chronicle*, which was disappointingly lacking in any updates on the woman or the diamond, when she heard a loud scuffling and scratching noise coming from the chimney. Was it a bird? Oh, poor creature. She hated to see animals suffer. As a child, her father used to read to her Thomas Percival's *A Father's Instructions to his Children*, and she had very much taken it to heart. She got up and stared at the fireplace, which was now emitting a blueish smoke. She was sure that it was not lit when she entered the room. Oh dear, the bird.

'Fredericka Elizabeth Swinglehurst, are you smoking my pipe?' A man's voice seemed to come through the fireplace, and in a flash there was the figure of her father, just as she remembered him before he died, dressed in his old-fashioned knee breeches, stockings and waistcoat, his powdered wig tied in a low ponytail. The figure, which was more a smoky outline than flesh and blood, wobbled slightly on its feet, before righting itself and standing upright.

Freddy laughed, closed her eyes and rubbed them. She must be even more fatigued and fevered than she thought, and the emotions triggered by her return home were conjuring up phantoms. She opened her eyes.

'And are you drinking my claret? And wearing long breeches? Egad, I knew that civilization was on the decline ere I went but I never expected this level of anarchy and chaos.'

'Father?' Freddy rubbed her eyes again, her heart pounding. 'Is it really you?'

'Of course it is, my dear. Who else would it be?'

Freddy stared and stared, but the ghostly figure of the admiral did not disappear. 'Oh, father.' She jumped up and ran to embrace him, but found her arms going straight through the thick, swirling smoke. 'Oh.' The smoke was a little chilly too. She shivered.

'I am sorry, my dear. I am not quite what I was in the old world. But sit down now and I will join you. And I shall have a glass of the ruby stuff and a smoke of that pipe. The smell must have pulled me through at last; I have been trying for some time now.'

Freddy continued to stare at the apparition of Admiral Swinglehurst.

'Well, sit down, dear,' continued the admiral. 'A man might die of thirst if he has to wait for his one and only daughter to finish gawping at him.'

The admiral grinned at Freddy, the remarkably good teeth he had in life still present and correct, and guided her back to her chair with the cold breeze of his arm. He picked up the pipe from the side-table, managed to re-light it using a taper, then, smiling dreamily, he part-floated, part-walked, wobbling slightly, over to his old desk, skilfully picked up the bottle of claret and the spare glass with his free hand, and took a few moments to position himself above his old tapestried chair, before slowly sitting down in it.

Freddy, her eyes still fixed on her father, mechanically picked up her own glass of wine, gulped back its remaining contents, then put the glass down. She smiled in wonder. If this was a dream – which it surely must be – she might as well enjoy it. Her father, her dearest father, come back to her after all these years. She now watched, fascinated, as the admiral poured himself a glass of claret and drank it back, a red glow briefly suffusing his smoky face. He put down the glass and smacked his lips, then took a deep puff on the pipe, exhaling orange wisps of smoke that gradually faded.

'Have the French invaded at last, daughter?' The admiral looked round the room, taking in the rococo flourishes on some of the furniture and drapery. 'What collection of Frenchified gewgaws, gimcracks and tinsel is this?'

Freddy laughed. 'No, father, dear. I wanted a pretty room and Mrs Gabriel managed it for me before I came home. She may have got a little carried away with the decoration. I fear it strays into the gaudy, vulgar and tasteless; everything a room ought not to be and so exactly what I currently cherish.'

The ghost of Admiral William Swinglehurst gave one of his familiar croaky laughs, a deeper version of Freddy's own, bending his shoulders forwards then throwing back his head. 'You always were a contrary little soul. I never quite knew what was really going on inside that lovely head of yours and could hardly ever second-guess you.'

'I do not know myself much of the time, dear father. But, where are you? I mean, where have you come from? Is it heaven?'

'Well, it would not be the other place, I hope. I should think you know me better than that. We are not at liberty to speak too freely on these matters, my dear. Rest assured, all is well. Tis just that we sometimes have a little hankering for the old world, so to speak, especially when a loved one is yearning, or we crave a taste of the old comforts; I have been thirsting after a nip of brandy and a puff on the old pipe. I have got myself quite lost, either stuck in an old door, or behind a gate, or tripping up in the grounds somewhere. How I ever made a sailor I do not know. Perhaps it is a landlubber matter. If I haunt a ship, I may have better luck. Well, well, I am here now.'

The admiral topped up his glass of claret from the bottle on the floor and took several large gulps. 'Oh, that feels quite heavenly.' He chuckled. 'Do not mind my little joke, dear. It is chilly work navigating the old world and the new. But I feel much more snug now.' The admiral glowed again briefly, in shades of red and orange. 'Now, my little sailor, I cannot stay long so do tell me what is in your heart. I am sensing danger about, and you must take heed. Yes, that is mainly why I came, I am sure – forgive me, dear, I get a little confused and forget my purpose.'

'Danger? Oh, father. You always did worry so. I am very well, and have nothing at all to vex me. I have come home to Hampshire to have a quiet life, and to be the village spinster. I have been living in London for many years and I am tired now, and yearn for a bit of peace. And, of course, it has tugged at the heart being back after all this time. Perhaps that is what drew you? Apart from the pipe, that is.'

'Perhaps, my love. But I am sure that you must take extra care. I have been feeling a pain here, and here,' – the admiral pointed at his head and heart – 'and it is easing a little now that I am discharging my duty, and warning you. What a relief. But do you still keep that pistol I gave you? And always on you? You must never let your guard down, you know.'

'Rest assured, father, I have the pistol somewhere nearby. But I really cannot imagine being in any danger here in Winchester, and snug here at home with the good Campbells.'

'No, but nevertheless I feel sure that you should be on the alert. Alas, there is more evil in this world than there should be.' The admiral punched a smoky fist in the air. 'Where is the pistol? Is it loaded?'

'It is in my workbox, I believe.'

Freddy glanced at her needlework box, made in the shape of a country cottage, which was positioned near her feet on the floor. She bent down to open the lid, took out a Manton pistol, flicked it round several times on her wrist, threw it into the air, caught it, and put it back in the box.

The ghost looked reassured, then grinned. 'Well, you have remembered my lessons, after all; that is something. But you must make sure you have a good supply of shot. Promise me.'

'I promise, father.'

The ghost sighed, and took a puff on the pipe. 'But what is this nonsense about spinsterhood, child? And you such a beauty. The most lovely, bright thing I ever saw, apart from your dear mother, that is. And to choose a spinster's life, and be the subject of ridicule and contempt.'

'I will never be that, for I am your daughter, and I

have position and wealth. I will not have to suffer that painful sort of dependence and mortification, or be subject to the whims and demands of others. But even if I wanted a husband, I am two and thirty years old, father, hardly the blushing bride. I believe I am considered ancient – practically dead - in terms of the market.'

'Nonsense, nonsense. Your life is only just beginning. And there need be no talk of markets.'

'Well, try not to be uneasy about me. I am truly well.' Freddy paused. 'I will admit that it was not always so. I found it very hard to lose you, but it was in the nature of things, and I had Charles. Then, the cruellest thing, he died from sickness at sea, when this war had barely begun. And it was not six months after you had left me. Did you know that?'

'Yes, dear.' The smoke of the admiral's eyes crackled slightly, and he held his glass of claret next to his heart, which made a mild, hissing sound.

'And I felt like one of those paper boats that you made for me as a child – do you remember? - bobbing on a great and stormy ocean. I wanted the waves to wash me away.'

'I know, dearest, I know it.'

'But they did not. And I reached land somehow. And I lived. I went to London, and, to be candid, was in quite the wild whirl of dissipation for a time. I grew steadier, but still independent. Now I am happy, indeed, and could not imagine my life any other way. And when I think of women like Lady Darby, about to take her sixth husband, I feel quite exhausted.'

'Now, my dear, nobody is asking you to take six husbands. One will be quite sufficient. But I suppose one can only admire the stamina of the countess.'

'You were a favourite of hers once, I think?'

'Ahem, yes, well. She was a fine woman, but a little too much for me.'

Freddy grinned. 'She has just had a great diamond of hers stolen, you know.'

'Indeed? Well, I am sorry for the lady. She always was fond of baubles, and the riches with which to procure them. But great wealth can be a great snare and a great evil, as I saw in the Caribbean, and as your poor dear mother experienced.'

'Will you tell me more about her life there?'

'Yes, dear, but not now; there is little time. Though I will say that she would not be over-fond of this peculiar gentleman's garb you are wearing – tis not quite fitting for a lady.'

'Oh, tis just for comfort when I am alone. You should try wearing stays all day.'

'I have worn them, once or twice.'

Freddy's mouth opened.

'Aye, indeed. Surely, I told you about the Crossing the Line ceremony on board ship, to commemorate a sailor's first crossing of the equator? Well, I made a fine Her Highness Amphitrite on those occasions. Then we put on all sorts of entertainments - plays and comedies and concerts - you know, when a man could be a woman. Tis true, I was not a very pretty wench, though that was likely for the best.' The admiral paused. Perhaps he had said too much.

'How delightful.' Freddy beamed at the ghost, imagining it in full female regalia. 'Will you not sing for me now, as you used to do? And dance the hornpipe?'

'Not now, dearest. I am afraid that it is time to go.'

The admiral's figure was starting to disintegrate, to get colder. Wisps of him were being pulled towards the fireplace.

'But, father, do not go. Or not just yet, at least. You have only just arrived. We have a great deal to talk about it, and I have so many questions.'

'Forgive me, dear, but I do not have a choice in the matter. However, I hope to come again, so do not fret. Perhaps keep the tobacco and the ruby liquid handy, and a tot of brandy, too, to keep an old sailor's heart stout. Oh, and a little Dr Johnson would be very welcome; the old volumes should be in my study. Above all, take care, and keep that pistol loaded! God bless you, my dear, and keep you safe this night.'

'Aye, aye, Admiral.'

'Aye, aye, sailor.'

Freddy stared at the last wisps of smoke as they disappeared up the chimney. She got up from her chair, walked over to the fireplace, knelt down and bent her head to look up inside the chimney, as if expecting her father's smoky legs to be hanging there. She stood up, went over to the chair where the ghost had sat, stroked it and then grasped the air around it with her hands, as if trying to feel her father's presence again. Nothing remained. She sighed, picked up the discarded glass of wine and the pipe, and returned to her own chair. She looked over at the fireplace, rubbed her eyes again, and smiled.

Chapter 7

Thursday morning came, and Freddy was stood in the driveway of the old manor house, shivering slightly with the cool wind, which was just blowing away the previous night's heavy rain. Flip, positioned next to her legs as was now customary with him, began wagging his tail with as much vigour as he could manage, as Gabriel drove through the gates, Affy beside him waving energetically.

'Affy!' shouted Freddy.

The gig stopped and Affy jumped out expertly before Gabriel could climb down to help. She hurried over to Freddy to embrace her, the pair looking more like mother and child than old friends, given Affy's tall stature. Affy pulled back and delivered a half-ironic curtsey.

'Foolish thing,' said Freddy, looking happily at her friend's familiar face, with its slightly protruding blue eyes, snub nose and wide mouth. 'You are no longer my maid.'

'I know it, but tis a hard habit to break. How are you managing without me? Very badly, I should think?'

'Not at all, Mrs Aphrodite, I assure you. I manage very well, indeed, and cannot think how I ever needed you at all. Though I will confess that Mr and Mrs Gabriel fill the breach quite well. In matter of fact, I am just as spoilt as I always was, if not more so. I have become quite tyrannical.'

'You always were a terrible tyrant and I do not know how I ever put up with you.'

Gabriel had climbed down from the gig and was stood by holding Affy's small box and a large sack of sugar.

'Poor Mr Campbell here is quite worn out, are you not, sir?' continued Affy, looking at Gabriel. 'He confessed all his grievances and sorrows to me on our journey and I quite sympathised. The only thing stopping him from throwing himself out of the carriage was the thought of Mrs Campbell's queen cakes, which I hear are famous all over Hampshire, if not the world.'

Gabriel, bewildered but happy with the friends' chatter, nodded at Affy and smiled at Freddy.

'Aye,' said Freddy. 'Mrs Gabriel lives in the kitchen, working day and night to satisfy the world's demand for the cakes, and wagons roll in and out twice a day to take them to Portsmouth, and from hence to our brave sailors all over the globe. But you must come into the kitchen directly, and try some. Mrs Gabriel will not be gainsaid. You must be hungry, dear, and very tired.'

'I confess I am very much of both, though I came only from Southampton this morning – I have been visiting my aunt, you know – so today's journey has not been so bad. Though judging from my somewhat wild appearance, you might think I had been accosted by highwaymen.'

Freddy took in Affy's dishevelled hair, damp clothes and pink face, and laughed. 'Indeed, you are quite the fright, my dear. I hope you did not scare Mr Campbell too much when he first laid eyes upon you.'

Freddy and Affy walked round the side of the house to the kitchen, Gabriel behind them balancing Affy's wooden box on his left arm and dragging the rather heavy bag of sugar with his right. Good gracious, he thought, what a strong and hearty lass this Affy was. As the ladies reached the door, Gabriel let go of the sugar and stepped forward to open it, and a warm, sweet smell filled their nostrils. Margaret, always happy to meet new people, beamed at them and took Affy's hand as they stepped in.

'Goodness, what a fine tall girl you are and what a quantity of thick red hair,' said Margaret, rarely one to refrain from sharing exactly what was in her head. 'Though you are looking a little knocked about, to be sure. Come in, come in, and sit by the fire. You'll catch the death of cold, my dear, and then where would we be? What would your family think of us?'

Margaret sat Affy down at the kitchen table, on a chair nearest to the dying embers of the fire, and took her dark blue cloak and bonnet, which were wet and heavy from the rain.

'Are you of Irish or perhaps Scottish descent, dear? You look just like my great aunt Annie.'

'My mother was Portsmouth born and bred, though her mother came from Spain,' said Affy, warming her hands over the coals, then turning to face the table. 'As to my father's side, that might be a possibility.' Affy paused, not sure what to say and wondering if she might shock Margaret and embarrass Freddy.

'Say no more, my dear,' said Margaret, winking at Affy. 'I shall claim you for one of my own. There's no mistaking that snub nose and those freckles.'

Affy laughed. 'My mother used to think they were very ugly, and tried to make me use Gowland's lotion to take them away. But it seemed to inflame my skin so I had to give it up. Then I met my husband, and he said that the angels had scattered gold dust on me and that I was the most lovely woman he had ever seen.'

'Well, and I can see why you married him. Mr Gabriel is the best man who ever lived but gallantry isn't one of his strong points. He did once remark on my fine eyes, but that was forty years ago.' Margaret now winked at her husband as she hung up Affy's cloak and bonnet on some iron hooks near the kitchen door.

Freddy sat down next to her friend and Mr Campbell pulled off his greatcoat, hung it next to Affy's cloak and sat down. Margaret bustled about, preparing the tea and placing the cakes on plates.

'Fetch me some of that new sugar, old man,' said Margaret to her husband, who had to get up again to undo the sack of sugar.

'It is mostly loaves, but we cut a bit for you so you can use it directly,' said Affy.

'There is our usual sugar in the cakes, if that is acceptable,' said Margaret, wondering if Affy might share the same aversion as Freddy.

'Of course, Mrs Campbell. We do try to have East Indian sugar at home when we can, but otherwise I do not fret too much. I went without sugar for a long time once, which was economical, at least, but I found I grew quite insufferable in my scruples and pride. I lectured my friends, and, indeed, anyone who would listen, on the evils of taking sugar in their tea, and then I began on my husband, about the evils of Caribbean rum, and he told me in no uncertain terms what he thought of that.'

'Affy could never be insufferable,' said Freddy, laughing. 'It is just that she is far too moral and humane for her own good, and so makes everyone around her feel keenly their own inadequacies.'

'I have the same problem,' said Margaret.

'Aye, and don't I know it,' said Gabriel.

'I can get a bit carried away, though,' said Affy. 'My husband and some of our friends have similar skin colours to Freddy's, you know,' – Affy turned to Freddy and pecked her on the cheek – 'and I wanted to help and to do the right thing by them. But sometimes too much zeal can do more harm than good, so I try now to be a little more moderate.'

'Well, my dear,' said Margaret, 'you seem just right to us, doesn't she, husband?'

'Perfectly so,' said Gabriel.

'How was your aunt?' asked Freddy. 'Is she very upset about your mother?' Freddy explained to the Campbells that Affy's mother had died about a month ago.

'Very sorry I am to hear it, my dear,' said Margaret, pressing Affy's hand.

'Thank you Mrs Campbell; how kind you are. It had been long expected. I have just come from my mother's sister in Southampton. I wanted to give her a few mementoes of my mother's theatrical career, which she was glad to receive.'

'I am sure that she was,' said Margaret, 'and we shall look forward to hearing all about your mother over dinner, when you've had chance to rest.'

'I hope you won't be too shocked, Mrs Campbell,' said Affy.

'Oh, nothing shocks me anymore, dear. Since Freddy returned, I am hardened to anything.'

Affy laughed. 'But have you heard all about the Celestial Light? There is much talk of it in Southampton, as well as in London. My aunt and her friends are quite thrilled with the story.'

'We know only what we read in the newspaper,' said Freddy, 'that it was stolen on the 26th last, and a member of the Countess's household, who ran away, is suspected. Is there more news?'

'Yes, well, possibly more speculation than news. It seems that that person was a very low fellow called David Barber, who worked as an under-butler in the Darby townhouse, and he has been seen and heard in Southampton blabbing about the theft – it went wrong, apparently – and now he's fled the country on a ship to who knows where.'

'Gracious,' said Margaret, wide-eyed. 'So he might have taken the diamond with him?'

'It is possible,' said Affy, 'though he claimed that the diamond was taken by someone else. Perhaps he is lying to put people off the scent. It is all rumour and confusion.' Affy looked quite serious for a few moments.

'Now, you need to take some rest,' said Margaret, noting Affy's slightly strained look, and despite her own desperation to pump her for every last bit of intelligence she had. 'Let me take you up to your bedchamber; it is next to Freddy's and is very pretty indeed. I chose the paper myself, rose-patterned with a grey border. Then you and Freddy can have a little time together, talking about whatever wild things ladies converse about these days.'

'Thank you, Mrs Campbell; that sounds delightful. But I promise to save as many wild things as I can to share over dinner.'

A few minutes later, when Affy's things were put away neatly in her bedchamber and she had duly admired the wallpaper, she and Freddy were sat in the latter's dressing room, sharing Freddy's tobacco pipe.

'What a dear pair they are,' said Affy, pulling on the pipe like an old seadog.

'Truly they are,' said Freddy. 'I never fully realised until I left them. I was too selfish and neglectful in my grief. They were so constant. Margaret wrote to me all the time, and now here they are, just as they always have been. It is a great comfort.' Freddy smiled, then looked concerned. 'But how are you feeling about your mother, dear?'

Affy thought about it. 'I am well, I believe. I feel calm. I miss her presence but it was time for her to go.'

'What was the cause of her death in the end?'

'She had very bad stomach problems, which had been worsening for years, as you know. I cannot help but think it was the white paint that finished her. She never would leave it off. It was so much the fashion in her day, and then she was so beautiful when she was young that she was desperate to stay that way. I never knew anyone go to so much trouble about their appearance. I remember coming back to one of our lodging houses as a girl and finding her, with blood on her hands, trying to behead some white pigeons. I thought she had done for the Lord Lydgate at last – and imagined the constable coming to carry her off to gaol - but it was just part of a recipe for preserving the complexion.'

Freddy smiled. 'Poor woman. Well, we have all committed many follies and nonsense for the sake of our appearance. I am quite relieved to have left all that off and to now let myself grow as old and ugly as nature intends.'

Affy laughed. 'You will never be ugly, you goose. I was never considered handsome, and, strangely, am quite glad about that now. A woman must have riches or beauty to get on in this world, they say, but I had neither, yet I am as content as can be with my lot.'

'Oh, Affy, now who is being a goose. But were you with your mother at the end? We did not get chance to speak about it.'

'Yes. She was in a great deal of pain – poor old girl – though dosed up on the laudanum, and it was a blessing, really, when she went. But she still wore her paint and patches, her wig, silks and flounces. I believe that she thought Lord Lydgate would come a courting her right to the end. She thought she was on the stage again, you know, and was catching flowers and pressing her hand to her heart.'

'Did Lord Lydgate never come?'

'No, at least not in the last few years. He was kind to her while they were together, as much as he was capable of being, but would never marry her. I think she always hoped he might do so; there has been the odd Lord who has married his stage mistress, but tis rare. He was quite generous with money, which helped us, but he never would acknowledge me, despite the likeness. If he had done the decent thing and died when he was most in love with her, he might have left her a bit of his fortune and she would have been more comfortable at the end.

But he grew bored and went on to several more mistresses; siring several more bastards, too, to judge by the amount of freckled, red-haired children running around the London theatres.'

'I am sorry, Affy. Are you bitter about it?'

'Nay. I find that I am not. And I never was, really. Mother was fond of me in her way, but never could love me passionately. I was too much Affy and not enough Aphrodite. I could not sing or dance or be graceful, as she was. Though with my height and bearing I could at least strike rather fine classical poses.' Affy got up, threw her discarded shawl over her right shoulder, put her left leg forward, her hands on her hips and her chin in the air.

Freddy laughed, and bowed her head.

Affy lay the shawl aside and sat down. 'I was happy. We moved around a lot, depending on the success of mother's career, and the handouts from Lydgate, but there always seemed to be interesting personages – originals, you might say - around, whether it was in the slums or better class of accommodation in Portsmouth, and then later in Covent Garden. Tis true, there are always villains abroad, but the good folks looked out for me, and conversed with me, and you know that I can outwit the wits, out-wag the wags, and out-talk the devil. Then when I was seventeen, a few years after we had moved from Portsmouth to London, my beautiful husband made his appearance, and ever since that moment I truly have felt like a goddess, and so lived up to my name at long last.' Affy got up again, shook out her copper hair, stretched out her arms and started to twirl round.

'Huzzah to that!' said Freddy.

Affy sat down, laughing, and picked up her glass of madeira. 'I fear that I am a little delirious with fatigue. And I really should be careful.'

'Why is that, oh Aphrodite?'

'The child might not like it.'

'The child?'

Affy tapped her stomach and smiled.

'Oh, Affy, truly? What happy news.'

'Is it not?'

Freddy got up, went over to her friend, bent her head to Affy's stomach and kissed it. 'God bless you, little one, and keep you safe.' She straightened up. 'But should you have been travelling hither?'

'Oh, yes, I am perfectly well.'

'I am glad to hear it, but I hope you will take the Collyer's Machine back to London – nice and comfortable – and Mr C will accompany you, at least some of the way. I insist.'

'Thank you, Freddy. I will not argue with you on this occasion, and will be grateful for the company.'

Freddy sat back down, relieved. 'That is settled, then. So how do you feel at the thought of becoming a mother?'

'Very happy. Though I am only about three or four months along, I believe, so I must not be too in love with the idea for the moment. In truth, Edward and I did try to reduce the chances of it happening for some time. And then about a year ago, we decided to throw away the sheath. Forgive me, dear, if I shock you by mentioning such things. I know they are not something that respectable women should know about, but my mother was always so exceeding candid in these matters that I had little choice but to learn. Have you seen those things?'

Freddy giggled. 'No, dear; I am far too respectable, though I confess I have seen something of the sort mentioned in handbills; I believe that a Mrs Perkins is involved in the trade.'

Affy grinned, and noticing a stray stocking on one of the chairs, got up, picked it up, put both arms inside to stretch it out, then waved it around and up and down as if she was stirring some broth with a giant spoon.

'I was the one who told Edward about them,' she said, 'and I had to send him off a-marketing to the druggists. I believe that he was a little shocked, but he is a rational man and saw the sense in it. They even come in three sizes. I did not like to enquire as to which Edward chose. A man has his pride.'

Freddy giggled again. 'Stop!'

'To be sure, I am my mother's daughter in some respects, and though I can barely sing and dance, I could always take to the stage to talk and pose, should times grow desperate. So, Edward and I set to in earnest, as it were, but nothing happened. And I did wonder for a time if I had somehow brought a curse upon myself by defying God's will to go forth and multiply – by using the sheath, you know. But then I thought, stuff and nonsense. Look at all the poor infants that come and go in this world, whatever the will of their parents, or their circumstances, or whether they are good or bad.'

'That is very true, Affy. And did your mother know ere she died?'

'No. It was a little early, and I was not fully certain; and then, at any rate, I do not know that she would have been pleased. She did not really love children. I do wonder if she might have – you know – disposed of a few, before and perhaps after me. Poor mother, I do not mean to be harsh towards her. She grew up so poor, and babies just seemed to come and come in that world. Sailors did like to leave a little gift on shore, and if it was not the pox it was a child. And some of the mothers were pickled in rum or gin, and some of the babies ended up in the gutters and some washed out to sea.'

'Oh, Affy.'

'It is a harsh fact of life. But I try not to judge. I am partial to a bit of gin myself.' Affy gave a half smile. 'But life was so hard, and we all need comfort. My mother tried to spare herself from that, and me also. That is why I speak so proper, innit, darlin?'

Freddy laughed.

'My mother insisted that I learn to speak properly – as she perceived it – and shouted at me when I pronounced any words with too strong a Portsmouth twang. People used to laugh behind her back and call her the "Queen of Bleedin' Sheba" and I was the "Queen of Bleedin' Sheba's Daughter". I did so rail against it as a girl, but, growing older, I likewise grew grateful for it. It has broadened my employment opportunities, I believe, for the nicer you speak, the better people seem to think you are – another nonsense of this world, but there it is.' Affy paused. 'But this is cheerful talk amongst old friends. Tell me how you do, and what you plan to do in this lovely and peaceful part of the world.'

'I do very well, and feel right at home again in my ancient castle; though I am not so very sure about the peaceful part. My dear, there is something I need your help with. Only conceive, on the day of my arrival in Winchester, a dead body was found in the grounds of the rectory. Gabriel and I drove right past the scene in the gig. It was dreadful. The body was that of a woman, who looked like me, you know, and was quite far gone with child.'

'Gracious. Who was she?'

'Nobody seems to know, or not, at least, at the rectory, and Margaret can discover no creditable information in villages nearby. I want to go into Winchester and ask around. The general suggestion seems to be that she came from that direction, and if she was a stranger to the area, she might have arrived there from somewhere else, possibly London. Somebody must have spoken to her, and she will have been noticed. People who look like me are not so heavy on the ground in this area.'

'Yes. What has been done with her body?'

'Oh, it is buried already. They held an inquest

two days after she was found and she was buried the same day.'

'What cause of death did they find?'

'Weakness of the heart, which I know is common enough, but I just feel that I need to discover more. I can't help but think of a poor husband somewhere waiting and anxious about her.'

'Husband? She was married?'

'She was wearing a wedding ring.'

'I see. Though that may not prove the fact.'

'Yes, I had thought of that.'

'Well, I am as intrigued as you are, and let us hope we can discover more tomorrow, for the sake of her, the babe that will never be born, and the friends still living.' Affy rested her hands on her stomach, and looked thoughtful. 'There is another mystery on my mind which I wanted to talk over with you. You know I mentioned earlier that there was much talk in Southampton about the diamond robbery?'

Freddy nodded.

'What I did not say before was that the vile fellow David Barber had mentioned another name in connection with the theft, Matthew Lane.'

'Isn't that the name of Edward's friend?'

'Yes, and there might be many Matthew Lanes in the world but this one works at the Darby townhouse.'

'Oh, my dear.'

'I am not sure what to think. I do not believe it, but then I have doubts. Imagine if Edward were caught up in something so dreadful, and we just beginning our family?'

'No, Affy, you do not believe that. Edward would never do such a thing. As to this Mr Lane, I do not know him, but do you think him capable of it?'

'No. He is a very good, agreeable fellow indeed. But then, if there was a motivation we do not know of. He is a former slave, you know, and was manumitted in his former master's will. Perhaps he is bitter, and has some personal reasons – and who could blame him? And the more I think about it, he, Edward and Tom Jackson – our other friend, whom I think you have met? – have been acting strangely recently – a bit secretive and furtive. Perhaps they have been plotting the operation for some time, and the diamond is now sat snugly inside the old, cracked blue teapot on our kitchen dresser, waiting to be transported to Amsterdam.'

Freddy giggled, and then reached out and took her friend's hand. 'I am sorry, Affy, but you remind me so of myself and my own wild imagination that I cannot help but laugh. Perhaps your sensibilities are a little overheated at the moment, dear, what with one thing and another?'

Affy laughed. 'Aye, perhaps you are right. I am very fatigued, and have a little nausea. I even caught myself thinking on the way here that my Edward has been looking exceeding well of late, and sort of glowing.'

'Oh, Affy. Do you believe those stories about the diamond?'

'Nay, they are for the credulous. But then.'

'Now, you go to your chamber and take some rest. You will need all your strength to enjoy Mrs C's dinner, which will be plentiful and exceedingly delicious. I will come and fetch you at about three. We dine early; the Campbells are old-fashioned and still stick to my father's habits. And we take our meals in the kitchen with Flip, and are very cosy together, despite us having a handsome dining room newly decorated. I had thought, when I returned home, that we would all eat together there, but Gabriel is horrified at the thought of servants – as he sees them - eating in such a grand place, and will not hear of it. Poor Margaret has tried every cunning trick to change his mind, to no avail. She is after becoming genteel, and is so proud of her newly acquired tastes. She has developed a particular passion for wallpaper and would try to paper over her husband if she could.'

'He is so sanguine, I do not think he would mind.'

'That is true. Now, come along to your room. You will need more energy yet for our outing tomorrow. I will expect you to ask a great many questions and help me get to the bottom of this mystery.'

Chapter 8

The next morning the sunshine made an appearance and Affy and Freddy, in great spirits, set off on their walk into Winchester, which would take about forty-five minutes at their slow, conversational pace. Before they left, Margaret invested considerable energy in warning them of the dangers of pickpockets, pilferers, the idle, the disorderly, vagrants, vagabonds, thieves, fraudsters, cheats, traitors and those women – and men, come to that – who were no better than they should be. Oh, and the soldiers, she called after them as they walked out of the kitchen – be on your guard against those red coats!

On arriving in town, they met the Reverend Millbrook, decorated with boxes and packages, walking down the High Street alongside another, younger man.

'Miss Swinglehurst,' Jonathan said, smiling, 'how do you do? This is my curate, Mr Frances Winkworth.'

'How do you do, sir,' said Freddy, smiling at the

curate, who was a slender, pale man of about five and twenty with large hazel eyes that looked like they bore all the sorrows of the world. 'And this is my friend Mrs Aphrodite Sweet, who resides in London, and is staying with us at the old manor house for a few days.'

The four exchanged greetings.

Affy smiled at the reverend. 'You have been enjoying your shopping, sir?'

The reverend laughed. 'Indeed, I have.' He waved a rose-coloured package from a confectioner's. 'My wife's cravings for sweet things must be satisfied.'

'They must,' said Freddy. 'And we will be matching you purchase for purchase. We are very determined shoppers today.'

'I wish you well of it.'

'Is there any news on the poor dead woman?' asked Freddy.

'Not much, I am afraid,' said Jonathan, 'only that our butcher, Mr Arnold, thought he saw somebody matching her description alighting from the London coach here in town around the date she was found.'

'She must have had business or friends in the city, then? Somebody must know her.'

'I do hope so. But, look, here is Mary, our housekeeper, coming from the butcher's now, and I must make haste homeward or poor Anne will be expiring for the want of sugar.'

'We cannot allow that,' said Freddy.

Mary came towards them, stiff and unsmiling, and

half-curtseyed at Freddy and Affy. Freddy noticed that the curate looked at Mary rather intently, though she could not quite make out the expression on his face – did it show concern, pity, love, or something else?

The reverend pulled out a fine gold pocket watch, carved with his initials, and examined it. 'Well, you will excuse us ladies. It has been a pleasure to meet you, Mrs Sweet, and I do hope we will see you at the rectory very soon, Fredericka. Anne is so looking forward to seeing you again.'

They said their farewells and when Jonathan was sufficiently out of earshot, Affy looked at Freddy in a knowing way.

'What a pretty fellow he is.'

Freddy laughed. 'I suppose he is.'

'He is very elegantly and richly dressed for a cleric. Are they all so smart hereabouts?'

'I do not think so. Though I suppose I have not seen so many since my return. When I attended balls and assemblies as a younger woman, one could not move without tripping over a man of the cloth.'

'I hope his wife is not too much of a spending woman; that can cause much trouble in a marriage. Though I suppose they must be quite wealthy?'

'I do not know. I have only met his wife Anne once, thus far. She seemed to be very amiable and gentle. Though they have a grand and richly furnished home, to be sure.'

'Oh, Freddy, do listen to me; I have turned into

quite the local gossip already and me not here above five minutes.'

'Ha! That is what happens when one moves to the provinces, my dear. One's neighbours, however dull, become intensely interesting. But let us not stand around wasting time. There are questions to be asked. A call at the butcher's is certainly in order but it may be wise to leave that to the last, rather than drag around the smell of meat.'

'Aye, aye, Cap'n,' said Affy. 'Where to first?'

'Perhaps the milliner's? There will surely be gossip to be had there, though how reliable it will be, I do not know. And I cannot imagine a distressed, ill woman popping into such a place to buy a few ribbons, but one never knows.'

The friends were disappointed at the milliner's, the pastry cook's, the draper's, the mantua-maker's, the watch-maker's and the circulating library next to the White Hart Inn. At place after place they only picked up the tales that Margaret had already solicited from the village, with perhaps a little less or more embellishment. Freddy was known everywhere. It seemed that the Campbells, in their pride, had been keeping most of the Winchester shopkeepers up-to-date on her life for the past eleven years, and so the friends had to remain longer than they might have wished in each establishment in order to satisfy people's curiosity. Some stared at Freddy a little too hard, and Affy became a little vexed in consequence, though tried not to show it. She and her husband were used to being looked at, and sometimes abused, and she was sensitive for her friend. Freddy, however, was sanguine; it was what she had been expecting, and she did not feel the victim of any particular malice, just a dogged curiosity about her life since she had left Hampshire. She was starting to feel weary, however, and suggested that they call at the silversmith's, since in any case she wanted to purchase a locket for Margaret; then they might stop by the butchers and call it a day.

They stepped inside the silversmith's, Hopkins & Sons, a handsome shop with a fine bow window and classical porch.

'Good day, ladies,' said a large man of around fifty years of age, appearing in front of them from behind the counter. 'It is a fine day, is it not? Will you not take a seat, and a glass of something to refresh yourselves?'

'Gladly, sir,' said Affy, sitting down immediately in a chair to which the man had gestured. 'We are quite fatigued.'

'I can see,' said Mr Harris Hopkins, who had very white hair but a rather smooth, boyish face. 'Come, come,' he said to Freddy, 'sit down next to your friend here. What will you have – tea, beer, wine?'

'A little wine would be very welcome,' said Freddy, sitting herself down in another chair.

Mr Hopkins turned his head towards the back of the shop. 'Silas? Two glasses of that nice cool Rhenish for our visitors, please.'

The three exchanged pleasantries, and Freddy told

Mr Hopkins her business, who brought out a lovely selection of lockets and advised on engravings. He asked a little about their history, and, like everybody, had heard of Freddy. Affy told him that she was a native of Portsmouth, though she had spent some time in Winchester as a little girl with her mother, who had appeared in the old theatre above the meat market hall. Affy could still smell the meat, she said, and had a vague memory of crying just outside the theatre at the sight of some poor man, probably a vagrant, being whipped at the post in the square. Mr Hopkins, delighted, declared that he remembered her mother, and her wonderful singing on the night of a performance of *The Merchant of Venice* in the year 1781.

A few minutes later, Freddy smiled to herself as Affy got to the point. ''Tis very sad business about this poor woman found dead at the Millbrook rectory. Do you know anything about it? Miss Swinglehurst and I are very anxious about any friends or relations who might be missing her. They must be quite distraught.'

Mr Hopkins frowned for the first time. 'Yes, it is very sad indeed. But I do not like all this idle talk around the business. Gossip can be an evil thing.'

'Yes,' said Freddy, softly. 'Indeed, we do not want gossip. We simply want to help, if we can, and to find her friends.'

Mr Hopkins looked at Freddy's kind face, then at Affy's open smile, and made a decision.

'I have not mentioned this to anyone thus far,' he

said. 'If the law were to come, I would tell them all I know, but I have been unwilling to encourage idle chatterers and possibly make things worse. I do not like what they say. She seemed like a good woman to me, if a little down on her luck.'

Freddy held her breath.

'Her name was Sarah Clarke – or so she said – and she had travelled from London. She came in just as I was thinking about shutting up shop. She was quite a handsome woman and very decently dressed, but looked tired and anxious. She wondered if I knew the whereabouts of a Josiah Clarke, who might live near here. She usually left messages for him at the Chequer Inn, she said. I had not heard of him, and said so, and she seemed in a panic. She told me that he was her husband, then immediately said that he was not, more her lover really, and that Josiah Clarke was not really his name, but she did not know his true one.

'She was so exceeding candid and talked so openly that I was quite shocked at first. She grew up in a very poor part of London around Covent Garden – St Giles, I think she said it was called - and had scraped a living here and there until she had met this fine gentleman, who was supporting her. She and this Clarke fellow had recently got up some plan together that had gone wrong, and she was very anxious to tell him about it, and had travelled hither in a hurry.'

'Did she say what the plan was about?' asked Freddy.

'No, and I did not press her. I suspected it was

something not within the law, and did not want her to incriminate herself, or to put me in a position of having to report her. Some would say that I did not do my duty, and I should have called the constable directly on seeing what sort of person she was. But I pitied her. She was heavy with child but also somewhat like a child herself. She was not bold in the way that fallen women can be; in fact there was a strange sort of innocence about her; it is hard to describe.'

'You are a sympathetic man,' said Freddy, gently.

'Thank you,' said Mr Hopkins. 'I cannot help myself, though the times can be severe on those who are unfortunate enough to stray from the path. Well, I gave her some refreshment and a few coins – though she refused the money - and tried to soothe her. Then her face lit up suddenly and she said, "Oh, but now I remember the direction of someone I once met who lives near here; they might be able to help me". And she mentioned a direction somewhere near the Millbrook rectory, though this person might have lived much further away. I was more than happy to guide her. Indeed, I offered to accompany her, for I do not like to think of a lone woman in distress on the road like that, but she would not hear of it.'

'And she did not mention the name of this person?' said Freddy.

'No, and again I did not want to press her. Perhaps I should have. But there was one other strange thing she said before she went. She asked if I knew anyone in the diamond trade, for she had a friend who might be inheriting a stone, which would want cutting. I said I did not. Again, I suspected that she was involved in something criminal. But if that were the case, she would be very bad at the business, for I never encountered anyone less discreet.

'She went on her way, and then when I heard what happened to the poor woman, I was quite sorrowful, and wondered what I could have done better to help her.'

'No, sir,' said Affy. 'You did all you could, I am sure. Many would have turned her away, and abused her, or even set the law on her, as you say. At least she had a little kindness before she died. My mother, you know, saw much of the world, and took all people as they were, and not how the world would wish them to be. If she were here now, she would shake your hand; I am sure of it.'

Mr Hopkins looked as if he might shed a tear, and smiled at Affy. 'Thank you, Mrs Sweet. That means a great deal to me. I have not spoken before because I wanted to leave the poor woman with some dignity, not throw her life to the gossip hounds to snarl and fight over.'

'You have behaved splendidly,' said Freddy, 'and it does my soul good to hear you. Be assured that we will only use this information to help us identify her friends, if we can, so that they may have some peace.'

Freddy and Affy left the shop, and stood outside for a few moments, quiet and thoughtful.

'Well, my dear,' said Freddy, eventually, 'that call certainly made up for hours of disappointment. Let us talk over it when we are at home, for we are both exhausted.'

They paid their final call, at the butcher's, Freddy having promised Margaret to bring back some chops. They learnt nothing new from Mr Arnold, who was a slick-looking fellow with a high forehead and a flushed countenance. He spent most of their conversation fishing for information about Mary, whom he clearly greatly admired.

Finally, Freddy and Affy dragged themselves to the coffee house in St John's House, in which Gabriel was waiting for them snug by the window, where he was talking a little business and pleasure with a friend. He had chosen the window nook so that he could look out for them, and Freddy put her face close to the glass and waved. Gabriel saw them and laughed, and he and his companion got up and came outside.

Freddy was a little taken aback by the sight of Captain Lefroy. Her stomach did a little dance, much to her annoyance; she had only met the man once.

'Captain Lefroy,' said Gabriel, 'you have met Miss Swinglehurst, and this is her friend, Mrs Aphrodite Sweet.'

'Miss Swinglehurst,' said the captain, staring a little at Freddy. 'I did not recognise you in your…' He paused.

'Gown, sir?' asked Freddy.

Affy shot her friend a quizzical expression, but was too tired to question her; she must do so that evening.

'Indeed,' said the captain, grinning quickly at Freddy. 'But I am afraid that I must take my leave again. You will think me always running away. I will procure that shot for you, Mr Campbell.' He shook Gabriel's hand, smiled and nodded at Freddy and Affy, then walked off with his long stride in the opposite direction.

'I believe that man is a little frightened of me,' said Freddy, smiling wearily.

Gabriel grinned. 'No, my dear; how could anyone be frightened of you? He is just a very busy man, I am sure; and he is getting some shot for your pistol; he knows the best place in Portsmouth.'

'Do you have a duel planned, Miss Swinglehurst?' asked Affy.

'Yes, but I am merely the second,' replied Freddy. 'Flip has challenged the farmer's dog, who has slighted his honour in some way. It is bound to be over a woman.'

Affy nodded. 'Agh, I see; yes, it usually is.'

Gabriel smiled at the women's nonsense, proud to be with them as they walked back to the waiting gig. He insisted on taking all their parcels, which were then piled into the cart, and a few tied onto the poor old nag, Molly, who did not seem to mind. The women closed their eyes on the journey home, their heads full of Sarah Clarke, Josiah Clarke, the mysterious friend, and, most strange of all, yet another connection to the Celestial Light.

Chapter 9

In the early hours of Saturday morning, a shadowy figure walked slowly towards the churchyard gate, stopped and leant his gloved right hand against the curled wrought iron to catch his breath. He coughed repeatedly, then looked around him as if expecting a spectre to appear and admonish him for disturbing the peace of the grave dwellers. He grasped the latch, lifted it up, fumbling, pushed open the gate and stepped into the yard. The gate swung back behind him and closed itself quietly. Some instinct of neatness within the man made him put the latch back on.

Mr Adam Short now followed the path which curved left and right to the church at the top, looking at the various graves by the dim glow of the moon. Some were white and grand and pompous, and he imagined the skeletons buried within them dining on game, washed down with claret. Some were a simple grey stone, some merely a wooden cross, and surely the skeletons that belonged to these graves would be dining on broth and small beer. Each man to his place, even in death. This reassured him. He smiled grimly as he made his way to the left side of the church, where he found what he was looking for, a newly dug grave, fresh and crisp. There was the spade, lying to the right of the grave, just as he was told it would be. He paused a moment and made the sign of the cross, cursing himself at the same time for his foolishness. Why would he not be done with these things? Of what use were they to a man who had, as some conjectured, a guaranteed ticket for the other place? But he did not believe that; no. He had done what he had needed to in this life. If God had created the world, and nature was red in tooth and claw, what had he done but obey its – and His - commands?

He picked up the spade, heavy to his weary body, and began to dig. It did not take long to turn up the soil and tap the coffin, which was made of an already degraded, cheap deal wood. The newly tacked lid gave way easily to reveal the shape of a woman's body wrapped in a woollen cloth. Short stopped to gasp more air, then put down the spade and bent to pull the body towards him. As he struggled to manoeuvre it into a large sack, the cloth fell away from the head of the body and he saw her face. The body had moved from the rigor stage back to a relaxed form, and the woman could have been sleeping except for the purplish colour of the skin and the slightly bloated face. The body smelt partly of decay but partly of spirits. Gin? No, it was rum. Strange. Short did not know that the soft-hearted curate, overseeing the woman's burial, had soaked her body in rum in the hope of putting off its putrefaction in the event of an anxious husband turning up to identify her.

Short had met Sarah only once, but she also looked a little like his love, the love he hoped to return to and die; it was something about the curve of the upper lip and the wide-set position of the closed eyelids. But he felt no pity for her. There. His heart was as hard as it should be, and so much the better for him. He got the body fully into the sack, secured it tightly with some rope, then proceeded to drag it back from whence he came.

As he stopped to open the gate, he pulled the cover from his fevered head to refresh it with the cold night air. The moon lit up his face, so that, as in Southampton, any onlooker catching sight of him might have been forgiven for thinking that it was the grim reaper himself doing his rounds.

That day Freddy and Affy, quite fatigued, eschewed all plans for chasing King Arthur and his knights round town, for seeing the sights – cathedral, college and the little ruins of castle and abbey – for striding up and down St Catherine's Hill, attending the New Theatre, and visiting Mundy's museum of classical artefacts, where Affy might have the opportunity to brush up on her classical poses. That would all have to wait for another visit. Instead, they would repose at home, and sit in the garden, conversing with Flip and the Campbells. They were not sure how much of what they had discovered to share with Margaret and Gabriel, but Freddy decided that it was best to be entirely honest and open. Though Margaret enjoyed gossip, she was silent as the grave when she needed to be, and it would be a help for them to talk things through, and to share the burden.

At around two in the afternoon, Freddy and Affy settled down to help Margaret prepare a curry for their dinner, which provoked much huffing, puffing and laughing.

'How glad I am to have my treasure and the Scottish relation helping me with this,' said Margaret (the Scottish relation was Affy), squinting at the recipe that Affy had scribbled, very badly, on a piece of paper and brought with her from London.

'Try my spectacles,' said Freddy, noticing the squinting.

'But do they work, my love? I've observed that you see just as well without them,' said Margaret, giving Freddy a knowing smile. She suspected, rightly, that Freddy mostly wore her spectacles to hide behind.

Freddy looked sheepish, and grinned. 'It entirely depends on the circumstances.'

'Do they eat a great deal of curry in London, dear?' said Margaret to Affy.

'Oh, yes, I believe so, though it is not something I have eaten much of myself.'

'Well, let us not be beaten, then. Whatever you can

get in that devilish London – that sinkhole of fashion and iniquity and vice – you can get here.'

'Perhaps not the iniquity and vice, Mrs Gabriel,' said Freddy.

'Don't be so sure, my treasure. I haven't set foot in that alehouse on the Romsey Road – and the good Lord strike me down if I should ever do so - but the stories I hear would make your hair curl, if it wasn't already the finest set of curls that any woman could wish for.' Margaret gave her husband, who had just stepped into the kitchen from outside, a stern look and then winked at Freddy and Affy.

Gabriel walked over to his wife and stood behind her, peering over her shoulder with fascination. He had eaten curry several times as a younger man, but not for many years since.

'Mr Campbell, stop hovering,' said his wife. 'Tis like having a ghost watching over me, and judging my performance.'

'I'm not hovering,' said Gabriel, grinning at Affy and Freddy. He went to the table, picked up an onion, threw it into the air and caught it.

'Well, my dears,' said Margaret. 'What did you discover yesterday? You both looked like you'd just returned from the wars, rather than a trip into town to procure some new ribbons and half a dozen chops.'

'A deal more than we expected, in the end,' said Freddy, and she and Affy related the tale told to them by Mr Hopkins.

Margaret's mouth opened, her jaw locked and she

held her spoon in mid-air. Before they could continue the conversation, they heard a knock at the door, which was already ajar to allay the constant heat and smoke of the kitchen. Flip flicked up one ear and wagged his tail slightly, indicating that the visitor was friendly. Gabriel went to the door.

'Hello young Joe. What brings you hither?'

'Hello Mr Campbell. If you please, I have a message for the lady.'

'Indeed, my boy. Well come on in and take a little refreshment while you're here.'

'Thank you, Mr Campbell.'

Joe entered the kitchen, adopting a curious expression as the smell of the cooking curry invaded his nostrils.

'What's that, Mrs Gabriel?'

'Curry, young man, curry.'

'What's that?'

'Curry, I told you. Have you got your ears stuffed up?'

'No, Mrs Gabriel, I mean that I don't know what curry is.'

'Oh, well, how could you? It's a fine, fancy dish from foreign parts eaten by gentlefolk and the aristocracy. Far too good for the likes of you. But, I tell you what, as a treat, you can be the first to taste it.'

Joe stared at Margaret. He was not sure whether to be glad or terrified.

'Come on, boy. Christmas is a coming and I've a pudding to make,' said Margaret.

Joe looked at Gabriel, who smiled at him and nodded,

then went over to Margaret, and hopped from one foot to the other. Margaret scooped some of the curry from the pot with her spoon, blew on it, and moved it towards Joe's mouth. Joe closed his eyes, screwed up his face and opened his mouth. The curry went in. He chewed. The meat – which was veal, though he would not have been able to identify it - was so good. He swallowed. Then he felt the fire, and opened his eyes. 'Arrgh!'

They all laughed.

'Is it exceeding delicious?' asked Margaret.

Joe nodded, then breathed out several times. 'It's fire,' he stuttered, 'like something from *One Thousand and One Nights* – those stories you told me.'

'It's magic, Joe,' said Gabriel and winked at him. 'Sit down, now, and take some more.'

Margaret always made it her business to feed Joe's stomach, as well as his mind and imagination with her stories. His family was very poor, though his father made what he could from agricultural labour and his mother gathered wood and gleaned the fields after harvest time. In good times they lived on bread, cheese and tea, with perhaps a little bacon once a week, but in bad times they would easily starve, and were dependent on the charity of the Millbrooks, the Campbells and the Dentons, the local farmers, to keep them off the parish.

Joe sat down, smiling at the company, and Flip came over to nuzzle at his legs and settle himself down under the table where there was hope of receiving a few choice morsels of meat. Joe grinned at Margaret as she scooped some of the curry into a pewter bowl and placed it with a spoon upon the table in front of him. He stared in awe at the bowl, then picked up the spoon. This was the most exciting day of his life. He closed his eyes, screwed up his face again and took a bite, waiting for the magic, then slowly repeated the exercise until the bowl was empty, graduating by the last bite to eyes fully open and face smooth.

'Good boy, Joe,' said Margaret. 'Now magical things are going to happen. But don't you have a message for Miss Swinglehurst?'

Joe had forgotten the message in his excitement. He now reached into his pocket and took out the letter, turning to Freddy, a little shyly, and handing it to her. He could not help but stare at her face. She was a little like that poor dead woman in her skin colour. 'Are you magical, too, Miss?'

Freddy laughed. 'Yes, of course I am, Joe.'

'She is very magical and very special, so mind your manners,' said Margaret, frowning at him.

'Yes, Mrs Gabriel.' Joe nodded and then turned to smile at Freddy.

Freddy took a few moments to look at her letter.

'Is everything alright, dear?' asked Margaret, half concerned, half hungry for information, as always.

'It is from the reverend, asking me to call over to the rectory tomorrow to spend a little time with Anne, who is not quite well and feeling low in spirits. Something very strange has happened. It seems that the dead woman's grave has been dug up, and the body taken.'

'Good Lord,' said Gabriel, 'as if that business were not terrible enough, and now this? The dear admiral always did warn about the evil in our midst. Tis such a wicked world, a very wicked world indeed.' Gabriel stood with his hands pressed to his head, and stared in front of him.

'Now, dear, sit down,' said Margaret, 'like a proper Christian, and stop that hovering, like some restless imp that's been sent to plague me.' Mrs Campbell pulled out the chair next to Joe, and encouraged her husband to sit in it. She patted him on the shoulder.

Gabriel looked up, remembering Joe, and tried to rouse himself.

'Well, Joe, don't be troubled by the nonsense of an old fool like me. Now that you've had your bowl of magic, you'd better be going. The Millbrooks and then your poor mother will be wondering where you are.'

Joe thought of his mother and sprang up. 'Yes, sir. Thank you kindly for the curry, Mrs Gabriel. It made me so happy.'

'Well, well, Joe; if you're a good boy, there'll be plenty more where that came from,' said Margaret. 'And stay a moment while I give you a parcel for your mother – there's the usual food, some linen shifts and a good sturdy bit of worsted cloth, which will serve for all sorts of things. Now don't drop it on the road or the dogs will be feeding on your supper.'

Joe turned to Freddy and Affy. 'Goodbye, Miss Swinglehurst and Miss Aph-ro-di-te.'

Margaret gave Joe the bundle and Gabriel saw him

out to the front path, and he hurried back to the rectory, his eyes still wide and head still full of adventure.

Gabriel returned, his face drooping with anxiety, his shoulders slumped, and sat down at the table. They all looked at each other, trying to process this further piece of the puzzle. Even Margaret, whose mind was bursting with questions, found that she could not articulate them, and kept opening her mouth to speak, then closing it. Affy, sensing that a change of subject might help Mr Campbell, decided to share her good news about the baby. Margaret started crying.

'We'll have a grandchild at last, husband, and a Scottish grandchild to boot,' she said. Gabriel rolled his eyes at his wife and grinned from one large ear to the other, and Affy, delighted with their reaction, got up and kissed them both.

'Well, we had better get my curry eaten, after me near killing myself to make it,' said Margaret, springing up. 'And Affy and our grandchild will be needing to keep their strength up.'

Gabriel Campbell, who hailed from the Scottish Highlands, had ended up in Hampshire via the somewhat circuitous route of the West Indies. He had gone out there in the year 1763, a gawky young man of one and twenty years of age, to work on a plantation, grateful for the opportunity to work and, please God, to make his fortune. He was to begin in Barbados, to spend some months with a bookkeeper cousin, before moving on to

Antigua, one of the new Caribbean territories acquired by the British under the Treaty of Paris, then being rushed on by many of his fellow Scottish countrymen.

He had left Margaret behind; they planned for her to follow him when he had established himself. To his shame, he had not thought over-much about slavery before he left Scotland. He was to have a very quick lesson – a lesson which had never left him – during the short time he spent in Barbados. He still thanked God every day that he had met Admiral Swinglehurst, who had been visiting acquaintances there as a sort of respite after the wars, and who noticed in him a kindred heart that could not be comfortable in such a place. The admiral offered he and Margaret positions and a home in Winchester in England, and he had been so grateful to accept, desperate as he was to get away, and not being willing to return home to Scotland as a failure.

Gabriel carried a lot of guilt, and felt himself a hopeless fellow, so sensitive to suffering – his cousin had called him womanish and effeminate when he had baulked at the realities of plantation life – yet so ineffectual at doing anything about it. He could not help but feel that the world was a very wicked place, and any sad or bad event that he heard of cut him deeply. The news about the poor dead negro woman and her unborn child had triggered one of his fits of gloom, and now this. What was happening in this quiet nook of England? Was nowhere safe from evil?

Chapter 10

The next day, before they went down to breakfast, Freddy and Affy re-confirmed their plans with regard to both the death of Sarah Clarke and the theft of the Celestial Light. After a little agonising, Affy told the Campbells about Matthew Lane, her husband's friend, and how worried she was about his potential connection with the diamond affair. Freddy and Affy asked Margaret and Gabriel to keep back this information, and what they now knew about Sarah Clarke, for a short time. Affy would make enquiries about Matthew as soon as she got home. There was also a chance they might even be able to track down any friends of Sarah, since she had grown up around St Giles, and another friend of theirs, Tom Jackson, was currently residing in that area. A black woman in certain pockets of London was not so uncommon as a black woman in Hampshire, but black women were generally less common than black men, and now they had names – or aliases – of the woman and her lover, and surely someone would be missing her. The Campbells were content to stay silent for the time being, not only to give the Sweets time to question their friend, but to honour the silversmith's delicacy in regard to Sarah, by avoiding triggering wild stories and nonsense that might do damage to innocent people.

Margaret, Freddy and Flip waved off Affy and Gabriel, the latter accompanying Affy on part of her journey. The Campbells did not entirely approve of Sunday travelling – Affy had been due to go home the following day - but understood the exceptional nature of the case, and Affy's need to set her mind at ease.

'You take care of yourself and our precious grandchild,' said Margaret to Affy. 'And let Mr C do everything, and keep an eye out for strange men.'

'I promise I will,' shouted Affy, laughing, as the gig rolled away, strands of her bright hair blowing slightly beneath her bonnet.

Margaret wiped away a tear. 'Why couldn't she come to settle with us, with that good husband of hers? What a fine family we would make.'

'That would be very agreeable indeed,' said Freddy, 'but her husband has his living in London, and Affy is not very at home in quieter places. We will see them as often as we can, though.'

'I hope so, my dear. It's so sorrowful to part with one's relations.'

Freddy grinned and kissed Margaret on her right cheek, who grinned back.

'Now, are you walking to the rectory?' continued Margaret. 'Though I don't know why I bother asking such a question, since you are so addicted to gadding about the country quite alone and unprotected.'

'Yes, Mrs C.'

'Well, mind how you go, and see what you can find out, as carefully as you can, but stay a moment whilst I get those cakes for Mrs Millbrook.'

Package in her left hand, and pressing on her stick with her right, Freddy set off on her visit. The weather was continuing fine, but she did not pay much attention on her way, preoccupied as she was with what she might find, and suspicious as she now was of everybody there.

Over at the rectory, Sam and Mary were sat at the kitchen table, taking a moment's rest from their duties. Sam looked at his companion, who was pale and seemed heavy somehow. He had known Mary five years now, since her arrival at the rectory with her two boys, then aged five and two. She was not always an easy person to like, but he had grown used to her, and they seemed to understand each other's ways. On first seeing her he had been struck by her beauty, as everyone was. But now he barely noticed it. She was Mary. He suspected that she bore some burden, something that was too difficult or perhaps even too shameful to share, and so he made allowances for her. He had been widowed young, and had no children, and understood when someone was carrying pain. His feelings towards her had grown tender, but he kept his own counsel. She was too locked into something else – whatever it was – to let anyone in. Perhaps that might change in future; for now, he let it be.

'Mary, are you quite well? You haven't been looking yourself for some time.'

'Oh, I'm perfectly well, Sam, just a little tired, what with all this running around over that woman, and now the body dug up.'

'It's very strange; I really cannot fathom it. Though I have heard of people who steel bodies from graves to sell to surgeons for dissection. Resurrectionists – that's what they call them.'

'I don't like surgeons. It's against God, I'm sure, to tamper with and defile those who should be resting in peace. I've not heard of resurrectionists in these parts, but it sounds like a reasonable explanation. For why else would somebody dig up a body?'

'I really cannot think.'

'Perhaps it was Mr Arnold, the butcher? He would certainly have the tools, and would be able to offer his customers a more interesting line in chops.'

'Mary!' Sam burst out laughing. Mary hardly ever smiled or laughed in the general run of things, but just occasionally she let slip a bitter, ghoulish humour, that had shocked and rather delighted Sam when he first encountered it. He wondered what she might be if she were less unhappy – there was surely a natural playfulness within her that had been long buried.

They were interrupted by the sound of the front door, and Mary sighed and got up, giving Sam a rare quick grin, which briefly lit up her strained face, as she went to answer it.

Freddy smiled at Mary as she opened the door, and was rewarded with a rather cold smile and stiff curtsey.

'Good day, Mary, is your mistress at home?'

'Yes, ma'am. We're expecting you. Do come in.'

Freddy stepped into the house and let Mary, in her rather rushed and slightly rough way, take her bonnet and shawl. She was shown through to the front parlour where Anne was sat, smiling, and Polly was stood proudly next to the tea table on which were perfectly placed all the tea and chocolate paraphernalia and some seed cake.

'Miss Swinglehurst,' said Anne, getting up, and taking Freddy's hand. 'I am so obliged to you for coming. You must think me most strange, summoning you in such a way. I am afraid that I was in a rather sad state yesterday, and dear Jonathan suggested that your company might do me some good, and I agreed. But I am quite well again today and so am feeling rather foolish.' Anne did not look well. She now glanced at Mary, nervously. 'You may go, Mary, thank you.'

Mary curtseyed again and left the room, closing the door loudly behind her. Anne winced.

'Please do not feel foolish, Mrs Millbrook,' said Freddy, who suspected that Anne was a little tipsy. 'I can assure you, I was most pleased to receive the invitation and to have the opportunity of spending a little time with you, well or otherwise. I am a stranger again, here, in some ways, and genial new company is always a pleasant thing.'

'Thank you, Miss Swinglehurst. But please do call me Anne. Do sit down.'

'And how do you do, Polly?' asked Freddy, smiling at the grinning Polly. 'Please take these queen cakes sent by Mrs Campbell. They are delicious; I find I am quite addicted to them.'

Polly took the parcel and Anne smiled and said, 'Yes, I can well imagine. I have terrible cravings for such things myself.' Indeed, poor Mrs Millbrook was so low in spirits generally that she could take little other food but sweet things, and in consequence felt a constant thirst, suffered from headaches and had dark shadows under her large grey eyes. 'What will you take?'

'Tea, if you please,' said Freddy.

'You may pour the tea and chocolate now, Polly, as I showed you,' continued Anne, 'and then you can take your leave.'

Polly very stiffly and deliberately poured a cup of tea for Freddy and carried it over to her.

'I have added sugar,' she said, proudly, to Freddy.

'Thank you, Polly, you are very good.'

'And can I offer you some seedcake, ma'am?' said Polly, smiling broadly.

'Not just at present, thank you,' said Freddy.

'Pour my chocolate, Polly, and then get along with you,' said Anne. She turned to Freddy. 'Mary makes the most delicious chocolate, with cinnamon and honey; and sometimes a little cognac.' Anne's voice was becoming a little slurred.

Polly did as bid, gave Anne her drink, picked up the parcel from the tea table, and gave an extravagant curtsey before leaving the room.

'She is such a dear creature,' said Freddy, sipping her tea. 'I feel that I am very fond of her already, and this only the second time we have met.'

'I understand you.' Anne drank some of her chocolate. 'I felt the same way after a very short acquaintance. She is awkward and untutored but I hope to make something of her. Her family are very poor, you know, much like Joe Carter's, and it is a big help for them to have her employed. Mary has no patience with her, and I believe John thinks our having her a little foolishness of mine. But she does my heart good.'

'Then you should keep her and cherish her.'

'I will, Fredericka. May I call you Fredericka?'

'Of course you may. But I would rather you call me Freddy, you know. Tis a strange name for a lady, and that is why I love it so.'

Anne laughed, something she did not do often. 'You are a very singular personage, Freddy. Oh, do forgive my boldness. I do not mean it as an insult; quite the opposite. It is so refreshing to hear you. I do not always enjoy the company of people as I should. When John and I were first married, and just prior to that, we went to so many things – balls, assemblies, Corporation feasts, charity festivals – John is so well connected – and I felt so alive.

'But now I do not go to things at all. I confess that I find the dinners and card evenings thrown by John's acquaintances in Winchester and thereabouts quite tedious, and I used to feel very fatigued at them. The men, you know, do so love the sound of their own voices, and seem to be experts on all sorts of subjects; and then the women rattle on about their fat infants, or speak spite against some poor, erring woman who has transgressed against their notions of decency in some trifling way.'

Anne giggled and put her right hand to her mouth. 'Do forgive me, Freddy; please do not mind me. I do not know why I am running on like this. They are really kind people; very kind. Oh dear; it is not good for poor John to have such a weak and ailing wife. I sometimes wonder if he could not have done better for himself by marrying elsewhere.'

'No, my dear, do not say that. He chose you. Surely, these acquaintances do not matter, only our true friends.'

Anne smiled weakly. Her eyes were starting to look a little glazed, the pupils large. She leaned her head back on her chair. 'True friends,' she repeated, slowly.

'I am sorry to hear that you were distressed, yesterday, to hear the news of that poor woman. Is it preying on your mind?'

Anne laughed. She looked around the room at the wallpaper. The spots were jumping around a little.

'Are you quite well, dear?' asked Freddy, noting that Anne was certainly drunk. Indeed, Anne had been awake most of the night, taking more and more brandy as the hours wore on, with the aim of inducing slumber, but creating only half-waking, half-dozing, fitful dreams, where ghosts wandered the grounds of the rectory carrying dead children in their arms.

Anne touched her lips, which were quite numb, then straightened up her head and body and looked directly at Freddy. 'Friends, you say? I do not have any. I have no children and no friends. No, that is not true; I have dear Henry, who has been quite my saviour. Please forgive me my self-indulgence and my weakness, Freddy. I am a poor, foolish creature, I know. But I am so melancholy; so, so wretched; and I never say the words, but I will run mad if I do not say them now. Oh, Freddy, I am so very unhappy. My heart is broken. Quite broke.'

Freddy was shocked. She had not suspected that Anne's suffering had reached such a pitch. She got up, went over to Anne and put her arms around her. Anne did not cry; she was still at the stupefied stage of intoxication. They both sat there for about ten minutes, saying nothing, when Freddy, hearing a little noise from outside the door, left Anne and sat back down in the chair she had previously occupied. It was the reverend, who had been discussing business in his study with Mr Winkworth, come to say hello. He saw immediately how things stood with his wife, smiled at Freddy, then took Anne's hand and guided her out of the room and upstairs to their bedchamber. He reappeared about ten minutes later.

'I am very sorry for this, Freddy. I am afraid that my wife is extremely unwell at the moment.'

'Pray, do not be uneasy. I like Anne very much and am sorry to see her suffer so.'

Jonathan sat down next to Freddy. 'I do get so very anxious about her.'

'If you do not mind me saying so, I believe that she is grieving for the loss of the children she has not had, and I wonder if she feels that she has failed you because of that. Could you not take her away for a while? It cannot be good for her staying in the same place, day after day. Perhaps you could both take the waters somewhere, or try a bathing resort? Or is there a kind relative that might take her?'

'She does have a cousin in Southampton of whom she is fond. Tis not the most fashionable place in the world, but she would have the benefit of both a watering place, and a friend. We met at a ball at the Long Rooms there, you know. It was a perfect summer evening, I remember, and she stood there in a rose-coloured gown, and I thought, she will make me a better man.'

'Oh, Jonathan, that is lovely.'

'Yes, and she was. I should go with her now but I cannot take the time away from business. If we try this measure and do not have success, I will do so. I shall write to the cousin directly.'

'Good, that is settled then. Are her mother and father still living?'

'Yes. They reside in Salisbury. Unhappily, we are a little estranged from them. They did not think me quite good enough for Anne at the start, and it has all been rather strained since. She might go to them but I think she would prefer her cousin.'

'And she has no brothers or sisters?'

'No. There was an elder brother who died in infancy. Of course, she does have the captain now, who is a comfort to her, and she speaks highly of her father's relations in Ireland, but that might be a little far for her to go just now. Thank you, Freddy, for your help and forbearance. I am sure that this is not quite the welcome home to Hampshire you would have wished for.'

'Nay, those near and dear to me are well, and so am I. I am only sorry to see others suffering.'

'You will stay for dinner, will you not?'

'Oh, yes, I would like to stay and spend a little more time with Anne when she comes down. Please do get back to your business. I spy Mrs Edgeworth's latest novel over there which I have not yet had sight of, and I might spend a little time with Polly.'

'That is good news about dinner. Captain Lefroy and Mr Winkworth will be dining too, and I hope we can cheer Anne a little. I will send Polly through directly. I see that you have warmed to her quite as much Anne has. I do not understand it myself, but you women must be indulged.'

Chapter 11

Freddy sat back, thinking of Anne. She was a little shaken at the sight of her suffering. One rarely saw such displays of feeling in polite drawing-rooms. But she was glad that Anne had unburdened herself. What a tragedy to want children so very badly and not to have them. And there was Affy, this morning, blooming with happiness in her expectant state. There was a quiet knock at the door, and Polly appeared, looking nervous.

'Polly,' said Freddy, 'do come in and sit down with me for a little while. Do not worry; there is nothing to be concerned about.'

Polly smiled, looking a little easier, and went to sit down opposite Freddy on the sofa. She sat down very hesitatingly and lightly, as if worried her lowly servant's body would tarnish the furniture.

'I thought it would be pleasant for us to have a little

conversation whilst your mistress is resting. You have such a bright smile that you cheer me up.'

Polly broke into one for a few seconds, then stopped when the door opened and Mary appeared. Polly jumped up, wobbling on her slender legs.

'Excuse me, ma'am,' said Mary, nodding briskly at Freddy. 'Polly, what are you doing idling in here? There's work to be done in the kitchen.'

'Yes, Mrs Harris,' said Polly, beginning to follow Mary.

'Mary,' Freddy said, interrupting, and firmly. 'It was I who detained Polly; I asked your master if I could have fifteen minutes of her time, and I promise you I won't keep her longer.'

'Oh, yes, of course, ma'am,' said Mary. Her cheeks glowed a little with annoyance, bringing the full beauty back to her face, which had looked a little pale, Freddy noted.

'I will bring her to the kitchen myself,' said Freddy.

'Thank you, ma'am.' Mary nodded and left the room.

Polly was stood on the spot, not sure what to do.

'Sit down again, Polly, dear,' said Freddy. 'Do not vex yourself. Mrs Harris is a very good housekeeper, I know, and wants you to do your duty and to train you up well, which can make her a little irritable. And then, you know, women as handsome as Mrs Harris have to worry a little less than the rest of us about being amiable.'

Polly grinned and sat down again. Unable to resist Freddy's warm manner and smile, she said, 'Mother says that the whole of the county is quite in love with her.'

'I am sure they are,' said Freddy. 'I am very surprised that she does not have a sweetheart.'

Polly coloured a little, looked a little fearful, and remained silent. She knows something, thought Freddy, but did not want to push too hard.

'How do you like it here?' asked Freddy. 'You have been with the Millbrooks one year, I believe? Mrs Millbrook is very fond of you.'

'I like it very well, ma'am, thank you, and Mrs Millbrook is the kindest mistress anyone could have. My mother says that she cannot credit how I've lasted so long with my gangly arms and legs, but she is very proud of me, and we are very grateful for the earnings.'

'I am sure that you do your mother great credit, Polly, and I am glad to hear that you are so happy in your position here. But have you not been a little upset by the business with this poor woman found in the front grounds?'

Polly nodded and squirmed slightly.

'Had you seen her before?'

Polly looked shocked, paused for a few moments, then shook her head. She is lying – poor girl – thought Freddy. It seemed as if nobody had bothered to ask Polly that question and she had not prepared an answer to it.

'Yes, well, it seems she was a stranger in town,' continued Freddy. 'It makes me sad to think of her wandering so far from home, all alone, and then her dying like that. I cannot help but think of her friends and family; they must be so worried about her.'

Polly nodded again, looking very worried herself.

'Polly, dear, if you do happen to know of anything, or hear of anything, would you tell me? I promise that you will not get into trouble. I just want to try and find her friends, if I can.'

A tear fell from one of Polly's large green eyes.

'Now I have upset you and I am very vexed with myself, for that is that last thing I intended. Do not be uneasy. Come, let me give you a kiss and say you will forgive me.'

They both got up and Freddy kissed Polly on the cheek and patted her hair. Polly smiled again; she was a little in awe of this strange, wonderful woman, with her dark skin, her spectacles, her funny laugh and open chatter, and the way she treated Polly as if she were an old friend, not a servant of a few moments' acquaintance.

'Now, let me take you back to Mrs Harris – you can guide me – and you can tell me about your writing, for I hear that you have learned to sign your name?'

Freddy and Polly walked through the passageway to the back of the house and the kitchen, which was a large, very smart affair with a new Rumford stove, Freddy noticed.

'Here she is,' said Freddy to Mary, who was scouring pots. 'I have brought her back to you in good time, as promised.'

'Thank you, ma'am,' said Mary, wiping her hands on her apron and turning to face them both. 'Now, Polly, take this cordial up to your mistress, and don't even think about dropping it. Then I wish you to dust the dining room and start preparing it for dinner, and then you can come and help me with the preparation.'

'Yes, Mrs Harris.' Polly looked a little ashamed of herself, took hold of the tray on which sat a cup of brandy-infused chocolate, and gripped it as if her life depended on it. She walked slowly from the kitchen, managing to give Freddy a quick smile as she went.

Freddy noticed Samuel Cole at the end of the kitchen, sharpening knives. He now turned and smiled at her.

'Mr Cole, I have heard a great deal about you from the Campbells,' said Freddy.

'Indeed, ma'am,' said Sam, putting down the implements he was holding and running his right hand through his sandy hair. 'They are very good people.'

'Can we get you anything?' Mary asked, wondering what this busybody was doing hovering in her kitchen.

'Yes, Mary, a glass of wine would be most welcome, thank you,' said Freddy, sitting herself down at the table, much to Mary's annoyance.

Placed next to a bowl of strawberries at the end of the table was a wooden and metal object. It was a gun. Was that her pistol, thought Freddy? It looked remarkably like it, with the carved leaves and branches on the metal. Her initials, FES, were carved upon the handle, so she would know for certain on closer inspection. Mary noticed her eyeing the gun.

'I believe this is yours, ma'am?' said Mary to Freddy.

'The mistress was looking at it earlier, and I thought it best to bring it in here, out of the way. She gets peculiar fancies, you know, when she is a little unwell.'

Sam looked at Mary sternly, who stopped talking. 'I believe that the captain is procuring some shot for you, Miss Swinglehurst,' said he, smiling at Freddy. 'He is a fine military gentleman, and knows his weapons.'

'Yes, I am sure,' said Freddy, angered at Mary's indiscreet and insolent comments about her mistress; and what was she implying exactly? There was silence for a few moments.

'This is a tragic business about this poor woman,' said Freddy, finally. 'It is very strange that she found her way here, is it not?'

'She may have been heading to Romsey,' said Mary, 'or much further. Or perhaps she had heard of the reverend. He does much good work for those less fortunate than ourselves.'

'Yes, that is a thought, Mary,' said Freddy.

'Aye,' said Samuel. 'Mr Millbrook is known far and wide for his efforts against the slave trade, amongst other things. He has become so busy in recent years that Mr Winkworth has taken on most of the parish duties. Mr Winkworth is a very good fellow, however.'

Freddy looked closely at Mary. She was nodding, and gave an almost tender smile, before turning to Freddy.

'Will you not be more comfortable in the parlour, ma'am? I will bring you through your refreshment. It is a little hot and noisy in here, but we are used to it, you know.'

Freddy almost laughed. Everything Mary said sounded like a confrontation. But she was happy to go.

'Yes, I will leave you now,' said Freddy, 'I can see that I am interrupting your work. I shall stay in Anne's pretty parlour until dinner time.' Freddy got up. 'A pleasure to meet you, Mr Cole,' and quit the kitchen.

Back in the parlour, she picked up the novel she had espied and settled down on the sofa. Mary soon appeared with a tray, on which sat a bottle of wine, a glass, and some plum cake. Freddy opened *Belinda*, excited as she always was about the promise in an unread novel, but found that she could not concentrate. She had not got much from Samuel and Mary. Sam seemed to be a very good, straightforward sort of man, though appearances could be deceptive. The insolent Mary could be hiding anything or nothing; she seemed to be such a misanthrope generally that it was difficult to tell.

Mary had suggested one thing that made sense to Freddy. Perhaps Sarah had encountered the reverend in a different setting? Something to do with the slave trade? And was he the friend she was referring to with Mr Hopkins? But then, why would Jonathan lie about knowing her? Could he, Freddy's dear old friend, be more involved in this business than she knew? She discounted the idea of his having a lover; he was too in love with his wife. Perhaps he was the friend referred to but simply did not remember her. He must encounter many people on his lecture tours, and may have spoken to her only once or twice. Or perhaps he did know her but suspected her involvement in the diamond case, and was trying to protect her, as an unfortunate woman in need of kindness.

As to Josiah Clarke, who was he? Could it be Captain Lefroy or the curate? Or someone else entirely who lived in this direction, near or far? She hoped that Polly would tell her what she knew, but she did not want to scare her away. A little time was needed there. A few hours later she was woken from her reverie.

'Fredericka, you are frowning. I hope you are not too vexed with me for abandoning you.' It was Jonathan, who had come into the room quietly.

'Not at all,' said Freddy, smiling up at him. 'I am simply thinking, and trying too hard. It cannot be good for my complexion, I am sure. I must cease!'

'I have come to take you through to the drawing room before dinner is served. I am afraid that my wife is too unwell to join us. She sends her sincerest apologies to you, especially, Fredericka, for wasting your time, as she put it.'

'Oh, no, she must not think that. I am very sorry not to have her company but there will be other occasions. I only wish her better, and speedily.'

Freddy got up and realised that she was herself feeling a little tipsy. She had forgotten that the rectory dined late, in the new fashion – not until five or even six in the evening – and she had now taken too much wine on an empty stomach.

'Thank you,' said the reverend. 'I hope you will not find dinner with three gentleman a little dull. Though they are men of information, and good men too. Perhaps your presence will ease the little awkwardness between myself and the captain, though it is a little unfair of me to lay that burden upon you.'

'Not at all, Jonathan; I will do my best to rise to the challenge. However, I am afraid that I am not properly attired for dinner. I hope I will not disgrace you?'

'Oh, no more than usual,' said Jonathan.

She took Jonathan's arm, and they walked through to the drawing room laughing together.

Chapter 12

The drawing room, decorated in a white and lilac paper with a dark grey border, was a very elegant affair, and the open glass doors letting in the late warm sunshine cast a soft glow over the furniture. Captain Henry Lefroy and the curate were sat rather stiffly on silk-covered, mahogany chairs. Henry frowned slightly when Freddy and the rector appeared, then got up to greet Freddy.

'Miss Swinglehurst,' he said, now smiling broadly, and touching her hand. 'It is a pleasure to see you here. I fear I have run away on the only two occasions we have met – you must think me most ungallant.'

'Not at all, Captain,' said Freddy, slightly disarmed by his warm greeting, when she had determined to be wary of him. 'Given the circumstances of our first meeting, I am surprised that you did not throw yourself out of the window on learning that I would be dining here today.'

Henry laughed. It was a warm, belly laugh, which surprised Freddy again.

'How do you do, Miss Swinglehurst,' said Frances Winkworth, who had followed the captain. He touched her hand and stared into her face with his large, soulful eyes. 'We have also met once before, very briefly, in Winchester.'

The reverend guided Freddy to a mahogany easy chair covered with brocaded silk, and handed her a glass of wine. Then he and the other gentlemen sat down. Freddy had a good view of the captain and the curate, and examined them from behind her spectacles. Henry Lefroy was, indeed, very handsome, yet in that slightly odd way that combines a number of unremarkable features – a long and slightly crooked nose, a pointed chin, small blue eyes positioned too close together – to create a very handsome whole. Mr Winkworth, too, was altogether well-looking, but in quite a different style. He was pale, delicate, almost feminine, and had a slightly lost air.

'Well,' said Freddy, 'here I am attending dinner with two clerics and one sailor. I wonder what subject of conversation shall predominate?'

'Oh, the sea, I hope,' said the captain. 'For your father was a great admiral, was he not, and so I think that counts as two sailors at table and so we are even.'

Freddy giggled, almost unwittingly. This man was rather charming, which was most inconvenient. But, then, she reminded herself, that was his power. She had learned to distrust charming men, and this evening she was determined to trust no-one at all. 'Yes, he was. My dear Mr Campbell said that you have heard of him?'

'Yes, we all – myself and my fellow sailors, that is – felt like we knew him, and of course some of the older men did, and spoke so highly of him.' Henry smiled his rather endearing, crooked smile. 'He was particularly renowned for his crossing-the-line ceremonies, I believe.'

Freddy felt tears suddenly coming; that was just what her father had mentioned in his recent visit, or whatever that was. Jonathan, sensing her emotion, endeavoured to turn the subject a little.

'Are you planning to settle on the land at last, Captain, and in Hampshire?'

'Nothing would give me greater pleasure, Reverend, and one day I hope to sit snug at the Admiralty sending green lads like myself off to war in rickety ships. But I have a few more tours in me yet, and these wars, you know, are far from over. I fear the tyrant Napoleon is only just beginning.'

'I quite agree with you there,' said Jonathan. 'I wish us clerics who stay at home could do more; we live too fat and easy.'

Henry looked at Jonathan with a slight curl of his upper lip. 'If that is what contents you, sir.'

'But the clergy is a most worthy profession,' said Freddy, irritated, 'and brings great comfort to people.' She glared at Henry, and he looked very sorry.

'Please forgive me, Miss Swinglehurst – and everyone – I really did not mean an insult,' said Henry. 'My own dear father was a clergyman, and no-one did more good for the souls in his care. I assure you I have a high respect for the profession. I only meant that for myself, being such a wild, rough and tumble, independent lad, the navy was the best place. Anne's father arranged for me to join the Royal Naval Academy at Portsmouth at the age of 13, in the year 1782, you know, and I came over from Cork, and they soon knocked me into shape. Then I was off to the East Indies as Volunteer on the *Hercules*, then midshipman on the *Perseus*, and I have not had the opportunity to look back since. I fear that I have become entirely fit for a life at sea, but entirely unfit for polite society.'

Freddy, softened, nodded at him. She was disarmed again, which annoyed her. She was feeling increasingly combative, and was quite ready to challenge the world on anything or nothing.

Mary now entered the room and declared that dinner was served. She smiled, briefly, but almost warmly, at the captain and the curate, who both looked at her intently.

'Come, Fredericka,' said Jonathan. 'In the absence of the mistress of the house I shall take you into dinner.'

Freddy got up, took Jonathan's arm again, and they walked through the connecting doors to the dining room, which was very grand indeed. The paper was of a regal red colour, which set off the gilt frames of the many portraits and historical scenes that hung from the walls, and the dining table was a long, mahogany affair weighed down with shining silverware and several covered dishes set on heated cross-shaped stands.

'We will not worry about precedence, and are all easy and comfortable this evening,' said Jonathan. He pulled out a chair for Freddy, and sat down himself to her right. The curate was opposite her and the captain to his left, facing Jonathan.

'Tis a very grand style of comfort,' said Freddy, smiling and looking round the room in wonder. 'The Campbells and I take a bit of mutton broth at 3 after noon in the hot and smoky kitchen, and Flip joins us at table.'

The captain laughed. 'I would find that quite comfortable. I am still not used to the captain's table at sea and yearn for a return to the mess table.'

'Do not listen to Miss Swinglehurst, gentlemen,' said Jonathan. 'For some motive known only to herself, she likes to give the impression of being a kind of wild gypsy. In truth, she has been in the whirl of the London *ton* these many years and has not eaten with less than a viscount for as long as she can remember.'

'You have found me out,' said Freddy, laughing and catching the captain's eye. He grinned at her, then looked down at the table.

'Let us say Grace,' said the reverend.

Grace was said, then Mary and Sam came forward and removed the dome-shaped lids from the dishes on the table, revealing a handsome spread of soles, roast fowls and rabbit.

'You see your dinner, friends,' said the reverend. 'We keep it simple today.'

He helped Freddy to the soup, while Henry and Frances helped each other. Mary and Sam filled wine glasses, cleared the soup bowls when the time came, then left the four diners to the rest of their meal.

When everyone was settled with full plates and glasses, Freddy said:

'So, Mr Winkworth, what drew you to the ministry?'

'I believe I was called to it,' said the curate, looking at Freddy with his usual deeply earnest expression. 'Though it took a little time for me to realise it. There are not many professions open to impoverished younger sons, and so that is how I began. But then I felt the spirit move inside me, and I vowed to devote my life to God. We live in a time of vice and corruption, Miss Swinglehurst. Whilst our honourable military men fight the war, we at home must fight a war against our inner demons, against the sins of the flesh. For if we do not reform, we are ruined. Only look what happened to the French.'

In the past few years, the reverend and his curate had come under the influence of the Evangelical movement within the Anglican church. Jonathan had not taken it in too severe a fashion. In some ways, he was a typical cleric of fifty years before; he did not abhor drunkenness, hunting, gaming, and many other pleasures besides; rather his spirit was evangelical in its sense of righteousness about good causes, and he was fully aware of the vanity within him that enjoyed the effects of his powerful invective on his congregants and audiences. Frances Winkworth, on the other hand, younger, naturally more earnest, was gripped by a fervour that almost consumed him, and made him prone to a morbid self-examination that filled his heart with guilt.

Freddy felt a little uncomfortable. 'Yes, I see,' she said, not entirely seeing. 'Well, I am sure you bring a great deal of comfort to people, sir. Think how that poor woman who died here came to a rectory in her time of great need.' Without intending to, Freddy had got onto just the subject she wanted. She examined the three men's faces, curious.

'Yes,' said Winkworth, looking grave. 'I hope she did find some comfort before her death; but most importantly, you know, in the great hereafter. I pray for her daily.' He paused. 'I am still most perplexed about the way her body was found, lying on the ground in the shape of the cross like that. It is blasphemous, I am sure.'

'She was found lying in the shape of a cross?' asked Freddy.

'Aye,' said Winkworth. 'She was on her front, face down, with both arms outstretched at right angles to her body.'

'Good gracious,' said Freddy, glancing at the captain, who was looking very uncomfortable. 'I did not know that. But then, how could she have died of heart failure? Or if she did, how did she end up in such a strange position on the ground?'

'We do not know,' said Jonathan quietly. 'We did

not want to make too much of it. I did not want Anne more upset than she was by dwelling on that aspect. We did wonder if it was some kind of revenge, or warning, against us, being so vocal as we are against the slave trade. There are many in the vicinity with vested interests, you know. Indeed, these include some clergymen, who claim that the institution of slavery is sanctioned by the bible.'

Freddy gulped back some more wine. She was drinking more than was considered seemly for ladies, who were meant to take a thimbleful of wine with their dinner and then turn to their tea and needlework. In fact, she was now quite drunk, but too drunk to realise that she was drunk. Her head was spinning with this whole affair – the dead woman and the diamond and all the possible secrets. She was confused, angry, belligerent.

'It is a terrible, terrible, business,' said Henry. 'I have seen something of it. But happily there are several fervent abolitionists amongst us naval men too…' He trailed off, looking a little defeated.

Freddy banged down her glass on the table, spilling most of its contents. 'Well, my mother was a slave,' she declared, as if they were playing a game of slavery one-upmanship and she had presented her trump card. She looked intently at the faces of her three companions. They were all glowing, she was sure. Any one of them could be a murderer and a jewel thief. 'She was a mulatto, you know, which is half black, half white.' She said this triumphantly, and waved her right arm in the air. 'And I am a quadroon. Yes, we are all labelled thus.

I had never heard of such a thing as quadroon – it is a mix of mulatto and white, I discovered - until some inquisitive fellow at a card party questioned me until he had established the fact quite to his satisfaction.'

'I am sorry to hear that you are subject to such impertinences, Fredericka,' said Jonathan gently.

'Oh, it don't signify,' she said. 'I have grown used to it. I asked the fellow what name was applied to the breeding of a pig and a cow, and whether he was half of each, or perhaps just a quarter cow, since there was less of the bovine and more of the porcine in his countenance. It was quite wicked of me.' Freddy giggled angrily, hiccupped, then put her head in her hands.

'Are you quite well, Miss Swinglehurst?' asked the curate with great concern. 'Can we do anything for you?'

'No, no,' said Freddy, looking up, and seeming to come to her senses. 'I am so sorry, gentlemen. I do not know why I am talking like this. My mind is troubled with lots of strange things, you know, and my emotions are a little heightened coming home to Hampshire after so long away. And, I fear, I am somewhat heated by wine. Mr Winkworth, I am guilty of indulgencies of the flesh, and am destined for the hell fires.'

The curate looked horrified. 'Good gracious, no, Miss Swinglehurst. That is not what I meant at all. Oh dear, I am mortified that I have…'

'Do not be uneasy, Mr Winkworth. You must forgive me being such an ill-tempered creature, this evening, for I feel like I am fighting a war but I do not know who is mine enemy. My father once said that I was a contrary little soul, and I am certainly proving him right today.'

Jonathan gave her a slight sardonic look she knew from old, and she laughed. 'You see, the reverend knows me very well.'

Mary's cooking was almost as delicious as Margaret's, and Freddy gradually found her heart and mind, as well as her body, softening, from its good effects, and her conversation softened likewise. The diners moved on to less contentious topics, and the evening ended peacefully.

Samuel took Freddy home in the Millbrook chariot. On arrival, she kissed the Campbells and went straight to her bed. It had been a tiring, unsettling day. She felt a little ashamed of herself, upsetting Polly like that, questioning Samuel and Mary, and ranting drunkenly at two clergymen and a captain of His Majesty's Navy; that was two drunken women the poor reverend had had to deal with in one day. She had learned a few things, though. She must write to Affy with an update on the morrow, and try to wait patiently for something from her friend in return.

Chapter 13

About two days after Freddy's visit to the rectory, Adam Short was waiting in a small, mostly deserted cottage – now more of a hovel – on the outskirts of Basing, Hampshire. He sat on a once fine but now battered and broken Windsor chair, which must have been handed down to someone many years ago, listening to the light rain tapping on the rotten roof, and staring at two crows pecking at the floor and a mouse which hurried along the skirting board under the window. Some travelling people had been camping there, but he had soon got rid of them with bribery and threats. A prolonged fit of coughing sent the crows flapping and fleeing and caused the mouse to pause a moment, before scurrying on its way. Short waited for his lungs to clear a little, then took out his silver snuff box, engraved with an elaborately curving A and S, pinched some snuff between his right thumb and forefinger, and pushed it up his right nostril.

Mr Short had once been a very rich man. A filthy rich man; a stinkingly rich man. A native of Hampshire, he had gone out to the Caribbean when a boy of not seventeen years of age, determined to make his fortune. And that he had done, surviving years of hardship, self-indulgence and disease, when lesser fellows had fallen, as if he was not made of human flesh but the hide of some specially-bred beast. And no one had more talent for the driving and flogging business than he. He had returned to England once before, when he was five and forty, with the aim of enjoying himself, and making his presence felt in the business and political realms. It had not been a success. Although he bought himself a luxurious townhouse, and grew used to fine drawing rooms, clubs, inns and coffee houses, he never felt entirely at home in them. He was considered vulgar, he knew. He was too overdressed; his strong Hampshire accent was still discernible; his manners were not quite proper. Above all, his money did not smell right – he was known as Short the Flogger, Short Torture or that Short Devil. It had angered him, briefly. Had he not helped to make the country great? Were not the many fine lords and ladies who turned up their noses at sight of him living off the back of his efforts? But, as his skin was thick, and his self-love great, he had brushed away all contempt and pushed on.

He had fallen greatly since then, and was back in the country on this occasion through necessity only. But even if he could have afforded it, his appearance alone would have made him no longer welcome in respectable establishments. Still, as he had grown up poor, he felt a sort of comfortable familiarity in the lowly type of places he was now frequenting. Even this shack was not so dissimilar to the place in which he had been born.

There was a quiet knock on the door, which was then pushed open by a tall, handsome man dressed in fustian clothing and cap.

'Mr Short,' said the man, nodding at him, and trying not to recoil again at the sight of Short's sickly, poxed face.

'Sir.' Mr Short nodded back. He raised one of his heavy brows and smirked at the gentleman's costume.

'You got her safely away, then?' asked the gentleman.

'Aye. It was not so difficult, though heavy work for me in my current state of health. I planned to do it sooner but was forced to take to my bed for a few days.' Mr Short coughed, then took a few moments to breathe in some air. 'I don't believe I was observed.'

'That is good. Where is she?'

'Just through that doorway, in the other room.'

The gentleman looked in that direction, his face full of fear. 'And you have brought the tools?'

'I have.'

'Well, we had better get on with it, then.' The man's face grew paler, and he was already sweating and shivering.

Mr Short and the gentleman went through to the next room, which looked like it had once been a kitchen place. The woman's body was on the floor, still wrapped in its now filthy woollen shroud. The man breathed in sharply, and pulled a large red kerchief from his pocket and tied it round his nose and mouth.

'You're not used to bodies, sir,' said Mr Short. 'I have dealt with rather a lot, in my time. She will decompose quickly now that she's out of the box, especially in this warmth. The sight will become a deal uglier, I can assure you. Though one can grow accustomed to the stench.' Short was almost enjoying himself.

'Why am I not surprised that Butcher Short should be accustomed to these things?' The man now turned an ashen colour, pulled the kerchief back off and stumbled to a corner of the room in which sat two old milk pails; he vomited into one of them. He stood there for a while, breathing deeply, then wiped his mouth with the kerchief and turned back to face his companion, whose scarred face was half-sneer, half-smile.

'You will have to get down on your knees,' said Mr Short, 'there is no table or other surface for you to use; we do not have the surgeon's luxuries.'

The man looked at the shrouded body and the sawing implement and two large knives lying next to it. He swallowed, then tied his kerchief back on, and knelt down. He pulled back the cloth to reveal the woman's face, its skin starting to blister a little, and tongue swelling inside her mouth; then her upper body, which was marked with the cuts and stitching from the partial autopsy, and the curve of her formerly pregnant belly. He looked at the implements, then back at the body, then up at Mr Short.

'You should do this, sir,' said the man from behind his mask. 'You are already thoroughly debased and degraded. The task would be nothing to a man who takes pleasure in torturing black flesh, I am sure.'

Mr Short sighed and looked at his companion with contempt, but said nothing. The gentleman began to cry. He got up and took off the kerchief again, saying, 'I cannot do it. I thought I could, but I cannot. I was so fond of her. But even if I had not known her, I could never do this. It is abominable.'

'I knew you could not,' said Short. 'What did I tell you?'

'You should do it, I say.'

'Do not give me orders. I may be doing most of the dirty work in this business but I'm not your lackey. This is a partnership, and an equal one, whether you like it or not. You're as soiled as I am, even though you believe that you can stay clean. I told you from the beginning that I wouldn't do this, and that, in any case, it was an outlandish and foolish notion.'

'Agh, yes, I beg your pardon,' said the man, with feeble sarcasm. 'You cannot do it because you have grown exceedingly tender, sir; I forgot. You love your negro, and only want to take care of her and your mulatto bastards like a dear, good husband should.'

'Damme, sir, I don't have to stand here and listen to your ridiculous insults. They barely touch me; my skin is as thick as old rope; but it's a waste of my precious time. You will show me some respect.' Short's voice grew more rasping as he expressed his anger. 'You're a fool, sir, a canting fool; slavery is the way of the world and we all live off the back of it. I didn't come hither to be lectured yet again, and I'll not take lessons on morality from a corrupted gentleman like you. Oh, and, lest we forget, a man who's happy to have the cadaver of one of his whores sliced up in his desperate quest for money, even though he finds he cannot get his own delicate hands dirty with such a disgusting job. You're a great hypocrite, sir. It's often the way with you fine gentlemen and your soft feelings for the poor, oppressed negroes. But you have to be the worst I've ever met.'

The gentleman continued to cry a little. He found that he was not angered by Mr Short's words, and knew that he had no right to be. 'Perhaps I am,' he said quietly. 'I find that my pride cannot even rally against your accusations because they hit home. You are right, sir. I am a base, despicable hypocrite, driven by avarice.'

Mr Short sighed. Now the man would lapse into self-pity; what a child he was. 'You are simply a man, like any other, something you frequently forget, I think. Now let us decide what is next to be done.'

Mr Short and the man went back through into the next room, where the former took the same chair and the latter sat on the floor, his back against a crumbling wall. The mouse was still scurrying back and to, as if it was on very important business but did not know what. The gentleman took an expensive flask of brandy from his pocket, unscrewed the top, and took several large swigs, before offering it to Mr Short. His politeness would usually have made him proffer it to a companion before himself, but he was a little wary of Short's disease, even though he was assured that it was not catching. Mr Short guessed his feeling, but did not say anything. He took the flask, and drank back a good deal of the brandy.

'A fine vintage,' said Short, 'I once had one of the best cellars on the island, you know. Well, back to business; we must get a surgeon to do the job that neither of us are willing or able to do. He won't find anything – I'm sure of that - but we may as well see it through.'

'Yes. And we should have hired a surgeon to begin with, as you said. I am so nervous about this whole business being discovered that I hoped to keep it between ourselves. But it seems that we must involve others, and have no other choice but to trust them.'

'There are many others involved already. We cannot do this alone, and will have to take our chances. This is as crazed a scheme as ever madman devised, and there's no containing it now. I'll get a surgeon, and we'll have to pay him well, and then I need to get to London quickly to investigate what Barber told me about this Matthew Lane fellow.'

'Do you think Barber was lying?'

'He is a liar by nature, but I do not believe he was lying in this case.'

The gentleman sighed. 'Thank you, Mr Short, for all

your efforts. I hope you can forgive me my peevish outbursts. We think very differently on some subjects but are otherwise much the same, as you say. Well, I should be going.' The man's usually handsome face looked haggard, and he was devoid of energy.

'You take this all very hard, sir,' said Short.

The man smiled. 'Yes, I am not cut out for it – as you see – and I have nobody to blame but myself for the mess I have made. I am a desperate man, and ruin and shame loom ever closer.'

'Well, you may have to face them, sir, and like a man. But there is still a very small chance that we can both get what we need.'

The gentleman slowly pushed himself up from the floor. 'Keep the brandy, Mr Short; you look like you need something to fortify you.'

'I will, I thank you,' said Mr Short. 'I will write – care of the Chequers - when there is news.'

The gentleman nodded and quit the cottage.

Mr Short stared after him. What a ridiculous man he was, he thought, with his dandified airs and canting speech; it was as well that the man's father, who had been Short's friend, and who was a good, simple fellow, was no longer here to see it. Short took several more swigs of brandy, and stared at the mouse, still busy about its imaginary business. He pulled out his pocket knife and threw it quickly at the creature. It wriggled, then fell still, blood spurting from its body in a most satisfying manner.

Chapter 14

After her eventful visit to the rectory, Freddy spent the next few days at home. She was trying to work through what she knew, and waiting impatiently for news from Affy. She updated Margaret with what she had discovered – that Polly was keeping something back and the fact that Sarah's dead body had been placed in the shape of a cross – and left it to her to share the information with her husband in the way she knew best. Then she tried to concentrate on other things. Margaret was inducting her into the mysteries of household management, which she had begun to learn as a young woman before tragedy, and her flight to London, had taken place. She was shocked at the amount of work involved and about how much there was to learn. The task of laundry day alone astounded her, and that with only three of them in the house.

She felt ashamed for not paying more attention

during her long absence. Margaret had sent her regular updates and accounts, and Freddy had signed it all off without barely a glance. She was determined to make up for lost time, to get to grips with every household task, and to bring in more help for the Campbells, who seemed to have been doing every job in the house and grounds, with very little outside help. How good and uncomplaining they were. How fortunate she had been to have such honest, trustworthy people to manage her affairs whilst she had been so careless of them. Although she could not bear to think of it, she knew that they would not always be with her. She was head of the old manor house and was now determined to become a proper manager of her own affairs, at the very least in honour of them and her father.

She went to church that Sunday with the Campbells. Mr Winkworth was a good preacher, if, perhaps, a little over-zealous on some points of morality, and with a tendency to mumble a little. She felt that she must attend church, even though she had never quite believed in a god. She had not said this out loud, for why would she? She did not overthink the matter, and it did not arise in general conversation; she was happy to honour the forms, and to sometimes take comfort from them. Strangely, the appearance of her father's ghost – if that was what it was – did not fundamentally alter her feeling. At church, those of the congregation who had not known her before were getting used to her face, and ceasing to stare. Mr and Mrs Campbell would stand either side of her, Margaret both beaming with pride and ready to glare at anyone who might dare to defame her treasure. Freddy knew that she was the subject of gossip, but was not troubled by it. She knew also that she should really start calling on and receiving people. She had high connections, such as the Countess Darby, and her father's standing gave her position in the neighbourhood. Plus, she was rich; Margaret was already preparing to fight off fortune hunters. But all that could wait. She just needed a little more time in snug comfort with Margaret and Gabriel; then she would be ready.

The weather was a little cool that afternoon and Freddy went to her dressing room, put on an old bed cap of the admiral's, and settled down to read *The Mysteries of Udolpho.* She was quite convinced that a second visit from her father was due, and, sure enough, she soon heard scuffling noises coming from inside the chimney, followed by a smoky shape appearing in the fireplace, then curling itself upward and upward, finally settling into the form of Admiral Swinglehurst.

'Egad, daughter, did I leave you so poor that you cannot afford a good fire? My old bones – if I had any – are quite rattling – and my teeth – I do seem to have those, in fact – are quite chattering.'

'Father!' Freddy jumped up, ran to the ghost of the admiral and tried to embrace him, before remembering that this was not possible. She pulled back her arms. 'Oh dear, I forgot that I cannot do that. No, father, dear, but tis the seventeenth day of June today, you know –

summer – though, to be sure, it is a little cold. But even if it were the depths of winter, I would be hesitant to have the fire lit; I would not want you to catch alight.'

'Catch fire? I am a ghost, Frederica Elizabeth Swinglehurst, in case you have not noticed. Nothing can harm me. To be sure, I was forgetting the season, but then tis chilly work travelling from the other side and a few flames would be quite welcome.'

'Oh, well, this ghost business is all new to me, Papa, and if you did but have the decency to come out of your portrait, like proper ghosts in novels do, I might have had a better idea as to what to expect. My favourite picture of you is most conveniently placed above your old desk, there. And if you would but come at the proper time, that is in darkest night, or better, by the light of a beautiful moon, and not, in the middle of the day, when one has just taken a little cold partridge and is more attentive to one's earthly stomach than to the world of the spirits.'

The admiral arranged his smoky features into a mildly sardonic stare. 'Oh? And is there anything else I might do to accommodate you, my dear?'

'Now I think upon it, you might think of coming at a set hour and day weekly, or monthly, as will suit you, when the clocks chime. Perhaps there may also be a little thunder and lightning, and some lashing rain.' Freddy grinned. 'Oh, and you might try to carry a bible, a crucifix and a mouldering skull and some bones.'

'Upon my soul, my love, that is a deal of things to

consider, and if only it were so straightforward, I would be happy to oblige you on every count. But, for the moment, dear, those delights will soon set me right.'

The admiral had spotted a bottle of brandy, two glasses, a pipe, a tin of tobacco and a few volumes of Samuel Johnson's works resting on a side table next to his old chair. He settled himself into the tapestried chair and skilfully, if shakily, went through the motions for lighting his pipe and pouring himself a glass of brandy, whilst Freddy looked on in awe.

'Aye,' said her father, 'that does the heart of an old admiral good. But are you well, my dear? Are you safe? I have been feeling that you are a little jittery, and a wriggling, like a fish that has just taken the bit. What ails you, my love?'

Freddy relaxed into her own chair. 'Oh, I am very well on the whole. It is just that there is a very strange business happening here in the village, and then it might even be connected to the theft of the Countess Darby's diamond.'

'Did I not tell you that I sensed danger? Are you in immediate peril?' The ghost jumped up suddenly, its wig bouncing into the air and hovering there for a moment, before landing back on its head.

Freddy smiled. 'No, father, do not be vexed. I am on the alert, I assure you. It is just that my mind is so confused and, I must confess, a little troubled.'

'Well, you must tell me all of it.'

'But you do not have much time, father, and I would so like you to talk of mother.'

'Do not fret; I will stay sufficient.'

Freddy smiled, relieved, and told her father all she knew, while he, curious, held his glass of brandy suspended just near his mouth.

'Well, Freddy, my little sailor, it all sounds like a most melancholy and dark affair. But why are you fretting yourself about it, my love – you cannot carry all the troubles of the world on those little shoulders of yours.'

'No, father.' She paused. 'I did not mention that Sarah's skin colour was like mine, you know. It made me think how spoilt I have been, and how ignorant of the world I was growing up.'

'You, ignorant? Did you not have the finest governess? And that fine old noble French master, who had fled from the terror? And the dancing master? And the music lessons; and you can play very well, though the least said about your singing the better; even poor Mrs C struggled to love that noise.'

Freddy laughed.

'And did you not have,' continued her father, 'the one and only Admiral William George Swinglehurst himself to complete your education? Aye, you were a little spoiled, to be sure, but then you did not have a mother, and there is nothing so very wrong with being loved, and cared for, and comfortable, as any young lady in your position should be.'

'I know, father, and I am truly grateful for it, and for all that you gave me. I only meant in terms of my knowledge of how other folks suffer. Especially,' - Freddy touched her face and pinched the skin of her right cheek – 'those like me. I feel so guilty somehow.'

'Guilty? What have you to feel guilty about? The only guilt is that of the slavers, and the traders, and it is a great evil in this world, my love, and one day there will be a great retribution. But do not take this burden upon yourself. God sends us suffering enough, which it is our duty to endure. We need not take on additional burdens that are not ours to bear. Do not wear a hair shirt. You must enjoy, with a full heart, the good things that have been given to you. It would be a sin to deny them, for has not God given the world beauty and joy, as well as pain and suffering? No doubt, we must all do what we can to alleviate that suffering, and I am sure you will do that, my dear.' The admiral took several large swigs of brandy, then chuckled. 'Well, Freddy, what do you think about having a preacher for a father? I never could abide an over-zealous parson, but only hear me now!'

Freddy smiled, watching the orange glow inside her father's smoky head turn red as he had grown more heated in argument. 'You would be a fine preacher, sir, and I, for one, would walk miles to hear you.'

'I think you would be an audience of one, my love. But I hope that your heart is a little easier now?'

'Yes, father; it really is, thank you. I do give a little money to help people, which I am sure you do not mind. During my last few years in London, I saw so much. I had seen people like me before, but not really seen them, if that makes any sense. My dear friend Aphrodite – you would like her, I know - opened my eyes to another world. There are so many destitute, and they need food and clothing and shelter. And then there is the money for campaigns, legal expenses for court cases, medical bills, and cash for those escaping, and hiding, and some is needed for bribes, and fees and so many other things.'

'Well, then, Fredericka Swinglehurst, you are doing a great deal of good, and you should be proud. And your mother would die of pride, if she was not already – ahem – dead - that is.'

Freddy burst out laughing. 'But you are dead, too, father, are you not? It is very confusing.'

'Well, yes, I am, my dear. Quite dead.' The admiral chuckled.

Freddy laughed her throaty laugh again, and then found she could not stop. She continued for several minutes, her father's night cap falling off as she bent her head forward and clutched her stomach.

'Now, Captain Freddy, that is more like it. You look just like your mother in a fit of merriment. It gave me so much pleasure to see. They were rare when we first met, you know, but became more common as she grew easier in heart and mind.'

'Are you together now?'

'Yes, in a way. In a manner of speaking. But all is well.'

'You are a little vague, father.'

'I flatter myself I am; it is required, you know.'

'Did mother suffer all those years gone, when birthing me? I cannot help but think of that sometimes. What a terrible way to end. I know that you had ten years of happiness together, however, and that comforts me.'

'Aye, we did, my dear. There is no doubting that. She did suffer somewhat at the end. I will not lie to you. Childbearing is not a man's province, but every man can hear the screams if he chooses not to stuff up his ears. But the fever that took her afterwards was short, and the delirium masked the pain, I believe. I was relieved for her – if not for myself - that it was all over, and she did look peaceful at the last.'

'How did you bear the grief?' Freddy's voice was quiet.

'Not very well, at first. It is why I suffer so to hear of your own suffering. But you refused to let me sink. You were a bold, insistent thing from the get-go, it seemed. It was as if your mother had saved all her strength to put into you. And you bawled and gurgled and laughed at me, enough to drive me half mad. And then one day I started laughing, too, and life called me back. But I must not forget the Campbells. It is hard to put into words how much they did for us all. Margaret nursed both you and me when your mother went, you know.'

'I can well imagine. To my shame, I am only just realising their worth, and it amazes me. But, father, did you not want to blame me for mother's death?'

'Blame you, my love? No. You must never think that. We wanted you so very much. You were nine years in the making, you know.'

'Poor, dear mother.'

'Well, well, we were lucky to have found each other. Although I did sometimes wonder if I had been selfish in taking her so far away from her home. It is a very hard thing to leave behind one's home soil for ever. At night she used to dream of her island, and murmur in her sleep. But she liked it here in Winchester, despite her sickness for home. She loved the Campbells and the countryside, and we made such a cosy family here. She had a talent for managing the poultry and for growing potatoes and strawberries. We mostly stayed at home, and kept ourselves snug.'

'Did you not want to settle in Barbados with her?'

'Nay, I could not. I will admit that I was too frightened about what I would become. I only intended to visit the island for a short period. I was at a loose end after the wars, and the Darbys of Portsmouth – a distant connection of the Countess, you know - invited me to spend a little time on their estate.

'Well, I got to the island, determined to disapprove, being very much against slavery in my heart, and was overwhelmed by its beauty. The scenery was quite breath-taking. They called Barbados "the civilized isle", you know, as the plantation system was long established there, and the lifestyle was most pleasant – for the white planting class, you understand. They seemed generous and hospitable, which was a balm to a man long tried by war. There was riding in the morning when the air was cool, and some shooting of birds during my time there. Edmund Darby even had deer on his estate. And the dancing! I never knew a place where people so loved to dance; at every kind of social gathering you can imagine, the rooms would be cleared for it. Well, my dear, you know how I love to dance.'

The admiral clicked his smoky feet together, and Freddy smiled and did likewise.

'But it shames me to say,' he continued, 'I felt my heart start to weaken. I looked at the negroes, and all the types of black mixed with white, and I thought, they are happy enough. This works in its own way; perhaps it is not so bad.

'And then one day the men had such a terrible debauch. You can barely imagine how much drink they consumed generally, and I was a hardened sailor, used to my fair share. And I kept up, and I drank and drank and drank. And later in the evening when I was ready for my bed, I saw something truly evil involving the local women; I will not give details, dearest. I thank God I refused to take part, but, to my shame, I turned a blind eye, and went to bed.

'The next morning I woke up with such a fever and in so much pain from the debauch, and was desperate for relief. A maid came into my room and drew back the blinds. The sun was blinding. And I screamed at her, and raised my hand as if to strike her, you know.' A tear rolled down the admiral's left cheek, which hissed a little. 'And she looked so terrified but at the same time so accepting of it. I cried, and asked her for my forgiveness. And after that day I vowed to have nothing more to do with the great evil.'

'Oh, father.'

'And I opened my eyes, for I had been wilfully keeping them half closed before, I am sure. I will own to you that a sailor's life can be a brutal one, dear. One has to maintain discipline on ship, or there would be anarchy. But this plantation brutality is of a new order, sanctioned by the devil himself. Even children enjoy inflicting punishments, and I saw the little Darby darlings beat the female slaves in the house with as little feeling as if they were swatting at flies.

'Even the hospitality was a sham. I soon realised that Edmund Darby wanted to involve me in the trade. I am sorry to say that many a corrupt navy man gets involved in one way or another.' The admiral sighed. 'The whole thing is based on a greed that would eat up the earth, and the stars and the sky, and heaven itself if it could.'

'I am sorry, father.'

'Do not you be sorry, my angel. It was a salutary lesson for me. And how could I regret it, when I met your dear mother, and got my little Freddy?'

'You never told me the full story of your meeting. Will you tell me now?'

'I will, dear, though I am afraid that it is rather a tainted one, as everything was in that place. When you were growing up, I wanted to keep all painful things from you, and to surround you with nothing but affection and happiness, but tis not always the best way. It is perhaps better that we are all aware of the evil in this world so that we can guard ourselves against it; for it will come to us in whatsoever shape it may, whether we want it or not.

'Your mother was the daughter of Robert Darby, a cousin of Edmund Darby's, and a slave woman whom he had set up high in his household. The woman grew quite haughty with her power, and even became a little tyrannical. This angered the other slaves, and the white workers, and not least his poor wife who had come out from England. It was a poisonous, corrupted household, as many were, and he was a violent, capricious, drunkard, as many were again. Your poor mother grew up in this atmosphere. Sometimes she was spoilt and petted – she was at least given a good education – other times bullied and cowed. She was not allowed to forget her slave status, since children of female slaves are by that fact alone always considered slaves themselves unless their freedom is legally granted.'

'Poor mother.'

'Well, she was fortunate in the sense that she had so far escaped any abuse from the men around her. But her father was getting worse and worse, and in his drunken, maudlin moods sometimes threatened to sell her to a trader, or to put her to work in the fields; or in other moods would cry over her and call her his beautiful darling girl.'

'But what about her mother? Did she not stand up for her daughter, and try to protect her?'

'Yes, I think she did, a little, but not enough. She was not so heartless, my dear, but she was as addled on rum as Robert himself, and was so used to his treatment that perhaps she expected nothing better for her daughter. And she was likely preoccupied with her other children; there were three sons born, it appears, all of whom were taken by the fever, and she longed to have a son living, who might secure a stake in his father's business.

'Well, to get to your mother and I, the two households socialised together, and I saw your mother, and soon loved her, for never was anybody so easy to love.' The admiral smiled, and pressed his right hand to his smoky heart, which glowed red. 'I was reluctant to speak, however, being some years her senior, and concerned that I would be somehow taking advantage of her in such a difficult situation. But one evening something happened to force me to declare myself, for her father, in one of his bad states, had agreed that whichever of the single gentlemen present won a particular game of faro, could have her; in short, she was to be a prize in a game of cards. So I intervened, and had to give him a large sum of money to save her. It shames me not a little, for it might seem as if I was buying her, like the poor slave that she was, but I did not know what else to do. Well, I said that she was free, and could do whatever she so wished. She said that she would prefer to stay with me, and we talked, and I found that she loved me.'

'Of course she did, father, for who would not love you also?'

'I am sure she loved me, dear, as I loved her. But it was

not an easy beginning because she had so little choice. What could she have really done with her freedom?'

'Yes, I do see. But you were so happy together, and the Campbells have told me how much she loved you, and how good you were to her.'

The admiral smiled. 'Well, dear, and we made you, the best thing we did. So you must keep yourself safe, and that pistol cocked and ready. Always be on your guard! At the same time, try not to weigh your heart down over this local business. I am sure that this Sarah will find her rest at last, however much her body has been insulted. I wonder, now I think upon it, if she was dug up not for her body itself, but for something that she carried on it, and was buried with her.'

'Oh, the diamond!' said Freddy, 'that could be a possibility.'

'Aye, it could. A most fantastical occurrence, but possible nonetheless. But it is time, now.'

'Oh, I feared that it might be. You have not even glanced at your Dr Johnson.'

'No, and I cannot take the books with me. Leave them on that little table and I will try to call in again when the house is quiet. Goodbye, Captain Freddy, and keep that pistol hard by!' The admiral's voice faded away as his form swirled towards the chimney, and disappeared.

Chapter 15

The next day, Freddy received a letter not from Affy but from another friend in London, Lady Lavinia Ingram, who was feeling unwell following her lying-in with her second child, and requesting Freddy's company to help raise her spirits. Freddy had not been expecting to visit London so soon after her return to Hampshire, but was more than happy to oblige her friend. And now there was an added incentive to go; she could stay for a short time with Affy and pursue some more lines of enquiry into the mystery. She now seriously considered the possibility that Sarah had been buried with the Celestial Light, though quite how, she could not conceive. Had Sarah known David Barber, or, indeed, Matthew Lane? She might call at the Darby townhouse to see what she could find out. She wrote two letters, one to Lady Ingram informing her that she would arrive that Friday, and one to Affy, telling her where she would be, that she would arrive in Somers Town a week later, and sharing the information about Polly, Sarah's body having been laid out in the shape of a cross, and her notion that Sarah might have been buried with the diamond.

The letters went the next day, only for a letter from Affy to then appear. There was not much to relate, Affy said, only that her husband had laughed rather heartily at the suggestion that he himself was involved in the diamond theft, and could not believe that Matthew Lane could be so likewise, though he was a little concerned to hear his name mentioned in relation to it and would try to find out more. They had only just seen Tom Jackson, and he had agreed to see what he could discover about Sarah, if anything, in St Giles.

Lady Lavinia was stepdaughter to the Dowager Darby – she of the stolen diamond - from the latter's second marriage, and Lavinia and Freddy had met fully – she had seen her once or twice before in Hampshire - in the year 1793, when Freddy had left Winchester.

When Freddy had first arrived in London, she found herself taken up by a rather fast set, part of the so-called *ton*, or near enough to it. The set thought that it would be quite charming to have a female negro friend; how clever they were to find her. Pretty negro servant boys were common enough, and had perhaps become at trifle passé, but the beautiful, clever daughter of a decorated admiral was another matter. What a display of their originality and style. Besides, one had to be for the abolition, and what greater signifier of one's acute sensibility for the suffering of the negroes than to have one of them in their midst?

Freddy had not minded being taken up. She had not minded anything, really, in her grief and loneliness. She let herself be pulled into the circle, where she was petted, patronised and called 'the sooty beauty' by young Lord Huntingdon, who never failed in an attempt to be a little free with her whenever they were alone together. Whilst she was unusual where she had grown up, she had become part of the fabric of the local village, Winchester and its environs, and was so known and accepted that she had not felt especially different. Her father had educated her. She knew all about slavery and trade and sugar, though it did not feel quite real to her. In London, she saw men, and the occasional woman, similar to herself, and could not help but stare and compare their faces, skin shades and hair, to her own. She had never been so aware of herself, of the body her soul inhabited, and developed a degree of self-consciousness that would lessen as the years passed but never quite disappear.

She drank heavily, smoked, took opiates, gambled. She flirted, laughed, cried, raged. It was a sort of terrible pleasure. But she never succumbed entirely. She had been so loved and treasured growing up that she knew in the core of her being that the state she was in was not worthy of her. Then something occurred to trigger a change. Her spirits were low one evening after she had received some unhappy news, and she had indulged herself even more than usual, and finally succumbed to Lord Huntingdon.

It was a shock, and felt like a violation even though he had not forced himself upon her. It was as if she had wanted to punish herself, to suffer – for what, she knew not. Rather happily for her if not for him, he died three months later in a duel, and so her transgression died with him. Then, of course, she had got rid of its result. Not long after this time, she had extricated herself from the set and moved to a small house in a respectable but not very fashionable part of town, expecting to cut most of her ties. To her surprise, she retained – or, more accurately, now made – several real friends, who turned out to have beating hearts beneath the wigs and the paint. Lady Lavinia was one of these.

'How glad I am to have you here,' said the woman herself, holding her friend's hand as they sat in her oriental-styled front drawing room in the Ingram townhouse in Mayfair. 'With you one feels a peace that one cannot find with everyone.'

'Thank you, my dear,' said Freddy, 'and happy I am to be with you. But you do not look yourself.' Lavinia's usually bright blue eyes were a little red and swollen, and her whole face seemed to sag around her pretty, upturned nose. 'Has it been difficult? How is the child?'

'The child is well, I believe. It is in the nursery with the nursemaid. I find I cannot take to it. With George, I could not bear to leave him. Now I feel that I cannot bear to be near her. I say this to you only. Thankfully, my acquaintance does not see anything amiss, since it is natural to hand the child straight to the nursery and resume one's duties, unless one is a most determined disciple of Rousseau. But knowing how I felt with my first I feel sure that this cannot be right.'

'Oh, Lavvy, I am sorry to hear it. But surely, the feeling will pass. You must get well yourself, and that is bound to help.'

'I will try, now that you are here. I am not very pleasant company, I am afraid. I feel so listless and melancholy and find myself weeping worse than any addict of the poets. To think that we used to feign sensibility in order to be fashionable and now I find the tears coming whether I want them or no.'

Lavinia began to cry a little, and Freddy continued to hold her right hand and pat it. 'It is a relief to unburden myself,' she continued.

'I am glad of it. You talk of our foolishness in the early days. Do you remember our sugar boycott evening? It all comes back to me now, sitting here.'

'How could I forget?' said Lavinia, smiling. 'I never have been so ill in my entire life.'

'Not as ill as Lady Jane, perhaps. Do not you recall her vomiting into the chamber pot?'

'Oh yes, poor dear. She went quite green and rushed behind the screen just in time. I had to get rid of that screen, and the fine chamber pot adorned with birds and fishes. I could not bear to look at them afterwards.'

The friends reminisced about the evening, in early December in the year 1793, when they had decided to prove that they were not the frivolous and selfish – nay, fiendish and monstrous - women that the anti-slave trade campaigners suggested, taking the blood and sweat of slaves along with the sugar in their tea, by giving up sugar. And as they knew that the best way to put one off riot and debauchery was to indulge in those things to their extreme, they would indulge in an evening of sugar.

Ten brightly-coloured ladies had been shown into the red, stuccoed dining room to the sight of the large walnut table laden with sweet things. These included, but were not limited to: cakes (Plum, Seed, Guinea, Almond), biscuits (Savoy, Naples, Yarmouth, Ratifia, Orange Flower, Lemon), wafers (Peppermint, Violet, Lemon), drops (Chocolate, Bergamot, Seville Orange), jellies (Gooseberry, Raspberry, Apple), plus gingerbread, sugared almonds, barley sugar, chocolate almond conceits, caraway comfits and chocolate creams. In the centre of the display was a large silver bowl filled to the brim with sugar – the kitchen staff had devoted many hours grinding it into crystals - since some preferred their sweetness neat. The delights were washed down with a variety of heavily sweetened teas, chocolate, wines and cordials. The women, having come costumed in outfits dedicated to their favourite confectionary, looked like so many hot-housed birds in an aviary. Lady Ingram was a Judge's Biscuit, dressed in a gown decorated with caraway seeds – her poor dressmaker had worked into the early hours for several days to get it finished – and a judge's wig and black cap. Freddy, in a tribute to queen cakes, was sporting a crown and a giant, puffed gown patterned with currants and roses.

Freddy remembered feeling quite delirious and, finding that she could take no more sugar by mouth, had attempted to snort some into her right nostril. Not much effect was produced, excepting some coughing and a very sore nose. Then she had gathered a handful of crystals from the bowl, tilted back her head, and dropped them over her neck and décolletage. She scooped up more, and rubbed them into her face. She got up, picked up more sugar and tipped it over her head, twirling around as she did so, laughing with dizziness and delight. Lavinia, watching Freddy, felt it was time to bring out the piece de resistance, and rang the bell for her turbaned black boy, Gustavus, who entered the room shortly afterwards struggling to carry a large, red, velvet sack of sugar. He nodded to his mistress, his face showing no sign of the horror he felt at this waste of such a valuable commodity, placed the sack on the Persian rug at the end of the table, bowed and left the room.

Lavinia went over to the sack and began to pick up sugar and throw it over herself. Three of the group remained slumped into their chairs, their faces pale, their heads starting to ache. But the remaining ladies got up to follow suit and join Lavinia and a still twirling Freddy. Now there were seven women scooping out the sugar with both hands, throwing it into the air in different directions and jumping around to meet it as it fell. They danced, a mass of sugared, colourful bodies, flickering in the candlelight, until Lady L tipped the remaining half of the sack of sugar onto the floor, and the ladies fell down, laughing, licking the sugar and rolling in it.

'It was not even effectual,' said Lavinia, finally. 'I managed three days.'

'There I have the upper hand. I managed four.'

The women were interrupted by a tall footman wearing a little too much powder, who announced the arrival of Mr Augustus Grey.

'Oh.' Lavinia looked a little surprised. 'Do show him in.'

Mr Grey entered the room, smiling warmly at Lavinia, then caught sight of Freddy, and bowed.

'Why, it is Fweddy Thinglewhurst,' he said. 'How do oo do? I whop that you are quite well?'

'Mr Grey. What a long time it has been since we met. I am very well, thank you.'

'Will you take some tea, Mr Grey?' Lavinia asked, gesturing for him to sit down.

'That would be wery pweasant, Lady L.'

Freddy smiled to herself as she watched the exceedingly elegant and shapely form of Mr Grey seat himself on a Sheraton chair. He was looking particularly striking that day, she thought, a peacock above all peacocks, one who strutted into the room, and filled it with the splendour of his feathers. Augustus was the former black boy of a certain, notorious Marchioness, who was now approaching five and seventy, and with whom he still lived in Berkeley Square. He had been brilliantly educated and was probably the finest horseman in Europe. His only other talents were playing at faro, and being a rake. Freddy had spent some time in his company during her years with the *ton*. Seeing him now, she thought him quite ridiculous. But then, had she not been ridiculous also? Had she not spoken, for a time, in that strange, childlike way, that kept the group tight together and excluded vulgar pretenders?

'Pway, how do oo find Hampshire? I was there not a week since, widing with the Wiscount Wodney.' Augustus's face was glowing from the fresh air and exercise.

'How pleasant for you. I find my home country quite delightful and am very happy there. I am leading a retired life for the moment, however; perhaps it would be a little quiet for your tastes.'

'Aye, perwaps oo are wight. The countwyside has its limits; some wesidents shoot themselves in the head from the boredom, I believe. Still, that arwea does have its pweasing diwersions. I wisited the waces at Winchester last year, and found them most congenial, although the wiff-waff is wather swamping the waces these days. Still, I will go again this summer, followed by Salisburwy, if I can bwing my hairdwesser, that is. The town gets so twerribly cwowded at that time and one can be dwiven into using somebody gweatly inferwior. There are more than enough fwights, clowns and scarecwows about as it is.'

Freddy smiled, mesmerised by the movement – or lack of movement - of Augustus's lips.

'You will be quite shocked, Mr Grey,' she said, 'but

I dress my own hair now, with a little help from my housekeeper. I believe that there are some wery good hairdwessers in Winchester, however.' Freddy giggled, realising that she had mimicked Augustus. Another thirty minutes in his company, she thought, and I will have slipped back into that world entire. Augustus did not seem to pay it attention, however.

'Well, Fweddy. Wustic styles can be quite charming, I suppose.' He nodded towards Freddy's simply styled chignon tied up with a soft, muslin band. 'Evewybody is all for nature in their dwess these days. But I find nature a little wulgar. Ciwilisation should not move backwards.' Augustus paused to smooth down his hair. 'Pway, is the Dowager Darby at her estate? She must be werry cut up about the diamond.'

'I do not know. As I mentioned, I am living very quiet at home, and have not seen people.' Freddy looked at Lavinia, who seemed a little nervous. 'Perhaps you have heard from your step-mama, Lavinia?'

'Yes,' said Lavinia, 'she has retired to the country for the time being. Her marriage is still to take place, though I do not know if it will be in Hampshire or London.'

'That is good news, indeed,' said Freddy. 'Do you know how the theft happened? I was at the entertainment myself, that evening, though unfortunately I did not stay long enough to witness the drama. I must admit that I am very curious about the whole affair.'

'Yes, the town is quite abuzz with it,' said Lavinia. 'I

believe the theft took place very late, in the early hours, but I do not know the details. It is a great mystery.'

'It is thought that she was slipped a little something to make her sleepy,' said Augustus, 'and someone simply unclasped the diamond and wan from the house with it.'

A maid now arrived with some tea, and Freddy, Lavinia and Augustus prattled gossip and nonsense - or so Freddy thought – for another hour. How glad she was to be out of all this. When Augustus had taken his leave, she said, 'does he call to see Lord Ingram? I had not known they were so well acquainted.'

'Yes,' said Lavinia. Then, after a few moments, 'No. I confess that he comes to call upon me. We have grown friends, you know.'

'Oh?'

'You think him ridiculous, and I do not blame you, but I assure you that he is not. It is just his armour.'

'When you say friends, dear, do you mean a little something more, perhaps?'

Lavinia sighed. 'Yes, Freddy, I do. Are you not shocked?'

'No. Perhaps a little with the man, but not with the thing itself. I know you have been very unhappy in your marriage.'

'It has been very difficult. And I started with so much hope. Lord Ingram is not cruel, I will admit, and I am told that I should be grateful for that. But he is cold, so cold, and he has his mistresses. Miss Nutt, that pert, tiny creature with auburn hair, is the current favourite,

I believe. I have given him a son, and that satisfies him, though he is perhaps a trifle disappointed with this latest offering, not qualifying as the male spare.'

'Oh, my dear. Coldness is very hard to bear. I grew up with so much affection myself that I can understand how hard it would be to do without it. But how did it begin with Augustus?'

'I did not plan anything, though I am sure you know that I have had my flirtations with several others ere this. We simply got talking around the card table (I am afraid that he is an inveterate gambler). Then the talk happened to become a little less giddy, and a little softer, and then very real. I have seen the man, you see.'

'Oh, Lavinia. What will you do? You are not planning to do anything hasty?'

'I do not know. No. I am too fatigued to do anything at all just now.'

'That might be for the best. The infatuation may pass.'

Lavinia smiled weakly. 'Perhaps. If it is an infatuation. It feels very much like love.'

'Oh, that is very hard. But you must let yourself get well, in your body and your mind. Tis always safest to do nothing when one is not oneself, I believe, and wait to see what time brings.'

'True, Freddy; you are wise, as always. Upon my soul, what burdens I have put upon you, and you not here above a few hours.'

'Do not say it. I am glad to share them, as you know; and as you have shared mine.'

Chapter 16

One afternoon that week, when Lavinia was sleeping, Freddy took the opportunity to visit the Darby townhouse, which was only a few streets away from Lavinia's residence. She had not yet talked to her friend about Sarah and the Celestial Light, but would do so before she left. It was a warm, glorious day, but already she was feeling that the city, even such a pleasant part of it as Mayfair, was not the place to enjoy such a gift, and she was longing to be back in her Hampshire garden with Flip and the Campbells.

She was just approaching the Darby residence when she spied a strange-looking man walking towards her. He quite stood out in that part of town, and in the brightness of the day, being a short figure cloaked in a brown hood. As he drew nearer she heard his strained, hoarse breathing, and as he walked past, and nodded at her, she could not help but recoil at the glimpse of his scarred, broken face.

Shaking off an uneasy feeling, she walked up to the front door of the Darby house and knocked. After a few minutes, the door opened and she was greeted by a pretty, plump young woman with dimples, a yellow strand of hair poking out from under her cap.

'Good afternoon, ma'am,' said the woman. 'How can I help you?'

'Good afternoon,' said Freddy. 'It is Charlotte, is it not? I remember that we had a little conversation on the night of the Countess's last party.'

'Oh, yes, it is Miss Swinglehurst. Please do come in.'

'Thank you, Charlotte. Being in town unexpectedly, I thought I would pay a short call on the Countess, but now I realise that she will have gone out of town – how foolish of me.'

'I'm sorry you've had a wasted journey, ma'am. But will you not sit a while and take a little refreshment?'

'I will, thank you Charlotte.'

'Come through to the drawing room on the first floor. It is pleasant and not too much in the glare of the sun.'

Freddy followed Charlotte up the first staircase. At the top, a man, of around medium height, with broad, handsome features and slightly pointed ears, was stood, waiting to let them pass.

'Matthew,' said Charlotte, 'this is Miss Swinglehurst, a friend of the Countess.' She turned back to Freddy.

'Matthew has just come from Hampshire, where he accompanied the Countess.'

'Good afternoon, Matthew. May I ask, how is the Countess?'

'As well as she can be, I think,' said Matthew, smiling, but seeming a little nervous, something which his upright carriage and proud manner was failing to disguise.

Freddy nodded at him and let Charlotte escort her to the drawing room.

'What will you take, ma'am?' asked Charlotte, as she gestured for Freddy to sit down.

'Some tea would be very welcome, thank you. And how do you do, Charlotte? Tis a very bad business about the diamond, is it not?'

'Oh, yes, Miss. The house was in a terrible state of confusion, and we were all so terrified of being accused of the theft. It can be so difficult to get a good situation, and once something like that has happened it tends to stick to people. But then, David Barber ran, so we knew it was him, though we suspected as much before that. I did not like the man. He had a way of looking at a woman that made me feel very uncomfortable and a little fearful.'

'I am sorry to hear that, Charlotte, and glad that he is gone, for all your sakes. Perhaps you like Matthew a little better, however?'

Charlotte blushed. 'Yes, ma'am, how did you know?'

'Oh, just the way you looked at him, I think. I am sorry to embarrass you, dear; I can be most impertinent and vexing, I know. Do forgive me.'

Charlotte smiled, her dimples blinking. 'No, ma'am; I am happy to own it. But let me fetch your tea.'

Charlotte quitted the room and ten minutes later, Matthew Lane appeared, holding a silver tray, on which was placed a cup of tea, a bowl of sugar and some tongs.

'Miss Swinglehurst,' said Matthew. 'Charlotte has become caught up in some bargaining with a tradesman at the back door, and asked me to bring this to you, for she did not want it to cool.

Freddy, pleased to have this opportunity to be alone with just the man she wanted to interrogate, smiled up at him warmly.

'Thank you, Matthew. I will just take my refreshment and be on my way. Will you not join me for a few moments, if I do not take you away from your duties? It would be pleasant to hear a little more of the Countess, and I believe that we have some friends in common.'

Matthew felt uncomfortable, but felt that he could not refuse Freddy's request. Freddy gestured to a chair opposite her, and he sat down as awkwardly as Polly had done that day at the rectory, looking around as if expecting someone to appear and chastise him.

'You have a friend called Edward Sweet, I think?'

Matthew looked surprised. 'Yes, ma'am, he is an old friend and a good one. I have not seen him recently. I believe that he called here just a few days since, but I was in Hampshire with the Countess.'

'One of my dearest friends is his wife, Affy; in

fact, I will be visiting them for a few days at the end of the week.'

Matthew smiled, and relaxed a little, though he was surprised that a fine gentlewoman like Freddy should be friends with members of a lower rank. 'They make a fine pair,' he said, 'and are as good as two people could be.'

'You are right, there, Matthew,' said Freddy, sipping her tea and pausing for a few moments. 'Matthew, would you mind if I ask you a very bold question? Please try not to be offended; you must not mind a singular busybody like myself. It is just that I have got caught up in some very strange events.'

What else could Matthew do but agree, though he looked shocked and worried, and tensed up his body, making and unmaking the shape of a fist with his right hand.

'Your name has come up in a very strange way. It appears that David Barber, the servant who fled this house, you know, has lately been in Southampton, and, to be truthful, he mentioned your name in reference to the theft of the Celestial Light.'

Matthew now clenched and unclenched his left fist too, but did not say anything.

'I do not say that anyone believes him,' said Freddy, noting the fists, 'but perhaps you should know what he has said. It was Affy who heard this rumour, on a recent visit to her aunt in Southampton. She and Edward are a little concerned about you, and are trying to get in touch.'

'That Davey Barber was a very bad man,' said Matthew, finally, 'and an exceeding dishonest one. He bore a grudge against me, being a level above him, and also he does not like fellows like me.' Matthew looked a little embarrassed, Freddy's skin colour being the same as his own.

'I can well imagine it,' said Freddy. 'There are a lot of them about; but thankfully, not everyone is like him.'

Matthew nodded. 'Besides, what would a fellow like me do with such a thing? I would hardly know how to get rid of it, and it is not as if I would be wearing it myself. These baubles serve no purpose on God's earth, as I far as I can tell, except, perhaps, that their value might be put to use in some great cause.' He stopped. Had he said too much?

'Yes, I can understand that view,' said Freddy. 'There are many evils in this world that need righting.' She waited a few moments, hoping Matthew might say more, but he simply nodded, and seemed to have deliberately stopped himself from going further. She changed tack. 'Another name has come up in reference to this affair – Sarah Clarke – do you happen to know her?'

'No, ma'am; truly, I have never heard of her.'

'It is likely that Sarah Clarke was not her real name. She is a negro woman like myself, and was heavy with child. Sadly, she died.' Freddy wondered if this fact might provoke a reaction, if Matthew had been lying, but his countenance did not change.

'I am sorry for the woman and her friends,' said he, 'but I do not recognise anyone of that name.'

'Well, it is all wondrous strange,' said Freddy, sighing, 'but I can tell the Sweets that you are well – if you do not do so yourself before then – and there is nothing for them to worry about?'

'Not at all, ma'am.'

'And do you have any notions of your own in reference to this diamond theft? Did you see anything on the night itself?'

'No, I'm afraid that I didn't. As to the thief, I'm sure it was David Barber, for why else would he have fled? Positions in the Countess's household are sought after, you know, for she is a good mistress, and are not easily given up. Where he's gone or what he's done with the stone I do not know.'

'Well, thank you, Matthew, and please do forgive me again for my impertinent questioning. I had better get back to the Lady Ingram's.'

Matthew saw Freddy out. When the door closed, he took a deep breath, closed his eyes, and rested his head on the door. His heart was beating quickly, as if someone was rapping urgently on the door, and he had to wait five minutes for it to slow. This was the second time he had been questioned about the diamond, and he knew already about David Barber and his stories. A repulsive man called Adam Short had only lately accosted him several times, and had tried to bully him into revealing an involvement in the diamond theft. But he had not said a word, and Short, confessing that he had not entirely credited Barber's tale, relented, and left him alone. Miss

Swinglehurst was another matter. She was a little odd, to be sure, but had a way about her that made a man want to confess all, and he had almost been tempted. Should he have told her what he knew? No, it was too risky to say anything to anyone. But then what would he say to Edward, who would surely ask him the same questions? He really did not know.

Chapter 17

After a week in Mayfair, Freddy left Lady Ingram seeming a little brighter and easier in her mind, and went across town to spend a few days with Affy.

She travelled in the Ingram silver and scarlet barouche, and Affy was waiting on the doorstep of the Somers Town house, laughing at the grandness of Freddy's arrival. A glittering coachman handed Freddy down.

'My dear, are you sure that you are not now too fine to step into our humble home?' asked Affy, curtseying and bowing.

'To be perfectly candid, yes, I am; and I may well expire from the shock to my exquisitely fine sensibilities. However, as I am here now, I shall endeavour to make the best of it.'

Freddy gave an ironical grin and hugged her friend, who was looking fatter and very well indeed. They entered the house, which had become a little more interesting since Freddy's departure. It was scattered with mementoes from Affy's mother's theatrical career, including handbills, newspaper reports, prints and a gilt framed portrait of her as Sheridan's Mrs Malaprop. Freddy was glad to be there. It was the place where she had recovered herself, and had found a new, more steady type of happiness. But it felt right that now it belonged to Affy and Edward, who had already made it their true home. They all settled down in the light front parlour.

'We have interesting news,' said Affy. 'Tom has discovered who Sarah Clarke was, and we have an address of her former lodging house. Edward can explain.'

'That is good news,' said Freddy, leaning forward in her chair and peering at Edward.

Edward, a muscular man with large brown eyes and heavy eyelids, smiled at Freddy a little shyly. He was an earnest soul, his seriousness well balanced by his wife's vivacity and humour. He was a little intimidated by Freddy, whom he thought to be a very high, important personage, despite her warm and easy manners. He looked up to her greatly. Although he did not think too much about matters of race, it gratified him to see somebody with a similar skin colour to himself in such an exalted position, and, unconsciously, he held his own head a little higher in consequence.

'Tom, in his enquiries, came across a woman called Maria, who was very anxious about the disappearance of a friend, who turned out to match Sarah's description and situation. Her real name was Sarah Long, though she also passed as Sarah Clarke. The two women grew up together very poor, but Sarah had met a gentleman from a higher sphere of life, and was being kept by him in decent lodgings in the better part of Covent Garden.' Edward glanced at his wife, not sure how much detail to give on this point.

Affy had no such scruples. 'Unhappily, as we suspected, Sarah had lived as a prostitute, But it had been a long time since she had been forced upon the town, and she had been living in these good lodgings for about two years. Unluckily, this Maria had never met the gentleman, so could not describe him, but she knew that he went by the name of Josiah Clarke and said that he took very good care of her friend.'

'How intriguing, if a little frustrating,' said Freddy. 'But have you been to Sarah's lodgings? If not, surely we must go there, at once, and talk to the housekeeper?'

Affy laughed. 'No we have not, Fredericka, but yes we shall. You and I shall try our luck tomorrow, after church.'

Freddy smiled. 'Yes, of course, dear; forgive me my impatience.' She looked at Edward. 'I am sure your wife has told you that since leaving London, my curiosity has grown quite wild. I am clearly destined to become the local busybody and I shall relish the role.'

'That you shall,' said Affy, 'and Mrs Campbell will be your intrepid assistant.'

''Tis more likely to be the other way round.'

'Aye, that is true.'

'But I have some intelligence of my own. I am afraid that I have trespassed on your territory and have already spoken to Matthew Lane. The Darby townhouse is so close to Lady Ingram's, so I thought I would call and see what I could discover from the household staff about the theft. I found myself quite alone in Mr Lane's company, and so could not help but take my opportunity.'

'Good gracious,' said Affy. 'Edward has tried to meet him, but he had been away.'

'Yes, he has not long returned from Hampshire, to where he escorted the Countess.'

'What did Matthew say?' asked Edward, looking very anxious.

'Nothing to worry you, I think,' said Freddy. 'He said that this David Barber was very likely the thief, being a very bad man, and that Barber had taken against him and that was likely why he tried to implicate him in the theft in some way.'

'Agh, that is a relief,' said Edward. 'I'm sure he would not be capable of doing such a thing.'

'I hope so,' said Freddy.

'You are doubtful?' said Affy. 'Do you think he was lying?'

'No; I do not know. He seemed like a good enough fellow, but I got the impression that something was troubling him, and wonder if he was holding something back. Perhaps he knows something about the matter but is protecting someone. In fact, he did say something I found interesting, that an object like the Celestial Light was useless in itself, but that its value should go towards some great cause. Is he involved in anything in that way, do you know?'

Edward looked concerned. 'He did become a follower of James Wilkins for a while, but he is no longer, I believe.'

'Who is Wilkins?' asked Freddy. 'I have heard the name.'

'He is a radical preacher and campaigner, though a printer by profession,' said Affy. 'He is very involved in the anti-slave trade campaign, but has been known to go much further, and sometimes talks revolution. I heard him speak, once, and it was very powerful. Afterwards, I was almost inclined to set fire to the parliament and then chop of King George's head.'

Edward looked alarmed.

'Husband, mine, you know I jest.' Affy touched her husband's cheek and grinned at him. He relaxed and grinned back. 'Edward does not approve of Wilkins,' she continued, to Freddy. 'You are all for king and country, my love, are you not?'

'Aye,' said Edward, 'I do not like extreme talk, or extreme solutions, and I find him blasphemous. I believe that he is in gaol at the present time. I will talk to Matthew as soon as I can.'

'He might open his heart to you, Edward,' said Freddy, 'for now I think upon it, why would he tell an interfering stranger ought of anything on so weighty a matter?'

'Did you happen to mention Sarah's name to him?' asked Edward.

'Yes, I asked him if he had heard of a Sarah Clarke, and he said that he had not. Perhaps he might know a Sarah Long, however.'

'I will ask him,' said Edward.

'Has there been nothing further in the newspapers about the diamond?' said Freddy.

'Not that we have seen,' said Affy. 'I suspect that the law has given up hunting for it. But you said in your letter that you think that the diamond could have been buried with Sarah?'

'Yes, the notion has quite got a hold of me, for it explains the body being taken, and then we know she asked Mr Hopkins about stone-cutting. Or is it all just my lunatic thinking? This whole affair has quite got the better of me, I think.'

'We will solve the mystery, I am sure,' said Affy, 'for look how much we have discovered from knowing nothing whatsoever. Tomorrow, we call at Sarah's old lodgings, and then Edward will meet Matthew as soon as he can, and we hope to meet Maria, too. Then you have Polly back in Winchester, who may yet tell you something.'

'I hope so.' Freddy sighed. 'Well, well, let us talk of something else, before I run mad. I come bearing gifts for the infant Sweet. I have quite killed myself carrying them from Hampshire so the very least you can do is to open them up and look delighted. Do not take alarm. Margaret has made them. I did attempt to stitch something myself but it was so bad that Mrs C threatened to disown me if I offered up such an abomination of needlework as a representation of the Swindlehurst manor house.'

Later that evening, when Edward was doing some jobs in the kitchen, Freddy said to Affy, 'Do you believe in ghosts?'

'Of course, dear. You cannot spend half your life in the world of the theatre and not do so. Why, I saw my mother only last week at half-time at Drury Lane.'

'Really?'

'Oh, yes. She was stood at the edge of the stage, blowing kisses to the audience. She bowed a little too hard and her wig fell off.'

Freddy giggled. 'Oh, Affy, you are joking with me.'

'No, truly. I expect to see her quite a lot. It is normal.'

Freddy, fascinated, stared at her friend. 'Did she appear in her old shape?'

'Oh yes, but her form was a little hazy, and then gradually disappeared.'

'Were you frightened?'

'Not at all; tis perfectly natural. I believe that you cannot spend your lifetime somewhere and then detach yourself from it entirely. Have you seen something, dear?'

'I… I do not know… Yes, I believe that I have, but it is so strange and wonderful that I am not quite ready to share it, what with all these other strange mysteries still unsolved. But you give me comfort, Mrs Sweet, even though, undoubtedly, you are quite mad.'

Affy grinned. 'Oh, quite mad, I assure you. There is a place in Bedlam reserved especially for me. And glad will I be of it when my friends are dancing the Tyburn jig, or run up the yard arm – as I think you sailors call it – for the great jewel theft of the year 1804.'

'Pray, be easy, dear. I will visit you in Bedlam once a fortnight and bring you a pipe and some of Mrs C's queen cakes.'

Chapter 18

The next day, after church, Freddy and Affy set off on foot to Covent Garden. It was another fine, warm day, and Freddy looked about her with interest as the sun lit up the streets that she had known so well, but had barely seemed to notice until now. How dirty some parts were, and then there were the varying degrees of foul smells. How noisy it was, and this the sabbath day, too. She laughed to herself at how speedily her mind and body had accustomed themselves to their new Hampshire environment, and unaccustomed themselves to the great metropolis.

'What are you laughing at?' asked Affy, taking Freddy's left arm.

'Oh, at what a country mouse I have turned into already,' said Freddy.

'Yes, dearest, you look quite startled. Do buck up or we will be targeted by all the rogues and thieves in the city.'

The two friends turned off the Strand, then walked along a few short, twisted streets before coming to a small, quiet cul-de-sac, and Sarah Long's lodging place.

'It seems like a decent dwelling,' said Freddy, looking up at the plain-brick, three-storey building, with very clean, sparkling windows.

'Indeed,' said Affy, raising the brass knocker and releasing it several times.

A small, spare girl with a sallow complexion and an assured look answered the door. 'Yes?'

'Is your mistress, Mrs Fisher, at home?' asked Freddy.

'Who's asking?'

'My name is Miss Fredericka Swinglehurst,' said Freddy, 'and this is my friend, Mrs Aphrodite Sweet. We have come about Mrs Fisher's missing lodger, Sarah – Sarah Clarke.'

The girl looked curious, and noting the fine clothes of the visitors and their proper way of speaking, pulled back the door quickly. 'Do come in. If you'd like to take a seat inside the parlour here and wait a moment, I'll fetch Mrs Fisher.'

Affy and Freddy were led into a cosy room with heavy, green upholstery and it was not long before Mrs Fisher appeared, a tall, raw-boned woman dressed in brown, her long chin tilting upwards as her eyes tilted downwards to look at them. Freddy got up, giving her warmest smile, and touched Mrs Fisher's hand. Affy followed suit, admired the parlour and expressed their gratitude for Mrs Fisher's time. The latter, gratified by their graciousness and fine appearance, lowered her chin and relaxed her features a little.

'I believe you've news of Mrs Clarke,' said Mrs Fisher, sitting down.

'Yes,' said Freddy. 'It is a little complicated and confused, but I am afraid that it is very likely that Sarah has died.'

'Good grief,' said Mrs Fisher, looking truly shocked. 'Surely not? I simply thought that she had ran off with her gentleman, though, to be sure I was greatly surprised that she left her child behind, for she quite doted upon her. And it seemed quite out of character.'

'Her child?' asked Affy.

'Yes, she had a one-year old daughter, quite a plump, bouncing little thing, and of course, there was another one on the way.'

Freddy and Affy exchanged looks, surprised at this news, since Tom had not mentioned it to Edward. But, then, Tom was on the run from a vindictive former master, and likely had not had the time to tarry and discover all.

'Where is the child now?' asked Freddy.

'Oh, her friend, Maria, took her. She is rather a low person, I am afraid, but then better that than hand the child to the parish. I could not keep her myself; my hands are already very full.'

'I am sure they must be,' said Affy. 'Did you know Sarah's husband?'

'Mr Clarke? Though, to be truthful, I knew that he

was not really her husband. I run a respectable house, Mrs Sweet, but I must make my living, and the gentleman was very polite and genteel, and he always paid well in advance, including for extras.'

'Are you able to describe him?' said Freddy.

'Only in a general way. He was tall and handsome, but I did not see much of him, and cannot recall the details of his features.'

'You would not remember his eye colour, I suppose?' asked Affy.

'I'm afraid not. Blue, were they? No, they could have been brown. Oh, dear, I must confess that my eyesight is not what it was and so the pictures I see of people are rather vague. But how do you know Sarah? What makes you think she is deceased?'

Freddy related what they knew, mostly from the silversmith, keeping back the information related to the diamond.

'Oh, the poor girl,' said Mrs Fisher. 'You know, she was no better than she should be, but I was rather fond of her - and the child – for she had such an open, affectionate temper that she was hard to resist.'

'Yes, we have heard that,' said Affy. 'Do you happen to know what her gentleman did for a living, or where he lived?'

'I knew only that he travelled a lot for his business. I did not like to enquire further; it seemed impertinent somehow; he was such a gentleman.'

'And he or Sarah never mentioned a connection to Hampshire?' asked Freddy.

'No, I cannot remember anything; but, from what you've said, it sounds very plausible that he was based there.'

Freddy and Affy thanked Mrs Fisher for her time, and Freddy checked that Sarah's bill was settled. As they left the lodging house, Freddy spotted Bess, the girl who had answered the door, staring at them through the front window, her white cap lit up by the sunshine. They were a little disappointed not to have discovered more about Sarah and the gentleman, but were glad to know that she had been well looked after in the last few years of her life.

They were just a few steps away from the lodging house when they spotted a tall figure coming towards them clad in a blue frock coat and tricorn hat. Freddy felt her stomach flip over; it was Captain Henry Lefroy. The captain's glowing face turned almost white when he recognised them, but he soon recovered himself.

'Miss Swinglehurst, Mrs Sweet; I could not believe my eyes for a moment, there; one does not expect to encounter people one knows, at random, in the great metropolis, despite what occurs in novels.'

Freddy could not help but smile. 'It seems that my whole life at the moment is quite beyond the realms of a novel...' She checked herself, remembering to be suspicious.

'I hope I find you well?' said the captain, smiling at them both, but looking at Freddy especially. 'I fear that I may have offended you the last time we met, at the rectory, and I hope you can forgive me, for it was truly the last thing I intended.'

'Oh, not at all, Captain,' said Freddy, 'I was in quite a strange temper, I believe; you must not mind me.'

Affy smiled at them. 'No, do not mind her, Captain. She is a very strange woman. I am accustomed to it, myself, but it can take many years of close study.'

Freddy scowled at her friend and the captain laughed.

'What brings you to town, Captain?' asked Freddy, suspicious again.

'Oh, I am visiting friends, and, in matter of fact, I must now take leave of you yet again. Are you in London long?'

'No,' said Freddy, 'I return to Hampshire tomorrow.'

'Oh, that is a shame; well, I hope to see you soon in Winchester. Do give my best regards to the Campbells.'

In Somers Town that evening, Freddy and Affy told Edward what little they had discovered, that is, that Sarah had a child, who was now living with Maria.

'My heart goes out to that poor infant,' said he, 'which will likely grow up in filth and squalor, and that if it manages to survive.' Edward took his wife's hand.

'You are too tender hearted, my love,' said Affy, 'it is one of your many fine qualities.'

Freddy smiled at them and rolled her eyes behind her spectacles. 'You both have so many fine qualities, it is becoming quite shameful for the rest of us. I may have to give up our friendship; I do not think my vanity can bear any more knocks.'

Affy laughed.

'Oh, no, ma'am,' said Edward, looking very serious. 'There is no-one so good and as kind as you.'

'Why, thank you, sir,' said Freddy, 'I am much gratified, and glad that I am appreciated in one quarter, at least. But I am but in jest. And, Affy, will you never get this husband of yours to leave off addressing me so formally and call me good, plain, Freddy?'

'Never, I am afraid,' said Affy. 'He thinks you quite the grand, fine lady – not exactly contradicted by your dazzling arrival yesterday - and is amazed that you condescend to keep us company.'

'And you do not believe me to be quite so grand, I suppose?'

'Oh no, I know you far too well, my dear.'

Freddy looked thoughtful for a few moments, then frowned suddenly. 'Do you think it could be him?'

'What could be whom?' asked Affy.

'Sarah's gentleman, and the man involved in the diamond theft. I think it could be Captain Lefroy.'

'The handsome sailor we saw today, and in Winchester, who looks at you so intently? That would be a great shame.'

'Yes, no doubt it would be, and I have to confess that I am quite drawn to the man; but the more I think upon it, the more I am convinced. Was it not strange that he was so close to Sarah's old lodging today? What was he doing there? And did he not look affrighted at the sight of us? And then he is tall and handsome, and nobody really knows what he has been doing these past years – perhaps not even Anne – despite his proud tales of the sea. He is much at the rectory, where Sarah's body was found, and we know that her gentleman, or friend, lived in that direction. And then one day I saw him in a heated argument with Mary – you remember the Millbrook housekeeper, she of the rare beauty? They looked a little guilty together, and I suspect they are entangled together in some way. He could well be a rake, for he can be very charming, yet there is also something a little secretive about him.'

'Gracious, you have made quite a case against the poor man,' said Affy, 'though it does not follow that it is not a good one; this whole thing is strange enough. Let us hope that we can soon discover more, and that the handsome sailor is innocent, or I shall have to revise the plans I have already made for your wedding, and that would be most inconvenient.'

Despite having to say goodbye to her friends the next day, Freddy was very glad to leave London and return to Hampshire. Her mind was now full of concern for the Lady Ingram, as well as everything else. How relieved she was to reach Winchester, to see Gabriel's smiling face waiting for her, and to listen to him, all the way home and not for the first time, admonish her for travelling alone.

Chapter 19

The day after Freddy returned from London, at a quarter past six in the morning, Mary was sat at the kitchen table in the rectory, her arms folded in front of her, her head resting on her right forearm, when Samuel came into the room.

'Mary, are you unwell?' he asked.

Mary opened her eyes, and saw Sam looking at her with concern. She lifted her head up and straightened her arms.

'I confess that I don't feel quite myself. I'm just very tired.'

'Well, you need to rest, woman. You overdo things here, I'm sure. You've not been right for some time now. Don't think I haven't noticed. You need to see someone. The master or mistress will be able to help.'

'No, Samuel, please.'

Sam was surprised by the hint of desperation in

Mary's voice. 'Well, at least get to your bed and rest a while. I'll smooth things with the master and mistress.'

'Thank you, Samuel.' Mary's voice was softer than usual, and drained of her usual spirit. 'I will take your advice, for once.' She smiled quickly at him.

'Come now, let me help you to the cottage.'

Sam helped Mary up and took her arm, which was hot to the touch. She was feverish, he was sure, and felt very heavy, as if she was swollen up with some sickness he could not name. They made their way slowly out of the house and walked the few yards to one of the two small cottages in the grounds of the rectory estate, where Mary lived with her two sons. The boys, John, aged ten and Michael, aged seven, were already up and active, digging in a patch of ground to the side of the cottage, which was part of the rectory's smallholding. The boys had been given permission to grow their own plants and foodstuffs as a way of keeping them active while their mother worked. John looked up as Mary and Samuel came towards them.

'Now, boys,' said Sam. 'Your mother here is unwell and needs to rest. Be good, now, and stay nice and quiet. And you must take care of her, and help her when she needs it.'

John nodded, smiled at his mother, and turned back to his spade. Michael looked anxious and ran to Mary, who kissed him on the head as he clung to her legs.

'Now be a good boy and keep your brother company,' said Mary, seeming to struggle for breath. 'I just need a bit of peace for once and I'll be right as rain.'

Michael looked up at his mother, his brow crinkled, eyes wide with fear.

'Back to your brother, now,' said Sam. 'The sooner you let your mother rest, the sooner she'll get well. And I shall come back soon with a mess of broth to aid her recovery.'

Michael was not sure. He sensed his mother's suffering but then broth was a magical word to him, and surely that would help? He pulled away from her and re-joined his brother.

'They are good boys,' said Sam.

'They are,' said Mary, 'though John is a little wild sometimes. He feels the want of a father.'

'I know, Mary. Tis hard for you all but you do a good job. Now come inside.'

The cottage was small, with just two rooms, one on either side of the front door, and a garret upstairs where the boys slept. It was very clean and neat, and contained a few good, solid, if old-fashioned, pieces of furniture. The thick green Moreen curtains on the windows kept out the cold, and the cosy effect was enhanced by the samples of Mary's embroidery that were dotted about the place; she was as nimble and adept with a needle as she was with everything else involved in household matters, which only increased her contempt for her mistress, whom she saw as a poor, wishy-washy creature only fit for sketching, painting and trifling on the pianoforte. Sam settled Mary down on a low settee in the room that served as kitchen and house place, and covered her with the stone-coloured cotton counterpane that was folded nearby. Finally, he poured her a glass of fresh water from a full jug sitting on the dresser, and placed it on the floor easily within Mary's reach.

'Do try to sleep, now,' he said. 'I'll come back soon.'

'Thank you.' Mary struggled to speak. 'You'd make someone a fine husband, Samuel, if you weren't so old and ugly.'

Sam laughed. 'I'm glad you've not lost your capacity to insult me, Mary. Rest now.'

He went away, pained for Mary. He was now angry with himself for not paying sooner attention to her malady. It was clearly worse than he had thought. He would consult the master as soon as he returned from London. It might be wise to call in the apothecary sooner than the morrow.

After Sam left her, Mary closed her eyes, then screwed up her face and clutched her stomach in pain. She breathed deeply for several moments, then forced herself to sit up and take a few sips of water. Finally, she stood up, and took a minute or so to steady herself. It would be a fine day; she needed air. She put on her woollen shawl and an old straw bonnet and let herself out of the small back door of the cottage, unseen by her sons, whose busy chatter she could still hear coming from the other side of the building. She did not seem to be observed by anyone else, and made her way slowly down a narrow side lane off the rectory grounds, which led to a small sort of plantation then out into open fields. How the air would cool her.

Several hours later, the master still not home, Sam returned to the cottage with his mistress, who was determined to be kind and to help the woman for whom she felt a hearty, if unacknowledged, dislike. Anne carried with her a little of that numbing cordial which she found so beneficial herself. As they approached the cottage, she caught sight of Michael marching round the same patch of ground as before, seeming to play at soldiers. What handsome boys Mary had borne, Anne thought, with their thick brown hair and ruddy complexions, though she always felt a little uneasy when she saw them, a feeling she could not quite identify but one that was more than the jealousy and longing she often felt regarding other people's children. As they approached, John hurried out of the front door to the cottage and came towards them, his face stricken.

'Sam, Sam. Mother's gone.'

'Gone? Surely not,' said Sam, clutching at a bowl of broth intended for Mary.

'She has, she has, look!'

Michael looked up on hearing his brother, then started to cry. They all entered the cottage, Sam depositing the broth on the small kitchen dresser, and found that John was telling the truth.

'I shouldn't have left her,' said Sam. 'She was feverish and perhaps in a delirium. She doesn't know what she's doing.'

'You did your best, I am sure, Samuel,' said Anne, who was feeling calm and light, almost as if she was floating. She had taken a rather large dose of the cordial prepared for Mary. 'Why do not I take care of the boys, and you go out to look for her. She cannot have got far, especially in her current state. As soon as my husband returns, I will send him to follow.'

'Thank you, ma'am. Yes, that sounds like the best plan.'

'Mama, mama. I want to come and find mama,' said Michael, stamping one of his sturdy legs and wiping away his tears with his right sleeve.

'No, Michael,' said John firmly. 'I'll go with Samuel. You stay here with the mistress and await our return. We want to give mother something to look forward to when she gets back. You can defend the cottage from attack and make everything ready, like a good boy.'

This appeal to Michael's military might did the trick and he allowed Anne to take his hand and guide him back inside, where they sat together upon the seat on which Mary had lain, looking out of the small front window, which gave a good view of the courtyard and the road into Winchester. Anne put her right arm around the boy and held his left hand with her own. How soft and warm he was. She usually found the exquisite touch of children only so much pain, but now she felt pleasantly distanced from what was happening around her. Holding the boy seemed to be preventing her from floating away. She smiled as she looked out of the window at the bright blue sky, tempted to spread her arms and fly, the boy dangling beside her. Then the silver birch tree seemed to become extremely large and dark, and grew gnarled tentacles that spread towards her. She looked away and clung to Michael.

Samuel and John walked quickly down the lane.

'Why would she do this?' asked John.

'I'm not sure. But a fever can make someone a little crazed for a time, and desperate for air. She will be resting on a bank somewhere.'

John nodded but looked deeply worried. Although he was only three years older than his brother, he felt that the gulf between them was great, and that he was the man of the house. He was angry with himself for being neglectful earlier, when Sam had brought Mary home, having been preoccupied with his own boyish dreams of naval valour and battles. They continued moving quickly on together in silence, looking intently about them all the time. After about forty minutes or so, John spotted the shape of his mother under a white willow tree next to the edge of a stream.

'There she is, Samuel.'

Sam smiled, greatly relieved, and the two ran over to Mary, who was sat on the ground leaning back on her elbows, her eyes closed.

'Mama, what are you doing?' asked John, tapping her on her right shoulder, then putting his arms round her neck and kissing her hair. She was extremely hot, and her skin and hair were sticky with sweat.

'John, dear, my son and heir,' said Mary, turning to smile at him. 'And Samuel, there, as always.'

'Now, Mary Harris, what nonsense is this?' said Sam. 'Did I not tell you to stay at home and rest? But when did you ever listen to your old friend, Sam?'

'She doesn't listen to anyone,' said John, laughing, feeling slightly giddy with relief.

'Now, John,' said Sam, 'you must run as fast as you can to the Denton farm, as it's so close by, and bring back some help. We'll need to carry your mother back to the rectory as soon as we can. I'll stay here and make sure that she doesn't run away, for one of us has to.'

'Yes, Sam.' John smiled at his mother, kissed her quickly on the cheek, turned and ran towards the farm.

Samuel sat down on the ground next to Mary. 'Now Mary, dear, take my hand and we'll rest a while until the cavalry arrives.' He took hold of Mary's left hand, which felt clammy to the touch, and looked into her face, which was drained of its usual colour and health. 'And then we'll get that fine, expensive surgeon out to you and make you well again before you know it.'

'No, Sam, no.' Mary's voice was weak with exhaustion and it was clearly an effort to talk. 'I don't want any surgeons meddling with me. I don't like them. They do more harm than good, I'm sure.'

'You'll do as you're told for once, Mary, and get

yourself right for those sons of yours. You must think of them, if not yourself.'

'No, Sam, no.' Mary began to cry. 'Please, no.' She now tried to haul herself up from the ground.

'There, there, Mary,' said Sam, pulling her back down gently. 'Don't fret yourself. We'll not have the surgeon if it alarms you so. You rest, now.'

Sam, relieved to have found her, was now growing quite alarmed at Mary's state of health and state of mind. He had never seen her cry. No, not in all the five years he had known her. He had seen the bursts of anger and the outbreaks of bitterness, but never tears. As he held her hand, he looked at her out of the corner of his eye. Her old striped gown was wet and covered in stains. She must have fallen, or even dangled in the water. Good Lord, what had she been thinking? The poor woman smelled badly, too – of sweat stale and fresh, and some sickly sweet odour he could not make out – and this pained him nearly more than all else, for she was always so proud, clean and fresh, and this would degrade her in her own eyes, never mind anyone else's. He breathed in, squeezed her hand, breathed out again, and stared awhile at the stream, which was moving slowly by.

Help soon arrived, John returning with two strong farm labourers in smock frocks pushing a cart. With great tenderness from rough hands, they lifted Mary onto the straw which had been laid down for her, and wrapped her up in a coarse woollen blanket given to them by Mrs Denton. Mary seemed to have given up struggling, and given in to exhaustion; she closed her eyes and was quiet, her breathing growing more regular as they journeyed home.

'Mrs Denton is calling for the surgeon and will send him to our home,' said John, quietly, as he and Samuel walked behind the cart.

'That's good,' said Sam, 'she must see one whether she likes it or no. I hate to disoblige her when she is so sensitive on the matter, but her health must come first.'

'Yes. They were expecting me when I got to the farmhouse. Joe Carter was there, you know – he'd been running an errand at the farm – and on the way there had seen poor mother in her bad state. He was very upset, and the farmer and his wife were acting a little strangely, I thought. I do hope that they don't know something about mother's illness, and are too afraid to tell me of it. I'm a man, now, you know, Sam, and I must be brave. I have a right to know things.'

Sam smiled and patted the boy on his shoulder. 'Of course you do, John. But let's get your mother home and safe, and then we can listen to what the surgeon has to say. He'll be able to tell us all what to do for the best.'

On arriving at the rectory, Mary was lifted up and taken inside the cottage, this time into the room to the left of the door, which served as her bedchamber. The two labourers and Samuel placed her gently on the bed. She was still a little hot, but beginning to cool down, and they covered the lower part of her body in the faded, tapestry bedrug, the labourers trying not to pay attention to her stained gown. Michael ran in to her, crying, then stood next to the bed and put his arms around her body. Mary opened her eyes, smiled at him, patted his back, then closed them again.

'Come, Michael, you must let your mother rest,' said Sam. 'You want her to get well, don't you?' He walked over to Michael and gently took his arm.

'I will sit with her,' said Anne, who had been waiting at the cottage with Michael. She was determined to help Mary. 'She should take a little wine, and some cold water in the first instance.'

'Will you get the water from the kitchen place, John?' said Sam. 'I'll go to the rectory and get some wine.'

'Get the best one you can, Samuel,' said Anne. 'It will fortify her.'

Sam left the house and John went into the kitchen, returning with a tin of cold water for his mother, which he handed to Anne, who tapped Mary very softly on her right cheek. Mary opened her eyes briefly, saw the drink, and lifted her head up to accept, without any protest or even the slightest look of derision.

'There,' said Anne, 'and Samuel is fetching you some good wine, which will help you to sleep a sweet sleep now and feel so much better when you wake.'

Michael, still restless, was allowed to have another chair brought in from the kitchen and to sit next to Anne close by the bed. He reached over to cover his mother's hand with his own, smaller, rounder one. Anne looked at the hands together and felt the pain return to her heart;

the cordial was wearing off. Sam had taken the two farm labourers with him to the rectory kitchen to reward their exertions with apple cake and ale, and he left Polly to take care of them while he went to the cellar to select a good white wine for Mary. He returned to the kitchen, and as he entered the murmuring voices fell silent, and he noticed that the labourers looked a little nervous and embarrassed. Perhaps they felt uncomfortable at the personal office they had done for Mary, who was often so stern and repelling. He began to open the bottle, giving the lads a kind smile and his hearty thanks as he did so. Then he noticed that Polly was staring at him with an expression of shame – and guilt, was it? – on her face.

'Why, what is it?' Sam asked.

The labourers and Polly looked at each other, then Polly nodded slightly, turned back to Sam, led him through to the passageway and took a breath. Speaking very quietly, she gave him some shocking and distressing news. No; he could not believe it; would not believe it. Not Mary. And how could he not have known? No, it wasn't true. There had been some mistake, some muddle – everything was so confused and disorderly just now, but it would all be put right. Poor Mary; she would need her wine. He shook his head, but said nothing, then returned to the cottage with the wine, to see John stood outside the front door, kicking his right foot on the ground, waiting, longing, for the surgeon to come and make his mother better.

Chapter 20

Freddy arrived home and shared what she knew with the Campbells. She started to question them, as gently as she could, about Captain Henry Lefroy. They had nothing but praise for him but admitted that they were not entirely clear on his most recent history. Should she confront him? No; perhaps she would put herself in danger. Had not her father warned her? And could the captain have murdered Sarah? He had such an appearance of goodness about him, but what did that signify? She must check that her pistol was in order, but now she remembered that it was still at the rectory. Why had not the captain returned it sooner? He must have got the shot by now. How strange.

The next afternoon, she was sat under the shade of the beech tree in an old cotton gown with her corset loosened, drinking lemonade and patting poor Flip, who was panting with the heat. One of her father's volumes of

Doctor Johnson sat open upon her lap, but she could not concentrate, her mind being full of the annoyingly handsome captain and his probable villainy, when she would hear news from Affy, and how best she could re-question Polly without frightening her.

As if she had conjured up a phantom from her mind, she now saw the tall figure of the captain striding towards her in his breeches and shirt sleeves. Flip - the traitor - brightened up and scrambled slowly to his feet, his tail wagging and his tongue hanging from his wide, grinning mouth, as Henry approached and came to a halt.

'Good afternoon, Miss Swinglehurst; I hope I find you well on this beautiful day?' he said.

'Yes, very well, sir,' said Freddy, beginning to get up.

'Please do not discomfort yourself,' said Henry. 'It is so cool and refreshing under this tree. May I join you?'

'If you must,' said Freddy, sitting herself back down in a rather ungainly manner. 'I mean, of course.'

Henry looked a little confused and Freddy kicked herself for her bad manners. His face was slightly flushed from the sunshine and she noticed his long, slightly freckled forearms, the hairs bleached white. She must really take control of herself. She smiled brightly at him in apology.

'Do not mind me, sir,' she said. 'I am so uncivil lately; I do not know what has come over me.'

Henry grinned, sat down to the right of Freddy, positioned his back comfortably against the tree, and stretched out his long legs.

'Not at all, Miss Swinglehurst; you are little piquant occasionally, I grant you, but that is part of your charm.'

'And is flattery part of your charm?'

Freddy turned to look directly at Henry; his expression was serious.

'I hope not. At least, I hope that I speak as I truly find, rather than to deceive in any way.'

An image of Mary popped into Freddy's head. Henry looked tired, she thought. There were lines and shadows under his eyes. Was he embroiled in something terrible, the something terrible that had been occupying her mind for so long? She could not help but feel a strong surge of sympathy for him, and had an urge to stroke his head as she would Flip's; she told herself to get the better of it.

'Do you have something on your mind?' she asked gently. 'You look a little fatigued.'

He looked at her gratefully. 'How kind you are. I am just a little preoccupied with family matters. I will not burden you with them; I just want all to be well before I sail again.'

Freddy felt an instant gloom at the thought of this man going away. 'Is it your family in Ireland? You must miss them?'

'I do, though I have been away a long time. When a man is at sea he has terrible yearnings. I was one of twelve, you know; can you imagine the burden upon my poor mother and father?'

Freddy laughed. 'I find that I can.'

'How I long to return to my youth and be a well-behaved boy for my mother, who had to put up with the lot of us fighting day after day, and my sisters were worse than the boys.'

'Yes, us women can be terrible indeed! But I know a little of what you feel. I have been lucky enough to have a second chance with the Campbells, at least, who have given so much to a selfish and thoughtless girl. Are your father and mother deceased?'

'Yes – God rest their souls - and I only have a few siblings remaining. But I must not get sentimental. When I do return we are fighting again within the hour.'

Freddy smiled. 'I always wished for a sibling to fight with, but I must not be self-pitying given how much love I have had in my life.'

'You must be very easy to love, I think,' said the captain, softly, looking into Freddy's eyes, then turning away quickly.

Oh, I really am in trouble here, thought Freddy. But what if Henry was saying the same thing to Mary, and many more besides? She did not respond, and they were silent for a few moments.

'What brings you here today?' she asked.

'Oh, I was returning your pistol with the shot. I am sorry for taking rather a long time about it. I have been a little preoccupied.'

'I only remembered about it today, so have not missed it. Not that I am planning to use it, of course.'

The captain laughed. 'I had better be on my guard,

just in case.' He paused, and glanced directly at Freddy again. 'In truth, I have tried to return it several times, but you were not here, and instead of leaving it with Mr Campbell, I went away again in order to return with it and thus have an excuse for seeing you.'

Freddy was silent; she was thrilled, frightened, confused.

'I have said too much, Miss Swinglehurst,' continued Henry. 'Please forgive me for startling you. We barely know each other, I know, but I hope you will give me the chance to remedy that in the future. I have much to deal with at present.'

'I…, I am not sure who you are,' said Freddy, simply.

The captain looked confused again, or was it guilty? They were interrupted by Mr Campbell walking slowly towards them, waving at the captain, and Flip getting up to greet his master. Gabriel and Henry began to talk guns, and they all returned to the house, which Henry quit soon after having business elsewhere.

Once Freddy had recovered from the intoxication of the captain's presence, her doubts and suspicions about him began to reassert themselves. Her heart was in danger, she knew; she must harden it, for now, at least, until all was known about the current mysteries. She had come a long way in her life to find peace of heart and mind, and though she knew that these two things might still be battered and bruised along the way, she could never again let them be broken.

Chapter 21

That Friday afternoon, Freddy was sat in the very hot kitchen with Gabriel and Margaret, while the latter was preparing the dinner and mumbling that they would start taking their meals in the dining room, like civilised people, if it was the last thing they did, and Mr C was quite welcome to eat alone in this burning cauldron if it so suited him. Mr C was just thinking up a retort, when there was a knock at the kitchen door, which was slightly ajar as usual to both keep out the heat and bring in the summer day.

'Why, it's Joseph again,' said Gabriel, pushing the door fully open. 'You've come back for more curry, eh, son?'

'Hello, Mr C. No, sir. I've another message for the lady. There are sad things happening at the parsonage and they need her help.'

'Come in, come in and sit down, now, Joe,' said

Gabriel, noting his pale face and agitated manner. 'Take a little refreshment, won't you?'

'What is it, dear?' asked Margaret, going to the pantry, and pouring Joe a tin of small beer from the large orange jug.

Joe sat down at the kitchen table and smiled feebly at Freddy, who was feeling very uneasy at this news. She hoped that poor Anne had not done something dreadful. Anne had sent Freddy a letter from the residence of her cousin in Southampton, apologising for her behaviour at their last meeting, thanking Freddy for her kindness, and saying that she had been feeling much better and was ready to go home and take up her duties. Freddy wondered if, on her return to the rectory, she had fallen back into despair.

'Go on, Joe,' said Margaret, kindly, if a little impatiently, putting his tin of small beer on the table, then sitting down herself. 'Do you have a letter for Miss Swinglehurst?'

'No, Mrs Campbell, the mistress just asked her to come as soon as she could as there's such trouble at the parsonage.'

'What trouble?'

Joe stared at them, then put his head down and started to cry a little.

'Come, Joe,' said Margaret. 'Will you not take a little cold beef to get your strength up? That will surely help you.'

Joe nodded. He had learnt never to say no to food,

even though he could not imagine swallowing one morsel at that particular moment. Margaret went back to the pantry and returned with some beef and a hunk of bread on a green earthenware plate. Joe smiled at her through his tears as she put the plate on the table in front of him.

'Eat up, then,' Margaret said, sitting back down.

Joe looked at the food. 'Can I take it home for mother and father?'

'Why, of course you can,' said Margaret. 'And more besides. But at least swallow a little of that beer for me.'

Joe took a few sips of small beer from the tin.

'What is the trouble, then?' asked Gabriel.

'It's Mary Harris.'

Freddy was instantly relieved, but this was unexpected.

'What about her?' asked Margaret.

'She did have a child and put it in the river.'

'What?' Margaret looked astounded, and could say nothing for a few minutes.

Gabriel, who became strong when his wife became weak, sat down next to her and held her hand. 'Surely not, Joe,' he said. 'Perhaps there's been some mistake, some confusion?'

Joe shook his head. 'I saw her under the white willow tree. A child cried. Then Mary put the bundle in the water and I found it down stream near the bank. I took it to the farm.'

'Is the infant alive?' asked Gabriel.

Joe shook his head again. 'No. They say it's murder,

and I'll have to go to the Great Hall and tell people.' Joe began to cry again.

Margaret was still silent, her right hand held over her mouth. Freddy got up and stroked the boy's head.

'When was all this?' asked Gabriel.

'A few days since. Then they did say at the Fox and Gibbet today that it was murder, so the constable will be coming tomorrow to take Mary away.'

Freddy kissed Joe on top of his thick hair. 'You are not drinking your beer, Joe,' she said. 'Take a little more, now, if you can, and then run back to Mrs Millbrook and tell her I shall come within the hour.'

'No, dear.' Margaret now spoke. 'You're tired at the moment and I think that your mind is a little overwrought. Wait until the morning, at least, and go when you're rested. You'll not help them like this. In the meanwhile, Mr Campbell will take Joe back to the rectory and see if there's any help he can offer directly.'

Freddy felt relieved. 'You are right, Margaret. I will be of more use to Anne in the morning.'

'Come, Joe,' said Gabriel, jumping up. 'Help me saddle up old Molly and we'll ride together to the rectory. Mrs Campbell will get some victuals ready for you to take home to your family.'

Joe smiled, the thought of the ride in the cart and the food to come cheering him a little. He took a few sips of the beer, but could manage no more, then got up and went outside with Gabriel.

Freddy sat down and looked with concern at Margaret. 'How do you do, Mrs C?'

'I admit I'm a little shaken up, my dear. It's a common enough tale - and I should not be shocked at it – if, indeed, tis a true one, though I cannot see why Joseph should lie; he's a good boy.'

'Yes, he is. Poor thing; what a sight for him to witness.'

'A terrible sight. I just cannot imagine Mary doing such a thing, or even getting herself into such a situation. Good gracious, how did it all come about?' Margaret sighed heavily.

Freddy kept her thoughts to herself, though she immediately thought of the captain as a possible father of Mary's child. Had he not mentioned family troubles? She knew she should not trust him. She felt gloomy and heart-sore again, but also a sense of vindication and righteousness.

'Poor Mary,' said Freddy. 'And you, Mrs C; are you sure that you are well? I hate to see you suffer; it goes to my heart so.'

'God bless you, my love. How can I suffer when I have my treasure home? Now let us both have our dinner. Gabriel may be some time, and you need to keep your strength up to be able to help at the rectory on the morrow.'

'Shall we take it in the dining room?' asked Freddy, grinning at Margaret.

'Why, yes, my love; what a splendid notion.'

Some hours later, they were sat back at the kitchen table, Freddy yawning.

'Get you to bed, child,' said Margaret. 'I shall wait here for Mr Campbell's return; and perhaps I shall be called out to rescue him after he's tumbled into a ditch with that long-suffering horse.'

Freddy smiled. 'Very well, then, Mrs C. Would you like one of my scandalous novels to read whilst you wait?'

'No, most certainly not. However, I may just take a glance at one of those delightful lady's journals of yours. Just because we live in the countryside, does not mean we have to be hobbledehoys.'

Freddy grinned, and they both got up from their chairs. Margaret kissed Freddy on both cheeks; then Freddy put out her arms to hug Margaret and snuggle into her soft form, which smelt of flour and the sweet water – made with roses – that she had taken to wearing after Freddy had gifted some to her many years ago. Freddy pulled back, looked into Margaret's kind face and could not help dropping a few tears.

'You are so good to me, Mrs Campbell,' she said. 'I do not deserve it. I do not deserve either of you, for I have done bad things in my life.'

'You, dear?' said Margaret, wiping away Freddy's tears with her small, round right hand. 'Nonsense. I never will believe it. You are our own dear treasure. You are overtired and under the weather; that is all. You were just the same as a girl, you know; a good night's rest will put you right. Now do not set me a bawling, too. That would be the final straw. Mr C will come home to find the kitchen all a flood, and not even the Hampshire rain to blame.'

Later that evening when Freddy had gone to bed, Margaret sat pondering her talk of bad things. She was no fool, and during Freddy's eleven-year absence she had often wondered what kind of life Freddy led, the life that was outside the pleasantries she had shared in her letters. Margaret felt that some painful things may have occurred, but, unusually for her, she did not want to know the details, unless Freddy should ever need to unburden herself. She only wanted to love and to keep safe their treasure, believing that God had compensated the Campbells for their childlessness with the gift of Freddy; and she would only ever feel grateful for that.

Chapter 22

Freddy had a fitful night's sleep. Captain Henry Lefroy must be the father of Mary's poor, dead child. Had he encouraged her to get rid of it? No, that was too dreadful; her thoughts were getting wilder and wilder and her brain more disordered. But now there were two dead children in this terrible affair, Sarah's unborn and Mary's just born. And had Mary known about the diamond, or was that just Sarah? The next morning, Margaret looked at Freddy's tired face with concern and pressed her to let Gabriel take her to the rectory in the gig, which Freddy agreed to.

Anne herself opened the door for her.

'Freddy; it is so good of you to come; thank you.'

'Not at all, Anne,' said Freddy, following her into the house.

'Let me take your things. We are all managing for ourselves, just now. Jonathan is not at home, but we hope to see him tonight or early tomorrow, and Henry is in London on business. So I am in charge.' Anne laughed. Indeed, thought Freddy, Anne seemed more alert than usual and even cheerful.

'Will you take some tea or some chocolate?' continued Anne, as they went into the front parlour. 'Polly can prepare it for us; she is being quite the angel and has not dropped one thing since yesterday morning.'

Freddy smiled. 'Dear Polly. No, thank you. I am very well satisfied after one of Mrs Campbell's breakfasts. I will not be able to fit into Gabriel's gig very soon.'

They sat down.

'So tell me, Anne, what is this awful business?'

'Oh, Freddy; it is quite dreadful. On Tuesday this week, Samuel informed me that Mary was very ill and he had sent her to bed. He had promised to check on her several hours later, and I said that I would accompany him and take her a cordial. We did so, but she had gone away from the cottage. Samuel and John – Mary's elder boy – went searching for her and found her, in a very ill state, resting under a tree not far from the Denton farm. They brought her home in a cart with the help of two of the farmer's men. She was very weak and strange, most unlike herself. Then the surgeon arrived – called by Mrs Denton - to examine her and he said that she had been delivered of a child. Then he told us that poor Joe had witnessed some of it, and told it to Mrs Denton at the farm, and that they were quite sure that Mary killed her baby. It was found soon after in the river by Joe.'

Anne paused and took a breath. 'I am at a loss to know how a woman could do such a thing. It is so against nature. To be sure, I do find Mary a little flinty, sometimes, but had not thought her capable of something so wicked as that. It is unfathomable.'

'Yes, in some ways,' said Freddy, 'though I have seen very good women acquire a certain madness when their child comes, and they do not always know what they do. We have also to bear in mind her situation, and the terrible scandal. Her life would be as good as over; though now, I fear, it almost certainly will be.'

'Yes, Freddy, that is true. How thoughtful you are.'

'Joe mentioned the Hog and Gibbet yesterday. Was an inquest held there?'

'Yes. Mary has been too ill to attend but poor Joe had to say his bit. They found her guilty of the murder of her bastard child, and she must go before the summer assizes. We are expecting the constable to come at any moment to take her away to the gaol.'

'Poor Joe. He was very distressed when he came to us yesterday.'

'Yes, the poor boy is quite cut up. It seems that what he witnessed will serve as the main evidence in the case against Mary.'

'Oh dear. It is a very sad business indeed. And did no-one even suspect that Mary was with child?'

'I am not aware that they did. I wonder if at one point the thought may have crossed my mind for the very briefest moment – so brief that I was hardly conscious of it - and then my mind dismissed it. Do you sometimes have that experience? She seemed a little fuller, a little heavier, perhaps, but she is quite a fine and stout woman generally, so it did not seem particularly amiss. I always feel so paltry and insignificant when I am in her proximity.' Anne smiled. 'It all seems so impossible. She lives here at one of our cottages, and has worked very hard for us. She has her leisure time, and her leaves of absence, but I would never have suspected her of having a lover of any kind. Though I suppose that it would not be so strange or unnatural if she did, her being a widow, and such a handsome woman.'

'And do we know, or even suspect, who that man is, the father of the child?' Freddy was thinking about the captain, but clearly could not suggest it.

Anne looked Freddy in the eye for the briefest moment, then said, 'no. I certainly do not know, but I imagine there will be gossip around. I believe that Mrs Denton has a few notions, but how accurate they are I could not tell you. She can be a trifle malicious, I fear.'

'Yes, there certainly will be much gossip. Where is Mary now?'

'She is in the cottage, waiting for the constable. Samuel is with her. He has been nursing her these few days during her illness – he is so good - and is quite overcome by the whole affair. I think he is rather fond of her.'

'Do you think he could be the father?'

'No, he is far too honourable. Even if it had been the case, I am sure he would have married her before things got to this stage. I always thought that they would have worked rather well together, and wondered about it, but they have preferred to remain friends, it seems, or perhaps it is that Mary had this other love.'

Freddy looked thoughtful for a few moments, then with concern at Mrs Millbrook. 'And, Anne, can I ask how you are managing, dear? This whole thing must be especially painful for you, after your sorrows with regard to children. I hope I am not touching on too difficult a thing, but I thought it right to ask.'

'Thank you, Freddy. You are so very considerate and I am grateful for your concern. It does feel so unjust, and one cannot help but think of one's own situation and what might have been. And that poor, poor, child; it crossed my mind that John and I could have taken it, you know. But I am managing pretty well. My time in Southampton with my cousin did me a great deal of good, and I resolved to be less self-pitying. It has gone on long enough, and I must make a change.'

'That is very admirable of you, and I wish you well in it. Acceptance can be a very difficult thing to achieve, but if one does achieve it, or something near it, one can find happiness, I believe, even if it is not the sort of happiness we wanted or expected in our lives. And you deserve your happiness, dear.'

'Thank you. I will do my very best. And while I am about it, I must apologise to you, Fredericka, for my selfishness. I cannot regret my unburdening my sorrow to you, for I am sure that it has set me on the road to recovery, but I have only thought of myself, and have barely discovered more about you, who seem so interesting. I hope we can put that right, when this business is done. I want to know about your papa and mama, and your time in London. And perhaps you can inform me a little more on this slavery business, for though I hope and try to do the right thing I am not sure I fully understand, and fear that Jonathan gets a little impatient with me when I say something ignorant or misinformed.'

'I suspect you know more than I do, dear. But it would make me very happy for us to get to know each other a little better, when things are less difficult.'

They were interrupted by a knock at the front door. After a minute or so, it was opened by Polly, who showed the local constable, George Redditch, into the room. He was a slouching fellow with a sharp, pinched nose, teeth more rotten and foul-smelling than most, and non-too-clean linen.

'Good day, ma'am, and to you, ma'am,' said Mr Redditch.

'Good day, constable,' said Anne, getting up, and recoiling slightly from the smell of Redditch's breath.

'As I think you'll know, I'm here to get Mary Harris and I need to be quick about it for I have to get back to the shop.' The constable ran a small and not very well-stocked grocers on the road to Winchester, and was suspected of more than the usual food adulteration and of overcharging his poorer customers.

'I am aware of it, sir,' said Anne, quite sharply, for

her; then turned to Polly and said softly, 'you can get back to your duties now, Polly.'

Polly nodded, smiled at Freddy, gave a wobbly curtsey, and quitted the room. Anne looked at Freddy, who smiled at her encouragingly and got up to follow them through the vestibule, out of the front door of the house and over to the cottages.

They found Mary cleaned up and dressed neatly, sat very quiet on a chair, with Sam sat next to her, his face racked with shock and anxiety. The boys were stood by, John silent and pensive, Michael fidgeting, about to start crying again, which he had been doing intermittently since Mary was brought home by the farmer's labourers. On sight of Anne, Freddy and the constable, he burst into tears, ran to his mother, put his head on her lap and clung to her. Mary patted his head, almost absentmindedly. 'There, there, son,' she said. She looked up at Mr Redditch, wielding his warrant with a flourish.

'Now, Mary Harris,' the constable said, 'I think you know why I'm here so I hope we won't have any nonsense.'

Samuel got up and addressed him. 'There'll be no nonsense here, sir; and I'm not sure why you're suggesting there would be.'

'Hoity-toity, Sam; I have but come to do my job.' He looked tempted to say more, but glancing at Anne and Freddy, changed his mind.

'I'm ready,' said Mary, getting up, and trying to push Michael away from her, who screamed.

'I'll accompany Mary,' said Sam to the constable, a little in the manner of a challenge.

'You may do so, if you wish,' said George, eyeing Mary with contempt.

'Mistress,' said Sam, turning to Anne, 'would you be good enough to look after John and Michael here, until my return?'

'Yes, of course, Samuel,' said Anne, 'I will do anything I can to help.'

'Thank you, ma'am, we're much obliged to you.'

The constable tapped his left foot impatiently. Michael, still clinging to his mother's legs, began to scream again, and John went over to him.

'Now,' said he, gently, 'you must be strong, like me, for mother's sake. We want to make her proud of us, don't we?'

Michael sniffed and nodded, and John managed to pull him away and then stood with his arms around the boy's shoulders. Sam took Mary's arm, who smiled at him and then addressed her sons.

'Now, you be good boys for Mrs Millbrook, here, and you'll see me again before you know it.'

'Good boys,' said Sam. 'The mistress and Miss Swinglehurst will take good care of you, and I'll be home very soon.'

Mary and Samuel followed Mr Redditch out of the house and over to his horse and cart. Sam made Mary comfortable on the straw, then positioned himself next to her and gave the signal to the constable to set off, and they made their way slowly into Winchester to the gaol on Jewry Street.

'Now, boys,' said Anne, still calm and authoritative, 'will you not come into the rectory kitchen and have something good to eat? Miss Swinglehurst has brought some of Mrs Campbell's queen cakes, and I know that she will be most disappointed if you do not eat them all up.' She paused and looked at poor Michael, who was still crying. 'It is very hard for you both, my dears, I know.'

Michael gave out a great sob, went over to Anne, and put out his arms.

'Come now,' said Freddy, smiling at John, 'Polly is waiting to serve us and will be getting impatient. And I want you to tell me all about your learning, for I hear that you are doing very well. We have so many different kinds of books at the old manor house, you know. They belonged to my dear father, and they are going to waste, and I need to find a good reader to make use of them. My father was an admiral in the navy, and sailed the high seas, so there are lots of adventures to be found.'

John smiled weakly and they all removed to the kitchen of the main house where Polly was waiting. She was the middle child of ten, and for all her awkwardness, was used to dealing with children. She now fussed over the boys, serving up the cakes and prattling away. Anne sat next to Michael, and held his hand, while Freddy sat opposite John and continued to draw him out on his learning.

Around three hours later, Samuel returned home, and joined Anne and Freddy in the front parlour while Polly looked after the boys.

'How does she do, Samuel?' asked Freddy.

'She is very calm, ma'am; it is I who am agitated. I've barely taken anything more than my pint of ale the whole of my life, but I had to stop off at the Royal Oak on my way back for two tots of brandy.'

'I am sure you were greatly in need of them,' said Anne.

'That gaol isn't a fit place for Mary; I don't know how she'll bear it. I can hardly bear to think about it. I cannot understand why she is there. I cannot understand this whole thing, but it seems that I must try and believe what people are a telling me, and what is before my own eyes.'

'Yes, it is a very strange business,' said Anne. 'But the reverend will be soon home. He knows many important people and might be able to help.'

'You will not disown her, mistress? I know that most would, and will. Poor Mary will be greatly in need of kindness.'

'Of course not, Samuel. We will do our very best for her; rest assured.'

'Thank you ma'am; that's such a comfort to me. I hate to think of her being friendless, or treated cruelly. The world generally will be very hard upon her, and that barbarous constable is no comfort to anyone.'

'I am sure that you gave her comfort,' said Anne.

'Indeed, it is a shame that old Wilson is not still here. He was the local constable previous to Mr Redditch' – this to Freddy - 'and was such a civil, decent sort of fellow.'

'Yes,' said Sam. 'I fear that Redditch is only in it for the fees, which then go straight to the nearest alehouse.'

'Well,' said Freddy, 'happily, he is but a tiny and insignificant cog in the wheel of the law, and we know that there are much better men than him wielding justice in our county. The High Constable is a very good and just personage, I have heard.' Freddy was not quite sure that she was on safe ground, here, but felt the need to say something reassuring.

'That is something,' said Sam, 'though I do not know how these things are managed, and who is involved. I must apply myself to it. But I should go to the boys now. How do they do?'

'As well as they can do,' said Anne. 'Michael takes it very hard, which is only natural. Dear Polly is trying to entertain them in the kitchen while she prepares the dinner. I must go and help her.'

'I'll take the boys to my cottage,' said Sam. 'I don't think they should stay in their mother's house this evening. It will be too painful for them.'

'You are right. But they shall stay here,' said Anne. 'There will be much more room for them. We have so many empty chambers in this rectory. We quite rattle around.'

Sam looked unsure.

'They are close to you, Samuel, I know, and they are

very fortunate to have you as their friend. But we can manage them better here – it will be more comfortable - and we will make sure they are well fed and looked after.'

'Yes, mistress, thank you. That would be a great help, and better for the boys.'

'That is settled, then,' said Anne. 'Well, we must get on. Freddy, you will stay with us for dinner, will you not?'

'Yes,' said Freddy, 'of course; and tomorrow I will return hither with Mrs Campbell. She is the best manager in the whole of Hampshire – in the whole of the kingdom, I should not wonder - and will set everything in order for us. I am sure that she can also recommend somebody to help whilst Mary cannot be here.'

'Thank you, Freddy. I do not know what we would do without you. And, Samuel, you must join us for your dinner. We will have it in the kitchen, very cosy, just as Freddy and the Campbells do. And you will be a comfort to the boys.'

'Thank you, ma'am.'

'And then the reverend and Henry will be here before we know it. And between your master and Margaret Campbell, we will do the very best we can for poor Mary.'

Chapter 23

That same day in the late afternoon, a handsome gentleman with a haggard face and a distracted air left a smart inn in Portsmouth and set off to walk to a less salubrious part of town. He stopped along the way to press a coin into the hand of a black beggar slumped in a rotting doorway, his left leg stumped at the knee, and then threw another coin to a pair of boys, one black, one white, who might have been any age between nine and nineteen, both dressed in filthy pantomime costumes and tumbling over and over until the white boy caught the coin, and they bowed and laughed at him.

After around twenty minutes, the gentleman turned down a filthy lane to arrive at a ramshackle tavern – now more of an alehouse - the Powder Keg, which looked like it was about to be crushed by the other buildings surrounding it. As he pushed open the door he felt a hot rush of air and breathed in a strong tang of sweat, rum and tobacco. He looked around the room, spotted Adam Short, and went over to join him at his table in a poky corner, bending his head as he went to avoid a low-hanging beam. Some of the other customers stared at the fine gentleman, who had not bothered on this occasion to play the fustian rustic.

Mr Short pulled back the hood he was wearing, and nodded at the gentleman as he sat down and then pushed a glass of rum towards him. The gentleman looked down at it with a slight look of disdain.

'What's the matter, sir?' asked Short. 'Don't enjoy a bit of the old kill devil? Not genteel enough for a fine gentleman like you?'

'I will take it with pleasure, Mr Short; thank you.' The gentleman took a few sips. 'So, we have come to a pretty pass, it seems.'

'Yes, it rather looks that way. As I said in my letter, Matthew Lane has not had a hand in the business. He is dull and respectable – I doubt he would have it in him - and I have not discovered any talk around him, except him being a very fine, honest fellow. I believe that that low devil, Davey Barber, just mentioned his name to me to shut me up. And I seem to have exhausted every other line of enquiry. The jewel will be long cut up and gone away by now.'

'Do you think that the thief was one of the Countess's guests, that evening, rather than a member of her staff?'

'It seems probable. I have looked into them as far as I have been able, but it could take months, years, to properly investigate them all, without arousing suspicion. We may never know what really happened, or who was involved, unless the story spills out in time. Either way, it's too late for us, I'm afraid.'

'What about the surgeon you employed? Could he have told you a falsehood?'

'Nay, it wouldn't have been worth his while. I would have soon arranged his appointment with the noose. In any case, the stones were never going to be inside her stomach. How would she have even got them cut in time, as well as having the crazed notion to swallow them? Unless you think she could have eaten the diamond whole and let it lie there, pristine inside her, until she got to you? In both cases, Mr Barber would have told me that he'd given her the stone, as planned, and so claimed his share of the job. I've made sure that he did not take it himself, and hide it from us. He is a snivelling coward and would not have the courage to do something so daring, or foolhardy. I'm afraid the only thing inside Sarah Long was your bastard. You know it was an outlandish scheme on your part, as I told you time and time again. I'm not sure why I went along with it, digging up her body like a mad man. You've grown quite lunatic in your desperation, I think, and I've not left you far behind. We have both become fine candidates for Bedlam.'

The man laughed bitterly. 'It is quite true. I took some of Sarah's fanciful comments and drew my own lunatic reality from it. She once said that if she were a fine lady, she would not only cover herself in diamonds from head to toe but would eat them for her dinner every day, washed down with champagne, so that her whole self would sparkle. And then we got to wondering what would happen if one really swallowed a diamond. Would it harm a person? Could it sit in the stomach until one wanted to get rid of it? And I said that if one owned the famous Celestial Light, one would not need to swallow it in order to sparkle, but simply possess it, and one's whole being would be transformed. We didn't really believe any of this, of course, but then in after time, as my impecunious state worsened, this conversation came back to me, and the idea of the diamond lodged itself in my mind, and I could not sleep at night for thinking of it. It became a sort of mania, and I hit upon the idea of stealing it, which would solve all my money problems. Not only that, I began to think that the stories surrounding it might be true – for did God not work in mysterious ways? – and if I could only possess it, however briefly, I could be redeemed in some way, and my old purity and righteousness return.'

'If only it were that easy.'

'You are right. Strangely, I feel easier and freer now that I know it is all done with, and my fate is sure.'

'But can you not run? Get on a ship? I'm too sick now; my time is done; but surely you could find a new life? You are still young; rouse yourself, sir.'

'I cannot. I have neither the wherewithal nor the will to do so. I am done. I do not know what I have been about these past few years.'

'Well, sir, you found yourself fallen, and desperate, as did I. And when a man is both those things, there is no limit to the follies, absurdities and degradations to which he is willing to expose himself. But never mind it; it didn't work out as we hoped. It was a wild and probably not ingenious scheme to begin with and wasn't likely to meet with success when looked at in the cold light of day. Myself, I long to be at sea. I do not like this cold, ungrateful country.'

The gentleman nodded and looked for a few moments at his companion, repulsed by the sores on his puffy white face, the bald patches scattered across his scaly head, and the slight erosion of his nose near to his left nostril. 'Will you survive the journey? It is a late stage of the pox, I take it?'

'Aye, aye, there is no mistaking the pox. I thought I'd beaten it, for a time. I took the mercury treatment, and even bathed my cock in fresh milk several times a day, like some kind of perverted Roman god. But it's rushing back on me now and it cannot be long. You're disgusted by my face, I see. I am, myself, and wouldn't look in a glass now for all the sugar in the Caribbean. I was once rather proud of my looks, can you believe? They called me a handsome fellow. You're very fortunate, sir, not to have your sins written upon your face, as I have.'

'Yes, I dare say I am. And I am surprised, too, that I do not, since I have been so incontinent in my life. It is perhaps as well that I never came into contact with the diamond, for they say that it will either cleanse you of your sins or bring them into the light for the whole world to see upon your countenance.'

'Nay, sir; that diamond stuff is a fairy story for simpletons and the credulous. I don't hold with such things. If only it were so easy to judge the souls of us all, the world might be a very different place, or one in which we could not bear to look upon our fellow men.'

'You are a philosopher, Mr Short?'

'I flatter myself I am. We're not all ignorant fellows, you know. I'm a literary man, and have taken pleasure in studying many branches of the philosophic sciences, though I have not often had the leisure time to devote to such things as I would have wished. I'm also a practical man, sir, and take the world as I find it.'

'How did you come to lose it all? I have known only the fact, but not how you came to it. My father would have been sorry to know it, whatever my thoughts on the matter.'

The gentleman's father, now deceased, had been a humble clergyman, and a friend of Short's. He later speculated in his business in the West Indies, and had done very well from it, something which had caused many a heated argument between the father and his righteous son, even though the son willingly took the money when the time came.

'There were many reasons. I believe that my son, Nicholas, one of those ridiculous, Macaroni coxcombs – a curse on him – triggered the whole thing. He didn't like life on the plantations, and didn't even endeavour to overcome his dislike. His senses were too refined - he said - his constitution too delicate. Mark you, he had no objection to the business in principle, or to the wealth it gave him. I indulged him, for his mother's sake, who was as weak as he was. He left to travel and dabble in Europe, as all these spoilt dandies do, but finally decided to settle down, buying an estate in Yorkshire, and trying to play country gent. I continued to support him, even though his mother had died and there was never much affection between us, for I was proud to have a son put his roots in some good English soil and so do the family name proud.

'But, as I could have predicted, he idled away his time and money in glitter and show; he built so many follies in the grounds of his estate – even one in the shape of his mother's head, I believe - that the people thereabouts thought him quite the madman. I do not blame them. Then, to my great surprise and happiness, he managed to get himself affianced to a young lady with a high aristocratic pedigree. I released more funds, over-stretching myself a little, but believing it to be for a very good purpose. But then he managed to ruin things, as he did everything, by showing what he truly was to the world. He was so refined and sensitive, you see – such an epicure - that he liked to play the lady in his pleasures. His fiancé caught him in the act – he couldn't even restrain himself until after the marriage - and so it was all called off, and all my pride and triumph with it. He went back to the continent with some of his men friends, and died, debauched and penniless, in Italy.'

'I am sorry to hear it.'

'Don't be. I should have thrown him into one of the copper kettles in the boiling house when he was a sickly, muling infant, and saved myself this world of trouble. Well, his death was a blessing, but it wasn't the end of my troubles. I suffered loss upon loss. There were crop failures and storms. I speculated and trusted where I shouldn't have. I grew fat, and my eye wandered from the business, when I used to be so lean and orderly. How I used to scoff at those over-bred plantation owners, who left everything to their attorneys and overseers, and didn't know when they were being swindled. Well, it's all over now. I would have settled for leaving Grace a small estate, with her own slaves; she would manage the business better than anyone, I can assure you – there's nothing like a negro to drive a negro. She's been by my side these thirty years, and should have got her reward.' Mr Short sighed and drained his glass. 'And so I came back to England – though I never wanted or expected to do so – to see if there was anything final to be done, and so you found me, sir, in Winchester, somewhat surprised and not over-pleased to see your old godfather, I'll warrant.'

'I did not recognise you at first, so changed as you were. But it is true that I was not especially pleased, and I am sure that you felt no different on seeing your godson. We were never friends.'

'No.'

'But then we discovered our altered circumstances,

and I found myself sharing with you my outrageous notion for getting money. I remember not quite believing that I was saying it out loud to another human being. Then it became real, and so it was.'

'So it was. And our meeting was a chance encounter, for I had not planned to come into Hampshire. It was only after my failures in London to salvage anything from my business, that I had a hankering to see the old place. It were likely better for us both if I had got straight back on board a ship, as I had planned. Well, well, it has been a final, if fruitless adventure. But what about you, sir, how did you sink so low?'

'The usual story, I believe. A few youthful indiscretions – gambling, extravagance, women – no more than other young men. But then a further slide into more licentiousness and debt. I find that I get a sort of fever on me, and cannot resist temptation, however hard I try. To crown it all, I have quite the talent for siring bastards.'

'That we share, sir.'

The gentleman laughed. 'I was so moral as a young man, a fact I am sure will not surprise you. I wanted to be so good - I thought I was, thought that I was so much higher than other men, almost like some kind of saviour. I still cannot resist the idea. But the better I wanted to be, the worst I became. God has certainly enjoyed some dramatic irony at my expense. And now the world will know my shame, and I will die in a debtor's prison. Imagine how people will enjoy that.'

'Undoubtedly, some will. But nobody should want

the world to love them. That has been your downfall, I think. I never cared for other people's opinions or for their soft hearts. I only wanted money, and found I enjoyed inspiring fear rather than admiration. It's a power that intoxicates, worse than Kill Devil itself.'

Mr Short looked down at his empty glass. He had never talked in this way about himself, had not even thought in this way about himself. He was not inclined to honest self-examination – why should he be? But his illness and approaching end had seemed to trigger a propensity to thought and reflection, if not to true self-condemnation, for his only regrets were in relation to the weakness or treachery of others, and not to the life he had led, or the person that he had been.

'I have not experienced that,' said the gentleman. 'But, yes, I have wanted too much to be loved and admired. Perhaps, in fact, both our cravings are different types of wanting power over others. And I so prided myself on trying to take responsibility for my actions, by keeping my lovers and my bastards, rather than abandoning them. But I only sunk further into the mire, and became more entangled and indebted, and will now inflict greater pain on those I care for. I have become the perfect exemplum of many a scriptural tale of falling, and you have seen my defects as clearly as any god, or as if the diamond had, indeed, written them upon my features.'

'Well, we must both face the consequences of our choices now.'

'Yes, indeed we must. Well, I must get about my business, and face what is to come, for as with you, with me, and it cannot be long.' The gentleman got up and stared in the face of his companion.

'Goodbye, sir,' said Mr Short.

'Goodbye; I wish you peace, sir, for my father's sake, at least.'

Adam Short nodded, and watched the gentleman slowly make his way to the door of the alehouse, and quit the establishment. He would take another tot of rum, and stay a while. He was growing weaker by the hour, and needed to recover his breathing, which was feeling strained, and numb the general pain that was increasingly attacking every inch of his body. How he wanted his Grace, but he knew that he would not survive to see her again.

The gentleman made his way back to the inn, enjoying the sunshine on his face as he walked. He had planned to leave that day. But then what now signified one more evening away? The disgrace and pain would come soon enough. He would stay another night in the inn. He could wander out and fill his cups, and perhaps take himself to a favourite whore house. Why not? There was always one last, tawdry fling; it was too late to reform himself now.

Chapter 24

As soon as news of Mary's situation got out, gossip began to link her with the dead black woman found in the grounds of the rectory. Was it not odd that they were both with child at the same time? Perhaps they were rivals for the same man? If Mary was wicked enough to drown her own child, what else might she be capable of? They had never been convinced that that woman had died of heart failure. Who ever heard of such a healthy-looking, blooming woman – so people described her – dying in such a manner? And then the body being taken like that? There was great evil involved, to be sure – quite probably witchcraft - and people warned each other to be extra vigilant of their pregnant womenfolk, and babies, who might be snatched at any moment.

Mary had not been well loved in Winchester, and this great opportunity to really malign her was too good to resist. During the five short years since her arrival she had been diagnosed as being a little cool, haughty and unforthcoming. The farmer's wife, who had a habit of taking instant, irreversible dislikes to people, had been particularly vehement against her. Mrs Alice Denton had been very shocked that day when Joe came a knocking on the farmhouse door carrying that poor dead child, but she could not help but feel a little glee at Joe's relation of the tale, and more especially the part where Mary held the child under water. Joe had, in fact, been a little hazy on this point, but Mrs Denton had coaxed the story out of him in such a way that meant there was no going back for the poor lad.

Mary was always thought to be a little warmer towards the menfolk than the womenfolk of Winchester. Naturally, this did not endear her to the women. Every male she had but spoken to during the past five years was now touted as a possible father to her dead child, from the High Sheriff of the county, who had once nodded and said 'Good Day' to her during a procession in the city, to the last pedlar who had turned up at the rectory with his pots and pans. Poor Arnold the butcher, who had so openly admired Mary, was besieged by customers, which was very good for his business but not his heart, for he would have married Mary in an instant – how people could think he could seduce and then abandon her, he could not fathom.

Freddy, hearing some of these rumours, second-hand, from Margaret, was at one moment exceedingly angry towards the captain – who had surely got poor Mary into this mess, as well as poor Sarah – and at another doubtful and a little penitent. Had the two women known each other? And how had Sarah died? As soon as she had found out about the body being lain in the image of a cross, she had suspected foul play, that is, that she was murdered. When she went to the rectory to spend time with Anne, she barely knew how to behave towards Henry. At one moment she was trying to avoid speaking to him, at another eagerly listening to his conversation in the hope of picking up some little clues to the truth, or simply succumbing briefly to his warmth and charm, and his obvious pleasure at seeing her. He seemed as confused at her erratic behaviour as she was. This could not go on, she thought, in her more rational moments. She was becoming more and more troubled, sleeping badly, her mind always distracted. But she did not know what to do.

The Campbells and Freddy did all they could to help at the rectory. Margaret found a Mrs Hobson to help them manage their household matters, who, though she was not quite as brisk and efficient as Mary, did smile a little more. Mary's sons paid several visits to the old manor house. Freddy would play spillikins and cards with them. John also found comfort in the admiral's study, Michael in the kitchen with Margaret, and both of them with Gabriel in the grounds, looking at the plants, crops, tools and horse tackle, and feeding Molly too many apples.

Mary remained in gaol and continued to refuse

to say anything, or to see anyone – not her sons, not Samuel. She silently went through her days, cleaning her room, taking in a little needlework, and barely eating the bit of oatmeal, bread and occasional broken meat that was the prisoner's standard diet. She attended the small, low chapel for prayers on Wednesdays and Fridays, and for the sermon and prayers on Sundays, and ignored the attempts by some of the amorous men sat on the opposite benches to solicit her attention. She was as popular inside gaol as she was outside of it, being marked as aloof and superior, and was rewarded accordingly by rough taunts and physical affronts from some of her fellow prisoners. There was one young woman, however, who touched Mary's heart despite herself, a scrap of a girl of fourteen years old, who had been committed for house breaking, and who cried constantly, terrified at the prospect of the noose, or even being sent away over the oceans far from her beloved mother. Mary, who had never had much patience with female tears, sat with the girl, held her hand, and murmured little, soothing nonsenses to her.

One morning, the day before Mary's trial was due to come on, Freddy walked to the rectory to deliver some items from Margaret, and was shown through to Anne's parlour by Mrs Hobson. She did not intend to stay long. She did not have the strength to resist the captain, if he was there, and would let herself fall into his charm like claret into a glass. She had brief conversations with Jonathan – who came and went – and Mr Winkworth, who was deeply troubled by Mary's plight and looking more earnest than ever. They both looked as worn and tired as she felt herself.

Polly appeared to say that her mistress had gone into town with Samuel.

'That is fine, Polly,' said Freddy, 'I will see her again soon. I just came to deliver these things from Mrs Campbell and will be on my way.'

'Would you like some refreshment, ma'am?' asked Polly, looking nervous. If Freddy felt that she could not withstand the captain, Polly felt that she could not withstand Freddy.

'No, thank you, dear. But, how do you do, Polly?'

'Very well, thank you, ma'am,' said Polly, who looked far from well.

'Are you sure? Do not be frightened of me, my dear; I will not ask you any more questions.'

Polly smiled, and then started to cry.

'Oh, Polly, what ails thee? Come, will you not sit down with me a moment. You can tell me your troubles, if you wish, but, if not, you can just take a little rest.'

'Thank you, ma'am,' said Polly, sitting down, and sniffing.

Freddy knew that she might have pressed Polly at any time over the past couple of weeks to reveal what she knew, but, desperate as she was to acquire more knowledge of this whole affair, she found that she could not do it. Polly was too tender and eager to please – it would be cruelty.

'They are saying that the dead woman found here was murdered, ma'am,' said Polly, between sniffs.

'Yes, Polly, I am afraid that is a possibility. It is very sad, as it is very sad about Mary. But happy times will come again, you know. You are a good girl, dear; you do your duty and keep helping your mistress and we will all help each other likewise.'

Polly smiled weakly and brushed away a tear from her left cheek with her right fist. 'They are saying that she was poisoned. Is this true, ma'am?' Clearly, this subject was praying on Polly's mind and she could not help but return to it.

'Well, I do not know, but if she was killed, that could well be the case.'

'We have some arsenic in the house, ma'am,' said Polly, now speaking quickly. 'The mistress sent me to fetch it a long time since – to deal with the vermin and a little for the complexion, I think. It was kept in the back store room, very well hidden and marked. But then, just after that woman was found, I noticed that the jar had been opened and some was gone.' Polly stopped, and stared anxiously at Freddy.

'Is this what is concerning you so?' asked Freddy.

Polly paused, then nodded.

'Try not to vex yourself. The poison could have had any number of uses, you know – for the vermin, or even the complexion, as you say. There is no reason to believe it was used on the woman. At the moment, with all these strange things happening, our minds are apt to get carried away. You would not believe some of the strange fancies I have been having recently.'

Polly smiled a little.

'Are you sure that there is nothing else troubling you?' asked Freddy.

Polly waited a few moments, then shook her head. She is carrying much more inside her than concern about that poison, Freddy thought, but it is too big for her to say out loud.

'Well, dear, you can always tell me if there ever is anything. In the meantime, try not to upset yourself.'

Freddy wandered slowly back to the old manor house, now wondering, as was Polly, if that poison had been used to kill Sarah. But who would kill her, and why? On arriving home, she retreated to the old beech tree in the garden to read a letter from Affy, Margaret hovering somewhere nearby, pretending to examine the strawberries. The first part of the letter related to Maria, whom they had seen. She was a very good, but very poor and worn-down sort of creature, Affy said. Unfortunately, she had not been able to tell them any more than they knew already about Josiah Clarke, Sarah's gentleman. The Sweets had offered to help with Sarah's child, and planned to give what they could on a regular basis. At least Maria now knew what had happened to her friend, however tragic the news.

The second part of the letter came as more of a shock and a revelation. Matthew Lane had unburdened himself to Edward. He had, indeed, stolen the diamond.

Chapter 25

David Barber, if for entirely the wrong reasons, had hit upon the right person as the one who had taken the Celestial Light. Matthew Lane, formerly known as Scipio, was the former slave of a London banker, an Obidiah Lane, who had granted Matthew his manumission in his will, and even left him a guinea or two. Matthew had been fortunate, he knew, to be well-treated by his master, who had even been fond of him, but a slave was still a slave however gilded the chains. After Lane's death, Matthew had gained a place in the Darby household; he was a free labourer at last. In the Lane household he had been resented by most of the other servants; the fact that he worked very well for nothing did not recommend to their master their claims for decent wages. But in his new place, he was a waged servant like any other, and his fellow servants appeared mostly to be good sorts of folks, apart from that low fellow, David Barber, but one could not expect a state of perfection. He did his work well, was a little sweet on pretty Charlotte the housemaid, as was everyone else, and enjoyed his leisure time.

In January that year, he had met with a friend in a Soho alehouse, who wanted him to listen to a political meeting led by James Wilkins. Matthew was a little hesitant, having heard something of Wilkins's reputation and being a mostly conformist and law-abiding soul, but agreed to accompany his friend and listen to what was said. Stood in the hot, crowded room, amongst the smoke and beer and shouts, he had been stunned by the words of Wilkins, who talked nothing less than revolution: "I would gladly die for the pleasure of plunging a dagger in the heart of a tyrant." The tyrants included not only slave owners but kings and princes of any skin colour, who monopolised the land that should be shared with all, and bid the poor man to be quiet and grateful in his state of oppression, and to turn the other cheek.

After this first time, Matthew vowed not to return to the meetings; the experience had been too unsettling of his new-found peace. But as he carried out his duties, his heart and mind continued to race, and he found himself drawn back, almost irresistibly, and had become a follower of Wilkins. He was in a perpetual state of anger, but did not know quite what to do with it.

And then, on that strange night towards the end of May, the Celestial Light had appeared before him, as if it had been sent by God for the cause. He had suspected that David Barber was up to no good, and had watched him, and then followed him, that evening, until the point where he had placed the diamond in the sewing box and ran up to the next floor of the house. Matthew found that he did not hesitate in entering the Countess's room, taking the stone from the box, and tucking it into the pocket of his waistcoat. It gave him a thrill to handle the diamond, however briefly, and he felt a warm glow and general feeling of wellbeing. He walked back down the stairs with a strange feeling of calm and confidence. When the household was abed, he managed to slot the stone inside the ivory handle of a gentleman's walking cane that his former master had left him in his will. It had been too fine for him, a mere servant, to use, but he kept it both as a reminder of his former bondage, and as a form of insurance, knowing he could sell it if times became hard.

The next day, when the jewel's disappearance had been discovered, and the house was thrown into chaos, he woke from his dream, and now his heart and mind raced with fear and panic, rather than anger, and he could not rest until he had got rid of the jewel. Luckily, the Countess and her maid, groggy, horrified – no doubt drugged by Barber the evening before - could not fully remember the latter part of the evening. A search of the house had been undertaken and when this proved fruitless, the Countess screamed for the constable to be brought. Matthew, terrified, prayed that his fear did not show in his face and bearing. It did, but he was not the only one, since the appearance of the law made all the servants nervous and guilty about a crime they had not committed.

The constable, Mr Briggs, was a sardonic fellow, full of suppressed energy, which gave the impression to those whom he encountered that he was about to explode, and so he struck the requisite fear into the hearts of the criminal and innocent alike. He ordered another, more thorough, search of the house, pausing for a while to examine a petrified Matthew about his possession of the fine walking cane. Matthew explained its provenance, and indeed had a copy of his former master's deed to prove his rightful ownership of it, and Mr Briggs was satisfied. Mr Barber, however, was less fortunate. Briggs had had dealings with him in the past, and when he laid eyes upon him, he gave a half-sneer, half – rare – grin, and decided that he had his man. His interviews with some of the other servants only confirmed this opinion, since they did not like Barber and suspected him of dishonesty. He could not arrest Barber on the spot, but assured the Countess he would return to the house soon, and in the meantime he posted a man to keep watch on the house.

The next day David Barber fled the house, getting into a fight with the watch, but managing to escape. General suspicions seemed now confirmed, and the rest of the servants could breathe again, and go about their usual business. Nevertheless, Matthew, actually in possession of the diamond, was still sick with fear, and desperately awaited his next half-holiday, which, happily, was only a few days away. He took his cane to a pawnbroker's, who gave him a tiny fraction of what it was worth. Charlotte and another servant saw him quit the house with the cane – he did not attempt to hide it - and he told them that he was pawning it for a short time to help a friend in need. Charlotte looked at him tenderly and he felt a deep sense of shame.

Matthew had felt a little better once the diamond was away from him, though at the same time felt a strange pull back to the stone, as if it was emitting a beam of energy from the city in the east, where the pawnbroker's was situated, to the Darby townhouse in the west of the city, in Mayfair. He really must get it to Wilkins, and be rid of it once and for all. He found that the latter would soon be speaking at a meeting house in Soho, a more respectable, and tamer, affair, than that at the usual alehouse. He managed to get a few hours away from his duties, which were a little quieter than usual, the Season having ended and his mistress being so stricken by the loss of the stone. To the great disappointment of the pawnbroker, he re-claimed his stick, and went along to the meeting with the jewel in his pocket, as if it were a barley-sugar he had taken along to sustain him while he listened. And, at one moment, it really did feel sweet. He found that he was smiling as he went, and walking almost as if he was floating. But at another moment it felt bitter, like a hot coal that was setting his teeth on edge and his body on fire.

At the venue, he nodded at several acquaintances,

shook hands with a few. The room was almost full. There were black men and white men and perhaps a couple of women. One white woman was sat on a seat at the front with twin babies, one of the infants crying quietly. Occasionally, Mr Wilkins smiled at them and once went over to kiss the infants' heads. At the back of the hall, Matthew noticed a couple of fine gentlemen and a lady.

The speech began; it was less controversial than some of Wilkins's, focusing not on the overthrow of all authority but on his family's experience of slavery in Antigua, and the horrors of the trade. Matthew soon found himself, as usual, completely absorbed. The words began to take hold of him, lift him up, send him soaring and dipping, again and again until, finally, he rose up to stand on some beautiful green plain atop a mountain, looking at the bloodied bodies below, who would be washed away by the great waves to be cleansed and born anew. The speech ended, with the audience clapping and weeping.

Now Matthew must hand over the jewel, and so he rose to approach Wilkins. He had not done so before. But Wilkins was surrounded by several admirers, then his wife and the infants. What should he do? He had hoped for a quiet moment alone with the man to explain his case and hand over the stone. He could not do so in that company. They would think him a mad man, perhaps call one of the Runners. He felt himself sweating, beginning to panic. Standing frozen at the end of an aisle of chairs, he turned round, and noticed again the three members of the Quality, as his fellow servants called them. One of the gentlemen and the lady were turning towards the door. The other gentleman was about to follow when he noticed Matthew staring at him. This gentleman was a negro, like himself, only darker. He had never seen a black man dripping in satins and velvets. He could not quite believe the sight. But his eyes did not deceive him.

He did not have long to calculate and weigh the matter; he was so desperate to get rid of the diamond. He saw this black man in his finery and thought not that he was some spoilt potentate who must oppress his people, but a formidable, impressive personage in some way connected to the great struggle for justice. He must be an important ally of James Wilkins. He caught the man's eye, who looked at him as if he was a curiosity. Matthew quickly looked around, saw that they were unobserved, and said, 'Please give this to Mr Wilkins, for the great fight.' He pressed the stone into his hand and rushed away.

The usual disdainful expression on the gentleman's face was replaced for a moment by one of complete astonishment. But he quickly recovered himself, pocketed the stone, and sauntered outside to join his friends. The gentleman and the Lord and Lady Chester had gone to the Soho meeting house that evening by way of entertainment. They loved to compassionate with, and gape at, the poor and the mad, and had gone regularly to the Foundling and to Bedlam, which had then become a little dull. Lady Chester said that she had heard of a great negro revolutionary, whose speeches were finer than those of Mr Fox, and that it might be amusing for them to try that. They had been delighted at the idea, and had decided to call in to the meeting hall that evening before going on to a card party. They were a little disappointed not to hear the revolutionary talk, but were impressed, moved and roused nonetheless. Lord Chester said afterwards that it was better than the theatre, and if his blood was not as blue as a sapphire he might have turned rebel himself, and put the good king's head to the guillotine.

In the months that followed, Matthew's heart would sometimes ache in a yearning for the stone, and he would unconsciously grip and un-grip his right fist, a physical tic he became known for though he was unaware of it himself. At the same time, and although the thing had not gone quite as he had planned, he felt relieved that he had done what needed to be done. He would sometimes wonder about the man to whom he had given the stone, but he did not doubt that he was somebody important, connected to Wilkins. He heard that the latter had been committed to gaol, for the third time, for blasphemy and sedition. But he trusted that the jewel had got to where it should have gone, and that Wilkins would do right by it. He discovered Wilkins's address and wrote a short letter to him, confirming what he had done, which he delivered himself. He now wanted to forget the whole business, and to relish his life even more than he had done before. He was free, he was employed, and he was discovering, with great joy, that Charlotte was growing fond of him. He felt a little sorry about the Countess, who was kind, and who trusted him; but, he reasoned, she who had so much did not need that extra toy; she would be happy without it. He did not know if, given his time again, he would do the same thing, but what was done was done.

The power of Wilkins's oratory started to fade, and Matthew reverted to his essentially conservative and law-abiding consciousness. However, one thing had changed permanently within him. Before, he had tolerated insults and taunts about his colour and race, and had bowed his head, only wanting to stay clear of trouble. Now, he matched insult with insult, sometimes fist with fist, unless he thought that he would bring Charlotte into harm. His head was high and his heart proud: he would never be a spooney again.

Chapter 26

In July, Winchester was warm with the influx of visitors pertaining to the Western Assize circuit, which was sitting in the city from Tuesday, the 17th of July. Visitors arriving for the summer social calendar or on private business complained about the scarcity of beds, which were all taken up by gentlemen of the law and others with business at the sessions.

Mary's case came on that Thursday. The court was crowded as soon as the doors opened, in the expectation of her appearance; she had achieved a certain notoriety since her incarceration. She was called in the mid-afternoon, which was slightly unfortunate timing, as members of the jury, the public and even the judge himself, had all taken their more than sufficient share of refreshment at nearby inns, taverns and alehouses. The lavender scattered in the court did little to mask the foul odours of sweat and alcohol.

Mary came into the Great Hall, walking uncertainly and clutching a small bottle of smelling salts, which had been given to her by one of the charitable fine ladies of Winchester. She was escorted by George Redditch, who had attempted to scrub up and straighten up in honour of the day, and was looking rather proud of himself. Those present who had known Mary were shocked by her changed appearance. She had been in gaol not quite two weeks yet already she was haggard; her curves had disappeared so that she looked all angles in the simple green gown she had once worn for church, which hung from now prominent shoulder blades. Her face, however, though it had lost its pretty plumpness and bloom, had taken on a different kind of beauty; it was white, her eyes larger and nose more aquiline, so that she looked like some kind of suffering saint. Even her detractors paused for thought, before deciding that her look was bold and sullen, and with even a trace of witchery in it.

She stood in the dock, seeming barely to notice where she was, apart from a few moments when she stared at the reputed round table of King Arthur, decorated with his full-length portrait and the names of his twenty-four knights, which was suspended over the judge's seat. The Hall, where the court was held, was the former chapel of the Castle of Winchester, and the only thing remaining of that fortress. Margaret Campbell and Freddy were there, primarily to look after poor Joe Carter, who would be called to give evidence. Anne Millbrook was at home taking care of Mary's sons. John and Michael had discovered that their mother's trial was taking place on that day. They had wanted to attend and so to see her and show their love, but Anne, with Gabriel's help, had managed to persuade them that it was not in their mother's interests, since it would only upset her greatly.

The presiding judge, Lord Stanley, was both a deeply sentimental man and a hanging judge who did not hold with what he saw as the increased leniency shown in these sorts of cases in recent years. He thought Mary a thoroughly bold and wicked woman and would be glad to get her disposed of as soon as possible. However, he was also a lover of his profession and respected the law as much as he mostly disrespected the defendants, witnesses and members of the jury who came before him. Due process must be gone through. He sat, very comfortable in his seat, his tiny features in the centre of a round face sporting several chins, making him look like the man in the moon.

He now addressed Mary. 'Mary Harris, you are indicted for not having the fear of God before your eyes, but being moved by the instigation of the devil, on the Tuesday, the 3rd of July in the year of Our Lord 1804, on a certain female child, then lately born of your body, feloniously, unlawfully, and with malice aforethought, did make an assault, and that you, on the said certain female child, with both your hands, did wrap the child in your shawl, place it into the stream and hold it there for so long that it died, so that you, Mary Harris, did kill and murder the said child, against the statute and against his Majesty's peace. How do you plead?'

Mary looked at him, bewildered.

'How do you plead, Mary Harris?'

'Not guilty,' she said quietly.

The twelve jury members were sworn in, and the Counsel for the Crown, a Mr Alexander Aitken, began the examination.

'Prisoner, I must inform you that you are at liberty to ask any witness what questions you think fit, after the examination is gone through by the Crown.'

Mary said nothing. Mr Aitken, a tall man with a prominent chin and darting eyes, disguised a sigh. These sessions had been a disappointment so far. Apart from a short, spirited exchange with a sheep stealer, he had been given no opportunity to spar with anyone. There seemed little point in his presence.

The first witness for the prosecution, Mrs Alice Denton, was sworn in. She was a short, wide woman, with pretty hazel eyes, and was trussed up, today, in her finest stiff linen, her chin tilted upwards and her small mouth firm.

'Mrs Denton,' said Mr Aitken, 'please tell the court in your own words what happened on this 3rd of July last in relation to our proceedings here today against the accused, Mary Harris.'

'Well,' said Mrs Denton, 'I was in the farmhouse kitchen in the middle of making bread with my daughter, Eliza, and my niece, Matilda, when there was a knock at the kitchen door; it was Joseph Carter with one of our labourers, Thomas Worsley, stood behind him, and Joseph was carrying a wet bundle, and he put out his arms and gave it to me, not saying a word, and I took it, for I was quite shocked and could do nothing else.' Alice spewed this sentence forth very fast, in her eagerness to share what she knew.

'Mrs Denton,' interrupted the judge, 'if you could try and speak a little more slowly, that would be a great help to the court.' He nodded at her encouragingly. He had a fondness for good clean farmers' wives with well-run kitchens, especially when making bread. The image signified to him all that was right with the old country, and the old ways.

'Yes, your honour; sorry, your honour.' Mrs Denton smiled and took a breath. 'Well, I took the bundle, and stared at it, and could not believe my eyes; it was a poor, dead child. Then Thomas told me that Joe had found it in the stream just near the farm, and that he had seen Mary Harris under a tree putting it in the water.'

'Did Joseph also tell you this himself?' asked Mr Aitken.

'Oh, yes. We put the bundle on a kitchen chair, for I could not bear to put it on the table. Then I gave Joe another chair, and Matilda brought him a tin of small beer, and Thomas stood behind him, patting his shoulder. And I said to him, "Joe, is this true?" and he said "yes, ma'am", and that he'd seen Mary Harris sitting under the willow tree, and that he heard the cries of an infant. Then he saw her put a bundle in the water, and hold it down for a long time; then she let it float away. And he picked the child up further down the stream and didn't know what to do. He was coming to me in any case, on an errand, and hoped I would know what was best.'

'And then what did you do?'

'I asked Thomas to move the bundle into the cellar, where it is cool and dry, for I could not stand the sight of it in our good, warm kitchen, and it still gives me the horrors to think of it there, and in our cellar. I don't think I'll forget that sight for as long as I live.' Alice sniffed.

'You are doing very well, Mrs Denton,' said Lord Stanley. 'Take your time, and then do continue.'

'Thank you, your honour. And then I asked Eliza to get my husband in from the cattle sheds, so that we might decide on the right course of action. She found him and we all sat and had a good talk about it, and thought that we should call the surgeon and the constable. Then the next thing, another knock at the door, and it was John Harris, Mary's elder son, saying that his mother had been found under the willow tree, having been taken ill and wandered off, and could he have some help from the farm to transport her home. We weren't quite sure what to do then, sir – beg your pardon, your honour - but I am a Christian woman and thought it right to send a cart and a blanket, and Peter, my husband, agreed with me. So we sent Thomas, and Arthur Ridge, another one of our farm hands, out to Mary, who was waiting with Samuel Cole. Then my husband said that he himself would go off to the surgeon in Winchester, and explain everything to him, and send him to Mary back at her homestead, and ask him what we should do with that poor infant in our cellar, and then let the law take matters forward from there.'

'Thank you, Mrs Denton,' said Mr Aitken. 'Now, there are two points upon which we must be absolutely clear in this case, for a woman's life may depend upon them. We will be calling Joseph Carter himself as a witness. But you must also tell the court, are you absolutely sure that Joseph said he heard an infant's cries?'

'Oh, yes, sir, for I pressed him on the matter, and he stuck by what he said. He's an honest boy, sir, and I don't see why he would lie about this.'

'Thank you. That is the first point, and we have established that the infant was alive when it was born. The second point is to establish without doubt what was the cause of the child's death. You say that Joseph told you that he saw the accused, Mary Harris, hold the child under water for a long time? What length of time, exactly, do you mean to suggest by "a long time"? A minute, several minutes, longer?'

'I could not say exactly. Joe said about five minutes, I believe, but will be able to answer best for himself on that. I only know that the poor mite was dead when it got to us, so it must have been held under the water for a good while.'

'How long have you known the accused?'

'Five years.'

'And what sort of woman would you say that Mary Harris is?'

'She is a woman as kept herself to herself, as they say. I found her to be a little haughty, independent and secretive.'

'Secretive? What makes you say that?'

'Well, sir, for a start, she said that she was a widow, but would never tell us anything of her dead husband. I'm not one to pry into other people's affairs, but as a Christian woman I only wanted to help, her being a widow and all, and she rejected all my kind advances and told me to mind my own business. And I have a cousin in Oxford, you know, who knew Mary's mother – now sadly passed – who never mentioned a husband in regard to her daughter. It wouldn't surprise me if those poor sons of hers were bastard born. Well, well, she does have a certain way with the gentlemen, which I found a little uncomfortable to notice, especially with my daughter and niece nearby; I don't like them to witness anything unchaste; they are at such a delicate age.'

'We are now veering off the point of this case,' interposed the judge, 'with the good woman's conjectures. Nevertheless, I would ask that the jury take note of a probable further indication of the accused's licentious character. Incontinence in women, as we know, is the most heinous of sins. The health of our society rests on the purity of our women, and once that is gone, the very foundations of our civilization will crumble.'

He looked around the court, his watery eyes resting a moment longer on the females present. He turned to Mr Aitken. 'You may continue. And let us get to the nub of the matter.'

'Thank you, my Lord. The purpose of my previous questioning was to establish how well Mrs Denton knew the accused, and whether she thinks her capable of murdering her own child. Mrs Denton, do you think Mary Harris capable of slaughtering a child to which she has given birth?'

Alice Denton paused, looking a little unsure for the first time. 'It's difficult to imagine any good, decent woman doing such a wicked thing, but I do know that once a woman falls, she is liable to sink so much into vice and bad ways that she becomes capable of anything. And then the evidence was there before our eyes, however much we might not want to believe it. So I say yes, I do.'

'Thank you, Mrs Denton. I have nothing further. You may step down.'

Alice stepped down, still firm and now, additionally, quite pleased with and proud of herself. Poor Joe Carter was called and sworn in, and he stood there, dressed in a borrowed suit of clothes that was too big for him, his face pale, his dark hair sticking up, shaking as if himself were on trial for murder.

Mr Aitken said to him, 'How old are you, Joseph Carter?'

'Eight years old, sir.'

'And do you know the nature of an oath, and what

will be the consequence if you swear falsely, that is do tell a lie?'

'Yes, sir, I shall go to the naughty man.'

'Good boy. Now, Joseph, can you tell the court in your own words what happened on the day of the 3rd of July last?'

Joe's lips moved but he could not get anything out. He looked around him, then tried again, to no avail.

'It is a very hard thing for you to do, Joseph,' said Mr Aitken, who felt most sorry for the boy. 'It might be easier for you if you can corroborate – that is, agree with, or indeed, disagree with – what Mrs Alice Denton has told the court. Did the events happen on that day as Mrs Denton has told us they did?'

Joe nodded, and managed to croak out, 'Yes, sir.'

'Now, Joseph, this is very important. Will you take it upon yourself to swear that you heard the cries of a child?'

'Yes, I did.'

'And you are sure that they were most definitely the cries of a new-born child and not, for instance, those of a woman, such as Mary Harris herself?'

The judge frowned at Mr Aitken, and Joe hesitated. He was sure that he knew what were the cries of children; he was the eldest of eight, after all, and had heard them often enough. But then it had not crossed his mind that the sounds could have come from something else, or even from Mary herself. Could they have done? He now doubted himself. His mind was muddled, and he was terrified of saying the wrong thing. Still, what else was there to do but agree with the gentleman, and with Mrs Denton, who was so very firm about everything? 'Yes, sir,' he said very quietly, and began to cry.

'You are doing very well, Joe, and we will not be troubling you for much longer. Now, you must tell the court exactly what occurred after you heard the infant's cry. What did Mary do with the bundle?'

'The water,' stuttered Joe. 'She put it into the water.'

'So, Mary put the infant, wrapped up in her shawl, in the water. Then what happened? Did she hold the child down under the water, as you told Mrs Denton she did?'

Joe put his head down and cried a little more.

'Joseph, you must find the courage to tell the absolute truth on this matter before the Court and before your God. Did the accused woman, Mary Harris, hold her infant down in the water?'

Joe nodded, then looked up. 'Yes, sir.'

'And can you tell us for how long she did so?'

'I cannot be sure.'

'Perhaps it was a few minutes? Or five minutes?'

'I don't know.' Joe sobbed. 'Yes, perhaps five minutes.'

'And then she released the infant and let it float on the water?'

'Yes, sir.'

'Thank you, Joseph. You have done very well. I have no more questions.' Joe was led away, crying, to be received by Margaret, who was ready with a large handkerchief and a bag of cakes.

The judge looked after the boy, shaking his head at the wickedness of the world, a single tear rolling down his fat cheek.

The other witnesses were called and quickly dismissed. Mr Peter Denton and the two farm labourers corroborated Mrs Denton's account. The surgeon who had waited on Mary confirmed that she had lately been delivered of a child. A friend of Alice Denton, a midwife, who had been given sight of the infant girl's corpse, gave her opinion that the child had been born alive, in a perfect state, and had perished from drowning. She also stated that it was impossible that Mary could have been ignorant as to the coming birth of her child, given that she had twice birthed sons. It was also noted that Mary had seemed to make no preparations – no fresh linen or any other items could be found in the cottage - to show that she had intended to care for a child, which was seen as further proof that she intended to destroy it.

The Reverend Jonathan Millbrook had been due to speak for Mary's character, but was prevented from appearing in court due to a severe illness of the stomach, and so had been forced to instead send a written statement, which was read out to the court. It stated that Mary Harris had come to the Millbrooks with a very good reference from a former employer in Oxford, that following the death of her husband she had wanted to move away, and that as she had a friend in Winchester – now deceased – that seemed a good place to try for a position. Mary had been with the Millbrook household for five years and had proven a most diligent and honest housekeeper. She did not appear to mix with many people and had certainly entertained no gentlemen as far as they knew. They had nothing to say against her character.

Mary looked up, briefly, when this statement was read, and seemed to concentrate on the words. She looked towards the entrance to the court, as if expecting to see someone come in, then put her head back down.

Samuel Cole was therefore the only character witness present.

'I am Samuel Cole, a widower, from Romsey, Hampshire, and I live in the second cottage on the rectory estate, where I work in a general capacity in the grounds and house for the Reverend and Mrs Millbrook. I have known Mary Harris these five years. She is a widow, with two fine boys, and I believe her to be a good and an honest woman.'

'Will you tell us what happened on the day in question from the time you realised that Mary Harris was missing?' said Mr Aitken.

Samuel did so in a slow, steady voice.

'Did you ever know her to consort with any gentlemen?' asked Mr Aitken.

'No, sir, I did not.'

'But you knew her to have several admirers?'

'Yes, but only in the sense that some called her a very fine woman, which anybody is free to observe. I never saw her flirt with anyone.'

'But there must have been someone?' interposed the judge. 'Although her name be Mary, she was not touched by the divine intervention, one assumes?'

Lord Stanley gave a wry smile, very pleased with his little joke. He was enjoying himself. It was the last case of the day, and his favourite kind, a woman accused of child murder. No subject more touched his soul, or gave him a greater thrill of horror, and he believed that he was doing the business of the Lord in smiting those who crushed the poor, unprotected infants of this world. The court laughed obligingly, and the judge looked Samuel in the eye.

'If you perhaps mean to suggest myself, your honour,' said Sam, 'as the father of the child, I must tell you that that is not the case. I was very fond of Mary.' He looked over at her bowed head and smiled. 'And I freely confess to the world that I would have made an honest woman of her, and at any time, if she would only have taken me. I would never have let this happen.' Mary looked up for a very brief moment and caught his eye.

'I see,' said the judge, 'well, then, tis a great pity that she were not wiser. And did you not notice that she was with child by someone? You saw her every day, did you not?'

'Yes, your honour, but I didn't notice. It seems very foolish, now, I know. I saw that she grew a little bigger, and sometimes she didn't look well, so I began to think she might have been swollen with illness, perhaps a case of the dropsy. The most obvious cause didn't even cross my mind, for it would have seemed impossible, and so I wasn't looking for it, and I believe in any case that women have more of an eye for these things than do the men.'

The judge nodded. He approved of Samuel. 'Aye, that is true. Continue, Mr Aitken.'

'Mr Cole, did you realise that Mary had birthed a child when you found her near the Denton farm?' Mr Aitken asked.

'No, sir, I'm afraid that I didn't; not even then. I thought that it was a severe illness, and I was very worried. I realise now that her fever and her disordered appearance were the signs of the birth of a child having taken place. She was so weak and confused in mind, I believe, that she did not know what she did, and was, perhaps, trying to wash the infant in the water. She could never kill anything deliberately.'

'You think that she was insane?'

Samuel hesitated. 'I don't know exactly, but I do believe that her mind was not right.'

'But she had not shown signs of mental instability ere that day?'

'No, sir, none at all.'

'I have nothing further.'

Mr Aitken had noticed a look from the judge that suggested it was time for the trial to be wound up. Samuel felt that he had let Mary down. There was so much he had wanted to say in her defence, but had not been given the opportunity, and then he was not sure if it would have done her any good, for it was all his own emotion and nothing as to the facts of the poor child's death. Mrs Millbrook had told him that she had heard cases of something called milk fever, which was a form of insanity following the birth of a child, and he wondered if he could suggest this. But then it seemed that this diagnosis needed clear and prolonged evidence to be proved. Even if Mary had agreed to having a counsel, the time between the baby's birth and death was too short to allow for such a defence. It was all too much for Sam. He still could not fathom how Mary had been got with child in the first place, never mind that she had birthed one and murdered it.

'Mary Harris,' said Mr Aitken, 'the evidence against you is now closed; this is therefore the time for you to make your defence if you wish to do so.'

Mary looked up, her face still distracted, and said nothing. Mr Aitken shrugged, and wondered how soon he could get back to London on the morrow.

The judge addressed the jury and summed up the case, directing them towards the verdict already given by the coroner, but noting, as he was legally bound to do, that they should not convict the accused of child murder if they had any cause to doubt, since the penalty was death; and there was still an opportunity to convict on a lesser charge of new-born child concealment, which incurred a sentence of incarceration.

The jurors huddled up to deliberate in not very well disguised whispers. Freddy looked at the beautiful Mary, who was brought so low, and her heart was full of anger at whoever – probably the captain - was responsible for this. For whatever the verdict, Mary's life was as good as over. Margaret closed her eyes and prayed for the sinner. She prayed harder for Mary than she had prayed for anyone before, since she felt that a woman who had killed her own child must be much farther out of reach of God's mercy, and therefore would be greater in need of prayer. Samuel prayed too, simply, fervently, but he did not hold out much hope.

After only five minutes, the jury reassembled themselves in their former position and looked at the judge.

'How do you find the defendant?' asked Lord Stanley. 'Guilty, or not guilty?'

'Guilty,' said the jury spokesman. There had been no doubt. The jury believed that the evidence was clear, and that silence could only be the refuge of the guilty; Mary refusing to say not one word on the matter since it happened showed that she had no defence to give.

On the pronouncement of the verdict, Mary started, for just a moment, looked at the door of the hall again, then back to the round table above the head of the judge, and stared at the image of King Arthur, as if expecting it to come alive and to jump down and rescue her. Then she looked at the judge, her face impassive.

Lord Stanley, pleased, put on his black cap, and now looked at Mary as an object of his pity.

'The crime of child murder is a particularly heinous one,' he said. 'You stand before the court, and before your God, convicted of having violated the most sacred ties of nature, by putting to death a child, the offspring of your own body, and the fruit of your own criminal passions.' Lord Stanley felt his tears coming, as he frequently did at this point, and most especially when he had imbibed a little too much claret.

'Who will care about the little children if we do not?' he asked, looking round the court, as if imploring them. He thought about the divine service at Winchester cathedral, attended, as was customary, by himself and his fellow circuit judge, before the sessions opened, and he felt as if he himself were preaching to the congregants.

'Day after day,' he continued, 'we turn a blind eye to their plight, and think it as nothing. We turn away from our religion, and our women grow abandoned, becoming as savages in their guilty lusts.'

He turned back to Mary. 'You were not an innocent maid, poisoned by a flattering tongue and seduced from the path of virtue, but an experienced woman, and one who knowingly took part in a criminal intercourse with a man whom you refuse to name. If the result of your vicious indulgence had lived, you might have lost your place, and been forced to live in poverty as well as shame. You can claim no benefit of linen, having made no preparations to rear the live offspring of your depraved appetites. You can claim no want of experience in the matter of childbirth, such as sometimes results in sad accidents, having born two healthy sons. You fully intended to rid yourself of the child. Unhappily for you, but happily for the justice of this country and of your God, you were witnessed committing the vile and heartless murder of your bastard child. Had you escaped, many other girls, thoughtless and light, or women, bold and wanton as yourself, would have been encouraged by that escape to commit your crime with hope of impunity. Let us hope that they will be saved by the merciful terror of your example.

'Mary Harris. You have refused to engage with this court, and have offered no explanation or defence for your crime. Instead, you have remained sullen, bold and, it appears, unrepentant. The law allows you but a very short interval. Let me earnestly exhort you to confess your great sin before it is too late, and to implore, through the merits of your Redeemer, the mercy of that God whom you have offended. You go into eternity, and for your soul's sake, do what you can, that that eternity may be an eternity of bliss instead of misery.' The judge craned his neck to stare at Mary, and his tears fell.

'I have only now to pronounce the painful sentence of the law which I am bound to do, and I accordingly judge and order that you shall be taken to the place from whence you came, and on the day after tomorrow, you will be taken from thither to the place of execution where you will be hanged by the neck until you are dead, and afterwards your body will be delivered to the surgeons for dissection.' The judge sniffed. 'Do you have anything to say as to why sentence of death should not be passed upon you?'

Mary was silent.

'Then the Lord have mercy upon your soul.' Lord Stanley pulled a dirty handkerchief from his pocket and blew his nose. 'Court dismissed.'

The constable escorted Mary back to gaol, where, in accordance with the law, she was to be held in the condemned cell, to be sustained on bread and water only, until the time of her hanging. There were jeers as she went, and cries of 'whore', 'murderer' and 'witch', but some felt sick with compassion for her, and perhaps thought about their own experiences, or those of somebody they knew and loved, who had begotten and rid themselves of their own unwanted bastards, and got away with it.

Chapter 27

The next afternoon, when the western assize circuit was packing up for its onward leg to Salisbury, James Wilkins was sat in one of the finest inns in Winchester, waiting to meet Mr Augustus Grey. He had travelled from London especially for the purpose.

A few days after he had given his talk at the Soho meeting house back in early June, Mr Wilkins had been arrested on another charge of sedition and blasphemy, and had languished in Newgate gaol for a month until a wealthy well-wisher paid for his bail, and then the charges against him were dropped. During his time in prison, James instructed his wife, Hannah, to keep back most of his correspondence; it was thought too dangerous to take it to him in his confinement, or even for Hannah to open it at home, since this might implicate her in any illegal doings. Wilkins did his best to protect his long-suffering wife from the consequences of his actions; but he could not change who he was, and nor did his wife want him to do so. So it was that a letter from Matthew Lane lay unopened in a box in the Wilkins lodgings near Cheapside, London, until a few weeks ago, when James was released.

Wilkins was a voracious writer and receiver of letters, and corresponded with men and women across the country, the continent and the United States on any number of subjects personal and political, but he confessed to his wife that this short letter from Mr Lane was the most curious he had ever received. Lane, in very simple language, said that he had heard Mr Wilkins speak on several occasions, and had been most moved and stirred by the experience. A strange chance had brought the famous jewel, the Celestial Light, in his path, and he had taken it on a whim, believing that Mr Wilkins, of all people on the earth, could put this bauble, so useless in itself, to the best use for mankind. He had attended Mr Wilkins's talk at the Soho meeting house, hoping to pass the stone to him. However, Mr Wilkins had constantly been in company, and Mr Lane, losing his chance and now in a state of terror about the jewel, had given it to a very handsomely dressed negro gentleman, who was present at the lecture with some other fine folk. He would be grateful if they would never mention his name in relation to the stone, since he was a humble, cowardly fellow and only wanted to return to his everyday life, and be content with his lot.

Mr Wilkins remembered with distaste a man fitting

Lane's description in attendance that evening with some aristocratic friends, as if Wilkins's life work were a sideshow at a fair. Further enquiry soon produced the name of Augustus Grey, and reinforced the instant dislike Wilkins had felt, the general opinion being that Grey was just another rakish fop, a parasite feeding on the fat of the land which the poor killed themselves toiling to produce. He had written to, and called upon, this parasite to no avail, until finally, to his great surprise and satisfaction, Grey had agreed to meet him, but only if he was willing to travel to Hampshire, where Grey would be residing with the Lord Rodney.

Augustus felt no obligation, or need, to meet Wilkins. The man would be hanged sooner or later, he thought. Still, after consideration, he decided that it might be an amusing encounter for him. He was taken into Winchester by the Lord Rodney's phaeton, where he idled away a pleasant hour purchasing some little trinkets, then hired a chair to take him to the meeting place, Robert Wagstaff's inn on the High Street. This was barely a few feet away, but he did love to be served by the toil and sweat of others, especially on such a hot day as this one. The chair stopped outside the inn and various lackeys ran to his aid, dazzled by the splendour of his dress. He was a man who was stared at wherever he went, stared at as a black man, stared at as a luxuriously dressed, apparently very rich man, but, above all, stared at as the combination of these two things. He had learned to deal with this state of affairs by enjoying the attention, and raising his head a little higher, and arranging his face into the utmost expression of disdain for everything about him.

He was shown inside, where he was espied by Wilkins, who was sat near the bar, and they were moved to a splendid little side-room, where it was cool and private. He ordered a pint of Rhenish wine for himself, and Mr Wilkins requested some of the inn's own ale.

'I thank you for agreeing to see me, sir,' said James, looking anything but grateful, and eyeing the pastel coloured, silk form of Augustus, as if he was some kind of exotic animal just brought ashore from a long sea voyage. The man also seemed to have a strange glow on him, as if he had recently imbibed some magical elixir of youth.

'Tis nothing,' said Augustus. 'Your letter was so wery mysterious and curious that, I confess, I was quite intwigued to discover your meaning.'

Augustus eyed James in return, thinking him quite a well-formed fellow, with his tall frame and high cheekbones, even though he did look like a scarecrow.

'Was it really so mysterious to you, sir?' asked James. 'A most curious and remarkable event, certainly, but I believe that you know exactly to what I was referring.'

'Do oo, indeed, oo impertinent wascal.'

The bowing and scraping waiter appeared with the drinks, smirked a great deal, then backed out of the room as if he had been serving royalty.

Wilkins took a sip of his ale.

'Mr Grey,' he said, 'I mean no impertinence. I had imagined that you agreed to see me because you understood the meaning in my letter, or I do not comprehend why you would squander your time in such a meeting. I have travelled from London in good faith, and ask only that you are candid with me in return.'

Augustus looked at his glass of wine, sniffed it, sipped it, then took several mouthfuls.

'And what if I did understand the meaning?' he asked.

'Well then, I would come right out and ask you the question, do you have the object, sir, and, if so be the case, what do you plan to do with it?'

Augustus glanced around him, then moved his eyes to Wilkins's, and looked at him intently. 'Oo know that I am not able to answer that question.'

'I see. And I understand your meaning.' James took some more gulps of ale. 'Are you interested in the poor and oppressed of this world, Mr Grey?'

'No, I have not the slightest interest in them.'

'I suspected as much. You have no fellow feeling for men like you and me, enslaved and tortured on the other side of the world?'

'I have nothing in common with oo, oo wetch, and even less with any wetched slaves.'

'Do you look in the glass? I had thought you did so, and frequently, but perhaps I have been mistaken. Are you not a black man, sir? We have that in common, though you would deny it.'

'Upon my soul, Mr Wilkins, your impertinence is intolewable. Why should I deny it? It is pwetty clear for all to see. I am wery pwoud of who I am. A bweautiful black fellow, as I have been told many times, and I enjoy it.'

'Then why can you not find a little compassion inside yourself for the suffering of your fellow blacks? You have in your hands the power to help them.'

'What are they to me? It does not signify to me what colour the suffering is. It is all the same; it is repugnant to my feelings and I avoid it.'

'Are you really so unfeeling? Do you feel no obligation?'

'Obligation? No, I do not. Why should I? I do not like all this fashionable pweaching and mowality – it is wulgar. Just because our skin is alike oo think I should think like oo, and, indeed, that we should all think the same. I am a man, endowed with my own mind. Black or white; tis all the same to me, and I will do what suits me.'

'You don't even believe in the abolition?'

'I have no thoughts on the matter.'

'And no thoughts on the enslavement of your race?'

'As I have said, I do not hold with wace. There are only men and women. Oo are the one who twies to make men diffewent, I believe.'

'Not so, on the contrary; I have always known that a prince in gold thread is a fool whether he be black or white. I only care for the poor man and the oppressed man, who one day will cease to bow to princes. You are corrupted, Mr Grey. Tis riches that do it, I believe; they harden the heart.'

'And oo are the most widiculous canting fellow I have ever met. Oo will soon find your end on the gallows, sir, and there oo will have a fine opportunity to speechify, and entertain the swinish multitude with your twacts.' Augustus laughed, drank back his wine, and poured the rest of the bottle into his glass.

They were both quiet for some moments.

'Mr Wilkins,' continued Augustus, relaxing his austere pose and clarifying his speech a little. 'I do not know why I bestow explanations upon a low fellow like yourself. I should shoot you straight through the heart with my pistol. But I have found our talk quite invigorating. You are mistaken about my heart, at least, though it does not take a black or white hue; it is as red and tender as any other man's.'

'The Lady Ingram?'

Augustus smiled slightly. 'Perhaps.'

'I wish you well of it. Love improves a man.'

'There, I will agree with you.'

Wilkins smiled.

'You think I have not suffered?' asked Augustus. 'You think I been closeted in silks and satins all my life?'

'No, sir. I imagine that you suffered much, at one time. You are a former slave, are you not? How could it be otherwise? That is why I have tried to appeal to you. But you have shrugged off your suffering all too readily, it seems.'

'I have done what I have needed to do. A man must mind his own affairs, and let others mind theirs.'

'You will not change your mind about the stone?'

'I repeat that I do not know of what you speak.'

'Well, then, Mr Grey, it is time for us to bid each other good day.'

James finished his drink, got up, and grappled in his pocket for a coin.

'Do not insult me further, Mr Wilkins,' said Augustus.

'Thank you, sir.' He left the coins in his pocket, nodded, and was gone.

When Augustus got back to the great house, he retired to his chamber to prepare himself for the dinner hour. He pulled off his cravat, waistcoat and shirt, then slowly undid his stays. He had been wearing a corset for fifteen years; it had been quite usual for dandified men to do so, though was not so fashionable now. He had continued the practice because he had not been able to curb the high living that had made him a little corpulent, but remained vain about his figure. He breathed a sigh of relief, sat down on the great divan bed in his pantaloons, and fanned himself with the discarded cravat. Then he smiled and took a small white satin bag from his waistcoat pocket, untied the cord and tipped out its contents onto a rosewood card table next to the bed. Twenty perfect stones scattered across the wood. He stared at them and laughed.

It had not been such a difficult business to get them cut. One did not acquire vast gaming debts without rubbing shoulders with some exceeding disreputable fellows. And, unlike some of the ineffectual aristocrats who got themselves into similar straits, he knew how to handle himself, how to bargain and to really fight, if necessary, with the additional advantage that his gawdy appearance and foppish manner made people underestimate him. He had been forced to repay a few dues that he would have rather fled from, but otherwise he was now set pretty fair for the next stage of his life.

He got up from the bed and looked at himself in a long glass hung between two tall windows overlooking the park. He picked up one of the stones with his right hand and rubbed it slowly from the top of his forehead, down his face, neck and upper torso to his naval, then back again and down his arms to his hands, dwelling on each long finger. He felt himself glowing, growing younger. Cutting the stone had not cut away its powers; on the contrary, perhaps it had increased them. He put the stone on the curve of his belly, and thought he could see it shrinking a little – it would not be long before he could throw away the stays.

He stared and stared at himself in the glass, intoxicated, bewitched; he had never seen so handsome a creature. He was a demigod: look how those rays of sunshine came through the window at that moment to worship him. He bowed at himself in the glass, and began to perform a minuet, that most elegant and difficult of dances of which he was perfect master. He put out his right arm and touched the reflection of his hand in the mirror, as if taking a partner's hand, then moved around the room with exquisite grace and control, arriving back at the mirror and bowing again.

Then he laughed at his own absurdity, and thought of how he would narrate his current thoughts and feelings to his love when they met. She was as fond of follies, nonsense and absurdities as himself – for what else was there in this world? - and they would laugh together, as they often did.

He rang the bell to call a servant to help him to dress for dinner.

Chapter 28

That same day, the day before hanging day, Mary attended the service for condemned prisoners in the gaol chapel. The Gaol's Ordinary, or Chaplain, Mr Cotton, was a good enough fellow, but having been at his profession for many years, he had acquired a certain hardness and efficiency in the care of the prisoners' souls, which was not conducive to opening up Mary's heart. Mr Cotton sermonized generally in the manner of a schoolboy reciting his Latin grammar, saving his energies for his condemned sermons, when he exhorted, ranted and finally dispatched most of his hearers to the hell fires -– best place for them – where they would burn for all eternity. Unmoved and impassive, Mary returned to her condemned cell, a small, airless room with a tiny, high, grated window, containing a straw-in-sacking bed with a blanket, two deal chairs and a pewter chamber pot.

Later in the day, Frances Winkworth was let into

Mary's cell, carrying a parcel of clothes for her. He had not been able to attend her trial, and was struck by the rapid replacement of the bouncing, glossy Mary of old with this new, gaunt beauty.

'Mary, tis Frances Winkworth here, come to spend a little time with you.'

Mary, who was sat very still on a small, deal chair, looked up at him and smiled. 'You are come, then; I knew you would.'

'I have been only waiting for you to let me come, Mary. You should not be bearing this grief alone.'

'You're right. I'm a stubborn, foolish woman at times, as you know. You will help me, won't you? And the Reverend Millbrook? He's an important man, and has influence, doesn't he? For it has all been some terrible mistake, and I realise that by refusing to see people I haven't given anybody the chance to put that right.'

Mary spoke calmly and brightly, and finished her little speech with a smile. The curate sat down on the second chair, took Mary's right hand with both of his and looked at her tenderly with his pale, woebegone face and large eyes.

'Mary; I am here to help you, and to give you all the comfort I can in this time of trial and sorrow. I will not abandon you at the last, my dear.'

'I knew you could not.'

'But I must tell you that I cannot change what will come tomorrow. We have all tried; but it seems that there is nothing more to be done.'

'Nothing more to be done?' Mary now grew agitated, got up off her chair and paced a little.

'I thought you were all my family,' she continued, 'but it seems that I'm not even worthy enough to be one of you fine causes, for which the reverend travels up and down the country with no expense and energy spared, and for which you preach so very passionately in church.'

'Tis very hard, I know, Mary.'

'Hard?' Mary stopped still, bent forward and let out a loud, hoarse cry.

Frances got up, put a firm hand on Mary's left shoulder for a few moments, as if anchoring her to the time and place, then slowly put his arms around her while she cried.

The guard, Nathaniel Smith, alarmed at the noise, appeared.

'Is everything alright, sir?'

'Yes, Mr Smith,' said the curate. 'Mary is a little distressed, as is only to be expected.'

Mary stepped away from the curate and screamed at the guard. 'Let me out! I must go home.' She moved quickly towards him and tried to get past, but he stopped her easily, gripping her arms. He was a tall, large man with a shining bald head and a slightly squashed face; his appearance had helped him to secure his position at the gaol, though, in fact, he was a rather tender man.

'Sit down, now, Mary,' Nathaniel said softly, and pushed her gently back to her chair, where she continued to shake and sob, but with less vehemence.

'We will be well together now, Mr Smith. Thank you,' said Frances.

Nathaniel nodded, left the cell and locked the door. Mary's behaviour was perfectly natural; he usually found the strange states of calm in the condemned more unnerving. He felt very sorry for the woman. It was a bad case, but not an uncommon one, he knew. She had done a great wrong but the truth was that she had been unlucky in being discovered so easily.

Frances sat patiently, holding both Mary's hands in his own.

'Mary. You know that if I could save you, I would, and if I could take your place now, I would gladly do so.'

Mary looked into his eyes and nodded.

'As to poor Samuel…' Frances smiled kindly, and Mary nodded again.

After a few moments, Frances continued. 'I know you understand the great magnitude of your situation and of what is to come tomorrow. But if you open your heart to your maker and to me, be absolutely truthful and repent any wrongdoing with a truly penitent heart, the kingdom of heaven will be open to you.'

Mary was silent, looking down at her hands enclosed in Winkworth's.

'Do you believe in the Lord, Mary?'

Mary nodded.

'And of the better world to come?'

Mary remained silent for a few moments, then said, 'what better world can there be for me?'

'There is hope of a better world for any poor sinner who confesses their sins and asks God for forgiveness. Do you think you can tell me the absolute truth, Mary?'

'I will try.'

The curate squeezed her hands gently.

'Let us begin with that sad day when the infant girl was born. Was she born alive, Mary?'

Mary looked directly at the curate and nodded.

'There, Mary, you can rid yourself of this burden now. Please go on.'

'The baby was alive. It screamed very loud, just like its brothers before it. And I saw their faces in its face. I wrapped it in my shawl to keep it warm, and then wrapped it a little tighter, to stop the noise, for I was fearful of passers-by. It grew more peaceful, and didn't cry. Then I looked at the stream and remembered Moses and the bulrushes, and thought that it could sail away to a better life. I placed it on the water. It sank a little, then floated, and I watched it go.'

'Did you hold the child under the water, Mary?'

'I don't know. It seemed to sink for a short while.'

'Now, Mary, remember your vow to the tell me the absolute truth. Did you want the baby to die?'

'No. How could I? I don't know.'

'Did you deliberately kill the child?'

'I'm sure I don't know. No. I'm sorry. I wanted the child to be quiet and peaceful and happy.'

'By placing it in the cold water of a stream?'

'I wrapped it in the shawl to keep out the cold. I thought it would go to somewhere good.'

The curate did not press the matter further. He believed that she had killed the child, but unconsciously, in a sort of madness. She was not able to confess further, since she did not know what to confess. There was still a small chance that she was lying, of course, but he could not see a reason for it now that her end was so near at hand and she must face the great judgement to come.

'She has gone to somewhere good; you can be sure of that. Now, Mary, will you now see your other children? I can bring them to you.'

'But how will I bear it?' asked Mary. 'I really think my heart will burst to see them and then to say goodbye.'

'I know, Mary. But you do it for them, and for their hearts. I will be here to bear it with you, and God will give you strength.'

Frances stayed with Mary another hour or so. They held hands, and talked quietly together, saying things that they had never said before.

Frances went away, his heart partly eased, his pain only increased. His own burden was heavy; for a long time he had been examining his conscience almost every few hours, and offering his heart and soul to God as penance, but never feeling any better.

That night, over at the old manor house, Freddy could not sleep. Her mind was racing faster than it ever had since this whole business began. She needed to do something about the captain, but what? Had not her dear father warned her of danger? If Henry Lefroy really had killed one woman, surely he could kill another? And he must know that she was suspicious of him. She got up; perhaps a glass of milk would help her sleep. She pressed her small feet into her silk slippers, reached down to her workbox and took out the pistol, now loaded – thanks to the captain, she thought grimly – and quietly went down to the kitchen. She pushed open the door, and Flip, snuggled on his usual blanket near the stove, cocked an ear, wagged his tail and roused himself to come and meet her.

'Oh, my dear old Flip,' said Freddy, patting him and bending down to kiss his head. 'How could anything bad happen when we have you to protect us? Look at your old friend, Fredericka, stood here in her nightgown with her pistol. She is stark, raving mad, to be sure. Now go back to your bed, you silly old thing, and get your sleep.'

Flip continued to stand where he was, gently wagging his tail, and Freddy laughed at him, opened the door to the larder, and found half a jug of milk. She then took a glass from the dresser, filled it, and sat down. She yawned broadly, took a sip of her milk, then jumped slightly; was that a noise outside? Flip pricked up his ears, but there was silence. Perhaps it is my father, thought Freddy, come a different way; but she felt too uneasy; it could not be him. She thought of Mary, condemned to die on the morrow, and those poor boys of hers, about to lose their mother. She thought of Sarah, whose daughter had also now lost a mother, wandering far from home to find her lover, carrying her never-to-be-born child, to end up in a strange grave, then dug up and taken away to who knows where. She thought of Matthew Lane, and the strange way he had got and got rid of the Celestial Light. She thought of Affy, full with baby and with love and life; she thought of Lavinia, weighed down with love for one child and indifference to another. She thought of Lavinia's lover, Augustus Grey, and only now realised that he was likely the grand black personage who had received the stone.

Above all, she thought of the captain, whose handsome face was interweaved with all her other thoughts, so that he was at the heart of all, and somehow the cause of all. Her eyelids fluttered and blurred images of dancing children juggling diamonds flickered before her eyes.

There was a knock at the kitchen door. She jumped and dropped the glass. Flip, instead of raising his hackles and growling, simply wagged his tale feebly and started licking up the milk. She listened intently.

The knock came again. Surely no person with good intent could be knocking at this hour? But then, what if someone was ill or frightened? Anne, or perhaps Polly?

Her heart beating quickly, her hands shaking, Freddy picked up her pistol and walked slowly to the door. Raising the gun in front of her with her right hand, she gradually opened the door with her left.

'It is you,' she said. 'I knew it would be so, but I so did not want it to be.'

'Miss Swinglehurst? Goodness, what are you doing?

I am so sorry to be calling at this late hour but I have something very important to…'

Captain Henry Lefroy did not finish his sentence. Just as he was stepping into the kitchen, Freddy's shaking hand lost control of the pistol and it went off.

Freddy screamed and dropped the gun. She had shot the captain.

Chapter 29

At 8am on Saturday the 21st of July, crowds were already gathering in the centre of Winchester and over on gallows hill, which was about a mile away from the city centre. The day was already warm, and promised to be hot, a fine day for hanging, though inclement weather rarely put people off from attending the spectacle.

Mary dozed a little through the night. The passion of grief she had felt in her boys' presence had exhausted her, but she had consoled herself with the thought that they would soon be together again. She also felt a strange calmness, and her body, its secret suffering long ground into her bones, sinews and flesh, felt light and inconsequential. This was her special day, the day she had longed for since she had first laid eyes upon her love, and now it had come.

A patch of sun came through the small, grated window of her cell, and Nathaniel brought her a drink of chocolate, which she had requested, but she could take no food. As a condemned murderer she was supposed to be fed on bread and water only, but Nathaniel, in his pity for her, had even tried to tempt her with sweetmeats, to no avail.

She sipped the chocolate very slowly as she dressed herself from the parcel of clothing that the curate had brought for her. She was pleased with the freshly washed and pressed white linen shift, which she luxuriated in putting on, and added her stays and stockings. Then it was time for the cream-coloured, muslin gown, her pride and joy. It had been hidden amongst her belongings for ten long years, never worn in public, but once or twice put on in private, in the rare idle hour that her life had afforded. As she touched it, her mind wandered back to the early days in Oxford, when she had earned her living charring, nursing, making, mending and cooking for any number of bachelor students, bewildered by the absence of female relatives to do for them.

And then she had met him, as overwhelmed as the next man as to the great question of linen, and they had laughed together, and he had taken an interest in her as no man had done before, and really listened to the tale of her simple life, the death of her father and the sickness of her mother. One day he had asked her to share the simple dinner she had prepared for him – she still remembered that plate of roast fowl and boiled potatoes - and the sun had shone into the open window as warm as the colour of his hair, and they had kissed, and no other man had turned her head since that moment.

She gave a small smile of triumph as she fastened on the gown, knowing how well its colour became her and how ill it made her mistress look. The dress was now a little big, but what did that signify? Then she sat on one of the chairs and painstakingly laced up a beautiful pair of lilac boots. Now she smoothed the skirts of her gown and looked at her final item of dress, a fine, ivory-coloured cap trimmed with lace, which was lying at the end of the bed. She reached out to pick it up, place it on her lap, and stroke it as if it were a cat. Anne Millbrook, desperate to help – that silly, pathetic woman – had written to her several times begging her to let Anne do something for her. Finally, Mary had requested this cap, giving precise details of the sort she wanted, and Anne had happily agreed to purchase it for her.

Mary now pinned the cap onto her head, leaving her hair loose down her back. It was not a style for a respectable matron, to be sure, but she was but a maid again, and this was her wedding day, and her thick, chestnut hair had always been her crowning glory. How proud her mother would have been to see her. She used to brush Mary's hair with one hundred strokes before bedtime, then kiss her on the top of her head and say, 'what hearts you will break, my love, but take care that somebody does not break your own; I'm not sure tis fitting, or safe, for a girl in our station to possess such rare beauty'. Mary was ready, and sat on her chair touching the silver cross hanging around her neck, an old gift from her lover.

The cell door opened and Mr Winkworth, looking

pale and anxious, came into the room. He was stunned again by Mary's beauty as she sat peacefully in her bridal costume, looking like a fallen angel, a shaft of sunlight picking out copper tinges in her hair.

'Good morning, Mary,' he said, going over to her and taking her hand. 'How well you look this day, and how I honour your calm composure. But Mary, dear, you know that the man who is to perform the deed today will only have your clothing. Perhaps it would be better to wear something a little more humble and leave these fine things behind for your friends.'

'Good morning, Frances,' said Mary. 'If a woman cannot look well, and fine, on her wedding day, then I don't know when she can.'

The curate was quiet for a moment. 'Your wedding day, Mary?'

Mary smiled. 'Oh, do forgive me my little follies and foolishness, Frances. My mind is somewhat distracted and you must be so good as to indulge me a little today, if you will.'

Frances looked at Mary with compassion. He was relieved to see that, despite the finery she was wearing, she was clutching at her cross. He would not admonish, or try to reason with her. She had come to a full repentance the previous day, he was sure, and so what harm could this do? If it took her to her death with peace in her heart, perhaps it was a blessing from God himself.

'Will you say a prayer with me, Mary?'

'Oh, yes, Frances.'

Frances seated himself in the other chair opposite Mary, took her right hand, and read to her in his soft tones, his voice shaking a little at the magnitude of the occasion: 'Yea, though I walk through the valley of the shadow of death, I will fear no evil; For You are with me; Your rod and Your staff, they comfort me.'

Nathaniel then appeared, indicating that it was time. He started on sight of Mary in her finery and had to swallow repeatedly to keep back his tears; he must really put himself to another profession, he thought, growing, as he seemed to be, rather softened than hardened to it. He led Mary and the curate into an antechamber, where the Yeoman of the Halter approached Mary with his ropes. She stood patiently whilst he tied her hands in front of her, pulling her hair back obligingly so that he could more easily put the noose around her neck and wind the free rope round her body. She was then led outside to the courtyard and so to the carts in which sat the other condemned prisoners, similarly tied, and sat on their coffins.

Mary was to share a cart with one Isiah Mackay, who had been convicted of uttering, or forgery. He looked at Mary, nodded respectfully and smiled weakly. She smiled back, despite herself. Another cart contained the other three condemned prisoners. The first one of these, convicted of highway robbery, had managed to drink a good deal of liquor through the night and was now thoroughly drunk. He laughed a great deal and, on catching sight of Mary, shouted a lewd insult. The second occupier of that cart was a boy of not sixteen, convicted of arson, and he sat on his coffin, pale, quiet and terrified. The third man, convicted of horse theft, was a sailor, and still dressed in a ragged version of the costume of a tar. He had taken his death sentence very badly, and had raved so madly for several days that he had to be straitjacketed. On coming to himself he had got religion, and was now sat on his coffin shouting to the crowd that he was going to a better place, and exhorting them to mend their ways and to learn by his example. Whether this was a genuine conversion or something feigned in the vain hope that he would achieve a last-minute reprieve was not known.

Frances and Nathaniel helped Mary into the second cart, and onto her coffin. Nathaniel stepped back unwillingly, having an urge to lift Mary up and run away with her. Frances positioned himself next to Mary and took her hand. He nodded at her companion, and said 'God be with you, sir'. For the first time Mary seemed to be really gripped by fear, the coffin on which she was placed suggesting, as it was intended to do, her imminent death. She looked at the curate, who rubbed her hand and patted her shoulder. No, this could not, would not be a death, thought Mary. It was the opposite; it was a union with her love, the man to whom she had devoted her whole life, forsaking all others.

One of the turnkeys now opened the elaborate, Tuscan-style gate to the east of the gaol. The procession, led by the under-sheriff of the county and other city officials, and surrounded by constables and officers, armed with pikes, set off, and Mary's cart followed the first out of the gate. Its starting jolt nearly pushed her off the coffin, until Frances put out a hand to balance her. She closed her eyes for a moment, and began humming an old folk tune that her father used to play on the fiddle when she was a girl. Then she opened her eyes and pushed up her chin. This was her day, her special day. She would not be cowed by the baying crowds. She was a good woman. She had been loyal to one man the whole of her life, and had borne him two handsome sons, as any proper wife should. They were as good as married in the eyes of God, if not the law. But the day had come to put that right. This was her reward at long, long last. Everything that was confused and wrong about her life would fall away. He would forget his strange infatuation for those dark women. They would move far away from Hampshire, and away from that spoiled mulatta at the old manor house. She did not like the familiarity that woman shared with her lover. It might lead somewhere that she could not bear to think upon.

And, of course, she had got rid of that other one, Sarah. Always in a precarious position, and suspecting she had rivals, Mary had long been a jealous woman. In January that year, in a stronger fit of passion than usual, she had begged leave of her mistress and taken a few days' absence from her duties to follow her lover to London. She had been shocked and sickened to discover that her suspicions were right, and that he kept one of those negresses in a lodging house in London, a woman with an infant daughter, and another child on the way. No, it would not do.

When her lover had left Sarah, Mary had approached her, coming near, then stopping, clutching her stomach as if in pain. Sarah had stopped too, looking concerned, and offered to assist her. They got talking and Mary was invited into Sarah's lodgings to take some tea. It was so easy; Sarah seemed to be an innocent, credulous soul. Mary tried to hide her shock and sickness of heart as she sat in the place that her lover shared with this woman, and heard about their life together. Sarah and Mary seemed to be at about the same stage of pregnancy; their unborn infants must have been begot very close together. Mary was amazed to hear Sarah speak, so open, so free, so unashamed, when she, Mary, had made silence the work of her life. Keep mum, keep mum, Mary, had been her injunction to herself for so long that silence had become more than a habit with her; it was her very nature. And people had wondered why she had not spoken in court. How could she, when the truth was so long stopped up in her very being?

And then Sarah was so happy about her second pregnancy, so looking forward to the arrival of another child, when Mary, notwithstanding her own shame, had mostly been concerned about the burden another infant would place on her love. She had considered trying to rid herself of it, but had kept putting it off, not quite acknowledging to herself that she was trying to force his hand, to get him to take action, and settle things, once and for all. Sarah told Mary her lover's assumed name, and that she knew he had another life, perhaps other lives; she did not seem too troubled by this. She knew only that he lived in Hampshire, but she did not know exactly where – perhaps Mary had heard of him? Mary said she had not. When Mary quit Sarah, she gave her the rectory address, which Sarah committed to memory, not being able to read or write, and Mary told her to look her up should she ever be in that part of the world, and she would return her kindness. Mary did not know why she did this – perhaps, again, she was hoping to force something to happen at last.

The procession continued to move forward, and began to slowly ascend the Andover Road, the crowd, comprising men, women and children of all estates, shouting cries of approval or disapproval, as they saw fit, and throwing rotten fruit and vegetables. Some of them, reserving their finest insults for the baby-murdering whore, waited for the first cart to pass before opening their mouths. In the latter cart, the gaol chaplain blandly intoned prayers whilst thinking about his forthcoming dinner. In Mary's cart, the curate said his prayers very softly and sincerely, looking into the faces of Mary and Isiah. Mary remained stoical. She would be dignified; they could not harm her. It would not be long before her happiness was complete.

But now they reached the place of execution, and Mary's cart drew to a halt behind the first. It was time for the condemned to be placed in the final cart, from which they would be pulled to their deaths. The three men in the first cart were prepared by the hangman and a few strong men. They were placed in the new cart, their backs to the horses' tails. Then the free ends of their ropes were uncoiled from around them and the ends thrown up to a young man lying on top of the cross beams, who secured them, leaving very little slack. The drunken man continued to laugh and babble, the young man soiled himself, and the third man's proud declarations of conversion grew fainter and he began to struggle with his ropes.

Mary looked around. Where was the church, the flowers and well-wishers? She thought she saw Sarah in the crowd, waving at her and smiling. Sarah, who had arrived at her cottage, that fateful Tuesday, to Mary's horror and perhaps relief – the great moment had come, something would happen. The boys had been staying with Sam that night, which was an occasional adventure for them, and Sarah had arrived unseen from the lane at the back of the rectory, so that it was just the two of them. Sarah was in a panic-stricken state about the diamond. Apologetic about her sudden call on Mary, she was also voluble as ever and told Mary about the whole plot and its failure. Her lover had told her that if anything terrible happened with regard to their plot, she could get a message to him via the Chequers in Winchester. But it would take time to get to the friend who wrote her messages for her, and she was desperate to get to her lover and tell all.

Panicked, Sarah had set off for Winchester, she said, and on arrival asked at the inn if they knew the whereabouts of Josiah Clarke. They did not, and she was not well received. She next tried the silversmith, who, as luck would have it, turned out to be kindness itself. He had not heard of Josiah Clarke, but then Sarah had remembered Mary, and the direction she had given. It turned out that it was not that far away, and so she had determined to go to Mary, who had seemed such a good woman, and who might be able to help in some way, until she could find her lover.

Hiding her shock, Mary had welcomed, sympathised, consoled, and insisted that Sarah stay the night and on the morrow they could think what was to be done. Sarah, exhausted from her journey, her anxiety, her late stage of pregnancy and the heat, felt quite ill, and gratefully accepted the tonic that Mary pressed upon her, a mixture of wine, sugar, arsenic and some compound that Sam used in the garden. Before they went to bed, Mary made the settee comfortable, kissed Sarah on the forehead, and gave her more tonic. Through the night, Sarah's sickness worsened, and Mary nursed her convulsing, spewing, leaking body, and cleaned up the mess with tender care. At the same time, she gave her more and more, and stronger and stronger tonic, until she died the next morning. Before death, Sarah had clutched at her heart, so perhaps she had undergone some kind of heart attack, after all.

Then Mary had used all her strength to drag Sarah's

body outside and over to the front grounds of the rectory, where she positioned it on its front and with the arms outstretched. She did not flinch, and felt no fear about discovery. If someone saw her she would simply say that she had found the woman, dead, and was trying to rouse her. He would soon know – and what could he do? – it would serve him right.

But look, now, Sarah was holding something; it was an infant wrapped up in a shawl, and she laughed and held the bundle with both hands above her head. Mary began to scream, and scream, and tried to get down from her cart, but then she fainted. Frances put some smelling salts to her nose, and she came to herself after a few moments. Frances uttered some soothing words, but Mary began to shout.

'Jonathan, Jonathan,' said Mary. 'Where's Jonathan Millbrook? Where's the reverend? He must come and take me away; he must. He is my husband in the eyes of God. I've given him two fine sons, Jonathan and Michael, and yet he's not here. He abandons me, leaves me to this at the last. I must suffer for his fornication, his great fornication. For he sires other bastards. That poor woman, Sarah Long, who died in the grounds of the rectory, was another of his creatures, and she did have his child, and had another on the way. And he didn't care that she died; no, she was only a problem got rid of. And he tried to involve her in a great theft. A famous diamond, I tell you – the Celestial Light – but it did not come off; for he's not only a rake but a great spendthrift, who cannot control his appetites, and must needs live in luxury.'

The crowd closest to the cart had fallen silent. At first they thought that Mary was simply raving, but gradually some of the words made sense to a few of their number. But it was too late to change Mary's fate. The hangman had his job to do and must do it. He now prepared Isiah, leaving the curate a few minutes to sooth Mary as best he could.

'It will be better whither you go, Mary, dear,' Frances now said. 'All suffering and sorrow will be banished. Ask forgiveness again at this last moment and surely the Lord will turn his face towards you.'

Frances felt a deep inadequacy, but Mary, seeing the true compassion and love in his face, this man to whom she had unburdened her soul and yet had not been judged by him, grew quiet and compliant. The hangman, Mr Hillier, now approached her and, as many others had been before him, he was struck by her beauty, and also moved by her suffering. He was patient and gentle with her as he took her to the big cart, and seated her next to Isiah.

'Let me tie your gown around your legs,' he said to her, quietly. 'It will preserve your modesty.'

Mary, who had a faraway look, nonetheless recognised and was moved by this seeming acknowledgement that she was not some kind of whore.

'Thank you, sir. I am a modest woman, despite what they say of me. I only loved too much.'

Mary turned to look properly at the man next to her, Isiah, and smiled lovingly at him, as if this was the husband she had been long waiting for. The people who were about the cart now took heartrending leave of their friend or family member. The gaol chaplain and the curate sang their final psalms and intoned their final prayers and moved aside from the cart. The hangman drew the white cotton nightcaps over the faces of the condemned. Mary, who had spotted a young girl in the throng nearby – it could have been her own dear daughter – took off her fine lace cap and indicated to the hangman that she wished the girl to have it. This was done, and then the hangman, smiling kindly at Mary, put the usual nightcap over her head.

The signal was given to the driver that the condemned should now be turned off. He nodded, lashed the horses, and the cart slipped away from under the feet of the four men and Mary, leaving them to swing.

The men underwent various degrees of struggle on their ropes before dying, but poor Mary, now just skin and bone, was too light to drop, and so to die, quickly. She writhed and convulsed, heaved and made choking and gurgling sounds, her feet paddling the air. The crowd could not see her beautiful face becoming engorged and her eyes protruding, which was hidden by the cap, but those close enough might have noticed the soiling of her gown caused by the contents of her bladder and bowel being expelled, and her womb rupturing and bleeding.

A weeping man with sandy hair now ran forward,

grabbed her legs and pulled on them as hard as he could for several minutes. There were choking noises and then the body went limp.

'There, there, Mary, dear,' said Sam, between sobs. 'Take your rest, now. God bless you, my love, and save your soul.'

After the bodies had hung for the requisite hour, they were cut down and claimed by the family and friends. A hooded man and woman moved among them, begging a touch from the hands of the dead as a cure for their wens and marks. Another group of people positioned nearby, who had been so recently shouting loud against Mary, that evil witch, now began to wonder, after hearing her speech, if there had not been some mistake, or even a deliberate conspiracy against her, and so began to turn against the authorities.

Two messengers from the hospital, sent by the surgeons, now tried to claim Mary's body for dissection, the only one they were due to take that day since Mary was the only convicted murderer. Surgeons did not often get the opportunity to cut up a woman, and were anxious to gain what knowledge from the body they could.

'Do not take her, sirs,' Sam said, composing himself. 'She does not deserve it. She was a good woman and it would shame her at the last to have her woman's body so exposed and treated.'

'I understand your feelings,' said the tallest of the men, 'but we are but doing our job and obeying the law.

Tis an unpleasant thing, but the men of science must have their corpses.'

Sam was about to respond when the four drunken revellers – three men and one woman – who had been discussing Mary's case, now approached.

The woman addressed the tall man. 'Leave her be, and let this good man here take her home and give her a decent burial.'

'We only obey the law, madam; let us get on with our job.'

'Oh yes, the law,' said one of the men. 'Cutting up us working people and doing who knows what with us, I shouldn't wonder. Perhaps we should cut up a few of the quality and see how they like it?'

'That's nothing to us,' said the shorter of the messengers. 'Now let us be on our way.'

Another of the drunken men, broad and brutish-looking, stepped forward and said, 'Aye, why don't you get on your way?' and punched the man in his right eye.

A brawl ensued, from which the hospital messengers did not come off well. Sam was distressed by the scene, but his priority was Mary, and he used the distraction to get her away. He had already bought Mary's clothes from the hangman, whose property they became on death. A wagoner, whom he had hired, helped him get her body into the wagon, which they did with great delicacy. Then they drove away to the house of one of Samuel's friends, which was just on the edge of town, before getting her to Oxford, to be buried with her father and mother.

Though the hospital messengers did not get Mary, they were allowed to bargain with the hangman for any unclaimed bodies, and so got that of the man who had gone from madman to apparently repentant preacher on his way to heaven.

It had been a good hanging day. There had been cheering, dancing, singing, fighting. Some had been injured amongst the jostling crowds, but nobody had died who was not meant to. The pickpockets took rich pickings; and there was yet the prospect of more enjoyment, with riot and debauchery at local alehouses. Not everyone revelled in the day. Some watched in awe and horror, and vowed to mend their ways; others experienced a grim satisfaction to see this visual confirmation that the justice of God and man was done, so that they could rest safe in their own beds.

Frances went home and took to his bed. Before she had confessed all to him, he had long suspected Mary's relationship with the reverend, and had tried to help her. For he understood what it was to love, and to love that man in particular, the Reverend Jonathan Millbrook. As a young man, Frances had fulfilled his physical desires to the full, surprisingly, for one so earnest, giving little thought to what he did. He restricted the satisfaction of his needs to parts of London where discretion was mostly assured, and got on with his life. However, as the time came for him to take his profession more seriously, guilt and remorse began to creep in, and finally to overwhelm him. But the new form of faith within his church seemed to provide a hope that he could redeem himself at the last, by committing himself to a pure life in, and for, his God. Then he had become Mr Millbrook's curate, and for the first time in his life had loved as well as physically desired a man. He thought that he was being tested by God, and it was a cross he was willing to bear in order to be saved at the last. Jonathan did not know, and he would never disclose his secret to him. But he had shared it with Mary, just the previous day. He did not think that she had entirely understood, but she had recognised that he somehow shared her pain, and they had comforted each other. And now she was gone, crucified for all their guilt and shame.

Chapter 30

At about 11 o'clock on the night before the hanging, the Campbells had heard strange noises coming from the kitchen, and was that the sound of shot? Good Lord, thought Margaret, the robbers are come at last to murder us in our beds. Still, frightened that Freddy might be in danger, Gabriel agreed to get the old hunting gun, which lay under their bed and was kept for just such a purpose, and to go downstairs to investigate. Margaret insisted on accompanying her husband, and they both crept slowly down to the kitchen in their white linen nightshifts and nightcaps, looking somewhat like two ghosts who had just been visiting the admiral. They could hear poor Flip yelping, and something else? A man, also yelping, and then a string of most eloquent and naval curses. It was Captain Lefroy. Gabriel pushed open the door, the gun raised, and Margaret peered into the kitchen from around his right side.

'Fredericka Elizabeth Swinglehurst, what have you done?' asked Margaret.

Freddy turned to look at the Campbells. 'I, I… quick, Mrs C; we need some linen to bandage his wound, and perhaps some brandy to null the pain. Help me! Help him!'

Henry, his face drained of colour, was sat on the brick floor leaning his back against the kitchen door, pressing down on his left leg with his left hand. Freddy knelt down in front of him and looked into his face.

'I am so, so sorry,' she said. 'I do not know what, why I…' She could not now think of a rational explanation for shooting the man. 'The pistol, you know, it just went off. Oh, what have I done?'

The captain pointed with his right hand to a piece of shot that had lodged itself in the kitchen door. 'I will live, Miss Swinglehurst. The bullet did but graze me. You were lucky.'

Margaret came closer. Henry smiled at her and showed her the wound, which was, indeed, very slight.

'I will get a little vinegar and honey to clean the wound, and a bandage, sir,' said Margaret, 'and Mr C will get the brandy, for I imagine that will be more to the purpose given the shock you have had. Then we will get you moved somewhere more comfortable, and you must sleep here tonight.'

Margaret cleaned and bandaged Henry's wound, and after he had taken two large shots of brandy, he was ready to get up and be accompanied to the drawing room, where he would sleep on the sofa. Freddy hopped from foot to foot, not sure what to do, then sat down at the kitchen table, thinking that the captain would likely not want her anywhere near him at that moment, if ever again.

Margaret returned to the kitchen about fifteen minutes later. 'There, my love,' she said, ''tis but a scratch, and a fine, hearty man like the captain will soon be right as rain. Mr C is having a little conversation with him, then we can all get a good night's rest and talk in the morning.'

'Oh, Mrs C, do you forgive me? I know not what I do of late. I have become so muddled by all these strange events, that I have been imagining all sorts of wild things. I thought that the captain robbed the Celestial Light, murdered Sarah, and fathered Mary's poor bastard child. But now, somehow, these ideas seem preposterous.'

Margaret went over to Freddy, stood behind her and put her arms around her neck, as Freddy often did to her.

'Freddy, Freddy, Freddy. I really should be angry with you, but I find I am not.'

Then, to Freddy's great surprise, Margaret started laughing, which was a sort of quiet gurgle. She rested her head on Freddy's shoulder and laughed and laughed and laughed. Freddy, bewildered, turned round to look into Margaret's face, and started laughing too. Margaret then sat down at the table next to Freddy, laid her hands on the tabletop, put her head on top of them, and continued to laugh. Freddy could not help but follow. Flip, delighted, snuggled between them and cocked his head from side to side.

When Margaret's shoulders had finally stopped shaking, she raised her head and looked at Freddy.

'Oh, my dear child. I've never laughed so much as I have since you returned to us. It feels wrong to do so now, given all the terrible things occurring, but I cannot help it. Sometimes, you know, Mr C and I giggle in our chamber like children, at something you've done or said.'

'Well, I am not sure how I feel about being a laughing-stock,' said Freddy, trying to look stern.

'We have never been so happy. Now, get thee to bed, child, before the constable comes to carry us all away.'

Freddy, dazed, relieved, happy – despite the fact that she had nearly murdered someone – kissed Margaret on both cheeks, grinned a bit sheepishly, picked up her candle and went upstairs to bed.

The next morning, Freddy slept late, and had slept well, her mind strangely calm. On waking, she remembered immediately what had happened with the captain, and was thoroughly ashamed of herself. At the same time, she felt happy. She was not entirely sure why but sensed it could be that she knew that she had been entirely wrong about him. She did not further examine the feeling, just enjoyed it. As if hoping to demonstrate her contriteness, she put on her most sombre, dull brown gown with a high collar, and tied her hair back rather severely. She toyed with the idea of a white linen cap but dismissed the idea as a step too far.

She arrived in the kitchen wearing as serious face as she could muster. The Campbells and the captain were sat round the table eating muffins and boiled eggs. The captain did not look particularly distressed; in fact, he was smiling broadly, and the colour had returned to his face.

Margaret looked at her. 'Have you turned puritan on us, dear? I have never seen you looking so prim and proper. It is quite as a virtuous lady should look and I am delighted to see this reformation come at last.'

Freddy gave her a mock scowl and sat down. She grinned at Gabriel and turned to the captain, a little shy.

'How are you today, Captain Lefroy?'

'Remarkably well,' he said, 'considering I was nearly murdered last night.'

Freddy looked sheepish, then rallied. 'Well, sir, accidents will happen, and perhaps you should try not take them too personally.'

Henry laughed. 'I should hope not, for if I believed that someone was deliberately trying to murder me, I should have to wonder why.'

'Now, Fredericka,' said Margaret, looking more serious, 'the captain has some things to tell you which are very important. Mr C and I are going to the rectory to help with Mary's boys, for, as you know, poor Mary has left us this morning, and it will be a very sad day indeed.'

The Campbells left, and Freddy and the captain were alone together.

'I cannot tell you how sorry I am,' said Freddy.

'I know,' said the captain, 'but it was an accident, and I believe that I am to blame. It was rather foolish of me to turn up here late at night when everyone is so nervous and frightened. Especially wearing only my shirt and breeches.'

Freddy laughed. 'It is entirely the sort of thing I would do myself.'

The captain laughed too. 'Yes, I cannot disagree with you there.' He became more serious. 'I have been trying to talk to you on these matters for some time, but the timing was never right, and then I was sure you harboured some antipathy towards me, and might not hear me fairly.'

'I am truly sorry, Captain. I have been so confused of late that I have been harbouring all sorts of suspicions against everyone.'

'It is understandable. I finally rushed here last night because it occurred to me that Mary might just make some revelations today, rather than go to the grave in silence, and I did not want you to discover the truth from local gossip. For the truth will be hurtful to you, Miss Swinglehurst, I am very sorry to say.'

'Do not be sorry. Please, go ahead; I am ready to hear it.'

The captain proceeded to tell Freddy all that he had suspected, and discovered, about the reverend, and his involvement with Mary and Sarah. He had tried to tell Anne, but she had not been ready to hear the truth, and so all he had been able to do there for the time being was to look out for her. He had also been trying to help Mary for some time by securing her a position elsewhere, away from Winchester, but she had refused his aid and insisted on staying wherever Jonathan was.

When he had come across Freddy in London, he, too, had been about to call on Mrs Fisher's; it turned out that the maid Bess had been involved with David Barber, and the latter, hardly the most discreet of fellows, had dropped a few, bragging words in her ear about the diamond, and what a fine, rich man he would soon be. The fact of Jonathan's involvement, whilst shocking, was not so surprising given that a life of wild extravagance might lead to any desperate measure. He had discovered the Mrs Fisher connection from the landlord of the Chequers Inn, in Winchester, who, having previously kept silent with the general run of persons as to what he knew, had grown confidential with a Captain of His Majesty's Navy over a bottle of rum.

Freddy received all the information very quietly, and when Henry had finished, she was able to fill him in with some missing bits of information of her own.

'There is one thing that I am not sure about,' said Freddy. 'For all the evil he has done, I cannot imagine that Jonathan murdered Sarah. Perhaps I am still grasping at some hope of a little goodness within him. Do you believe that he did it?'

'No. In fact, I think it was Mary, though it cannot be proved. She was growing more disturbed, I fear, and could not help herself. He was certainly involved in the digging up of Sarah's body, however, though he would not have done the deed himself. Of course, we know now that the diamond was never with her.'

Henry looked with concern at Freddy, and continued. 'This must be very distressing for you to hear, Miss Swinglehurst. I know that you and Jonathan were great friends for a long time.'

'Yes; I am shocked. We were great friends as children, and he knew my father well, which bound him to me in a way. But then he went away to study, and I eventually fled to London for all those years, and I suppose people change with time. It seems that I have not really known him.'

'For what it is worth, I do not think that he was ever a truly evil man. When Anne first met him, I liked him a great deal and could see how much he loved her. I think bad habits grew upon him over the years so that he could find no way back.'

'He has inflicted incalculable misery and suffering on so many. And poor Anne. Have you told her what you know?'

'Yes; it was but yesterday. She took it calmly; she amazes me sometimes. Well, Miss Swinglehurst, I must be going. I want to help Anne at the rectory, but I must call at my house beforehand to attire myself properly.'

Freddy grinned. 'Let me get you one of Mr Campbell's coats; it will become you very well, I am sure. And if you get arrested on the way home, I shall come and bail you out wielding my pistol and will be forced to become highwaywoman before the day is out.'

Chapter 31

Over at the rectory, the atmosphere was very sombre. There was just the Millbrooks, Mrs Hobson and Polly in the house; Samuel would be gone for a few days, taking Mary's body to Oxford.

The Campbells arrived with Flip, hoping the dog would help comfort Michael, who had grown attached to him. Polly let them in; her master and mistress were upstairs in their chamber, she said, the master being very unwell with a stomach complaint. Margaret and Gabriel were relieved not to have to face the reverend directly, the captain having told them a little of what he was now telling Freddy. The main thing now, they thought, was to help Anne and the boys, and they followed Polly round to the back of the house, where the boys were tending their vegetable garden.

When John saw them, he stopped, looked Gabriel in the eye, and knew that his mother was gone. Michael immediately sensed that some tragedy had occurred and started to cry. Margaret put out her arms to the boy and she and Gabriel steered both boys to an old seat in between the two cottages, where they sat down. Flip settled himself between Michael and Gabriel, and the younger boy wiped his tears on the dog's fur. There, Margaret told them as gently as she could that their mother would not be coming back. It had been decided that the boys should be told initially that their mother had died in gaol. Then John would be told the truth, apart from his brother, and Michael might be told the full story in time. John was too curious and intelligent to be deceived, and likely already suspected that his mother had been hanged. Even if he did not, the cruel gossip of local children might soon furnish both the boys with the truth, so it was as well to prepare them for it. Michael sobbed and sobbed, and John sat very quiet, clutching Gabriel's bony hand.

Upstairs, the reverend was lying in bed in his nightshift. He was thinner than he had been, and his handsome, unshaven face bore the shadows of sleeplessness and the lines of someone constantly frowning in pain. His wife, fully dressed, was sat on the coverlet next to him.

'My dear, during our marriage, you have not often had the honour of your wife waiting upon you in our bedchamber,' said Anne.

Jonathan smiled. 'Well, I was never in need of it, my love. But, see you now, the perfect nurse.'

Anne laughed. 'I flatter myself I am. And what with Mrs Hobson and dear Polly, who is becoming quite the housekeeper, we are set fair to be the finest run establishment in Hampshire.'

They were quiet for a few moments. 'I only wish,' continued Anne, 'that poor Mary did not have to leave us in this terrible way.' Of all the things her husband had done, his treatment of Mary at the last was the most abominable thing to her. But it was not entirely incomprehensible; she knew that it was merely the most extreme manifestation of his desperate and degraded state. And her knowledge of it helped to harden her resolve to become a stronger and more self-respecting version of herself.

'I know, dear.' Jonathan looked Anne in the eye, and she held his gaze.

'Those poor boys,' Anne continued. 'But they will be safe with me; you can be sure of it, husband.'

'I know it, and it gives me peace.'

'I will love them as I have loved you.'

'I have not deserved it, my dearest Anne, but I am truly grateful for it – please believe me.' Jonathan clutched his stomach in pain, and began to cry a little.

'There, my love, of course I believe you.'

'I loved you straightaway, you know, when I saw you in that rose-coloured gown, looking a little lost amongst the throng.'

Anne smiled. 'Yes, I did not thrive in those environments. I was a little bashful and awkward, I suppose, and did not know quite what to do or to say. I did not know the fashionable talk, and no doubt I said something quite nonsensical to you.'

'You said that it was such a beautiful evening you wished that you could grow wings and fly up, up, up into the sky and across the oceans.'

'Did I really say that? I had not known I was such a poet, if a rather commonplace one.'

'Indeed you did. I can see your grey eyes now, looking out on the evening, and can imagine you floating away over the sea, your pink gown flaring out in the starry night.'

'I am surprised that you did not attempt to fly away yourself, at meeting such a whimsical and fanciful woman. "The fancy is all very well in poetry and novels," Mama used to say to me, "but do not reveal too fevered an imagination to a potential suitor; it will only scare them away. A sensible man wants a sensible wife".'

The reverend laughed, then winced and clutched his stomach.

'Oh, my dear, we will call for the doctor to come again.'

'No, Anne, there is nothing more he can do for me; truly. In any case, I will not be here long.' He looked his wife in the eye again, and she steadily returned his gaze.

'I know.'

'How will you ever forgive me? I have done so many grievous things in my one lifetime that I would need ten lifetimes to try to atone for them, and it would still not put things right. But I want to try and explain to you what…'

Anne put her fingers to her husband's lips. 'Now is not the time for confessions and recriminations, my dear. Let us have our little peace here and now, while we can. For it cannot be long.'

'It cannot be long. But, Anne, why do you not despise me? I could hardly blame you if you did.'

'I do not know. I will confess that I did despise you a little for a while, but it did not stick, and now it has long been gone. Rest now, dear, you are most unwell. I will go and see about our dinner, for I am becoming quite the cook, as well as the nurse, and I will also see if I can find a little something to ease your stomach.'

Anne smiled at her husband, stroked his hair, then closed his eyelids and kissed him on the lips. Then she went downstairs to the kitchen, with her step firm and her head held high.

That Monday morning, the Reverend Jonathan Millbrook was arrested for debt. It was a relatively small thing – a couple of trinkets from Mr Hopkins, the silversmith in Winchester – but he knew that this was the beginning of the end, and so it proved. His many other debtors, large and small, rushed in, and he was consigned to the debtor's gaol in Winchester. Since the reverses in his fortune, and principally the failure of the diamond affair, he could have made the decision to flee his creditors, and his current life, but, as he had told Adam Short, he found that he no longer had the will or even the desire. He was very ill, the stress of the past few years – of half a life's debauchery and deception, in fact – contributing to his painful and often debilitating stomach complaint. Perhaps there was also a part of him, even up until the last, that hoped for some kind of divine intervention, for an angel to come forth and sweep all his troubles away; for he could never quite shake off the feeling that he was special, chosen.

He had once thought of confessing all his troubles and sins to Freddy and of asking for her help, but found that he could not do it. The old manor house, and Freddy herself, had always represented to him all that was amiable, natural and good in this world, and he did not want to sully them with his mess – he had done enough contamination. He had loved her – in the romantic sense - once, as a young man, though she had not known it, and he had envisaged their marrying one day, if she would have him. But their lives had gone in different directions, and then he had met his true love, Anne, whose life he had so damaged.

So he went quietly when he was arrested, Polly crying, Mrs Hobson shocked, Anne still, calm and ready. He thought that Anne must know, now, the extent of his profligacy and licentiousness. She had begun, recently, to examine the household accounts, after not doing so for a long time. Several years ago, he had taken the task from her, meaning, at first, to relieve her of a duty she found onerous, being so frequently ill and low in spirits. But then he found that it had suited him, enabling him to hide his uncontrolled spending, and most especially the expenditure related to Mary, Sarah and their children.

He did not want his wife with him in debtors' gaol, as many men were forced to have theirs. She could not bear it, and did not deserve it. He was sure that her parents would take her back now that he was out of the picture, though they would not help him personally. He knew in his heart that their dislike of him at the start was based on a recognition of his character, and where that character might lead him, and that they truly loved their daughter. The accounts aside, he suspected that his wife may have had some suspicions about Mary, and perhaps even Sarah. Henry certainly had, and must have mentioned some of them to her. In fact, Henry had attempted several times to lecture him on his duties as a husband and figure of the community, referring obliquely to what was probably his knowledge of the affair with Mary at least. He, base fellow that he was, had simply laughed at him. Well, what Anne did not know already she would discover soon enough. He was not yet aware of Mary's dying confessions, but suspected that local gossip would furnish everyone with the truth eventually. It was incredible that he had managed to keep his ship afloat for so long, and in secrecy, as it grew more and more battered and ridden with holes. It had finally ground upon the rocks, and so be it.

He was sure that Mary had contributed in some way to poor Sarah's death. He did not know how she had made the discovery of her rival, and she had never confronted him about it, but the laying of Sarah's body as if on the cross could only have been Mary's work. It was a message to him: that she knew what this Sarah was; that he, a Minister of God, was a foul hypocrite and a liar; and that she would never let him forsake her. He had encouraged the coroner, out of delicacy for the woman's state and case, he had said, not to complete a full autopsy, terrified that some foul play might be discovered, and had been relieved when a heart weakness had been soon found, so that she was only half cut up. He had been amazed, as well as relieved, that Mary had not disclosed him during her pregnancy, after the birth of their child, at her trial, or even in gaol, and he had been only waiting for the revelations to happen. He had tried, briefly and with only half a heart, to secure a defence attorney for her. Henry had tried harder, but she had refused all aid. Sunk so low as he was, he was quite ready to let her hang and for their secrets to die with her, whilst hating himself all the time for his cowardly, unmanly and deplorable behaviour.

He had loved Mary in his way, as he had loved Sarah. But he had loved his wife most truly, despite what he had done to her. Sarah and Mary had known him too well, known what he was. With Anne, he could be that pure, heroic figure that he had always wanted to be, and she had looked up to him accordingly. That was over now.

Chapter 32

THE DAY AFTER the reverend's arrest, Freddy walked slowly to the rectory to call on Anne.

Polly opened the door, and smiled brightly at her. She looked almost like her old self, and seemed to have grown a little taller.

'Miss Swinglehurst,' she said. 'Please do come in.'

'Thank you, Polly,' said Freddy, following her into the vestibule, then through to the front parlour. 'How well you are growing into your position now; you could almost be mistress of the house.'

Polly beamed. 'Thank you, Miss. Please do sit down, and I will fetch Mrs Millbrook. Can I get you some refreshment?'

'Yes, Polly. Some tea would be very welcome.'

'Of course, Miss Swinglehurst.' Polly nodded and left the room.

Anne appeared a few moments later looking tired

and pale, but at the same time, she, too, seemed brighter, and also had about her a determined air.

'Freddy, dear. Are you well?' She kissed Freddy on her right cheek, then sat down.

'Yes, Anne, but I am more concerned about you.'

'Please do not be anxious on my account; rather strangely, I feel better than I have in a long time. I am a little dazed and still disbelieving in some ways, but also relieved. Yes, I do believe that that is the word – relief.'

'I am very happy to hear it. How are Mary's boys?' Freddy felt a little awkward once the words were out; she could equally have asked, how are Jonathan's boys? Anne did not seem to pay it heed.

'They are not in a good way. Michael cries all the time; John remains silent; neither are eating well. But tis very early, and I hope they will improve with time.'

'You can be sure of that, Anne. What will happen to them now?'

Anne's face brightened. 'Oh, they will come with me to Salisbury. I am returning to mama and papa. I wrote to them setting everything out, as I knew it – before John was taken, for I knew what was coming - and mama sent the kindest letter in reply. Papa should be here in a few days. I am quite overwhelmed with emotion about it all, for we have been estranged for so long. They knew, you know, what sort of man Jonathan is, and tried to dissuade me from marrying him, but I was stubborn, and foolish.'

'Well, we have all been that in our time. But I am so

glad to hear about your parents. It will be such a comfort to be around your family again. I have felt that since returning to the Campbells.'

'Yes, the Campbells must be the kindest people on this earth, I think.'

'I quite agree with you. And your parents are happy to take the boys?'

'Yes. I suggested it a little tentatively in my letter, but mama says her and papa will be very happy to welcome them, and they will also arrange for a good schooling. I am so happy about it. For they are my husband's children, and so they are my children also, in a way.'

'That is very generous of you, Anne, and more so than I can imagine some being in a similar situation. They are such dear boys, and it will be quite the best thing for them in helping them to bear their loss.'

'I do hope so. Mama and papa are such kind people; I had forgotten. I was terrified in writing to them, thinking that they would be severe. But they seem to have softened with the years, and say that they are only glad to have their daughter home. They have even agreed to employ Samuel, if he will go with me, for it will be better for the boys to have someone they love close by, and Samuel will no longer have his position here.'

'That sounds like an excellent arrangement. Poor Samuel will be grieving greatly, I think.'

'Yes, it is very hard upon him.'

'Good servants are so invaluable. I blush with shame when I think how cavalierly I have treated the Campbells, who have taken care of the old manor house for all these years with such prudence and economy. I am quite determined to employ an army of servants so that they can rest a little at last.'

Polly interrupted them, entering the room with some tea. She conducted the tea ceremony with perfect efficiency, presented Freddy and her mistress with their cups, and quitted the room in a state of great dignity and pride.

'What a wonder that girl is,' said Freddy.

'Indeed she is. You, know, Freddy, she has known something of what has been going on here. She has seen my husband and Mary together and drew her own conclusions about Mary's sons. We had a talk yesterday, after Jonathan was taken away, and I encouraged her to speak. She is such an intelligent girl. She observed much, but was fearful of telling anything, or misconstruing what she saw, so kept her own counsel.'

'Poor girl; I have suspected that she was carrying some sort of burden.'

'Yes, and I think she is also feeling a relief to have got rid of it.' Anne paused. 'I think also that she half suspected me of poisoning that poor woman, with the arsenic I sent her out to fetch many months ago.'

'Oh dear, poor Polly.' Freddy thought it best not to mention that the thought had also crossed her own mind, if only very briefly.

'Perhaps she sensed a little of my anxiety around that purchase, and then drew the wrong conclusion later on. Oh, Freddy, you seem to have become my priest, whether you like it or no. I did procure the arsenic for a reason other than ridding the house of vermin, and certainly not for use on my complexion. You have been a witness of my suffering, and can perhaps imagine that sometimes I did not want to carry on. You know of what I speak. It is a great sin and a wickedness, I know, but I have to confess that I was tempted for a short time.'

'Oh, Anne, many things are considered a great sin and a wickedness in this world, but we are all susceptible to them. I am only sorry that you felt almost driven to that.'

'Thank you, Freddy; I knew you would not judge me.' She giggled suddenly. 'Once I had decided against that course of action, I almost considered another – putting the arsenic in my husband's tea.'

Freddy laughed loudly. 'I do not blame you. I would have stabbed him through the heart with one of Margaret's kitchen knives a long time since.'

Anne giggled again. It was a pleasure to see Anne laugh, her pale skin crinkling slightly at the edges of her eyes and in the middle of her brows.

'You are not wearing your usual jewellery,' said Freddy.

'No. I have laid it all aside, and I feel wonderfully light. The debtors are crowding in – you know - to take the household goods, as well as all the trinkets that Jonathan was addicted to buying. He really could not resist spending money and it became a quite vicious extravagance. He purchased all sorts of luxuries for the house, for himself, and for me, few of which I wanted or needed. His latest thing was an elaborate folly, which he wanted to build on one of the meadows, and he was even considering a hothouse. You may have observed that we manage here with very few servants, considering the size of the house and grounds. We have employed several over the years – butlers, housemaids, groomsmen – but they did not stay. It puzzled me, but now, of course, I realise that they would not have received their proper wages. Mary clearly had her own reasons to stay, and Samuel is such a good and loyal fellow, and obviously felt an affection for Mary.'

'Oh, Anne, what a time you have had. But you are bearing up remarkably.'

'I flatter myself I am. I have, however, acquired some peculiar habits.'

Anne put down her cup of tea, which had remained untasted, picked up several pieces of sugar and put one in her mouth, which she chewed on for a few moments, smiling.

'I am blaming you for this, Freddy. I am happily becoming more and more singular, which your fine example has given me permission to do. I am not sure how the wives of Winchester would feel about it.'

'Oh, they would enjoy it a great deal if only they knew, I am sure. I used to do it as a child. It is most comforting.'

'At least we can be grateful that I am not dipping the sugar pieces in cognac.'

'Quite, my dear, but do not stop yourself doing so on my account. When will you be leaving Hampshire? I will miss you. We have not known each other long, but I feel as if we are firm friends.'

'We are, indeed, and I will miss you too. But you will visit in Salisbury, will you not? And I will visit you at the old manor house. Tis no great distance.'

'No, indeed. I may consider sitting on Flip's back, and letting him carry me to Salisbury, and then Michael will get two old friends at once.'

Anne laughed. 'I can well imagine you doing it, Freddy. But I am forgetting the gift I have for you, if you would like to take it, that is.'

'Oh? I am all curiosity.'

'Cannot you guess?'

'No, I cannot think, unless it be that spotted wallpaper I so admire, but pray do not go to the trouble of stripping it off; it would quite spoil your gown.'

'Oh, it is better than the finest wallpaper in the kingdom, I can assure you. Well, you know how much I love Polly, and I wanted her to come with me to Salisbury. But she is torn about leaving her mother, who has great need of her, and so does not know what to do. And then I remembered that you had talked of hiring a lady's maid, and I know how fond you are of Polly, and I thought you might like to employ her yourself.'

'Oh, Anne, I would be so glad to do so. But it would not feel right for me to take her from you.'

'It is not as if you would be stealing her from me.

I will miss her greatly. But, truly, it would be the best arrangement for her, and I know how happy she will be with you. You will bring her when you visit me, so it will not be a real parting. Besides, I do not want to further try the patience of my parents; my mother's nerves have not always been good, and Polly's slippery hands might not contribute to the soothing of them.'

'Yes, I will need to warn Margaret to lock up our china. But, verily, it will make me very happy.' Freddy paused. 'Will you see your husband ere you go?'

'No, I do not think I will. We have made our peace with each other, you know, and I think it is best that we do not meet again. It pains me to think of him rotting in that jail, but I can do no more for him. One condition of my parents' help is that he must manage alone. He has caused enough suffering, and I have sacrificed enough of my life to him.'

'I agree with you, Anne, and with your mama and papa.'

'One thing you could do, Freddy, if you were minded to help a little? I know that you and Jonathan were once good friends, and he had a great fondness and respect for you, despite what he has done. I do not believe that he will ever get out of jail, for the debts are enormous, and he can never pay, but perhaps you could arrange, now and again, for him to have a little decent food and medicine. For everything in the gaol has to be paid for, and he will be left in the meanest conditions. It would console me to know that he will have at least a bit of physical comfort.'

'Of course, Anne. I will be glad do that. I am still struggling to come to terms with what he has turned out to be, myself, and the anger within me would let him rot, friendless and forsaken. But we were such good friends as children, and my father was very fond of him, and thought him a fine boy. Which he was, indeed, at that time. But even leaving aside that connection, I would do it for you, for you are so accepting, and generous in heart, despite all he has done.

'I have been very angry, believe me, Freddy, but it was an anger expressed in my silence and misery. Now, I find it has passed, and I feel only sorry for him that he has wasted all his talents, and brought himself to this. Thank you, Freddy, for everything. You have been my angel, you really have. Well, before I start weeping, we should fetch Polly and tell her the news.

That evening Freddy sat in the kitchen with the Campbells and told them what had transpired at the rectory. They were very pleased, and relieved, for Anne and for Mary's boys.

'That's a very good arrangement, indeed,' said Margaret, fanning herself with a silk and ivory fan, an old present from Freddy.

'Aye,' said Gabriel, ''tis the best thing we could have hoped for, in the circumstances, though I confess I'll be sorry to see them go. We could have taken them, you know.'

'Yes, we could, dear Mr C,' said Freddy, 'and how

like you to think of it. It crossed my mind too. But I think it will be best for Anne and her family to take them. She feels no resentment, you know, despite all, and in fact seems to feel more of an obligation to John and Michael, them being her husband's children. And it sounds a little as if her mama and papa are lonely, and have been missing her, and it will do them all good to have the boys.'

'Yes, it's for the best,' said Margaret, looking tenderly at her husband and patting his left shirt sleeve, which was rolled up to his bony elbow. 'But we will see them again, I am sure.'

'Oh, yes,' said Freddy. 'Anne will bring them to us and we can pay a visit in Salisbury whenever we so wish. Though, to be sure, it will be better when we have our fine new carriage and horses, for poor old Molly will not survive the journey.'

Margaret beamed at the thought of the carriage. 'Well, that is a thought to cheer one, after all the recent sadness.'

'Yes, and there is another thing, which I hope will please you both.'

'What is that, Miss?' said Gabriel.

'I will be taking on Polly as my lady's maid. Anne wanted to take her to Salisbury, but Polly was torn about leaving her family. As you know, her mother is sickly and there are so many children to take care of. So Anne wondered if I might take her, and I thought, Margaret is constantly telling me that I am not living up to my position, as mistress of the manor, and perhaps I should have a maid, after all. Polly is a little clumsy, to be sure, but I know that you will train her beautifully, Mrs C. I hope that neither of you object to the scheme?'

'Object, my dear?' said Margaret. 'How could we object? You are seeing sense at long last. I will take her in hand and she will become the finest lady's maid in the country.'

'I have no doubts that she will.'

'She will be most welcome,' said Gabriel. 'She has a sweet way about her, and it will be a pleasure to have her here.'

'So, although the boys are leaving, you will have another young person about the place, after all. It is just that you will still be surrounded by women.'

'Tis my fate,' said Gabriel, smiling, 'and I am long resigned to it.'

'Aye,' said his wife. 'Mr Gabriel knows who is in charge in this world, or who should be, at least.'

Freddy laughed. 'So, Mrs C, you will have another room to decorate.'

Margaret's face lit up again, and she clapped her hands. 'Oh, yes, I will give it some thought. Perhaps something simple in blue. A maid's chamber must not be too extravagant, yet it must be dignified enough to signify her position as a lady's maid.'

Freddy smiled. 'I leave it all to you, Mrs C. But I have another thing in mind. I would like to go to Affy in London for a few days, and talk all this strange business through with her, and to see if I can offer some help to Sarah's friend, who is taking care of her daughter. They may need money and clothing, and other things.'

'That is a kind thought, dear,' said Margaret, 'and it will do you good to spend some time with the Scottish relation.'

'Thank you,' said Freddy. 'I will be away but for a short period. I will write to Affy directly and set out at the end of the week.'

Chapter 33

Freddy arrived in Somers Town on the Friday of that week, to greet the ever-growing Affy, who was now about seven months along.

'Why, my dear,' said Freddy, looking at Affy's rounder face, 'you have a slight look of Mrs Campbell. Perhaps you truly are related, after all.'

Affy laughed loudly. 'I do hope so, for I could have no better relation. But, Freddy, where is your cane?' They were stood in the narrow vestibule of the house.

Freddy looked about her, but she had only her box with her. 'Oh, I must have left it in the post chaise, in which case I fear that I have seen the last of it.'

'I fear you have.'

'Well, never mind, it will be an excuse to go a shopping for a replacement.'

'Do you really need a replacement?'

Freddy smiled. 'And now you look even more like Mrs Campbell, with that penetrating stare she has.'

'Ha! I have been practising it in front of the glass. It is part of my new repertoire of classical expressions to go along with the classical poses.'

'You goose. But I confess that you are right, as always. I no longer need the stick; I just find it comforting.'

'Well, there is nothing so wrong with that. But perhaps you could see how you manage without one for a short period, and then purchase another if you do not like it.'

'I will do that.'

'And what about those spectacles?'

'What about them?'

'Perhaps you could leave those off as well.'

'Do you not care for them?'

'I like them very well. But I do not believe that you need them.'

'Oh, Affy, you are right again; it is really quite tiresome.'

'So, they are merely for comfort also?'

'Yes, I am afraid that they are. And I enjoy hiding behind them. After all, I no longer care what impression I make to the world; it is not as if I am a hunting for a husband, after all.'

'Yes, and you are making quite sure that they are not a hunting for you.'

'Aphrodite Sweet, it is as well that I do not come to

you for flattery, for I would be sorely disappointed. But, indeed, I think that is partly true too.'

'Well, dear, if you want to hide your most lovely face, that is up to you. I will not say another word on the subject.'

'Oh, so now comes the flattery. I cannot keep up with you, woman; I never could.'

Affy giggled and pinched her friend on her left cheek. 'Now, dear, I am not sure why we are still standing here. Come into the parlour and take your rest. We have much to talk about, and then we have a visitor coming here tomorrow, who will greatly interest you, I am sure.'

On the Saturday evening, the visitor rang the front doorbell. Edward got up to answer it, leaving Freddy and Affy sat in the front parlour waiting. The visitor was a thin, short black woman dressed in a ragged, greatly patched dress and brown boots with holes in. She was carrying a girl of about one year of age, who looked remarkably well and stout, though her once pristine smock and cap was thick with dirt and grease. The visitors' smell preceded them into the room. Affy had warned Freddy in advance that it would be so, that the stench of the slums was more than the general stink of London; it had a quality all of its own and could be quite overpowering to those not used to it.

'Good evening, Maria,' said Affy, 'and little Henrietta. Do sit down, both of you.'

'Thank you, Mrs.' Maria did as bid, propping up Hetty on the floor next to her feet so that she could look at the room. Hetty looked around her with a slightly gormless, haughty expression, as if she was a Lady So and So from the Great Hall patronising a poor, sick cottager with a visit.

Freddy smiled at them and tried not to take too deep an intake of breath at the smell. She was glad that she had been warned; she did not want to offend.

'Will you take some tea, or a little wine, Maria?' asked Affy, who had met her once before.

'A good cup of tea, with plenty of sugar, would be very welcome, ma'am, thank you – it's a real luxury for us. Sarah used to give me the odd cup when her landlady was away, and it was quite heavenly.'

'Well, then, a very good cup of tea you shall certainly have. And Hetty?'

'She can have a sip of my tea, when it's cooled down. Or perhaps a little milk would do her good, if you have it?'

'Oh, yes, and we have some fresh from the country, so it will be very wholesome. I will bring it for her.' Affy got up slowly, patted Hetty on the head and left the room.

'Maria, this is Miss Swinglehurst, a very good friend of ours,' said Edward, sitting down.

Maria nodded at Freddy, and stared a little, fascinated to see someone like herself so fine and elegant with her green silk dress and soft, clean skin. Perhaps she was a whore done well, like Sarah. But then if she was good friends with these respectable people, perhaps not. She might be one of those religious types. 'Pleased to meet you, ma'am.'

Freddy smiled at her. 'How do you do, Maria.' She looked at her, and thought, that could have been me. She was a little repulsed, a little horrified, and a little ashamed of herself for those feelings. But she was determined not to flinch. 'What a fine child she is' – this, looking at Hetty.

'She is that; she's a proper handful, too, aren't you, dear?'

Hetty started wriggling, as if to indicate consent.

'Miss Swinglehurst knows something of Sarah's story, Maria, and also knew the gentleman in question,' said Edward. 'She would like to help you both, if she is able.'

Maria smiled at Freddy. 'That's very good of you, ma'am, I'm sure. But if it's God you're offering, we're alright as we are, thanks. I've nothing against God, mind, other than that he doesn't seem to have done much for us; but let that be.'

Freddy laughed. 'It is not God, Maria; I was thinking of something more practical – money, food, clothing.'

'Well, that's a different thing altogether, Miss, and would be very helpful. We get by, you know, but I won't say no to some help for this one. She's used to a comfortable life. I'll say this for the gentleman; he provided. Sarah and the child were as snug as you like in that lodging house, and didn't want for a thing. Sarah was always dressed nearly as fine as yourself, and they had good victuals and plenty of coals.'

'I am glad to hear it,' said Freddy, which she was, though she could not help but wonder about the losses of the poor tradesmen who had been paying for Sarah's comfort.

Affy entered the room with a cup of tea for Maria and a tin of milk for the child.

'Here you are, dear,' said Affy, placing the drinks on a side table near Maria. 'Shall I give the child her milk so that you can enjoy your tea in peace?'

'Thank you, Madam; I would like that.'

Affy picked up Hetty, gripped her with her left arm, took the tin of milk, then sat down with the child on her lap. Hetty burst into tears, but calmed a little when she was given the milk, even though most of it ended up dripping down her chubby neck as she squirmed.

'I had better get used to this,' Affy said, laughing, and looking at her husband.

'As had I,' said Edward, smiling at her. 'We were just explaining to Maria that Miss Swinglehurst would like to help her and the child.'

'Miss Swinglehurst is the kindest person in the world,' said Affy, 'though she does not like to hear it said.'

Freddy grimaced at her, smiled, then turned back to Maria. 'Do you have children yourself?' she asked.

'Oh yes, ma'am, five,' said Maria, gulping her tea with great pleasure. 'Well, there were five, but now there are just two. Some of them don't stay long, ma'am, and I do not blame the poor things. It was George, Harry and Eliza that went, but there is still Kitty and Sally.'

Freddy swallowed. 'I am very sorry to hear that, Maria.'

Maria shrugged. 'They're better out of it; though I won't pretend it don't break my heart when they go.'

'Well, we will try to make sure that you can keep Kitty and Sally – and this one, of course – as strong as they can be,' said Affy.

'Thank you, ma'am.'

'Will it be a great burden for you to keep Hetty?' asked Freddy.

'Children are always a burden, ma'am, in the way of keeping them fed and the sickness away. But you can't help loving them, even though you try not to, sometimes, in case they're minded to pay you only a short visit. And I'll love this one just as well, for Sarah's sake, as well as her own.'

'I am sure you will.' Freddy swallowed again, wondering if she was really quite up to facing the cruel realities of life, after all. 'You and Sarah grew up together, I believe?'

Maria took another gulp of tea. 'Yes; well, as far as I can remember. We were just scraps of things, playing together, when we had the chance to. Poor old dear.' A tear rolled down Maria's cheek. 'But I'm glad she had a few comfortable years towards her end. That's more than many of us can hope for.'

Hetty now started wriggling and crying, then turned her head towards Freddy. Affy put the child on the floor, so that she could have a little crawl, and she headed at pace towards Freddy, who picked her up. Hetty stopped crying and stared at Freddy's face, then began to draw on it with a podgy, milky finger.

'Come, now, Hetty,' said Maria, 'let the fine lady be. Don't you be smearing your dirty fingers all over her beautiful gown.' She went to get up.

'She is fine,' said Freddy smiling. 'Do not concern yourself. Please do enjoy your tea in peace.'

'Thank you, ma'am.' Maria relaxed back into her chair. 'I must admit that it's pleasant to have a moment to rest, however short.'

They conversed a little more about Maria's and Sarah's lives. Maria seemed to enjoy talking about her friend, and perhaps it eased her heart to do so. Then it was time for her to leave. There was a husband and the two children, as well as a bundle of other infants that she was minding for friends, waiting at home. Edward got up, went into the kitchen and came back with a parcel of things paid for by Freddy.

'Maria, this is for you and Hetty, from Miss Swinglehurst,' he said. 'There's some food, clothing, medicine and a little money – not too much, in case it gets taken, but there will be more.'

Maria shed a few more tears. 'Thank you, Miss Swinglehurst. It will be such a help.'

'It is a pleasure for me to do it,' said Freddy, feeling ashamed and guilty, as she often did, usually when she was trying to help people.

'I will walk with you, Maria,' said Edward, as he got up and took Hetty from Freddy.

'There's really no need, sir.'

'Let him go with you,' said Affy. 'I insist.' She patted her husband's stomach. 'The walk will do him good.'

Maria grinned. 'Thank you, then.'

They all moved into the hall place, and Maria, stood close to Freddy, and staring at her still, could not resist reaching out a hand to touch her face.

'Do forgive me, ma'am. I cannot quite credit my eyes and so I tried my hand. You're like a dream; like me, but such a fine lady.'

Freddy could not stop a few tears from coming. She looked at Hetty, now nodding off in Edward's arms.

'I will take her,' said Freddy.

There was silence.

'I will take her,' said Freddy again. 'The child. Hetty. I will take her to Hampshire, to live with me, and to have a good life. That is, if you will allow me, Maria, for I do not want to cause you more suffering.'

Edward and Affy were exchanging looks.

'Perhaps we should all sit down again, just for a moment,' said Affy, and they trooped back into the parlour and resumed their seats, Hetty now sleeping peacefully on Edward's lap.

'I am in earnest,' said Freddy, smiling at Affy, then looking at Maria. 'Would you be sorry to part with the child?'

'Why, yes, ma'am, in some ways, but I could not prevent her from having this chance, if you are really minded to take her. She won't have much of a life with me, poor mite.'

'She would not want for anything that money can buy, you can be certain of that. But I promise you that she will always have love and kindness, too.'

'Freddy, dear, will you not step into the kitchen with me a moment?' said Affy.

Freddy smiled at her, got up, and followed, grinning at Edward and Maria as she went.

'You think I have gone quite mad,' said Freddy, laughing at Affy's bewildered expression. 'And perhaps I have, a little, but I am truly in earnest; never more so, in fact.'

'Are you sure that you are not a little carried away in your desire to help? You do not have to do this, dear. It will change your whole life, and forever. I had thought that you were happy to remain without children?'

'I was, very happy. And it is true that I had not planned this. It is a little sudden, I know, and so you are naturally incredulous. But it is more than sensibility got out of hand, I can assure you. I have no intention of fainting, swooning, eloping, throwing myself into a lake, fighting a duel, or stabbing my lover with a bloody dagger.'

'You disappoint me, dear. You could think of beating your breast a little, then swooning, at the very least.'

'Well, alright then, I will try one little swoon, to oblige you, my dear. But, Affy, I promise you that I am sure of this thing in my heart.'

Affy cupped Freddy's face with her hands, and stared into it with a part quizzical, part comical expression. Then she laughed. She knew that Freddy truly meant what she said.

'Well then, Fredericka Elizabeth Swinglehurst, you had better do it.'

'I will. But, Affy, could I ask you and Edward to take Hetty for a few weeks? I think it would be best to wait until Anne and the boys have left Winchester before Hetty comes to me. I would not want Anne to be upset further by sight of another one of her husband's children, though she will, of course, know in time.'

'Yes, I understand you. What havoc that man has wrought. Let us hope that there are not many more of his children running around, of which we are not yet aware. But, yes, my dear, we will be very glad to take her. And tis best that the parting is done now, if Maria is agreeable. It is not a good place where they live, you know, and there is danger of infection and other accident. I wish we could take Maria too, and them all, for that matter; but there it is.'

'Thank you, dearest Affy.'

Freddy kissed her friend on the cheek and they returned to the parlour. Edward, still looking at them in amazement, offered to get more sweetened tea for Maria, and gently put the sleeping Hetty down on his chair, placed a coverlet over her, and went to the kitchen. Freddy told Maria about her life and situation, not forgetting the good Campbells, and Affy said that she and her husband would take good care of the girl until it was time for her to go into Hampshire. Freddy made absolutely sure that Maria was not feeling pressured to give the child to her. Maria said that although she had grown a little used to the child's face, and her gurgles reminded her of Sarah's incessant chatter – she was a real talker, Sarah - the kindest thing she could do for her friend was to give her daughter this chance. How amazed Sarah would have been to think of her daughter growing up a real fine lady, with silks and a gold carriage and as much tea and chocolate as she could ever wish to drink, and to learn her letters and read books.

Edward returned with the tea, and Maria drank it very slowly, not only in her relish but as if putting off the moment of departure. Then she put down her cup on the small table and got up, abruptly, now desperate to get the farewell over with. She went over to Hetty, kissed her on the head and left the room, clutching her parcel and mumbling thank yous and goodbyes. Edward followed her, to escort her home, and Affy and Freddy stared after them, tears in their eyes.

Chapter 34

Freddy arrived home late that Monday, and the next morning she was sat in the newly-decorated drawing room on the west side of the house, waiting for Margaret to join her, so that she could relate to her the latest news.

She heard a knocking upon the front door, and to her amazement, a few moments later, Margaret ushered Lady Lavinia Ingram into the room.

'A visitor for you, dear', said Margaret, staring at Lady Ingram in her silks and jewels, who was clearly a very high personage indeed.

'Lavinia! How delightful to see you. I was just in London but you were not there. What brings you hither?'

Freddy got up, hugged Lady Ingram, then took her hands and looked into her face, which was glowing with a sort of elation mixed with fear. 'Come, come, sit down, dear. Will you take anything?'

'No, no, Freddy, thank you. I cannot stay long, I am afraid.' She sat down on a settee near to her friend.

'If you do not need anything, I will leave you,' said Margaret.

'Thank you, Mrs Campbell,' said Lavinia. 'It has been an honour to meet you, however briefly. I have heard so much about you from Freddy, and how very dear you are. And what a lovely home you have made here; it is quite charming.'

'Well, thank you, madam,' said Margaret, beaming. 'It is always such a pleasure to meet Fredericka's friends.' She curtseyed and left the room.

'What is it, Lavinia?' asked Freddy.

'I have fled my husband, and am running away with Augustus Grey.'

Freddy stared at her.

'Are you terribly shocked, dear?' asked Lavinia.

'Well, I confess I am a little. Are you sure about it? Could you not reconsider? Surely there is still time to change your mind.'

'No, my love, and I do not want to. At any rate, it is final. I left the Lord Ingram a note, and am already here in Hampshire with Augustus. We fly to the continent today, then will perhaps try the Americas.'

'Oh, Lavinia. I had not realised that your situation had become so desperate, and I am very sorry to hear it. What decided you in taking the action?'

'The situation had become quite intolerable. The Lord Ingram had begun to flaunt his mistresses before me. I am not sure why. I did not think he was cruel – as I have mentioned to you. I wonder if he suspects me about Augustus, or just in general terms, and was trying to goad me. Or perhaps he no longer cares enough to take the trouble to follow the forms.

'But, to be candid, even if things had not taken that turn, I could not have gone on in that same way. It is a sort of sameness, a bleakness of heart that one is forced to bear. One's children are meant to be the compensation, the passion and purpose of our lives, and to bring us our peace. But, unhappily, that has not been the case with me. Perhaps I have something lacking as a woman, and I am unnatural in some way – well, that is what they will say. I know that what I am doing is a sort of madness, but I verily believe I would have run into another kind of madness if I had not taken some desperate measure.'

'I am so saddened for you, dear, that it has come to this. The world can be a cruel place for an unhappy woman.'

'Aye, it can indeed. But I do not mean to be so self-pitying. When I think of you, my love, and some of the cruel taunts you have had to suffer, I feel a little ashamed to complain. You seem to have such a core of strength inside you, and a peace that is not easily disturbed by the world.'

Freddy smiled. 'It was not always the case, dear, and has taken practice; it is hard won. I appear to have become a very rational and content sort of creature, though I may surprise you yet, and run to Gretna Green with the butcher.'

'Well, at least you would not be wanting for meat. But nobody deserves contentment more than you, dear. I think I had things too easy for a long time, and so was not prepared for the knocks. I have such a restless and impatient nature.'

'You were born to travel the seas, my dear; we could have been pirates together.'

Lavinia laughed. 'Ha! What a pretty pair of pirates we would have made.'

'Very handsome, indeed. And thus dressed as men, we would pass all our time with them, and so learn their dreadful secrets.'

'Aye, and so we may discover at last, the perfect remedy for our sex in driving away love.'

'Are you very fond of Augustus?'

'Yes, very fond. But do not think that I am flying with an excess of sensibility - all raptures, transports and ecstasies - though, heaven knows, I love the man well enough.' They both laughed. 'I go with my eyes fully open, and know that it will be very hard for such a pair as us in this world. I dare say it will end badly. But we can always blow our brains out.'

Freddy giggled. 'Oh, my love; yes, there is always that.' Lavinia and Freddy used to joke about blowing their brains out as a solution to all difficulties, small or large.

'But, do not fret; I will not do so now, and ruin this perfect drawing room.'

'Thank you for your consideration, dear; Mrs C will be much obliged to you.'

Lavinia mimed putting a gun to her head and started to laugh, and laugh and laugh, her body shaking, her perfect small teeth on display. Freddy joined her, until Lavinia's laughter turned to tears, and she started to sob.

Freddy moved closer and put her arms around her friend, until her crying had eased a little. She took both her hands. 'Oh, my dear, dear Lavvy. I am sorry that you are suffering so. At least your uncertainty is over; you have made your decision; you are prepared for what may come, and you are going with love, at least. Let us hope for the best, and not think about endings.' Freddy smiled into her friend's face. 'But you will have had to leave behind the children? How have your borne it?'

'Badly. I have left behind Master Ingram, and only you know how much it tore my heart to do so. But I found that I could not deprive the Lord Ingram of his heir, and he is less likely to follow us if he has the boy. However, we have the girl with us, a fact which may surprise you. I could not leave both my children. Augustus is fond of her, and says that I will grow to love her. I am hopeful that he is right. I do not think the Lord Ingram will come after us for the sake of a girl.'

'That is very painful for you to lose George. But I am glad that you have Sophia, and hope she will soon bring you comfort. What will you do for an income?'

'We have money. I have my settlement from my father.' Lavinia paused. 'And, as to the rest, it has come about in a most strange and remarkable way. I am a little ashamed to own the truth of it.'

'You do not have to tell me, for I believe that I already know the truth.'

Lavinia looked incredulous. 'You do? Nay, I do not think so. This story is more crazed than that contained in any of our favourite novels.'

'Is it the Celestial Light?'

'Why, yes. How on earth did you know?'

'By a story even more crazed than your crazed story, my dear. I will tell you of it someday. There is a local connection, and I discovered more about the London side of things from Affy. But, pray, do not make yourself anxious; nothing will be said; I promise you that.'

'You are too good, Freddy. I am very curious as to the story, but, as you say, it can wait. I hope you do not feel too hard on us about it. As you may know, it was a most strange, chance opportunity that came in the way of Augustus, and he could not resist. We will need to live as well as we can, and he must also pay off his debts. The Countess has not lost much, with the insurance, and I believe she is very happy in her new marriage.'

'I do not judge you, my love. Only know that you can always come hither if the worst occurs. It is a haven from the world and its opinions.'

'As are you, my dear. I so wanted to see your dear

face again ere I go, for I do not know when we will meet again. I cannot thank you enough for your friendship.'

Freddy and Lavinia hugged for a while, then the latter said that she must make haste. They went to the front door, and parted laughingly and tearfully, Lavinia promising to write as soon as she and Augustus were settled for a time. She stepped into the hired post-chaise, waved at Freddy, blew her a kiss, then was driven away to join her love.

Freddy returned to the drawing room, a little overwhelmed by this meeting with her friend. She could not blame her, but thought that the chances of such a couple finding peace and happiness in the world as it was were not high. The scandal of a woman of rank leaving behind her husband and child was bad enough; that woman would not get a welcome in many respectable households. But that woman running with a notorious negro rake was of another level entirely. Where would they find their haven? It was brave and foolhardy on both their parts; Lavinia had forever lost her child, her reputation, security and place in society, Augustus an unusually pampered and privileged security in the household of his Marchioness. She feared that it would end up with more unhappiness, as well as in bitterness and recrimination. Had Lavinia really thought through the long-term consequences of such an irreversible action? Well, well, it was too late now, and her friend knew that there was a home for her at the old manor house should it ever be needed. Even Augustus would be welcome, though

Freddy smiled to herself at the thought of him in the kitchen with the Campbells, drinking small beer and toasting some cheese or frying up a hash for his supper.

And how strange that she, Freddy, should be so connected to the infamous diamond that one old friend had tried to steal it and another had ended up with it. She should write it all down in a novel, but even by the standards of the present day, no-one would believe it.

Chapter 35

Margaret, having spotted Lavinia's departure, now entered the drawing room with some tea.

'The Lady Ingram has departed, I see,' she said. 'What a fine lady your friend is, and so charming. I hope that nothing upsetting has occurred?' She looked at Freddy with her usual concern and her usual curiosity.

'Well, yes, tis a little upsetting,' said Freddy. 'It is yet another curious and dramatic tale, I fear'. Freddy sighed and gave a half smile. 'It seems that there are a lot of them about. I will tell you of it, by and by, but there is other news to discuss.'

'You have left off your spectacles, my love, and what a beauty you are, just like your mother before you.'

'Oh, Mrs C, you wicked flatterer. Yes, I have left them off. They are locked safely in my father's old desk, ready to come out again should I ever feel too exposed to the big, wide world.'

Margaret smiled. She was trying desperately to contain her impatience regarding Freddy's news, and calmly put the tea things on the new walnut tea table. 'How do you like the room, my dear? Is it quite ready?' She looked around her with great pleasure and pride.

'It is perfection, Mrs C, thanks to you. That blue spotted paper is just the thing. Anne does not mind our stealing her taste in wallpapers. And with the fine green dining room, too, we must be the most elegant home in Hampshire.'

'I am quite sure of it. Now, if only we could get my husband out of the kitchen.'

'I do not think it will happen. He is as much part of the kitchen furniture as the old stove.'

Margaret sighed. 'I fear you are right. When he dies – God forgive me – his skeleton will be a hanging over the kitchen range until the end of the time, shaking one of its long fingers to warn people never to get above their station.'

Freddy laughed. 'Never mind. The new rooms will be well used, I am sure, for I think we are ready to throw open our doors at last.'

Margaret gave Freddy a well-sweetened cup of tea, and sat down next to her treasure on the pale green settee, where Lavinia had been sitting. 'You don't know how it fills my heart to hear it.'

'I do know it, Mrs C.'

'Now, what is this other bit of news you have for me?

I could barely sleep last night, in anticipation, and kept plaguing poor Mr Gabriel with my conjectures.'

'Forgive me, Margaret, dear; I was so fatigued yesterday and wanted to wait until the morning, when I would be a little more alert. And then somewhat unexpectedly, the Lady Ingram came.'

'Yes, quite, my dear. Well?'

'Well, I will need you to help me to alter my chamber and closet a little, and, in time, prepare yet another room.'

Margaret looked puzzled, and took a sip of tea. 'Upon my soul, the mumbling curate has not made you an offer, has he? You are not taking him, surely? Mr Winkworth is indeed the kindest fellow in the world but I do not think he is quite good enough for... Oh, forgive me, my dear, if I speak out of turn. My mouth will run away with me.'

'Do not fret, Mrs C. If the good curate should ever propose marriage, I shall kindly but firmly tell him that Mrs Margaret Campbell thinks him not good enough for Miss Fredericka Swinglehurst of the old manor house, and that he should take his mumblings elsewhere. But, no, the news does not relate to marriage.' Freddy paused. 'It is a child. I would like to adopt a child. To be candid, I am adopting a child.'

'Oh, my dear.' Margaret held her cup of tea suspended in the air. 'That is news indeed, but quite delightful news.' She stopped. 'Oh, my dear,' she said again, smiling.

'I should really have talked it through with you and Gabriel beforehand, but it was quite an unexpected decision. It will affect you greatly and I do not want you to be needlessly burdened. You have borne enough on my account.'

'Nonsense, my dear; you must not say such things, or I will become very cross. Besides, nothing would give us greater pleasure than to have a child about us.'

'But the child is a negro – or a mulatto, if you will, like mother. It is the Reverend Millbrook's bastard daughter, the first born of Sarah Long, that poor woman. There will be much gossip and judgment around it.'

'Let anyone dare share any malice in my company.' Margaret clenched both her small, round fists, forgetting that she was holding a cup in one of them.

'Try not to break the china, dear Mrs C. But you give me courage; thank you. She will be so safe and cosy here, I know, though the world will not always be kind. We will have to help her to bear it.'

'Of course we will.'

'I must also tell that you that I have had no plans to have a child. I have had no urge, felt no pang, you know, when it comes to children. I hope it does not you pain you to hear this, Margaret, dear, but I want to be candid to the most important people in the world to me. Affy and Edward found the girl staying with Sarah's friend, Maria, in St Giles, an impoverished quarter of London. The friend has nothing, and the child would have been a burden to her, though she would have done her best for it. She is a very good sort of woman, and I feel quite ashamed thinking about her situation when set alongside mine. But the life chances of children are not good in that unhealthy place. Affy and Edward thought about taking the infant themselves, but they have enough to think about already, and I thought how much I have to give, and how much wealth to share.'

'That is very honourable of you, dear. But you do not have to take the child from a sense of duty. There are other ways you could help, you know.'

'I know. But when I saw her face, my heart cleaved to her. I thought of my mother.'

'Agh, well then.' Margaret smiled. 'How old is the girl? What is her name?'

'She is just over a year old, I believe. And then, what do you think? Her name is Henrietta - Hetty.'

'Your mother's name. Oh, that is fitting. There, my love; that is settled then.'

Freddy was quiet for a few moments, then said. 'I will not know what to do. I am terrified. You will help me, will not you, Margaret?'

'You silly, foolish child. What a question to ask your second mother.'

'Not only that, but I am already terrified of losing her, even though she is not yet here. I am quite nonsensical. But so many children die, do not they? Maria has lost three already, though I know being so poor does not help. But everyone, rich or poor, loses them, it seems. How do people bear it?'

Margaret put her cup down, and stretched out her arms to Freddy.

'Oh, Freddy.'

Margaret kissed Freddy on the top of her head, and put her arms around her neck. Then Freddy knelt down and laid her head on Margaret's lap, and they stayed like that for several minutes, Margaret smiling and thinking how much Freddy, with the slight tang of soil from the garden mixed with her perfumed lavender water, smelt like her mother.

'Little sailor, do not vex yourself,' she said. We none of us know what will come in this life, but it is our duty to do the best we can each day and be thankful. The Lord gives, and the Lord takes away, and I cannot pretend to understand his reasoning. But it would be sinful to spend our lives in fear of every possible loss, instead of being grateful for what he has given us in each moment. We would drive ourselves quite distracted.'

'Yes, that is true. You are far too wise, Mrs C. Perhaps you should replace poor Mr Winkworth. You would stun the congregations with your amazing sermons; and without mumbling once, I am sure.'

'You are quite right, my love. But until the great world recognises my talents, I shall have to remain contented with applying them here in the old manor house, and continue to preach to Mr C, who is growing a little deaf, though he will not admit it, and dear Flip, who is as attentive a listener as anyone could wish for, and who quite approves of everything I say.'

'As do I. Will you tell Gabriel all this news? I thought it might be best that way. Then, if he is agreeable, I will write to Affy to confirm the plan. They will bring Hetty to us in a few weeks' time. I wanted to wait until Anne and the boys are gone, rather than confuse them and give Anne any more pain at this time.'

'That makes sense, dear. But as to Mr C being agreeable, why, it will be the happiest moment of his life, excepting the day he married me, of course. I'm bursting to tell him all this news, though he will be away a while yet this afternoon. Once he gets upon the subject of horses and tackle, and stabling, there will be no end to it.

'But I have intelligence of my own to share. Mr and Mrs Cooper, Anne's papa and mama, came a calling with their daughter just yesterday, while you were gone. We had thought that Mr Cooper would come to Hampshire alone, but his wife decided to join him. And what a fine, handsome couple they are, and such bearing and manners. Well, you will meet them by and by. But best of all, they seemed so glad to be reconciled to their daughter, for Mrs Cooper could not stop kissing her, and Mr Cooper smiled constantly, and was all civility and benevolence. I had not expected it; it was very touching. And they are very kind to the boys, and take a keen interest in them, and so our hearts are easy at their going, and Mr C, especially, is reassured. Samuel is back from Oxford; the poor man is still quite distressed. But he has agreed to go to Salisbury, and so be useful to Mary's sons, and that will comfort him.'

'Well, that is all good news indeed, and as happy an outcome as one could hope for after all the suffering. Poor Samuel; how different things might have been for Mary, and them both, if she had taken him.'

'Yes, that is so; he would have been such a good husband for her, I am sure. But unhappily her head was long turned by the reverend, and she could not see clearly. Well, it is not the first time that such a thing has occurred, and it will not be the last, I dare say.'

'Still, there are happy changes coming for us all, and you, especially, are going to be a very busy woman, Margaret Campbell.'

'Indeed I am, my treasure. And now I have two dozen more items, at the very least, to add to my list. And, that reminds me, I must look into that Rose Brown from the village as a possible new kitchen maid. She is a little greasy looking, to be sure, but we can put that right if she proves creditable.'

Freddy smiled. 'Mrs C, you are a wonder. You should be managing the royal estate. The king himself could not do better.'

'Aye, but I'm sure he would not be half so interesting as Mr Campbell, and would not obey me as Mr C knows he should. But, see, I am already growing quite puffed up with my power; tis quite intoxicating and I will very likely have turned tyrant before the year is out.'

'Yes, I have observed it, and am thinking of buying you a crown. You are livelier than ever, Mrs C; it is doing you good.'

'Yes, I feel quite the girl again, I assure you. And with all this happy news, I feel almost fit to dance a hornpipe. Your father taught me to do that, you know.'

'To dance a hornpipe? Why, that is delightful.'

'Yes, and he complimented me on my footwork. Poor Mr C attempted to dance with us but just tripped over his feet. Molly the poor old nag has more lightness of leg, and has better legs generally if one is to be strictly candid about it. But your mother, now, was grace itself. She and your father used to dance together at home, not being so fond of public places. Well, well, that gets me a thinking that I hope that the admiral will be at peace now, and so stop his wandering.'

'Wandering?'

'Yes, around the house and grounds; he must have been uneasy and restless, I should think. When I first heard the noises in the house, I thought that we were to be set on by a gang of housebreakers and murdered in our beds, and my hair quite stood on end at the very thought. You may have noticed when you looked at the accounts from London that the bill for our household locks increased? I was so anxious to keep us safe, and poor old Flip, with the best of intentions, was never formed to be a guard dog. Then one night I saw your father in the kitchen, lifting the cloth from a plate of my queen cakes and trying to sniff at them, it appeared. Silly Flip, who was lying in front of the hearth, just grinned and wagged his tail. Then the ghost floated down to the cellar and I followed it.'

'That was very brave of you. Were not you frightened?'

'Of your father? Nay. The good admiral could only ever be a friendly spirit. I think he was after the best madeira. At any rate, he passed the cheeses and the beef, smelling them a little, and settled near the wine bottles. There was a half a bottle of good port nearby, and do you know, he took off the stopper and drank back several gulps straight from the bottle, which made his form all a glow. I was quite mesmerised. Then he turned and smiled at me. My heart stopped for a moment, then, I can tell you. It was such a peculiar feeing, but not an unpleasant one, and I think I laughed, ere he disappeared.' Margaret paused to look at Freddy. 'You have seen him, dear, have you not?'

'Why, yes, I have seen him, and twice. How did you know?'

'Oh, there is no special reason. It is only natural, you know, that you should.'

'He drank some wine – as he did when you saw him – and also smoked his pipe, and talked to me, quite as if he was alive and well, though he was formed of nothing but smoke.'

'Well, then, that is what he came for, to spend some time with his daughter, and to settle his mind. I feel sure that he will be an easier spirit now.'

'Yes, I hope so. It is all wondrous strange, is it not?'

'It is indeed. Wondrous strange and strangely wonderful, not unlike the dinner I am planning for this evening, which, now I think upon it, I must make haste about and begin preparing.'

Margaret got up, kissed Freddy on the top of her head and pinched both cheeks. 'My dear child,' she said, and left the room.

Chapter 36

After dinner that day, Freddy went up to her dressing room to take some rest, a pipe and a glass. She wanted to gather her thoughts, and make the most of her peace before all the changes to come. She changed into her man's clothing, sat down, then reached into her workbox and took out the letter written by her mother before she died, the customary practice for women about to give birth, being such a dangerous and unpredictable life event that it was. The letter was written on a now crumbling piece of paper in a neat, elaborate hand, and was short.

> *My Dearest Life*
>
> *For that is what you are, even though you have not yet arrived into the world.*

If you are reading this, you know that I was never able to meet you, which I am so longing to do, and I am truly sorry for it.

Whether you be boy or girl, know that you are truly loved. Promise me to always love and honour your father, who is the dearest man that ever lived, and do the same for the Campbells, who match him in goodness.

Always be kind to those weaker than yourself, and always value your own self, and never let yourself be bullied or humbled.

Your mother will always be with you, and kisses you endlessly with this letter.

Henrietta Swinglehurst

Freddy touched the words on the page, smiled, then kissed the letter and put it back in her needlework box, and settled down to re-read *The Monk*. Perhaps she really should write that novel, after all. *The Reverend; or The Wicked and Marvellous Adventures & Crimes of Jonathan Millbrook; with some Elegant Effusions & Observations on that Subject by a Lady Who Knew Him.* Then she heard some scuffling noises coming from the chimney and looked up. Oh, her father. She smiled. She had not been sure if she would see him again.

The familiar blue-ish, whirling smoke emerged from the fireplace and began to spiral upwards and outwards, then settled itself into human shape in front of the desk.

Freddy stared even harder than usual. It was certainly her father, but gone were his old breeches, waistcoat and tail wig; in their place were a dark blue gown, over which were loosely fastened some grubby stays, and a woman's tall, powdered wig, decorated with miniature glass ships, each with their own tiny guns. The gown was a little too short, showing the admiral's hairy calves, and heavy brown boots. Freddy laughed with delight. The admiral was also proudly carrying a small skull, which he placed on the floor. Then he stood straight, grinned at Freddy, saluted her, and beckoned her to join him.

She got up, saluted, then went over to where he stood, curtseyed and stood opposite him. The sounds of a harpsichord and a fiddle now struck up, seeming to come from out of the fireplace; they were playing the hornpipe.

'You are safe now, my dear, I know,' said the admiral, 'so there is just one thing left for us to do: dance!'

He put out his arms and crossed them at the elbows. Then he jumped, cutting his right foot towards his left knee, and repeated the action six times, whilst turning in a circle and alternately leaning his body from one side to the other. Then he proceeded through the various moves of the hornpipe, flicking and stamping his feet, raising his hands above his head to mimic climbing a rope, rocking back and two as if he was rolling and swinging about on a stormy ship, and pretending to row. All the while, he was executing very neat turns, and moving slowly forwards and backwards across the room.

Freddy was doing her best to follow, until a combination of doffing her cap, hitching her trousers, and moving backwards, sent her flying to the floor.

'Drunkenness will not be tolerated!' shouted the admiral, and attempted to help her up, but as he was not composed of anything very solid, this took some time.

Freddy, giggling, got on her feet, and righted herself. They set off again, until the admiral then shouted, 'Now speed it up!' and flung his wig through the air until it landed with a thud on *The Monk*, which was lying on Freddy's chair. He began to repeat the actions of the very first steps, but at double speed, his gown and stays bouncing madly as he did so.

Freddy tried to follow, getting more and more dizzy, and finally fell over again.

'Man overboard!' shouted the admiral. 'This is what comes from slovenly, slipshod steps. The moves of the hornpipe are jolly, rousing and invigorating, but they should also be very smart and neat, my dear.'

'Aye, aye, Admiral,' said Freddy, from her position on the floor, her hair wild, her cheeks glowing, her shift, pantaloons and face smeared with dust.

'Up you get, little sailor.' The admiral did his best to help her up again with his smoky arms. 'Not a brilliant performance, but certainly tolerable. You are sprightly, my love, but there is much work to be done.'

Freddy, still laughing, saluted her father, who floated over to the small table near Freddy's chair, poured himself a glass of brandy, knocked it back, then gave a deep sigh.

His body had turned completely orange with all the exertion. He smiled tenderly at his daughter, gave her a quick salute, then his smoky body began to disintegrate and move over to the fireplace, where it finally disappeared.

Freddy picked up the skull from the floor, grinned at it and placed it on her small table next to the brandy. Then she flopped down into her chair, poured herself a drink, and lit her pipe. She closed her eyes, tapping her foot softly, still hearing the music and seeing in her mind's eye the ghost of her father dancing.

The next day in the early afternoon, Captain Henry Lefroy called at the old manor house. He was carrying a very fine stick, which was a present for Freddy. Margaret answered the front door.

'Captain, how do you do? How delightful of you to call, given the potential danger to life and limb. Do come in, sir.'

'Thank you, Mrs Campbell.'

'Are you here to see my husband, Fredericka, or my own good self? Oh, and not forgetting Flip.'

'Oh, all four of you certainly. But perhaps I could have a word with Miss Swinglehurst to begin with?'

'I shall let her know you're here. Will you take anything? Some tea, or perhaps some lemonade? It's a warm day.'

'Some lemonade would be very welcome, thank you.'

Margaret took the captain through to the drawing room, where it was cool, and set off to find Freddy. The latter appeared five minutes later wearing an old linen dress and cap and a large, striped apron of Margaret's, now covered in soil.

'Captain Lefroy. How do you do? Do forgive my frightful appearance, but then you are used to that. Mr C is trying to teach me a little gardening and farming, but I appear to be a hopeless case – Flip is doing rather better than me - and I have already killed several shrubs and a crop of peas.'

The captain laughed. 'It is a relief that the good folk of Hampshire are not relying on you for their sustenance.'

'Yes, quite; we would all be half starved.' Freddy sat down. 'How is your leg?'

Henry grinned. 'Entirely back to its old self. How is yours?'

'Entirely back to its old self.'

'That is a shame, for we could have had matching bad legs, and just two good legs between us.' Freddy giggled. 'I hope you will do me the honour of accepting my present, nonetheless. I heard that you had lost your stick in London.'

The captain handed Freddy the cane, the ivory and amber handle of which was carved into the shape of a dog's head.

Freddy took it, laughed with delight and ran her hands over the handle.

'Now I hope that you are not too amused by the poor dog's features,' said the captain. 'It was meant to be a likeness of Flip, but I fear it could be any animal within the entirety of God's creation.'

'Tis quite perfect,' said Freddy, 'and I shall treasure it, though I hope Flip will not become too jealous.'

Margaret appeared with two glasses of lemonade.

'Upon my soul, what a fright you are, Fredericka. I hope you're not getting clay on that fine rug.'

'No, Mrs C, I took off my boots. See, just my stockinged feet.'

Margaret sighed. 'I must beg your pardon, Captain. I have tried my best, but the girl is quite wild, and there is nothing to be done with her.'

Freddy laughed. ''Tis only the captain, Margaret, dear; he has seen me looking worse than this.'

'That is no excuse.' Margaret grimaced at Freddy, then grinned at them both, and quitted the room. Henry smiled after her, then turned back to Freddy as they both sat down.

'The Campbells are such fine people,' said Henry. 'It has been a pleasure getting to know them, and it has been a respite here when my mind had been very troubled about Anne.'

'I am glad to hear it,' said Freddy.

'There is a sort of seduction in this house, being so informal and unstuffy as it is, and it makes one feel quite drowsy and free in spirit. Jonathan, to his credit, used to refer to the times when you were children, and the admiral was still here. He said that you all seemed to have the secret of the most simple and happy form of life, enjoying worldly things but not being governed by them, enjoying the company of others but not depending on their judgements, or thinking overmuch about the opinions of the world in general.'

Freddy smiled. 'That is exactly it; and I feel my good fortune, I can assure you, though it was not always so.'

Henry drank back some of his lemonade and sighed a little. He seemed a little nervous, and was tapping his fingers on the edge of his chair.

'I am adopting a child, you know,' Freddy blurted out suddenly.

'Oh, indeed?' Henry looked a little taken aback. 'But that is very good news.'

'It is, is it not? Though it has been a little unexpected.'

The captain smiled. 'I would expect nothing less than the unexpected from you, Miss Swinglehurst.'

'Will you not call me Freddy, sir? Anything else feels a little formal, you know, when a woman has shot at a man.'

'Quite. It would make me very happy to call you Freddy, Freddy.'

'Splendid.'

The captain took a deep breath. 'It would make me even more happy to call you something else, too.'

'Oh? Well, Mr C has recently been calling me Crack Shot Freddy, which has a nice ring to it, I think.'

'It would make even more happy to call you my wife. Do you not know that I love you, you nonsensical, lunatic woman?'

Freddy stared at him, and opened and closed her mouth several times.

'Could you love me, Freddy?'

Freddy nodded, then shook her head.

'I fear I will need some clearer signals.'

Freddy shook her head, then nodded.

The captain got up, knelt down in front of her and took her small right hand with his own, taking great heart that she did not pull it away.

'Do you think you can love me, Freddy?' repeated the captain.

'Yes,' said Freddy. 'I can love you. I believe that I do love you.' She laughed, as if surprised. 'But, tis all so unexpected. I had come home to remain Miss Swinglehurst, and my heart was at peace.'

'Well, so was mine, to be candid, until you fired a hundred-gun frigate into it with your shift and pantaloons.'

Freddy giggled. 'These things usually have the opposite effect; I will have to re-think my strategy for scaring away the opposite sex.' She was quiet for a moment. 'How do you feel about the infant? Her name is Henrietta, she is one year old, and she is the bastard child of Jonathan Millbrook and Sarah Clarke.'

'Fredericka; you are quite determined to shock me and to put me off. But you will not do so. If the child is yours, she will be mine, too, and I will love her just as well.'

'Well, that is just typical of you. I suppose if shooting you did not put you off, your heart must be pretty stout.'

'My heart is as hail and as hearty as any old sailor's should be.'

'I do believe it is. But I regret that I cannot say the same for my own. You will go away, and die. I could not bear it.'

'Freddy, you have endured much loss, I know, and I am very sorry for it. But I am a little concerned that you are quite so quick to settle the matter of my death. And some might say that there is as much danger in a certain quarter of Winchester as there is on board a man of war.'

'That is quite true, sir.'

'Will you have me, Freddy?'

Freddy paused, cocked her head to one side, and grinned.

'Oh, I dare say I will.'

The pair sat together for an hour or so, going over their short acquaintance and its misunderstandings. They agreed that they needed to take some more time to get to know each other before marrying: suspecting someone of murder, theft and grave robbery was hardly the ideal start to a courtship. Henry confessed that he had thought about their getting a license and marrying quickly before he sailed again - his ship, the Poseidon, was awaiting orders at Spithead – but he realised now that this was too hasty a scheme. Freddy said that she must put her daughter first for now; she needed time to get to know her, and settle her into her new home, so that Hetty became as firmly planted in the soil of the old manor house as the Campbells, and would know she belonged there. Freddy had also to get used to the idea of having a husband, after all, for she had been rather vocal on the subject of spinsterdom, she said, and it was all rather embarrassing. Despite the hazardous profession of the sailor, they both realised that there was no need to rush, for this love would not be of that kind; whatever the fates brought, it would grow steadily and freely in its own singular way, much like Fredericka Elizabeth Swinglehurst herself.

When the captain had taken his leave, Margaret appeared, smiling knowingly and looking a little puffed up with pride.

'He loves me,' said Freddy.

'Of course he does,' said Margaret. 'Even Flip could have told you that. Did I not tell you what a handsome, charming man he was?'

'I suppose you did.'

'And I'll wager you no longer consider him to be quite so shiny?'

'No, Margaret, dear; I do believe that he is quite the least shiny, least glowing person I have ever met.'

Acknowledgements

Professor Hilary Fraser and Dr Ella Dzelzainis for inspiring in me a lifelong love of all things long nineteenth century.

Dr Jonathan Gibbs and my MA Creative Writing: First Novel cohort (2017-2019) at St Mary's, Twickenham, for guiding me through the craft of novel-writing (special thanks to Clare Rees).

Laura Gerrard, for her hugely insightful and very practical editing skills.

Dr Susan Civale and Jackie Hughes (it's all about the dogs) for their no-nonsense feedback on the early chapters of this novel.

Last, but by no means least, my partner Stuart, for his love, patience and for never letting me – nor anyone else in the vicinity – go hungry.

About the Author

Author photograph by Helen Rushton

R S Leonard was born in Cheshire, England, and after a long stint in London now resides in Hampshire.

She has a PhD in nineteenth-century literature and culture and an MA in Creative Writing, both of which eventually inspired her first novel, The Body, the Diamond and the Child. She is currently working on her second novel, a mystery centred around a Victorian lunatic asylum.

Her other career is in philanthropy.

rsleonardbooks.com

Printed in Great Britain
by Amazon